INCUBUS

DAUGHTERS OF LILITH:
BOOK 2

Jennifer Quintenz

SECRET TREE PRESS

Copyright © 2013 Jennifer Quintenz
Cover design by Jennifer Quintenz

All rights reserved. This book or any portion thereof may not be reproduced or used in any manner whatsoever without the express written permission of the publisher except for the use of brief quotations in a book review.

Printed in the United States of America

First Printing, June 21, 2013

ISBN-13: 978-0615829135
ISBN-10: 0615829139

Secret Tree Press
www.JenniferQuintenz.com

PUBLISHER'S NOTE: This is a work of fiction. Names, characters, businesses, places, and events are either the product of the author's imagination or used in a fictitious manner, and any resemblance to actual persons, living or dead, business establishments, events, or locales, is entirely coincidental.

Please purchase only authorized electronic editions, and do not participate in or encourage piracy of copyrighted materials. Your support of the author's rights is appreciated.

*To my sister, Manda.
Chance. Choice. Love you.*

CONTENTS

Acknowledgments	i
Chapter 1	1
Chapter 2	15
Chapter 3	29
Chapter 4	45
Chapter 5	59
Chapter 6	75
Chapter 7	87
Chapter 8	101
Chapter 9	117
Chapter 10	133
Chapter 11	143
Chapter 12	155
Chapter 13	175
Chapter 14	193
Chapter 15	217
Chapter 16	231
Chapter 17	243
Chapter 18	253
Chapter 19	261
Chapter 20	267
Chapter 21	283
Epilogue	289
Excerpt from "Sacrifice"	293
A Note From The Author	305
About The Author	307

ACKNOWLEDGMENTS

Book two, and my list of acknowledgements continues to grow. I'm seriously indebted to a supportive network of family, friends, and fellow story-tellers.

To my parents, who nurtured my sister's and my interest in writing from the beginning. Dad, who hinged our allowance payments on creative writing tasks - not just chores. Mom, who journeyed with us to bookstores at least once a month to load up on new stories. Dot, who subscribed us to the magical TLB Enchanted World Series. Clyde, who never tired of my questions on religion and philosophy.

To some truly excellent friends. Bethany Lopez, whose support and sense of story was invaluable. Josh Feinstein, who volunteered his mad-ninja editorial skills. Marc Manus (both manager and friend), who gave excellent and thorough story notes from outline through drafts.

And finally, to Asher and James, who sacrificed in little and not-so-little ways to give me the precious gift of time to write.

He has inscribed a circle on the face of the waters at the boundary between light and darkness.

- Job 26:10

1

The late September sunlight had its own kind of magic. Spears of mid-morning light broke through a heavy bank of clouds to strike the leaves of an expansive aspen tree, setting each one aglow with an emerald fire. I tilted my head up, eyes closed, letting the warmth seep in, welcoming it beyond my skin, through sinew and muscle, into my bones. Some hidden part of me had been cold since last December. I lived with this fist of ice around my heart, unable to pry free from its hold.

Winter solstice.

My eyelids snapped open. I felt the muscles of my back knot up. With effort, I forced myself to pull in a long breath. As I let it out, I willed my body to relax.

In answer, I felt his warm fingers lacing through mine. Lucas stood next to me, distracted by the stream of kids pouring out of the newly arrived school bus behind us. I don't think he even realized he'd taken my hand. It was an unconscious gesture, but it did more to warm me than the sun. I leaned closer, breathing in the subtle spice of his scent. He sensed the motion and turned to look at me. I smiled but he read something in my face. Concern clouded his eyes.

"It's nothing," I said, then, tasting the lie, I shrugged. "It's nothing new."

Lucas nodded. There was nothing else to say. The only reason he wasn't having sheet-twisting, sweat-drenched nightmares every night was that I policed his dreams. Even then, more than a handful of times the Lilitu demon Ais had risen up before us, conjured by Lucas's sleeping mind. In many dreams we'd battled her together, fighting teeth and nails that glinted like steel, staring into glassy black eyes. These fights were always epic and acrobatic—loosed from the laws of physics that dictate everything in the real world, Lucas and I could run faster, leap farther, and fight tirelessly. Our dream fights were much more glamorous than the actual night we had faced Ais. The night we had nearly died.

Fragmented memories of that night rose up, knife-sharp and aching to shred my forced calm. I turned my attention back to the reason we were all here.

The Mission of Puerto Escondido sat perched in the foothills, about 15 miles away from the center of Old Town. The monks who'd settled here hundreds of years before had picked a beautiful vantage point. Piñon and juniper trees dotted the mountains that enclosed our little valley. Most of the town was nestled comfortably in the lowest dip between the peaks. Standing in front of the mission, I could see across the bowl of our valley, from the glimmering stand of old oaks that edged my neighborhood to the wealthy foothill community on the other side of town.

As if glancing at his neighborhood was some kind of summons, Royal's brand new, platinum two-seater cut across the unpaved parking lot, kicking up a dusty plume in its wake. The kids nearest the parking lot coughed and waved dust away from their faces, irritated. Irritation changed to interest as they got a good look at the car. The Corvette Stingray convertible had been a present from Royal's father. If you asked Royal, he'd say it was an attempt to compensate for being chronically absent—but that didn't mean it wasn't fun to drive.

"Told you." I grinned at Lucas, feeling some of my anxiety melting into the background. Royal was a grounding force in my life. Safe. Familiar.

"You said he'd make an entrance," Lucas replied, unable to wrench his gaze off the gleaming roadster, "but now I'm thinking you left out a few key details."

"What?" I said innocently. "I told you he got a car for his birthday."

"A *car*—?" Lucas glanced at me, incredulous. "That's like calling the Hope Diamond a pretty rock."

"Which is technically true," I shrugged, "depending on your taste in gemstones."

Lucas smiled, shaking his head, then draped an arm over my shoulder. "Okay. Now I'm thinking I put too much thought into your

Christmas gift." I elbowed him in the ribs. Lucas grunted, but his grin deepened.

In the parking lot, Royal emerged from this gleaming work of art, seemingly oblivious to our classmates' stares. He walked around and opened the passenger door for Cassie. She unfolded from the car, smoothing her long black hair back from her face. She was beaming, flushed from the ride, and when she spotted us she waved brightly. We moved forward to meet them at the edge of the parking lot. Royal approached us casually enough, but as he got closer I could see the twinkle of excitement in his eyes.

"Well?" he asked. "First thoughts. Brutal honesty."

"Hm." I said, tilting my head to one side critically. "I thought it'd be more—" I glanced at Lucas.

"Awesome," he supplied.

"Yes. I thought it'd be more awesome," I said. "I mean, don't get me wrong. It's okay, for a car. I'm sure it will get you from point A to point B. Maybe you can upgrade it in a few years. Get something a little—"

"Awesomer," Lucas said.

"Right."

Cassie bit her lip, muffling a giggle.

"It's an incredible ride and you know it," Royal said, unruffled. He held up his car keys. "Just for that, Cassie gets to drive it first."

"Me?" Cassie squealed.

"I'd like to amend my former statement," Lucas said.

"Too late." Royal tossed the keys to Cassie, who plucked them out of the air gleefully. Lucas looked forlorn.

"Although I do need a favor, so if anyone wants brownie points—" Royal jabbed his thumb over his shoulder at the car behind him. "To be clear, brownie points get you behind the wheel."

"Let's hear it," Lucas said.

Royal lowered his voice. "My dad's hired some SAT dude to come over and tutor me three times a week. I could really use some company. This guy is way, *way* beyond plastic. Just watching him smile all afternoon makes *my* cheeks hurt. Isn't there some saying? 'If you're going to suffer, you might as well make your friends suffer, too?'"

"I don't think so, no," I said.

Royal snapped his fingers. "Misery loves company."

"Yeah, that's not exactly the same thing."

"Whatever. My misery basically demands your company. It's the first rule of friendship." Royal turned beseeching eyes on Cassie. "Save me from Academic Ken Doll. You'll have my eternal gratitude."

"All right. I'm in," Cassie said.

"Thanks, study buddy." Royal grinned, catching my eye for the briefest moment. I knew—and I knew Royal knew—that if Cassie was going to go to college, she'd need some serious scholarships. The kind of scholarships that started with an excellent score on the SATs. Which made me suspect that this tutor might not be as lame as Royal would have us believe.

"Count me in, too," I said.

"So these brownie points," Lucas began.

"Don't worry, pretty boy," Royal said, grinning. "There's plenty of road to go around."

Behind us, Mr. Landon clapped his hands together, drawing everyone's attention toward the doors of the old mission. His portly stature and receding hairline—which might have made him the target of students' jokes—were easily overshadowed by a youthful enthusiasm for his subject. He was one of a handful of beloved educators at Coronado Prep voted among the "Best Teachers" year after year. Mr. Landon taught AP History to all the juniors at Coronado Prep, which was the reason for this class-wide field trip.

"All right, kids, I think that's everyone," Mr. Landon said. "Please direct your attention to our fabulous guide for the day, Annie Gerardo. Annie?"

I turned toward the slender, mousy woman standing next to Mr. Landon—but my gaze caught on another figure, hovering at the back of the crowd of students. Almost as soon as our eyes locked, the strange woman slipped through a gate into the mission's garden and was gone. A shivery tingle crept over the back of my neck. I'd only had the briefest glimpse of her, but something about the woman was off. She was human—that much I could see instantly. Approaching middle age, with a wide, kind looking face. But something in her eyes was missing.

"Braedyn?" Lucas looked at me curiously. I noticed the rest of the students were following Annie into the mission's main sanctuary. Royal and Cassie, a few paces ahead, trailed the bunch, waiting for me to catch up.

I turned back to the gate through which the woman had vanished. "Did you see...?"

Lucas followed my gaze, but of course there was nothing to see. "What am I looking for?" he asked, tensing like a coiled spring, ready for release. I realized I wasn't the only one with a hair-trigger these days.

"Nothing," I said, forcing a smile. I squeezed his hand, still laced through my fingers. "Let's catch up before we miss the whole tour. Knowing Landon, this is probably going to end up on a quiz."

Lucas and I were the last of our group to set foot inside the mission. The heavy mission doors swung shut behind us and a sweeping peace enveloped me. The outside world fell away, as though muted by a great distance. The sunlight, which had seemed so harsh moments ago in the parking lot, was at the wrong angle to beam directly into the sanctuary. Instead, fingers of light shot through the high windows to reflect against the painted ceiling, bouncing aimlessly in the vastness above us and filling the cathedral with a reflected glow.

"Come in, everyone. Come on, don't be afraid to scootch a little closer." Annie waved us forward. When Lucas and I edged farther inside, she gestured at the sanctuary around us grandly. "This mission was first established in 1593, by a group of Spanish monks. This room we're standing in was the entirety of the original mission. Everything else—the dormitory, the gardens, the refractory—that was added later." Annie gestured for us to follow her deeper into the sanctuary. I stepped out from under the shelter of the foyer and got my first good look at the simple stained glass windows, depicting the lives and deaths of a variety of saints.

I heard a group of guys muffling laughter from the other side of the sanctuary. I glanced over and saw Dan Buchanan making a lewd gesture while a group of kids surrounding him snickered. One of the girls tossed her icy-blond hair back over one shoulder and noticed me staring. Her smile vanished in an instant.

Amber. She used to brag that she'd grown up getting most of the things she wanted in life. Until I came along, I suppose. She'd made a failed play for Lucas when he started at Coronado Prep, but that wasn't the reason for the icy rage that gleamed in her eyes.

This was about an ultimatum she'd given me last winter.

You were there when Derek died, she'd said. *You had something to do with Parker's meltdown. I don't want you at my school. I don't want you near my friends. I'm warning you. If you stick around, whatever happens next is on your head.*

With some effort, I let my gaze slide away from Amber back to our tour guide. Amber's threats were toothless. If she ran around telling everyone her theory that I was a Lilitu demon, they'd all look at her like she was nuts. Never mind the fact that it was true. Most of humanity wasn't willing to accept that people—things—like me existed. I'd had a hard enough time believing it myself when I'd found out. Steering my thoughts carefully away from this sensitive topic, I sighed. No, there wasn't much Amber could do to me, and we both knew it.

"And now for the *pièce de résistance*," Annie proclaimed with a wide sweep of her arm. She walked into the small alcove to the left of the altar. "Have you ever wondered why our town is called Puerto Escondido? Well, feast your eyes on this." Placing her hand on a carved wooden rose, she turned her wrist. The rose, which had looked like it was carved into one of the church's pillars, moved. It was some kind of latch. Behind Annie, a section of the rich oak paneling popped open. She pulled it open farther with a flourish.

While Annie was obviously excited about this revelation, the junior class of Coronado Prep did not share her enthusiasm.

Annie, struggling to win back her audience, attempted a "spooky" voice that came off painfully corny. "But why, you may ask, did the monks of Puerto Escondido need a secret door out of their sanctuary?"

"Booty calls?" Dan offered. The sanctuary rang with raucous laughter. Annie's face fell, and my heart went out to her. But seriously, we were in high school, not kindergarten.

"Okay, Mr. Buchanan, you're with me for the rest of this tour," Mr. Landon said. Dan shrugged and moved to join Mr. Landon near the front of the group.

"Um..." Annie struggled for a way back into her tour.

"Maybe the kids could roam a bit? Come to you if they have any questions about the mission?" Mr. Landon offered. Annie's face melted in relief and she nodded. "Okay, kids," Mr. Landon said, taking charge. "Try and remember this is a school field trip. There may or may not be a quiz on this mission so it might behoove you to take some notes." He waved off a chorus groans with good humor.

"Thank the Lord," Royal said, turning around to face us. "That poor woman. I was getting ready to dial emergency services to come and resuscitate her."

I heard someone approaching behind us, but when the newcomer spoke, even Royal's expression blanched.

"Cassie?" Parker's voice wavered. When she saw him, the blood seeped out of Cassie's face. Royal and I had made a pact to keep Parker away from Cassie as much as possible. We'd done a thorough job of it so far this year; Cassie hadn't come face to face with him once since school started. If she guessed why we'd sometimes steer her down a side hall, or forget a textbook and ask her to walk back to a locker with us, she hadn't let on. But here in the mission, outside the confines of school, we'd let our guard down. He'd gotten past our defenses. Royal locked eyes with me and I saw his flash of panic.

"Leave me alone," Cassie said to Parker, her voice suddenly cold.

Royal and I moved at the same time. Royal guided Cassie away. I stepped in front of Parker to block him from following.

"What are you doing, Parker?" I hissed. "She doesn't want to see you anymore, remember?" I felt Lucas move to stand beside me.

"I thought maybe—" Parker ran a shaking hand through his hair.

"Maybe she forgot that little video you made?" My voice crackled with quiet fury. "That's not likely, is it?" It had been almost a year since Parker had seduced Cassie on a dare and shared the videoed evidence of the deed with his friends. She'd never quite recovered. She put on a brave face, hung out with us like old times, but she'd stopped sewing, stopped designing those fashion-forward creations she'd been so passionate about before. And she'd stopped wearing her hair in the quirky twisted knots that had always seemed so *her*. Where she used to radiate her own personal brand of Cassie-ness almost unconsciously, she now struggled to fade into the background. It was the thing I hated most about what Parker had done to her. He'd stolen her from herself.

Parker squirmed miserably. "I made a mistake," he started.

Lucas didn't give him time to finish. "Don't worry. You're not going to get the chance to make another one."

Parker pulled his gaze off of Cassie and glanced at Lucas, as if seeing him there for the first time. "This has nothing to do with you, Mitchell."

"Come on, man," Lucas said, his voice soft and dangerous. "Walk away."

Parker gave Lucas a lopsided smirk. "Or what? You want to take a swing at me? I thought you used up all your second chances with Fiedler last year."

Lucas's shoulders loosened, the way they did before a practice bout with the Guard. I tried to catch his eye. Parker was an arrogant ass, but that didn't make him wrong. Lucas couldn't afford to push things with Fiedler, not after the rocky start he'd made at Coronado Prep last year.

Either Parker couldn't see how close he'd pushed Lucas to the breaking point, or he meant to instigate a fight.

"She's got nothing left to say to you," I said. Parker's eyes shifted to me a half-second before he shook his head and shoved me aside. I stumbled, catching myself on a column.

"Hey," Lucas growled. He caught Parker's arm roughly. Parker spun around, fist clenched, ready for a fight. Behind them, I spotted Mr. Landon wandering through the crowd, eyes peeled for any trouble. If I was going to diffuse this situation, it had to happen now. I fixed my gaze on Parker.

"*Leave Cassie alone*," I said, willing power into the words. The faint tinkling of chimes echoed strangely around my words as they tunneled through the space between us to settle inside Parker's mind. I saw Lucas tense out of the corner of my eye. I hadn't used *the call* since the night of Winter Ball—the last time I'd told Parker to stay away from Cassie. I shouldn't have had to tell him again, but I pushed that troubling thought down and willed my words to penetrate through Parker's own desires.

It worked. After a second or two he blinked at us, as though startled to see us.

"Um, hello?" Ally Krect snaked her arm through Parker's and glared suspiciously at me before turning an inviting smile on Parker. "Did you get lost, babe?"

"Clearly." Parker seemed to shake the last of his haze off. He looped his arm over her shoulders, turning his back on us.

I could feel Lucas turn to study me.

"I don't know," I said, in answer to his unasked question. I finally met his gaze, and saw my own worry mirrored in his eyes. "Maybe I didn't do it right the first time."

"I was there," Lucas said softly. "You did it right. He's resisting somehow." Lucas turned to stare after Parker, who was ignoring us, arm still comfortably circled around Ally. She flicked a suspicious look over to us, then angled her body so her back was facing us, too.

"Come on," I said, drawing Lucas back to Royal and Cassie, who were studying some old carved panels on the walls. Doing their best to act normal.

"It's so pretty here," Cassie said, glancing up as Lucas and I joined them. "I can't believe this place is over 400 years old."

"All right," Royal said, getting down to business. "I say we split up. You two take that side, we'll take this side, and we can compare notes tonight. Deal?"

I glanced at Lucas, more than a little willing to spend some time strolling through the beautiful mission alone with him.

As if he could read my thoughts, Lucas smiled. "Deal."

Cassie was right. The mission was beautiful. Everything, from the beams in the ceiling to the stones under our feet, had been hand carved by the monks who'd established this mission nearly half a millennium ago. Lucas and I wandered through the sanctuary, letting the peaceful beauty of the space wash over us. As we drifted back to the main sanctuary doors, Lucas spotted a crack in one of the massive columns framing the narthex. He examined it for a moment, then smiled.

"Huh," he said. "Apparently those monks were hiding more than one secret around this place." He hooked his fingers into the crack and what had looked like a carved section of the column turned out to be another concealed door. Lucas opened it, revealing a tightly curved spiral staircase leading up. "Where do you suppose that goes?" There was a decidedly mischievous glint in his eye.

"Well," I said, as if resigning myself to an odious task. "Mr. Landon did give us an assignment."

"True. This might be on the quiz."

The spiral staircase was so narrow you had to watch where you put your feet; each tread narrowed from about eight inches to almost nothing as it connected in the center of the spiral. It took a bit of concentration to walk up, and I knew coming down would be another challenge.

But the climb was worth it. Lucas and I reached the top of the stairs to discover we were in a cozy little viewing balcony overlooking the main sanctuary. Very cozy, actually—we could barely move without bumping into each other. Sheltered in our hiding place, we had the perfect view of the sanctuary. Just above us, a stained glass window depicted a beautiful saint, haloed in light, holding an arrow over her heart.

Something drew my attention back down to the level below. A lone figure stood in the center of the sanctuary. A familiar feeling pulled at the edge of my thoughts, but before I could place it, Lucas spoke.

"Beautiful." He was so close, his breath stirred the hair against my neck. I was suddenly aware of the warmth of his body behind me and ached to lean back into him. My heart quickened. I tried to tamp it down. We couldn't act on these feelings. We had made a promise to the Guard, to our families. But beyond that, I'd sworn to myself to never, *never* let myself risk Lucas's safety again. And yet, right at this moment, none of that seemed to matter.

I turned in his arms.

Whatever reassuring thoughts I might have had about Lucas's and my self-control, I overestimated it.

I don't know which of us moved first. Our lips brushed and I felt the sudden swell of the Lilitu storm inside me, straining forward, waiting for one moment's weakness in my self-control to drain Lucas of his vitality. I pulled back from Lucas as if stung.

"We can't." I cringed at the sound of my voice, hoarse with emotion. "We can't."

"Braedyn," he started. I traced my fingers across his lips, thrilled at the soft warmth of the touch. I bit my own lip and turned aside.

"We promised," I said.

"I know. I just wish—" Lucas pulled away from me, and I could see the struggle on his face. "This would be a lot easier if we knew when the waiting part would end." He smiled, that lopsided smile that made him look in the same moment vulnerable and worldly. "Too bad

Sansenoy didn't leave you his number."

"Right. Because, you know, why not just call and ask?"

Lucas pitched his voice an octave higher than normal, and I realized he was imitating me. "'So, Sans, that whole becoming human thing, when do you figure that's going to happen? 'Cause my boyfriend and I have some plans.'"

"I do not sound like that!" I said, punching him in the arm for the poor impersonation. But I couldn't stop myself from giggling.

"Ouch." Lucas smiled, rubbing his arm, clearly pleased to have won a laugh. "Hey, can I ask you a question?"

"What?"

"Why haven't you told Murphy?"

The question caught me unprepared. When I'd told Lucas of the angel's offer to make me human, he'd been so thrilled, I'd stopped halfway through. There was a part I hadn't told him. I hadn't told him about the caveat. Because if I slipped up, if I used my Lilitu powers to hurt someone badly enough, I would cross a line. My soul would be too tainted to ever be redeemed, and my chance of becoming human would evaporate as completely as a drop of water spilt on the hot desert floor. That was why I hadn't been able to bring myself to tell Murphy, my father. I couldn't bear it if Dad pinned all his hopes on me becoming human, and then I lost control and crossed the line. It would crush him. I'd told myself it was better he not know, but keeping this from him was getting harder and harder. I forced myself to smile. "I just haven't found the right time."

Lucas nodded, but I could tell he didn't believe me. "What exactly constitutes the right time to tell your dad that you might actually get to live a normal, healthy life?"

"It's—" I took a deep breath, then went for a half-truth. "The Guard needs me right now. As a *Lilitu*. I don't want to distract anyone with thoughts of what might happen someday."

"*Might?*" Lucas looked genuinely surprised. "What's this 'might' business? You got a guarantee from an angel that you could be human one day. How does that leave room for 'might?'"

I dragged my eyes back to the sanctuary. "Yeah. No, you're right." I forced a lightness into my voice, hoping that would put an end to the discussion. But Lucas heard the fear behind my words.

"Braedyn?"

I didn't respond, not trusting myself to speak.

"You don't have to hide anything from me."

"I know." Still my words came out too brightly to be believed.

Gently, he cupped one hand under my chin and lifted my face. "What are you not telling me?"

I reached up to take hold of his hand, but I didn't pull it away from my face. After a long moment, I came to a decision. "Okay," I breathed. "But not here."

Lucas's brow furrowed, but he didn't say anything. He simply nodded. I returned to the spiral staircase. I could feel him watching me all the way down.

I emerged from the hidden staircase, trying to get my breath back under control. It would be too humiliating to start crying on a school field trip. I turned to face a row of shadowy statues, pretending to study the carved figures while I quickly thumbed moisture out of my eyes. I turned back to the sanctuary, scanning the room for my friends. If I hadn't been so distracted, I would have seen her sooner. As it was, I only caught the motion of her darting from behind a statue out of the corner of my eye. I barely had time to react, shying to the side as she attacked.

That tiny movement probably saved my life, not that I had time to appreciate my good fortune. One moment I was twisting to shield myself from an unknown attacker, the next I was skidding across the floor, pain lancing through my shoulder, and she was there, on top of me, lips pulled back in a snarl.

I reacted without conscious thought, my muscle memory kicking into action. I drove my knuckles into the woman's throat, which should have flattened her. She barely reacted, but her grip loosened enough for me to plant my feet against her ribs and kick her off of me.

I heard someone scream. Lucas shouted. And then she was diving for me again. I threw my body to one side, rolling onto my feet and spinning around, hands up and ready for a fight. She was already mid-lunge. I was dimly aware that she was the woman I'd seen earlier, slipping through the gate into the mission's inner garden.

She collided with me before I could do more than block her punch.

The force of her blow sent me staggering back a few steps. I faced her, frantic, but hard as I wracked my brain I knew I'd never seen this woman before in my life. Could she be a spotter? Maybe a member of the Guard from a different unit? I held out my hand—a gesture of truce.

"I'm not your enemy."

She lunged for me again, swinging her other arm with more force. I saw the tire iron with just enough time to drop. It sailed through the air where my head had been moments before. Ice gripped my stomach. Whoever this woman was, she was not playing around. That blow was meant to end me. I tried to run past her but she caught me by the scruff of my shirt and jerked me back, hard. I hit the ground with a sickening *thunk*, red and black swirls overtaking my vision. When they cleared, I saw her standing over me, tensing to swing the tire iron for my head.

Lucas hit her like a freight train, bowling her over before the killing blow could fall. A wave of nausea rose in my throat but I pushed it down and forced myself to roll to my knees.

Lucas was wrestling with her for the tire iron beside a bank of stained glass windows. She released the iron suddenly and Lucas, unprepared, lost his balance. Before he could recover, she turned, punching him savagely in the solar plexus. Lucas dropped the tire iron. It struck the ground, impacting with the sound of a clanging bell. Something was wrong—Lucas gasped for breath with a horrible, wet sound. He dropped to his knees, unable to do more than struggle for oxygen.

The woman picked up the tire iron and turned back to Lucas, hunched over on the ground before her.

"No!" My voice sliced through the sanctuary. The woman turned toward me, and I saw again the lifelessness of her eyes. My breath came out in a ragged hiss of realization. "No."

The woman left Lucas, bearing down on me. I realized that I had to end this fight, and I had to do it now. Nothing would make her stop, and the next time I went down, there would be no one there to save me.

I charged toward the woman. She lifted the tire iron to strike, but at the last moment I dropped, skidding toward her across the slick, polished stone, feet first. I connected solidly, the force of my kick shoving her up and back.

No surprise flickered through those dead eyes as she hit the stained glass window. The glass exploded behind her like a shower of multi-colored gems, clearing the way for sunlight to flood the sanctuary with blinding intensity.

I skidded to a stop beneath the window and threw my arms over my head protectively. Tiny fragments of stained glass showered down. The silence was profound, but brief.

Screams sounded inside and outside the sanctuary. I couldn't summon the energy to look up.

"Braedyn!" Lucas called, voice hoarse.

I moved my arms away from my head gingerly, and slivers of glass tinkled to the ground. Glass littered the floor around me. Lucas was half-crawling, half-scrambling forward to meet me. I dragged myself up into a sitting position.

Lucas threw an arm around me. In seconds we were surrounded. Mr. Landon was shouting, his usually jovial face a mask of panic. Annie was screaming into the phone, eyes streaming. And beyond them, a shell-shocked crowd of my classmates watched in horrified fascination.

The only thing that felt real was Lucas's arm around me. I realized I was clinging to him ferociously when Mr. Landon tried to pull us apart.

"Are you hurt?" he was asking. "Braedyn, are you hurt?"

"Don't," I whispered, tightening my grip on Lucas's shirt. Mr. Landon pulled back helplessly.

"How long?" he asked Annie. "How long until the ambulance gets here?"

I didn't hear Annie's response. I was looking at Lucas's face. "Did you see?" I whispered. "Did you see her eyes?" Lucas nodded grimly. So I wasn't crazy. The woman who'd attacked us?

She was a *Thrall*.

We were still clinging to each other 15 minutes later when the paramedics arrived.

2

As far back as I could remember, the moon had been a comforting beacon in the darkness. But tonight, the thin crescent sliver seemed distant, unfeeling. My shoulder ached. A student who'd seen the attack reported that the woman had leapt for me, clubbing that tire iron across my shoulder. I supposed I was lucky that the fracture was my only serious injury from the day. Most of the large stained glass shards had fallen out of the window with the woman. The few smaller fragments that had rained down on me left only superficial cuts on the skin of my hands and my lower back. My jacket had ridden up during my slide across the floor; otherwise, I might have escaped with even fewer cuts. My arm was bound up in a complicated sling, but I knew I'd only have to wear it for a few days, not the month or more the doctors had prescribed. There were a few perks to being Lilitu. One good night's sleep would ease the pain, three or four would heal the fracture completely.

I glanced out the window to the Guard's house next door. Lucas's drapes were closed, but I could see the light was on. It was close to midnight, but he was still awake. Probably getting grilled by Gretchen again, going over the whole attack in excruciating detail. As the Guard's resident spotter in Puerto Escondido, Gretchen would have been on high alert just knowing there was a Thrall in town. But the Thrall had just attacked Lucas, the last family Gretchen had in this world. She'd drive herself to find the Lilitu responsible, no matter what it cost her.

A Thrall in town. We hadn't seen one since Ais's death. It hadn't surprised either Lucas or me to learn that after she'd fallen through the stained glass window, the Thrall had rolled to her feet and stood up. What did shock us was that instead of returning to the sanctuary to renew her attack on us, the Thrall had fled the scene. Thralls don't give up. Once they have their orders, they pursue their objective until they are killed or incapacitated—or until the orders are rescinded. I couldn't guess what the Lilitu who'd sent that Thrall intended. I only knew that it meant a Lilitu was back in Puerto Escondido.

I tried to tell myself we'd all known it was just a matter of time before the Lilitu resurfaced. Ais had made it pretty clear that a growing number of Lilitu were hell-bent on breaking through the Wall that separated our worlds. This war was ancient, but the final battle was coming.

Knowing it was coming and seeing it begin were two very different things.

I shivered under the blankets, wishing Lucas would fall asleep. I needed to see him, to feel his arms around me in the only safe place we could embrace—in the dream.

I heard a voice downstairs, full of tension. I tried to push it out of my mind, assuming Hale had come over to talk about the attack with Dad. Hale might have been the leader of this unit of the Guard, but he sought out Dad's advice often. More and more often, it seemed to me. I heard another muffled voice. This one sent a jolt down my spine. Thane was here, too?

I pushed the blankets back and crawled out of bed, slipping my feet into the cozy moccasins Dad had given me last Christmas. While the September days were still warm, the nights had grown sharper, heralding the coming New Mexico winter. I edged out of my room and walked down the hall, stooping to kneel at the top of the stairs.

I couldn't see into the kitchen from here, but I could hear the three men talking as distinctly as if I were sitting around the kitchen island with them.

"Marx split his unit into three groups," Hale was saying. "He's leading the search into Canada, but it'll still take some time to gather everyone together."

"How much time do you think we have?" Thane asked, his voice clipped even more than usual.

"Enough," Dad said.

"Even if we can gather everyone," Thane shot back, "that's only about 100 soldiers. If this intelligence is correct, and the Lilitu have found the way to open the seal—"

"We play it safe," Dad said. His voice was steady, but there was an anger behind his words that sent a shiver of alarm down my body.

"We don't even know where this seal is located," Thane growled.

"You're the archivist," Dad snapped back, losing his calm. "Isn't that your job?"

"How exactly do you suggest I go about finding information that's—as far as we can tell—all been destroyed?" Thane's voice grew softer, dangerous. "She is our secret weapon, but that only helps us if we use her."

A chair scraped the floor. "She's been through enough," Dad said hoarsely. "She and Lucas, they've already had to deal with more than any kid should be expected to handle."

"What do you suggest?" Thane asked, a mocking edge to his voice. "Asking the Lilitu politely if they wouldn't mind waiting a few years so our children have time to mature?"

"Thane's right," Hale said. "That Thrall went after her, Murphy. Keeping her out of the loop won't protect her."

"I'm not suggesting we keep this from Braedyn," Dad said. "I'm just asking that we not throw her directly into the lion's den." Hearing my name sent a jolt of anxiety through me. It drove the exhaustion out of my head in an instant. I strained to hear everything.

Thane made a disgusted sound. "This is what she was raised for, Murphy! Or have you forgotten that? She needs to be training. We've got a very limited amount of time to push her to discover what she's capable of."

"If it were up to you, she'd have no social life at all," Dad said. Warmth spread through my stomach. No matter what we'd been through, Dad still fought for me to have a life—a life as normal as we could make it under the circumstances. I bit my lip, suddenly feeling the urge to tell him about the angel's promise. He deserved to know.

"If it were up to me, she wouldn't even be attending high school," Thane snarled back. "What does she need with an education? There's very little chance she'll survive the final bat—" But Thane's words choked off abruptly. All the warmth that had flooded through me a moment ago vanished.

"Murphy." Hale's voice rang with authority. After a moment, I heard Thane drag in a ragged breath.

"You see this, Hale?" Thane hissed. "He's not fit for this task. He's let his feelings for the demon overrule his common sense. Give me charge over her training and I guarantee—"

"Go home, Thane," Hale said quietly.

"Hale," Thane began.

"We all need some sleep. Things will seem clearer in the morning."

There was a long moment of silence, then I heard another chair scrape the floor. I ducked back into the shadows at the top of the staircase as Thane marched to the front door. He placed a hand on the doorknob, then hesitated. He turned toward me, as though he'd known all along I was there, listening. His eyes found mine, steely and calculating. He lifted two fingers to brush his temple in a mocking salute, and then he was gone, pulling the door closed behind him.

I shrank back against the wall, frozen.

Hale and Dad walked to the front door a few moments later. They both looked exhausted.

"You know it's time," Hale said. "She has to start training again." Dad didn't answer. Hale put a compassionate hand on my dad's shoulder. "I give you my word, Murphy. I'll do my best to prepare her."

Dad nodded slowly. Hale opened the door and walked into the night. Dad closed the door, then leaned his forehead against the solid oak. After a few moments, I drew back into the hall and returned to my room. How long he stood there, I don't know. I fell asleep before I heard him move.

I found Lucas in his dream.

The campus of Coronado Prep loomed, threatening, against the background. Dark dream-clouds swirled with too much energy in the sky above us.

"Lucas," I called. He turned to face me, and I saw the anxiety melt in his eyes. Overhead, the roiling motion of the clouds slowed.

"Is this a dream?" Lucas asked. I nodded. He was getting better at lucid dreaming every night. His brow furrowed as his thoughts turned inward. "But today at the mission...?"

"That was real," I said.

"So they're back."

Around us, the campus of Coronado Prep faded, leaving us in the vague half-space between dreams. I reached for Lucas's hand. He took it, drawing me close. This time, when our lips met, I didn't have to pull away. There was no Lilitu storm to battle, because I couldn't hurt Lucas in a dream. His arms tightened around me and I let myself sink into the sensations, relaxing for the first time since the Thrall had attacked.

I pushed thoughts of tomorrow from my mind.

By Saturday morning, my shoulder was good as new. I slept in, luxuriating in the moment. For this moment, no one was expecting or demanding anything from me. Even when Lucas vanished, his dream-presence snuffed out as he awoke next door, I lingered in the sweet remnants of our night together. Moments like this would become harder and harder to hold onto.

When I finally made my way down to the kitchen, mid-morning sunlight was streaming through the windows and I had to squint against the glare off the countertop.

Hale was sitting with Dad at the kitchen island, looking over some handwritten notes. They looked up as I entered.

"Morning," I said automatically.

"Braedyn," Hale greeted me with a cordial smile.

"How would you like your eggs?" Dad asked.

"I'm not that hungry."

"Well, you might want to eat something anyhow," Dad said. "How about an omelet? Green chili and cheddar cheese?"

I glanced back at Hale, putting two and two together. "Training?"

Hale nodded.

"In that case, omelet me up."

"Sure thing, kiddo." Dad smiled and ruffled my hair on his way to the stove. I grunted, irritated, and pulled my fingers through the wild tangle, trying to smooth it back down.

"So what are you two conspiring over this morning?" I asked Hale. Dad cracked some eggs into a bowl and began whisking them.

Hale glanced at his notes. "Your dad and I were considering what made the most sense for your training regimen."

"We're not just picking up where we left off?" I couldn't keep my surprise out of my voice.

"I think, given the, uh, time constraints," Hale glanced at my dad at the stove. Dad, acting like he wasn't listening, poured the eggs into a frying pan where they hissed furiously. So this wasn't his idea. I turned back to Hale. "I think it makes more sense to focus on skills you'll be able to use sooner rather than later," Hale explained.

"Sooner?" I looked at the scribbled notes, hoping to hide my unease from Hale.

"I just want to be prepared," Hale said, smiling with manufactured confidence.

"What kind of skills?"

"More hand to hand," Hale said. "And I'd like to start training you against multiple opponents."

"What about sword practice?"

"No bladed weapons. Not for a while, at least."

"Order up," Dad said, sliding a steaming omelet onto a plate in front of me.

Hale stood. "I'll see you in the armory in an hour." He left, and I heard the front door close behind him.

I picked up a fork and started carving the steaming omelet into small chunks. Cheese and green chili sauce oozed out onto the plate and my mouth watered. I was aware of Dad watching me.

"So." I moved the omelet around on my plate, waiting for the curls of steam to dissipate before taking a bite. "You think we'll be fighting again soon?"

Dad sat next to me at the island. He studied his hands, trying to keep his voice light. "It's possible."

"Possible like it's possible we'll go for ice cream today—or possible like it's possible there are aliens living on Mars and we don't know it because they're just really good at hiding?" When he didn't answer, I nudged him with my elbow. "Dad?"

Dad looked up, and I saw tears standing in his eyes.

"Oh." I swallowed hard, suddenly not hungry. "This is it, isn't it? This is the final battle."

Dad looked back at his hands. "It's possible," he said again.

One hour later I was standing beside Gretchen in the basement of the Guard's house, taping my hands up for practice. Lucas and Matthew were already sparring on the mats behind us. Gretchen finished taping her hands and slapped them together, hard. As I'd feared, she seemed laser-focused on the job at hand. I sighed inwardly, knowing I'd walk out of here sore when training was over.

Gretchen turned on me abruptly. "So, listen," she said. "Mr. Landon told me you saved Lucas's life, drawing that Thrall away from him before she could split his head open." Gretchen put a hand on my shoulder, giving it a brief squeeze. "I owe you one."

"Uh, thanks?"

Gretchen wasn't much for displays of emotion, so it wasn't a surprise when she turned her back on me and walked out onto the mat. "You coming or not?" she called over her shoulder.

I hurried out to join her, growing more uneasy by the moment. It had been almost a year since I'd done any serious training. It had only taken a few weeks for me to recover from my injuries from our fight with Ais. Lucas's injuries had taken much longer to heal. But neither of us had resumed training after that night. As I faced Gretchen, I wondered how much I'd forgotten.

Quite a bit, it turned out.

Gretchen wasn't pulling her punches, so each time I moved too slowly or failed to anticipate an attack, I got an immediate reminder of why practicing was a good idea. Hale orbited the mat, offering suggestions and encouragement to both Lucas and me as we fought our respective sparring partners. Although, I noticed grimly, Matthew was taking it a lot easier on Lucas.

Distracted, I wasn't prepared when Gretchen landed a fist in my side. I doubled over, winded. Gretchen danced back, waiting for me to recover. "I thought you owed me one," I wheezed.

"Do you need to stop?" she asked.

"No," I sighed, straightening.

"Then less talk, more concentration." She moved forward, looking for an opening. This time I kept my eyes on her, so when she moved, I was ready. I blocked her punch and followed it up with a quick attack that forced her to step back, wheeling around to defend herself. As she struggled to regain her balance, I struck, connecting solidly.

She let out an *oooof* of air, then grinned. "Nice," she managed.

"Keep your elbows in."

We sparred for close to an hour, when Hale called a water break.

Lucas collapsed into a chair, letting some of his water dribble down the sides of his mouth as he gulped it in. I sat beside him, wiping sweat off my face with the edge of my t-shirt.

Matthew and Gretchen took their time with their water. A fine sheen of sweat gleamed along their brows, but nether was breathing heavily. Hale walked over to them to talk. I saw Gretchen glance at me, a calculating look in her eyes.

"Not looking forward to tomorrow morning," Lucas said, rubbing a sore shoulder with one hand. I smiled in sympathy. Lucas sighed. "Don't even. Tomorrow morning you won't even have a bruise."

"I don't have to heal fast," I said. "If you'd prefer, I can always leave your dreams alone."

"Don't you dare," Lucas murmured, catching my hand in his and giving it a warm squeeze. His smile was warm, intimate. If this were a dream I'd lean forward to kiss him. But we weren't dreaming.

"Okay, break's over," Hale said, turning. Lucas and I quickly released hands and Lucas let out a groan of despair. Hale saw Lucas's ashen expression and smiled. "Why don't you sit this one out?"

Lucas and I both sat back, relieved.

"Not you," Gretchen said, giving me a wicked grin. "Come on. Up."

"I'm going to show you a few techniques for handling multiple opponents," Hale said. "Then we'll get you started practicing them." He gestured to Gretchen and Matthew. "Okay. Come at me."

Gretchen and Matthew traded a quick look, evidentially agreeing on a plan of attack with a few terse gestures. They sprang at Hale, Gretchen from the front, Matthew from behind. Hale blocked Gretchen's attack, but while his attention was focused on her, Matthew came behind him, pinning his arms behind his back. Gretchen renewed her attack on Hale, who kicked out at her, using her body as leverage to shove Matthew backwards. Matthew lost his grip on Hale. Hale rolled free, sweeping a foot behind Matthew's leg and knocking the younger man flat on his back.

Matthew let out a grunt of surprised pain, and Gretchen's eyes narrowed. Lucas let a low whistle escape beside me. I glanced at him and he grinned ruefully. "She's pissed," he murmured. "Hale better watch it."

Gretchen danced back, judging Hale's movement. She sprang at him and Hale had to throw himself awkwardly aside to miss the attack. As he scrambled to gain his footing, Gretchen threw herself on the ground at his feet, catching him around the knees with her legs and twisting. Hale went down like a tree felled by an axe, sprawling on the ground. Gretchen was on him in half a second, pinning him to the ground, fist poised to strike his throat.

"Yeah, okay," Hale wheezed. "You win."

Gretchen rolled off him and walked over to Matthew, who was smiling broadly. She offered him her hand, then helped him stand. Hale stood and gestured to me.

"I don't know about this," I said.

"It's okay," Hale said. "We'll start slow."

Slow, I discovered, was a relative term. Hale had Gretchen and Matthew attack at one quarter speed the first couple of times while he talked me through some strategies for dealing with them both at once. The main technique Hale seemed interested in teaching me involved a fairly quick series of moves to redirect the first attacker while repositioning for the second. Even at quarter-speed, I found myself breathing harder.

After we'd run through a few slow-motion fights, Hale stepped back.

"Right, let's pick it up." He nodded to Gretchen and Matthew.

Gretchen met my eye. "Ready?" she asked.

"I guess?" I barely had time to raise my hands in a defensive position before they sprang. My first instinct was to turn and run, but Hale was there, shouting instructions, so I did my best to fight back. Only, my timing seemed completely off. I'd turn my attention to one, just in time to give the second the perfect opening to tag me with a fist. To be fair, Gretchen and Matthew were fighting half-strength at best, but facing twice as many fists and feet as I was used to was overwhelming. Each time they drove me off the mat, Hale would call a stop to the fight and we'd reset in the center of the room. We drilled the same attack and defense over and over and over. Each time I took more punches than I gave, and each time I ended up getting driven off the mat. It was demoralizing.

By the end of the session, my whole body ached and my mind felt like it had been forced through a strainer. It was my turn to collapse into a chair. Lucas had a small towel and a bottle of water ready for me.

"I feel like a boxer in the ninth inning," I groaned.

Lucas shook his head. "It's rounds in boxing, not innings. But you did kind of look like a boxer by the end there."

I was mid-gulp, so I couldn't laugh in disbelief. Lucas read my expression and shook his head. "Look," he said, pointing. I turned and saw Gretchen and Matthew, leaning against a table, gulping down their own waters. "You gave them a workout."

Huh. They did look kind of exhausted. I finished the bottle of water and smiled, taking a deep breath.

"You did well, you two," Hale said, joining us. "Why don't you rest? We'll take care of the equipment for today."

I sank back into my chair, grateful for the break. Lucas and I sat in silence for a few minutes, recovering from the grueling session. I finished my water and noticed Lucas eyeing me, as if he wanted to ask a question.

"What?" I prompted.

"That double step thing Hale had you do—" Lucas said.

"You want me to show you?"

Lucas nodded and we walked into the middle of the room. Hale, Gretchen, and Matthew were busy rubbing oil into the daggers they'd practiced with before Lucas and I had joined the training session. They ignored us.

"It'd be easier to show you if you attacked first," I said. Lucas, who'd had a chance to relax and recover while I was fighting Gretchen and Matthew, nodded. He attacked as Gretchen had done. I blocked him, then caught his arm in one of my fists. "From here, if there were a second opponent, you'd reposition your foot like this," I settled back into a deeper stance and twisted Lucas's arm, turning him on his heel. "Then while the first attacker is recovering, you have a few seconds to deal with the second." I "fought" a second imaginary attacker as Lucas watched, curious.

"Okay," he said. "You come after me."

I waited for him to raise his hands, then rushed him. Lucas blocked my attack, but when he reached to grab my hand and reposition his foot he lost his balance and tripped back, pulling me down on top of him. My squeal broke into a peal of laughter as I looked down into Lucas's chagrined face.

"You make it look easy," he said, flushing slightly.

"Hale," Thane called from the staircase. Lucas and I froze as Thane descended into view. "Marx is asking for details about the accommodations we'll be able to offer the Guardsmen—" Thane's voice broke off as his eyes found Lucas and me.

Suddenly self-conscious, I rolled off of Lucas. We got quickly to our feet, but the damage had already been done. Gretchen looked over, sizing up the situation in half a second. She walked quickly onto the mat, placing herself between Thane and us.

"You," Thane hissed, turning on Gretchen. "You're supposed to be chaperoning them."

"It's fine, Thane," she started. "They were just sparring."

"I have eyes, Ms. Mitchell. And I'm not a fool."

"They know the rules, Thane." She turned to face us, crossing her arms. "Right?"

I felt my cheeks reddening and lowered my eyes. "Yes," I said. "We were just messing around."

"This is not a game," Thane said quietly, advancing toward me slowly. "What seems innocent could cross the line in the blink of an eye. One mistake might cost Lucas his life. And if he dies, you would face the wrath of the entire Guard."

I felt hot anger swelling inside, but I refused to blink, determined not to let Thane see how his words had affected me. Gretchen planted her hand on his chest, arresting him in his tracks. "They get it, Thane. Back off."

Thane shrugged. "I'll leave them in your capable hands, then," he said, smiling slightly. He turned toward Hale, who was frowning at Lucas and me thoughtfully.

"Actually, Lucas," Hale said. "We could use another hand with the equipment."

Lucas glanced at me wordlessly, then went to help Hale. Stricken, I fled up the staircase to escape the armory, Thane's judgment, Hale's suspicion.

Gretchen followed me. "I know you two are being careful," she said quietly. "Don't let him get to you."

I froze in my tracks. Someone had left the TV on in the living room. It was muted, but I didn't have to hear the newscaster speak. The words "MISSING WOMAN" scrolled beneath a smiling photo. The next moment, the screen changed and a home movie of the missing woman began playing.

"Braedyn?" Gretchen said. She followed my gaze to the TV.

"She was a mother," I whispered. On screen, the woman played with two little girls at a birthday party. Smiling. Happy. Alive. Her husband came onto the screen. They kissed, and the touch was one of deep and genuine love.

This missing woman, this loving wife and mother, she was the Thrall who'd attacked me at the mission.

News of the Thrall's identity energized the Guard. Thane and Gretchen went to canvass her neighborhood, trying to find out what they could about her life before she'd become a Thrall. Whatever they'd managed to learn, it wasn't enough to satisfy Gretchen. If anything, she seemed more puzzled after their research trip. I heard her talking to Dad in a low voice after dinner.

"As far as I can tell, the marriage was real."

"Really?" Dad sounded surprised, which made no sense to me.

"I don't know," Gretchen said. "Maybe she played both sides?"

Before I had the chance to find out what they were talking about, Hale asked Lucas and me to help with the dishes. By the time I remembered the conversation later that night, I was already in bed. I laid my head down on my pillow, making a mental note to talk to Dad about it tomorrow.

I closed my eyes in my bedroom, and opened them in the dream.

As always, I found myself in my own private dream within the larger, universal dream that all living things share. A field of roses ringed a tiny meadow. The flowers had once been pure white. Now, every petal gleamed a rich blood red, except for a small white spot at its base. I touched one of the roses absently. They were my warning. Each time I fed on the spiritual energy of a living human in the physical world, the petals grew a little more red, a little less white. I didn't know exactly how it worked, but I knew that it was connected to the angel's caveat; there was only so much damage I could do to others before I'd cross a line. If that happened, I would never become human.

I turned from the roses, meaning to search out Lucas and join him in his dream.

She was standing in my meadow, arms crossed, watching me. I took an involuntary step back. Honey blond hair cascaded down her shoulders, framing a perfect face. There was no denying her beauty. Karayan. The only other Lilitu ever to have been raised by the Guard.

A jumble of emotions crashed through me, but I fought them back. "What are you doing here?"

"I see you haven't changed much," she said, grimly amused at my reaction. "Not that I was expecting a warm welcome. Maybe your basic 'hello' or something."

"Actually, I never got the chance to thank you," I said in a rush, interrupting her. "For the night Ais died."

Karayan's beautiful lips narrowed in a small frown. "Whatever."

"No, seriously," I breathed. "What you did—If you hadn't been there—" I took a step toward her. "We owe you our lives."

Karayan turned away abruptly. "I didn't want to see you get killed. It doesn't mean we're BFFs or anything."

I stopped in my tracks. "Sure, my mistake." I crossed my arms awkwardly. "So, what *are* you doing here?"

Karayan flipped her hair over one shoulder and fixed her piercing green eyes on me. "Something's brewing on the Lilitu side. I don't know the plan, exactly, but it involves some kind of weapon."

"Okay." I waited, unsure how to respond to this.

"You don't get it," Karayan said, eyes narrowing in irritation. "This is important. Like, 'it could decide the War for the Lilitu' important."

"Okay." A thought struck me. "Karayan, do you know where the seal is?"

Karayan gave me a disgusted look. "Are you seriously telling me you're still playing the Guard's devoted lap dog? They don't own you, Braedyn."

"Um, I'm confused," I said. "Why are you telling me about this weapon thing if you're not trying to help us win?"

"Us," Karayan snorted.

"The Guard," I snapped back.

"I'm not trying to help the Guard, you idiot. I'm trying to help you."

"And I'm trying to protect my friends and family." I got the distinct impression Karayan wanted to roll her eyes, but I pressed on. "We could really use your help."

"My help?" Karayan's voice sounded incredulous. "Those people aren't my family, remember?"

"They could be," I said.

Karayan turned to look out over the field of roses, but not before I saw the stricken look in her eye. After a long moment she spoke again. "Watch your back, Braedyn." Karayan glanced over her shoulder to meet my eyes. "I don't know how, but you're a part of their plan."

And then she was gone.

3

Karayan's words still shrouded my thoughts the following Monday when Lucas and I arrived at school. I'd told Dad what she'd said as soon as I'd woken up. He hadn't liked it any more than I had, and had looped Hale and the others into the conversation at breakfast. After an entire Sunday spent deliberating, we'd reached no conclusions about what to do. Karayan's warning that I was somehow a part of the Lilitu's plan was too vague to act on, and too frightening to ignore. Hale had even questioned Karayan's motives, suggesting she might have wanted to upset me to keep me distracted and unfocused. That had given me pause. What did I really know about Karayan? On the one hand, she had basically delivered Derek to the Guard for execution as a Thrall. On the other hand, she had saved all our lives the night of Ais's death. Would Karayan have gone to the trouble of sparing us once in order to have the pleasure of watching us destroyed later? In the end, whether or not upsetting me had been Karayan's aim, it was the end result of our conversation.

Lucas curved his arm around my shoulders protectively while we walked from the parking lot to school. We had to part ways for first period, but he lingered with me outside my class until the last moment.

"We're going to figure this out," he said. He brushed the hair back from my forehead, smoothing it behind my ear. I felt a twinge in my middle when he withdrew his hand.

"You sound so sure."

Lucas gave me a crooked grin. "Come on. You're Braedyn Murphy. You went head to head with an ancient Lilitu and emerged victorious."

"One," I said softly. "And I had a lot of help." He heard the unspoken fear in my voice. His smile dimmed. If the final battle was drawing closer, it was unlikely we'd be facing just one powerful demon.

"When Gretchen and I first discovered the Guard, we hooked up with this unit. Their oldest soldier was this guy Anders. He must have been 60. Tough." Lucas smiled faintly at some memory. "He had this saying; 'don't go looking for tomorrow's trouble, it'll come find you. Just be ready when it does.'"

"That's supposed to be comforting?"

Lucas laughed softly. "Right. Yeah, it sounds pretty terrible, doesn't it? But I think what he meant was worrying about what might happen doesn't help." The bell rang, and Lucas sighed. "When trouble comes, I'll be standing right by your side." He leaned his forehead against mine and we stood there for a long moment, drawing strength from one another. Then he turned and walked down the hallway.

With a leaden stomach, I walked into first period. I spotted Cassie and dropped my books onto the empty desk beside her. She looked up, startled, then smiled.

"Hey, rock star."

"Huh?" I saw Cassie's grin deepen and she pointed down to the school newspaper on her desk.

"You're kind of a big deal," she said. Her eyes flicked lightly around the room.

I turned and noticed most of the class staring at me with varying degrees of interest. More than one guy straightened when my gaze passed over him. I groaned under my breath and snatched the paper up off Cassie's desk. Someone had snapped a picture in the mission. It must have been just after the Thrall had attacked Lucas, but neither of them were in the shot. I was standing in the middle of the sanctuary, hair streaming back from my face, my eyes shining with furious power.

Someone slid into the desk on my other side. I braced myself, expecting to find a dreamy-eyed boy giving me a watery smile. I'd learned from experience that the best thing to do in these situations was to end the crush before it had a chance to grow. But as I turned, my prepared speech died on my lips.

It was Amber. She gave me a cool glance, then turned her attention to the front of class where Mr. Landon was writing today's lesson on the board.

At 8:05, morning announcements began as they always did.

Headmaster Fiedler read through the day's notes with his usual cheerful efficiency, but I wasn't paying attention. I was trying to figure out why Amber was sitting next to me, ignoring me. There were other seats available, including one by her friend Missy.

Headmaster Fiedler finished with the day's announcements and his voice brightened. "Okay, last but not least, we've got a special announcement from the drama department for you this morning."

A tinny recording filled the room.

"*I'm ready,*" came a girl's hushed voice.

"*Are you sure?*" a boy asked. Something prickled on the back of my neck.

"*I think I love you, Parker,*" came the sweet reply.

Cassie gripped the desk beside me, her body going rigid with shock.

The muffled sounds of kissing, the rustle of sheets, then a pause.

"*Cassie?*" Parker's voice sounded exasperated. "*I thought you wanted this.*"

"*It's just— I've never done this before,*" the recorded Cassie breathed. Students started giggling, a few glanced at Cassie. Cassie's face could have been carved from stone. Her eyes found mine with silent, desperate pleading. "*Can we go slow?*"

Titters spread throughout the classroom.

"Um," Mr. Landon realized at last that this was not the drama department's special announcement. "Okay, clearly there's been—" he rushed to the speaker, trying to locate an off-switch he'd never needed before. The recorded sounds of movement grew louder. Cassie leapt to her feet, knocking over her chair in her haste to escape. She fled the classroom, horrified. I stood to follow her.

"No, just— Stay in your seats," Mr. Landon said, racing out the door after Cassie.

I grabbed Cassie's and my bags, ready to drive her away from this place, my heart pounding.

"He told you to stay seated," came Amber's calm voice. I turned. Of everyone in the classroom, only Amber wasn't reacting to the sounds issuing over the loudspeakers. She sat, calmly, while our peers clamped their hands over their mouths or laughed outright in disbelief.

"You?" Realization came in an icy rush. Amber's eyes didn't waver.

A shrill whine screeched over the speaker and students clutched hands over their ears, wincing in pain.

"...said turn it off!" roared Fiedler. The speaker finally fell silent.

"I told you not to come back to school," Amber said. Her eyes hadn't left my face.

I felt my hands balling into fists at my sides. A growing rage clouded my vision. "Why Cassie?"

"Be honest, Lilitu," Amber said, lowering her voice to a hiss. "You didn't think I was any kind of threat, did you? Sure, maybe I can't do anything to you. But you better believe I can make your friends suffer. If you don't decide to leave Coronado Prep, things are going to get a lot harder for the people you love."

For a moment, the only thing I could hear was the rush of blood in my ears. I lunged for Amber, but she was faster than I'd bargained for. She jumped out of her seat and grinned at me. The class spun around in their seats to stare at us.

"Girl fight!" one of the guys called, and another round of laughter filled the class. I was too pissed to care. Amber didn't take her eyes off of me. She was grinning with malicious glee.

"Do it," Amber said. "I dare you. You'll be doing me a huge favor by getting yourself expelled."

It took all of my self-control, but I forced myself to turn my back on her, pick up Cassie's and my things, and walk out of the classroom.

***

It took almost 20 minutes, but I finally found Cassie sitting on the bleachers overlooking the school's soccer field. Royal was perched next to her. As soon as I saw them I texted Lucas, then ran across the field to join them.

Cassie looked up as I arrived, winded from my sprint. She held a long blade of grass in her hands, carefully shredding it into tiny fragments.

"I'm okay," she said. I glanced at Royal behind her, and he shrugged helplessly. Cassie sensed the motion and smiled wearily. "Guys, I'm okay. I mean, this isn't going down in my diary as one of the best days ever." She studied the mutilated blade of grass in her hand then sighed, letting the pieces fall to the earth at her feet. "But I've already wasted too much of my life thinking about—" she bit her lip, betraying exactly how close she was to breaking. "Besides," she whispered, "everyone knew already." She reached up to wipe away a tear as it slid down one cheek.

"Oh, Cass." I sat on the bench next to Cassie, fully aware that I was helpless to ease her pain.

"Cassie sandwich," Royal said. He reached his arms toward me and we pulled each other close in a group hug, squashing Cassie between us.

She struggled between us, but she was laughing. "Okay, okay. I need to breathe."

As we released her, Lucas appeared at the edge of the field. Cassie saw him and waved. Lucas waved back, jogging over to join us.

"No meltdown pending," Cassie said as Lucas scooted next to me on the bench. "Pinky swear." She looked up into the wide, blue sky. A few brilliant white cumulus clouds edged one horizon, fat and lazy and comforting. Cassie watched them for a moment. When she next spoke, her voice was wistful. "I just wish I knew why."

It was like a knife turning in my gut. Maybe I should have told them the truth right then; Cassie had been punished for my crimes, and Amber was threatening to hurt the rest of them, too. And I had the power to stop it, I just had to give up the one normal thing in my life: high school.

Instead of speaking, I squeezed Cassie's hand and vowed to myself to do everything I could to stop Amber from hurting anyone else I loved. Even in my head, the promise sounded hollow.

Cassie refused to leave school, and so when lunch rolled around we took our seats at our usual table. Cassie sat with her back to the wall, facing out into the dining room.

"Let them all get it out of their system," she murmured, facing the gawking student body fearlessly. But I saw her hand shaking as she reached for a roll, and she couldn't keep herself from jumping a little each time someone laughed in the dining hall. "Butter?" She said, forcing a cheerful note into her voice.

I grabbed the butter dish and handed it to Cassie, leaning past Lucas. I'd overestimated my reach, and had to brush against him to pass the dish to Cassie. I felt his intake of breath as I pressed against him. I sat back quickly. Lucas's fingers twitched on the table, and I could practically feel his desire to touch me. In the dream we might spend an entire night entwined. But the sensations of the most intimate embrace in a dream were dwarfed by the sensations of the simplest touch in reality.

"Sorry," I whispered.

"Don't be," Lucas answered, forcing a smile. "I knew what I was getting into. Besides, as hard as this is right now, think how great it's going to be when we can be together for real." He reached under the table to give my hand the briefest squeeze. I squeezed back.

"Shut up! Just shut up!" Parker's voice cut across the din of the dining hall.

Lucas and I turned to see Parker standing beside Amber's table, furious. Ally said something to Parker that we couldn't hear, but Amber and her friends snickered. Parker brushed Ally's arm off his shoulder and strode away from her. Ally stared after him, pissed. Parker shot an agonized look at Cassie.

I looked back at Cassie, but she was steadfastly ignoring Parker. Devastated, Parker walked out of the dining hall. Lucas looked at me again, worried. I shook my head. There'd be time to talk about Parker—and how he might be resisting the power of *the call*—later.

Royal cleared his throat as though nothing had happened. "So," he said. "Chuck Norris marathon at my house this weekend. Who's in?"

"Depends. Who's Chuck Norris?" I asked.

"Chuck Norris," Lucas said, looking at me like I was an alien. "Chuck Norris."

"Repeating his name isn't actually helping," I said.

"Cassie? Chuck Norris." Lucas turned to Cassie for backup.

She shook her head. "Sorry. I'm with Braedyn on this one."

"How do you not know—?" Lucas turned back to Royal.

"I find it's best not to ask that question," Royal sighed. "The gaps in their education are really quite shocking." Royal turned to us, steepling his hands like a professor addressing two errant school kids. "Ladies, prepare yourselves. After this weekend, Chuck Norris will be a permanent fixture in your minds. You're welcome in advance."

Cassie and I traded a smile, and I felt a wave of relief wash through me. Maybe she really was going to be okay.

Suddenly, a rich, masculine voice cut through the dining hall chatter.

"Hello, Coronado Prep!" We turned, along with the rest of the school, to see a handsome man stepping up onto a chair at the front of the dining room. "For those of you who don't yet know me, my name is Mr. Hart, and I'm the new drama teacher for this august institution." Someone whistled and the room filled with giggles. Mr. Hart waved in the direction of the whistle, unperturbed. "Listen up, you talented masses. If any tiny particle of you yearns for the spotlight, come audition for our fall production of *Camelot*. I can guarantee passion, heartbreak, and everlasting love. Maybe even a little hero-worship. Will it be corny? Yeah, maybe, but in that fuzzy-no-one-gets-hurt kind of way that reaffirms your faith in humanity."

Laughter swelled throughout the dining hall again. Mr. Hart evidently knew how to make an impression.

"Recap: Audition! You know you want to! Go Wildcats!" He raised his fist in the air, eliciting a roar from the crowd, then bowed dramatically from the waist. The roar swelled into another round of laughter as Mr. Hart stepped back off the chair. As conversation returned to the dining hall, I saw several girls straining to catch another glimpse of Mr. Hart while giggling with their friends.

Whether he was aware of it or not, Mr. Hart had done us a huge favor. No one was staring at Cassie anymore. The subject had been officially changed.

The final bell couldn't come fast enough. It had been a trying day, and I just wanted to meet up with my friends and escape from campus. I stopped by my locker to drop off some books and pick up a few others I'd need for homework. Lucas leaned against the locker bay next to me.

"What a messed up day," he said.

"You can say that again."

"I don't know how she kept it together today." Lucas shook his head in wonder. "When I heard that tape this morning, man, I wanted to find Parker and grind his face into the ground."

"It wasn't Parker," I said grimly. Lucas's eyebrows jerked up in surprise. "It was Amber."

"What?" He looked genuinely bewildered. "What does she have

against Cassie?"

"Nothing," I answered. "It's me she's trying to hurt. She couldn't go after me directly. So she went after my friend."

Lucas's jaw clenched in anger. "Wow, that's low. Even for the ice queen."

"She wants me gone. Out of Coronado Prep." I closed my locker, keeping my eyes focused on the lock while I turned the dial. "Do you think... do you think I should leave?"

"*No.*"

"She's threatened to make all my friends suffer." I shrugged miserably. "Before today I just kind of wrote her off, but if she'd do that to Cassie—?"

"She's sick, Braedyn," Lucas said. "I don't know what's wrong with her, but it's—you can't give in to her."

"And if my friends get hurt?" I asked quietly. "Royal? You?"

"I can take care of myself," Lucas said. "And we can watch out for Royal and Cassie together."

Lucas offered me his hand and I took it. We walked outside together, huddling closer as a cold breeze rustled the leaves of the aspens soaring above us.

Cassie was sitting on the stone retaining wall at one edge of the parking lot, hunched over a notebook. As we drew closer I saw what she was working on. It was a long, elegant gown with a swirling, full skirt that gathered loosely around the feet. Sleeves hugged the upper arms tightly, then opened like trumpet flowers from the elbow to the wrist.

"Cass, that's amazing," I said, awestruck.

Cassie looked up, slipping another paper on top of the drawing.

"Wait," I protested. "Let me see."

Reluctantly, Cassie handed the drawing over. I noticed that the dress was just one of the designs she'd sketched on this sheet. Next to the gown was a rich tunic, trimmed in faux fur with a sweeping cloak to match it.

"What is this?" I asked, awe-struck.

"Just doodles," she said, embarrassed. "I guess I got inspired."

"Mr. Hart?" I guessed. Cassie blushed but nodded, flashing me a small smile.

"Cassie," Lucas said. "These are awesome."

"And when are you going to show them to him?" Royal asked, gliding up beside us and plucking the drawing out of my hands.

"What?" Cassie squeaked. "No, this is just—doodling." Cassie quickly snatched the drawing back from Royal. He crossed his arms.

"Uh huh," Royal said flatly.

"I didn't even know we had a new drama teacher," I said, throwing Cassie a lifeline.

"Yeah," she said, eager for the change of subject. "Ms. Stevenson had some kind of accident this summer, she's going to be out the rest of the semester. I think they said she had a broken collarbone or something."

"Yikes," I said.

"And on that cheerful note," Royal said, "SAT tutor at my place this afternoon. Who's in?"

A skinny boy bounded up to us. Rick had been one of Derek's best friends. I felt a wave of emotion and struggled to force my thoughts back onto happier ground. Derek had died in my home, killed by the Guard because he'd been turned into a Thrall. It was yet another reminder of how I put the people around me in danger. "Yo, Braedyn."

I forced myself to smile. "Rick, what can I do for you?"

"You see today's paper?" he asked, beaming. "I took that picture. Pretty kick-ass, huh? You looked like, I don't know. Like some kind of super-chick. Like Catwoman or Black Widow."

"Yeah, it's a nice shot," I said, trying to keep the irony out of my voice. It was hard enough keeping the Lilitu powers in check without an army of teenage boys identifying me with comic-book heroines.

"Wonder what that lady was looking for," Rick said. "So weird, right?"

"What?" Lucas and I said at the same moment.

"Yeah, I was watching her. She kept staring at the ground, walking around in circles right in the middle of the sanctuary. Then you came down and she just lost it. Well, you know the rest of that story. Am I right?" Rick raised his fist up, clearly expecting me to reciprocate. I bumped my fist against his with a strained smile. "Awesome."

"What makes you think she was looking for something?" Lucas asked, trying to get Rick to focus.

"Well, she had that thing drawn on her hand. You know. Like

those weird carvings on the floor. I figured she was looking for something specific." A horn honked from the parking lot and Rick turned, waving at a car. "That's my ride," he said. "Catch you guys later."

As Rick raced away, I looked at Lucas. I didn't even have to ask.

"You drive," Lucas murmured.

I turned back to Royal and Cassie. "Catch you guys tomorrow?"

"So, that's a 'no' on the SAT prep?" Royal asked.

"We—there's this thing," I started.

Royal held up a hand. "Spare me the details." He turned to Cassie. "Please tell me you're not abandoning me, too?"

"I'm actually looking forward to meeting your academic Ken doll," Cassie said.

Royal smiled and threw his arm over Cassie's shoulder. He glanced at us and shrugged. "Their loss," he said to Cassie. "Toodles." Royal held my gaze for a moment, and I could see his disappointment. Then he turned and led Cassie toward his gleaming platinum two-seater in the parking lot.

While part of me wanted to stay and do my part to cheer Cassie up, I had to go back to the mission. If the Thrall was searching for something in that sanctuary, we needed to know what it was.

Twenty minutes later the town was receding in my rearview mirror. We headed across the natural preserve that separated the mission from Puerto Escondido proper. I stepped on the gas and the Firebird leapt forward beneath us, shooting down the ribbon of asphalt that wound up the far side of the valley.

We reached our turnoff and I eased up on the gas. The road to the mission had never been paved, and if you didn't know where you were going there was a good chance you'd miss it. You couldn't see the mission from this point on the road. It was higher up the mountain, shrouded from view by scrubby Piñon trees. Up farther, the trees would thin out, providing that amazing view from the mission's front door. I turned onto the dirt road. Dust and small rocks kicked up behind us.

"You know, it's possible that Rick just saw this woman acting crazy and made up a theory that she was looking for something to explain it," Lucas said.

"Yeah."

"Or maybe she was there to attack us, and she was just walking in circles, waiting for us to come back down from that balcony."

"Maybe." I kept my eyes focused on the road. "Or maybe," I said, "she *was* looking for something. Something she didn't want us to find. Maybe that's why she didn't come into the sanctuary until it looked like we'd left. Maybe that's why she attacked us," I glanced at Lucas. His jaw was tight. "And maybe that's why she ran away after her fall, instead of coming back to finish the job."

Lucas looked at me, his eyes full of questions.

I turned back to the road. It curved around in a gentle arc, and as we came out of the turn, the view opened up revealing the mission. The parking lot was empty. I pulled to a stop in front of the sanctuary and killed the engine. Neither of us moved for a moment. The last time I'd seen the mission, I was being escorted into the back of an ambulance by a group of EMTs while Mr. Landon hovered by my side anxiously. I felt a sudden pang of uncertainty. Maybe we should have told Dad what we were planning.

"Well, here goes nothing," Lucas said. I pushed down the doubt.

We got out of the car and approached the building. The doors to the sanctuary were closed but not locked. There was no lock built into the doors, actually. If you wanted to keep someone out, you'd have to lay the heavy crossbeam through the metal brackets bolted to the inside of the doors. Lucas held one door open and I walked inside, scanning the space.

It seemed empty. Darker than the last time we'd been here. The shattered stained glass window was boarded up, blocking a good part of the late afternoon sunlight. Without the warm glow of sunlight the sanctuary seemed colder, more foreboding than peaceful. I shivered against a sudden chill.

Lucas took my hand wordlessly. We moved forward into the space. Walking out from under the foyer's coved ceiling, I was suddenly aware of the hidden balcony, unseen in the shadows above us. I had the creepy sensation that someone was watching. I shook it off.

"Let's get this over with," I whispered. We walked into the center of the sanctuary, coming to a stop before the altar. The floor was stone but not, as I'd assumed earlier, paved. I wandered across the floor but could find no seams in the rock.

"It's all one stone," Lucas said, echoing my thought.

We examined the floor, and discovered that we were only partially correct. The massive stone, roughly circular in shape, stretched clear across the sanctuary. But smaller stone tiles filled the gaps beyond the round stone, extending the floor to the edges of the room. The surface of the stone had been worn down over the centuries, but we could still make out faint marks carved into its face. I recognized one mark, partially hidden under a pew, and froze.

"Lucas," I called. "Look." I pointed down to the mark I'd spotted and heard Lucas's sharp intake of breath. "Help me?" Together, Lucas and I pushed the pew back, revealing a string of symbols we both knew all too well. Symbols that were carved onto the blades of every set of daggers a new member of the Guard received. The symbols were older than mankind; they'd been handed down to the Guard from the three angels charged with hunting down Lilitu—Senoy, Sansenoy, and Semangelof. These symbols were meant to protect humanity in the fight against the Lilitu.

"Why?" Lucas looked up, meeting my eyes. "Why here? Do you think the monks—?"

I stood suddenly, electric fear shooting through my nerves. "Lucas. What if *Puerto Escondido* isn't referring to a secret door in the sanctuary? What if it's referring to a door between realities?"

Lucas looked up at me, brow furrowed, trying to see what had suddenly become clear to me. "I don't—" He stood, glancing back down at the ground.

"I think the monks built their mission directly over the seal." I stared down at the massive stone, ringed with ancient symbols. "I think *this* is the door they were trying to hide."

Lucas reacted, grabbing my hand and pulling me off the massive round stone. We retreated to the side of the sanctuary, huddling against a wall, staring back at the seal with sick fascination. Lucas had shielded me from the stone with his body instinctively, but as the adrenaline of the moment cleared, he turned to face me, realizing he had me pinned against the wall. His eyes found my face, but he didn't move. Only our breathing disturbed the silence. I knew I should say something to break the moment, but I couldn't. Lucas brushed fingertips along my cheek, leaving a warm glow lingering at his touch. I looked up, finding his eyes. Somehow, even in the dim light of the mission, they gleamed.

"Tell me what you want," he said. I saw him struggling for self-control.

"What I want," I breathed. "What I want." My eyes flickered to his lips. "There's a caveat," I said at last. "To becoming human."

Lucas drew back a little to get a better look at my face. "What do you mean? What caveat?"

"I can't lose control," I said. "Every time I slip and let the Lilitu part of me steal energy from someone, it destroys another tiny bit of my humanity. If I lose too much, there'll be no changing what I am. No chance of becoming human for real. So when you ask me what I want—"

"It's hard," Lucas said. "I know. It's hard for me, too."

"I wouldn't blame you if you wanted to leave me."

"Don't joke about that," Lucas said.

"Right, you're the guy who flirts with danger." I smiled, but I could hear the edge in my voice. "Why not date it, too? What's the worst that could happen? I slip up, you die, I get executed by the Guard." Lucas's expression looked pained.

"Don't," he said again. "Don't manufacture a reason for us to break up."

"Fine," I said. I pushed against his arm and Lucas let me go. "We should get home."

"I'm with you to the end, Braedyn. Or until you don't want me anymore."

Something in his voice stopped me before I could walk away. He offered his hands to me. After a moment, I took them. Lucas pulled me close and this time I sank into him. He wrapped his arms around my back, holding me tight.

"There's something you're forgetting," Lucas whispered into my hair. "You've kissed me without hurting me before."

He was right. There had been one kiss after my Lilitu powers had blossomed. One kiss in his room, where I'd successfully battled down the Lilitu storm and kept it from siphoning off the essence that made Lucas who he was.

"I trust you," Lucas breathed. "If you tell me we have to stay at arm's length when we're awake, that's what we'll do. But if you ever want to try again..."

Tears seared the corners of my eyes as a swell of emotion threatened to break over me. Lucas, seeing this, started to pull back. I caught his hand, stopping him. I didn't need to speak. I tilted my head up, slipping a shaking hand up to Lucas's cheek. He let me guide him forward, lips parting.

Someone coughed pointedly behind us.

Lucas and I jerked back as if scalded. Adrenaline jolted my system, my heart wrenching painfully in my chest. The intruder was a slight boy about my age, with thin wire-frame glasses and fair, close-cropped hair.

"Assuming that's your car parked out front, you two could probably spring for a cheap motel. So, if you don't mind, some of us are actually here for the history of this place."

Without waiting for a response, the blond boy turned to a wooden panel and carefully placed a sheet of almost-transparent paper over it. He fished a bit of charcoal out of his pocket and started rubbing it lightly over the paper. With every stroke, the image of the panel beneath took shape on the page.

I turned back to Lucas, brushing my hair back from my face, embarrassed. "Come on. We should tell the others what we found."

Lucas nodded and we headed together toward the door.

Without looking up, the boy said something under his breath.

"What was that?" Lucas asked, stopping.

"I'm almost done here." The boy glanced over his shoulder at Lucas. "So if you're planning on getting the goods in the back seat of your car, do me a favor and drive somewhere else first. I'm not all that interested in the mating habits of the Southwestern suburban teen."

Lucas's eyes widened in outraged surprise. "For a skinny kid, you've got a pretty big mouth. Why don't you shut it, before someone shuts it for you?"

"Yes, you're very threatening," the boy said, flicking his eyes over me impartially. "But I'm guessing your girlfriend'll give it up without the macho display of manhood, so you might as well save your energy."

Lucas took a step toward the kid, fury snapping in his eyes. I grabbed his arm.

"Come on," I said quickly, surprised by Lucas's sudden rage. "Ignore him. He doesn't know what he's talking about."

"Right," Lucas said gruffly.

"Of course not," the blond boy sighed in a mocking tone. "How could I possibly understand? You're the only two people in the history of the world who've ever felt this deeply, this purely."

I felt Lucas stiffen with rage beside me, but we were at the sanctuary door. I pulled us outside. The sun had dipped below the mountain while we'd been inside the mission, and the sudden cool air was the slap in the face we needed.

"You okay?" I asked Lucas, who was still staring back at the sanctuary like he was brewing for a fight. "Hey. Lucas."

Lucas startled, then saw me watching him. He gave me a grudging smile. "Sorry. We've got way bigger problems than some undernourished tow-head with an attitude."

I smiled, letting some of the tension ease out of my back. I led the way to my car, but as I unlocked the doors I caught Lucas shooting one last glare at the sanctuary behind us.

4

By the time we got home, the Guard was already settled around the worn round table for dinner. Spaghetti. Gretchen must have been on kitchen duty tonight. Gretchen had many skills, but cooking was not one of them. Everyone looked up when Lucas and I entered, but it wasn't until I saw Thane's expression harden that I realized Lucas and I were still holding hands. I pulled my hand away quickly and shrugged out of my sweater, taking the seat next to Dad. Lucas sat between Gretchen and Hale on the other side of the table.

"Heads up." Matthew tossed him a dinner roll, which Lucas caught with a tight smile. Neither of us were in a very playful mood.

"Everything okay?" Dad asked, sensing our unease.

Thane's gaze flicked from me to Lucas, suspicion creasing the edges of his eyes.

"I'm not sure," I said. "We found something at the mission."

"When was this?" Gretchen turned on Lucas.

"You went back to the mission?" Dad asked with a frown, echoing Gretchen's disapproval.

"It was something one of the kids at school said," I pressed on. "We didn't want to bother you guys until we knew more, just in case it turned out to be nothing." I glanced at Lucas. He watched me, eyes mirroring the tension we'd both felt since leaving the mission. Only part of it was tied to our discovery, but the Guard didn't need to know about the almost-kiss.

"What did you find?" Hale asked, setting his fork down.

I looked back at Lucas. "You tell them," he murmured. "You're the one who figured it out."

"What if," I felt my cheeks redden, suddenly acutely aware of how crazy this sounded. But everyone was listening. Even Thane put his fork down, waiting. I cleared my throat. "The floor of the mission," I started again. "Most of it's covered by this one huge round stone. It's got these carvings, like the ones on our daggers. But there are more symbols that I've never seen before, all around the stone."

"When you say, 'like the ones on our daggers,'" Dad began.

"They're exactly the same," Lucas said, anticipating him. "No question. Braedyn spotted them first, but we both recognized the symbols immediately." Lucas gave Dad a humorless grin. "It's not like they're easy to confuse with something else." The room grew silent, dinner laying forgotten for the moment.

"Go on, Braedyn," Hale said quietly.

"We know Ais came to Puerto Escondido looking for the seal, hoping to open it for the Lilitu to come through, right?" I asked. Hale nodded, waiting for me to get to the point. I took another breath. "What if the monks found the seal centuries ago, and built their mission to hide it? What if that *stone is* the seal?"

For a long moment, no one spoke. Hale sat back slowly, lost in thought. Thane and my dad traded a glance.

"Hm. Interesting." Dad picked up his fork, spooling a strand of spaghetti around it absently.

"It does make a kind of sense," Hale said.

I'd expected a bigger reaction. Something closer to shock and amazement, not this calm consideration of the idea. Lucas glanced at me, sharing my surprise at the group's measured response.

"How does that make sense?" he asked Hale.

But it was Thane who answered us. "Puerto Escondido has been a stronghold of the Guard for centuries. This is one of the few places on earth where the Guard has maintained an almost continual presence." Lucas and I turned to stare at Thane. "We've long known that this place has some kind of significance to the Lilitu, but what exactly?" Thane shrugged unhappily. "Too much of the history of Puerto Escondido has been lost."

Gretchen gave a little laugh of disbelief. "Lost? If those monks knew they were sitting on top of the seal, how exactly do you lose track of information that significant?"

"Off the top of my head? I suspect the Lilitu had something to do with it," Thane snapped.

"Regardless," Hale said. "We've got our new priorities. Thane, I need you to dig into this. Find out whatever you can. Make some calls."

Thane nodded.

"Gretchen, you and Matthew swing by the mission tomorrow. Recon only."

"On it," Gretchen said.

"That means no hunting, you two," Hale said, gesturing at Matthew and Gretchen with his fork. "You find any trace of Lilitu presence, you report back immediately."

"I think it's time for us to do a full inventory of the armory," Dad said.

"Right." Hale and Dad exchanged a grim look. "We'll start tomorrow."

With that, everyone turned back to their food, lost in unhappy thoughts. Everyone except for Lucas and me.

"That's it?" I asked. "You're sending Gretchen and Matthew to swing by the mission?"

"We don't have the resources to put a guard on the place full time," Hale said around a bite of spaghetti. "But we'll add it to our rounds." He took another bite, ending the conversation.

"What about us?" Lucas asked. "What should we be focusing on?"

Hale looked up, but Dad answered before he had a chance to swallow his food. "School."

"But, we can help." Lucas looked at Gretchen, hoping for some support. She avoided his gaze. He looked around the table, frustration edging into anger. "You wouldn't even know about the seal if it weren't for Braedyn and me."

"So, as a reward for stupidly risking your safety, you want us to let you throw your future away?" Dad spoke quietly, but there was a dangerous edge to his voice. Lucas glanced at me helplessly.

"The boy has a point," Thane murmured. "What good will school do either of them if the Lilitu win?"

Dad's fork hit the edge of his plate with a sharp clatter. "School matters. Braedyn's education matters. It matters to me, because it means we live in hope. I am fighting to give Braedyn a future. In this future, she graduates high school. She goes to college. She builds a life of meaning for herself. I'm not giving that up. It's what she deserves."

I felt my chest tighten. Hot tears sprang into my eyes. Dad believed in me absolutely, and listening to him talk, I could almost see the future he dreamed of.

"How?" Thane glanced at me impersonally. "She is Lilitu, Murphy. What kind of future do you really think she'll have? Marriage? Children? These things are impossible for her."

"That's not true," Lucas said. His whole body was coiled tight with anger. Thane eyed him, unmoved.

"If you think the Guard will allow her to take the life of a human man in order to create a Lilitu child, you've missed the entire point of our existence," Thane said. He turned back to his plate, dismissing the entire conversation.

"This discussion is moot anyway," Hale said. "We've got bigger problems."

"You're fools if you believe that," Thane said around a mouth of spaghetti. "More immediate problems, yes. But bigger problems?"

"Enough," Dad said, pushing back from the table and standing to loom over Thane. "She has done nothing to earn your distrust."

"She's Lilitu, Murphy," Thane said, sounding almost bored. "She earned my distrust the day she drew her first breath."

"Sit down," Hale commanded. But Dad didn't budge.

"It's no wonder you drove Karayan away," Dad said through gritted teeth. "You don't have the capacity for fatherly love." That got Thane's attention.

"Karayan should have been a warning to us all," Thane hissed, lurching to his feet. "Instead of trying to raise up another demon, we should have drowned it at birth."

Dad lunged across the table, grabbing Thane by the throat. Chaos erupted. Gretchen and Matthew tried to pull Thane back while Hale worked to pry Dad's hands free from his throat. Everyone was shouting.

Lucas turned toward me, pleading with his eyes.

"If I ever have children," I said, surprised by the strength in my voice. "They will be *human*."

This pronouncement cut through the chaos, leaving a stony silence in its wake. Dad turned to look at me, uncomprehending. Hale took advantage of the moment to wrest Dad back from Thane. Thane was breathing hard. His hands lifted to massage his throat, but he kept his glare fixed on Dad.

Everyone else in the room was watching me.

"I don't—" Dad started. "Braedyn?"

"Sansenoy made me an offer," I said. Uncertainty edged a tremor into my voice, but the time had come to tell him. "He has the power to make me human."

Dad's face lit from within. Unbidden, tears glistened in his eyes. He grabbed me, pulling me into a fierce hug. "God... thank you, God," he murmured into my hair.

As Dad embraced me, I saw Gretchen and Matthew turn to Lucas. Gretchen's face broke into a rare smile as she pulled Lucas close. Matthew caught them together in a hug and ruffled Lucas's hair, beaming.

"That's, I'm—" Hale looked stunned. A slow smile spread across his face and he shook his head. "I'm so happy for you, Braedyn."

"Just like a Lilitu," Thane growled. Dad released me and turned to Thane, genuinely stunned. Thane's lips twisted into a bitter smile. "Have you forgotten why she was suffered to live in the first place?" Thane said. "Without a Lilitu ally, the Guard has virtually no chance of victory in this coming battle." Thane glanced at me, eyes simmering with outrage. "And she abandons her duties now, at the critical moment."

"I'm not abandoning anything," I snapped. "Why do you think I haven't taken him up on his offer yet?"

"No," Dad looked at me, urgently. "We can find another way to defeat them," he said quietly. "This isn't your responsibility."

"The hell it isn't," Thane said. "If you won't do your part, demon, then—"

"Thane!" Hale grabbed the front of Thane's coat, cutting the older man off mid-sentence. "Get out."

"You know what's at stake," Thane growled.

"*Out.*" Hale's voice left no room for argument. Thane straightened, summoning what dignity he could, and left. When we heard the front door slam, Hale turned back to me, eyes heavy. "It's your choice, Braedyn. But Thane isn't wrong."

"No," Dad said again.

"Dad, it's okay." I took Dad's hands in mine, willing him to listen to sense. "There are things I can do to help as a Lilitu that I wouldn't be able to do as a human."

"Those things put you at risk," he whispered.

"I'm at risk anyway," I said. "We all are." I glanced around the room. Gretchen and Matthew still had their arms looped around Lucas, but they were watching us with solemn expressions now. Lucas's met my eyes and nodded grimly.

"There's something else," I said, taking a deep breath. "A caveat."

Dad stiffened, drawing back to get a better look at me. "Which is?"

"I can't harm humans." I glanced at Matthew unintentionally. His expression hardened as our eyes met, and I knew he was remembering our kiss. I'd fed off his life energy, drawing enough to weaken him badly. That he'd volunteered to give me that energy to find and save Lucas didn't matter. It was after that kiss that I'd discovered the deep red petals on all the roses in my dream garden. "Every time I feed off someone's energy, I lose another bit of my humanity."

"I didn't know," Matthew said.

"Me neither." I smiled a thin smile and shrugged. Dad put a hand on my shoulder, drawing my attention back to him.

"Braedyn, think carefully about this. The longer you go on as a Lilitu, the more you'll face temptation." His eyes flickered to Lucas before he could stop himself.

"I know," I whispered. "But this is something only I can do."

After a long moment, Dad nodded. I could tell he wasn't convinced, but he held his tongue. Lucas met my eyes with a warmth I could almost feel.

"So," he said into the sudden quiet. "School. I think we can manage that."

The group chuckled, and returned to their seats at the table. As we continued with dinner, I saw Lucas staring wistfully at Hale and Dad. I could see how much he wanted to be included as a full member of the Guard, but for my part, I wasn't in a hurry to take on more responsibility. Deep down I knew Lucas would be getting his wish sooner rather than later. And even if I became human tomorrow, I didn't have that much longer to pretend to be a normal girl.

Finding the seal affected Lucas more than I would have guessed. When I went over to the Guard's house the next morning, Gretchen, sifting through a handful of mail in the living room, pointed wordlessly into the kitchen.

I found Lucas leaning against a cracked tile counter, picking through a bowl of dry cereal listlessly.

"Hey," I said gently. "You ready for school?"

He looked up and I felt my stomach twist a little. His beautiful eyes were drawn, tired. His hair even more tousled than normal. He didn't have to tell me he hadn't slept all night. I'd waited for him in the dream, but he'd never materialized.

"How do you do it?" he breathed. "How do you act like everything's the same as it was yesterday?"

"Because it is," I answered, my voice harsher than I intended. Lucas winced at me, raw emotions coursing through his features. Softening my tone, I moved to the counter beside him. "The seal was there yesterday. It was there the day before, too. If we're right, it's been there for centuries. That hasn't changed. The only thing that has changed is now we know."

Lucas nodded, letting his eyes drop to the floor. "I guess you're right."

"Lucas?"

"I don't know," he said, anticipating me. "I don't know what's wrong with me."

"Besides being exhausted?" I asked. "What kept you up last night?"

"We're practically living on the doorstep into the Lilitu world." Lucas looked up at me, eyes drawn with exhaustion. "That doesn't creep you out?"

"Sure it does," I said.

"I guess there are some benefits to being able to will yourself to sleep." Lucas pushed his bowl of cereal away. "We should get a move on or we're going to be late. The last thing I need is an after-hours detention." Lucas offered a weak smile. "I'm kind of looking forward to a normal day at school, actually."

We made it through morning classes before we saw him.

"No." Lucas came to a dead stop in the entrance to the dining hall.

"What?" I asked, sensing the anger welling inside him. I followed his gaze and stared. "No way."

Two steps behind us, Cassie and Royal peered over our shoulders, straining to see whatever it was that had stopped us in our tracks.

The skinny blond boy from the mission was sitting at a dining table alone, wolfing down a plate of enchiladas. He paused between bites to take a swig of milk. As he set his glass down, he saw us and froze. Lucas took an unconscious step toward him. The skinny boy stood abruptly, picked up his plate, and fled in the direction of the kitchen.

"I don't get it," Royal said. "What are we staring at?"

Lucas and I traded a quick glance. "Nothing," Lucas said. "My mistake. I thought I saw a cockroach." He gave Cassie and Royal a smile. "Let's eat."

"Oh, yay," Cassie said half-heartedly. "So hungry now."

"You guys sit." Royal had that look on his face he gets when he's planning something devious. "I'll grab the food." He turned on his heel and hurried away. I caught sight of something black and pink in his hands as he turned away from us.

I followed Cassie and Lucas to our usual table. Royal appeared with a tray piled with food a few minutes later. Coronado Prep served family-style lunches, so we took turns passing around the serving tray of enchiladas. One of the best things about this school was the kitchen staff. They didn't do authentic New Mexican dishes every day, but when they did they were spot on. I scooped two enchiladas onto my plate and the aroma of seasoned chicken jolted my stomach awake. Handing the dish off to Lucas, I took a bite. The tender chicken would have been delicious on its own, but coupled with melted cheddar and green chili sauce it was heaven. Judging by the sudden silence at our table, I wasn't the only one savoring the meal.

"You must be Miss Ang."

I opened my eyes at the rich masculine voice. Mr. Hart stood by our table, smiling down at Cassie. Cassie's eyes bulged slightly as she struggled to swallow a bite of food.

"Mind if I take a seat?" Mr. Hart pulled the empty chair beside Cassie out and sat, placing something on the table in front of him. Cassie and I saw the black and pink notebook at the same moment. Cassie's eyes widened, and she turned on Royal.

"What did you do?" Cassie looked mortified.

"Before you skin me alive, just listen." Royal glanced at Mr. Hart. "Talk fast, drama man."

"Royal," Cassie hissed.

"Your friend has done me a huge favor, Miss Ang," Mr. Hart said.

Cassie glanced back at him, her cheeks flushing a rosy red. "It's just Cassie," she mumbled.

Mr. Hart flipped open the notebook to a drawing I hadn't seen before. Cassie had taken her earlier sketches of the gown and fleshed them out. What had been beautiful before was simply stunning now. It seemed to be two dresses, one of which was worn over the other. The inner gown was snug from the shoulders to the waist, with tight sleeves long enough to cover most of the back of the hand. Below the waist, the dress flowed into a full skirt, which hung in luxurious folds all the way to the floor. The outer dress was open along the sides from the top of the shoulder to the hips, revealing the form-fitting curves of the inner dress beneath. One corner of the outer dress was tucked up into a low-slung sash across the hips, revealing the swirling skirt of the inner dress. There was something both simple and luxurious about the draped fabric. To top the entire costume off, an understated metal circlet rested on the figure's head.

"What were you thinking for this material?" Mr. Hart gestured reverently at the overdress.

"Uh," Cassie glanced around, looking like a deer caught in the headlights. "I was picturing a silk dupioni," she said.

"And for the detail fabric here?" He brushed the narrow sleeves peeking out from under the billows of fabric of the outer dress. "Satin brocade?"

"Actually, I was thinking cut velvet, since she's a queen," Cassie said.

Mr. Hart shook his head slowly. "That's fantastic," he said slowly. "What kind of palette?"

Cassie sat up a bit straighter, pointing out elements of the drawing as she talked. "Since it's a tragedy, I was thinking the costumes should all be in muted gem-tones. So the outer dress is a grayish sapphire color and the inner dress, the cut velvet, is a light silver. You could even use the inner dress on its own for the scene where the queen is almost burned at the stake."

"Perfect. You're hired."

Cassie looked up, startled. "Hired for what?"

"Costume design," Mr. Hart said, as though it were obvious.

"Royal's already told me you're completely capable of making all of these garments."

"But—" Cassie shook her head, struggling to process what was happening. "There must be 30 costumes in that show."

Mr. Hart looked aside, calculating silently for a moment before speaking. "46."

"I can't sew that fast," Cassie said faintly, her face falling.

"Of course not," Mr. Hart replied. "We'll get some parents to help with the chorus. You're in charge of the hero costumes. Guinevere, Arthur, Lancelot, Mortimer. Don't worry," he said when Cassie's mouth opened in protest, "you'll have plenty of hands to help." He placed a hand on the notebook, giving Cassie a confident smile. "If what I've seen is any indication, you're going to ace this class."

"Class?"

"Cassie, the level of skill you demonstrate in these drawings is worth an AP credit at the very least. I wouldn't be surprised if these costumes got you a college scholarship."

Cassie's mouth dropped open in surprise. "A scholarship?" We all heard the excitement in her voice. A smile broke out over her face, and for a moment she was the old Cassie, impish and confident and eager for a challenge.

Mr. Hart's smile broadened. "All in good time. Are you in?"

"She's in," Royal said, satisfaction shining in his eyes.

Cassie turned on Royal with a wicked grin. "On one condition," she said, holding up a finger. "I'll need an assistant."

"Done." Mr. Hart stood and offered Cassie his hand. She shook it, grinning. "I'm hoping to hold our first meeting with the design team on Friday after school. Does that work for you?"

"It does."

"Great. Don't forget to bring your assistant." Mr. Hart gave Royal a bland smile and left.

Royal looked between Cassie and the retreating Mr. Hart, suddenly finding himself on the spot. "Wait, you don't mean me?"

"You got me into this," Cassie shrugged. "Did you think you'd be able to walk away scot-free?"

Royal's eyes narrowed unhappily. "I admit, I hadn't thought it through that far."

"It does seem like a fair penance," Lucas murmured.

Royal glared at him, but I could tell his resistance was fading. After a moment, Royal sighed. "Right. I'll assist you. As long as you don't expect me to do any sewing. Or take notes. Or run errands. I don't make lunches. The occasional coffee is negotiable."

"Perfect." Cassie looped her arm through Royal's. "First step, fabric samples." She looked at me, beaming. "What do you say, Braedyn? Want to join us? It'll be just like old times."

I smiled at Cassie's enthusiasm. "Sure."

Royal glanced at Lucas. "You too, Lucas. You're one of us now. That means if you're in it for the good times, you have to take part in the crazy-girl escapa—ouch!" Royal made a face as Cassie kicked him lightly under the table.

"Don't scare him," she chided sweetly.

Lucas gave me a warm look. "I'm in." He took another bite of enchilada.

Cassie pulled her notebook closer and opened it to a fresh page. "Maybe we should try—" she started sketching, abandoning the thought mid-sentence.

Royal caught my gaze over the table and smiled. Silently I mouthed, *thank you*. Royal nodded, glancing back at Cassie. I had a feeling we'd all get pulled into the Coronado Prep theater scene this semester. But seeing Cassie this happy made it totally worth it.

After school, Lucas and I found a spot to sit on a retaining wall along one edge of the theater building. We were waiting for Cassie and Royal to join us. Cassie had wanted to run a few ideas by Mr. Hart before our fabric-hunt began.

"So what is this place?" Lucas asked.

"It's a specialty fabric store. It's near Old Town," I said. "It's got some material, but Cassie likes it because they've got books and books full of fabric samples that you can order. She knows that place inside out."

"You're telling me the whole store—all they sell is fabric?"

"Yes."

"So, I should bring a book."

I hit Lucas on the shoulder playfully. "Tread carefully, mister. Or else you'll be dreaming of pink taffeta for a month."

"You wouldn't do that to me," Lucas said, half-pleading.

I was getting ready to laugh at his forlorn expression when I heard something from behind the theater. Lucas and I turned toward the sound in the same moment.

"What was that?" But I knew, even before we heard another meaty crack, followed by a half-grunt, half-sob. We ran around the side of the theater.

Three seniors ringed a smaller, fair-haired boy. Two of them held his arms while the third, an athletic guy with his shirtsleeves rolled up, swung a fist hard across the smaller boy's face. The boy hung between them, taking the impact with a hoarse cry. His glasses were on the ground, but I recognized him anyway. That skinny boy from the mission. The athletic boy hit him again, and he gave another sharp grunt of pain.

"Hey," I called, rushing forward. "What are you doing? Leave him alone!"

The seniors glanced up at me. The skinny boy struggled to stand up between the two guys holding him. One of them, a freckled boy, recognized me and grinned.

"Dude," he said to the athletic boy. "It's the chick from that fight at the mission. You better do what she says or she'll beat you up."

The athletic senior frowned at me, his eyes flat and hard. "You're defending this prick?" I turned back to Lucas, hoping for some help. In answer, Lucas folded his arms across his chest, unwilling to get involved. The senior took this for an answer and swung at the boy again.

I darted forward and blocked the punch, redirecting the senior's momentum to send him stumbling to the side.

"What the hell?" he shouted at me. But the second he made a move forward, Lucas was there with a hand on his shoulder, preventing him from getting any closer.

"I told you," the freckled boy said, howling with laughter. He and his friend released the skinny kid, who stumbled to his knees, scrabbling in the dirt for his bag. He must have fallen earlier; I could see the dirt along one side of his head, matted in his short blond hair.

The athletic boy's features clouded with anger at his friends. "What are you doing? You're letting him go?" The other seniors hesitated, glancing down at the skinny boy.

"Come on, man," Lucas said softly. "You made a mistake. Don't make it worse."

The senior looked from Lucas to me and back, then shrugged Lucas off angrily. "Whatever. You want the little dweeb? You can have him."

He stormed off, with his snickering friends in tow.

I turned back to the new boy. He clutched his backpack tightly in one fist, avoiding my gaze.

"Are you okay?" I asked.

"If I'd wanted your help, I would have asked," he snapped.

Lucas snorted in disgust and turned his back on the skinny boy.

"Why are you being such a jack-hole?" I snapped back. "In case you didn't notice, I'm the reason those seniors aren't grinding you into a bloody pulp right now."

The skinny boy ignored me, kneeling in the dirt to collect the books and papers that had spilled out of his backpack when the older kids had attacked. With an exasperated sigh, I knelt beside him to help gather his things up. He glanced at me, his face red. I held a book out to him. After a long moment, he took the book from me gingerly.

Lucas shook his head but thankfully refrained from comment. He ran to chase down some loose papers before they could blow away. The skinny kid eyed me as we worked collecting his things.

"I'm Braedyn," I said. I picked another book up off the ground and spotted his mangled glasses.

"Seth," he replied.

I handed him the glasses, and when he took them our hands brushed. With the touch, Seth looked up, and I saw his unguarded expression for the first time. His eyes were a vibrant, warm blue I'd only ever seen on postcards of the Caribbean. But it was the emotion within his eyes that caught my breath. He looked vulnerable. Scared.

"Thank you," he said quietly. Stripped of its customary venom, Seth's voice was pleasant. It had a texture to it, a sort of raspy warmth I could listen to all day.

"Sure," I said, feeling awkward.

Seth put his glasses on and bent to grab another book off the ground.

I turned away to collect some more loose papers. But as my eye fell on the pages in my hands I froze. A drawing stared up at me. Inky claws, leathery wings, spiky silver teeth—there was no mistaking this for anything but a Lilitu. I let my eyes slip to the other pages papering the ground all around me. Page after page was filled with research on the Lilitu, symbols like the ones on a Guardsman's dagger, sketches of the old mission.

I looked up and saw Seth watching me with the strangest look on his face—a sort of curious surprise.

Lucas joined us, holding a stack of loose-leaf pages. "Here," he said, thrusting them at Seth.

Seth and I stood together. Lucas saw my expression and glanced at the pages in my hands. His eyes widened slightly before darting back to Seth.

"Thanks," Seth said, his voice hoarse. "I'll take those." He snatched the pages out of my hands, bent to retrieve his backpack, and hurried back into the heart of campus.

"He's researching Lilitu," I whispered.

"Why?" Lucas wondered aloud. We watched Seth's retreating back until he darted into a building and out of view.

"Hey, guys, there you are!" Cassie waved at us from the door of the theater building. Royal followed her out, slipping on his sunglasses against the afternoon glare.

Lucas glanced my way, a question in his eyes. I shook my head slightly. We couldn't go with Cassie and Royal to the fabric store. Not until we'd told the Guard about the new student at Coronado Prep with the backpack full of research on the Lilitu.

Cassie bounded over to us, face alive with excitement. Guilt twisted my insides, but this couldn't wait. Cassie would just have to understand.

5

The drive home was full of speculation. Lucas and I discussed the extremely remote possibility that Seth was some kind of random Lilitu hobbyist who'd just happened to move to Puerto Escondido on the eve of the final battle. Add to that the fact that we'd run into him poking around the old mission, and we couldn't dismiss the truth staring us in the face; Seth knew Lilitu were real, and he was actively researching them right now.

Which opened up a vast ocean of questions. Who was Seth? How did he know about *Lilitu?* What did he know about the mission? Why was he poking around out there - and how did he happen to be there just as we went back to investigate? Did he know about the seal? What drew him to Puerto Escondido in the first place?

"Hale will know what to do," Lucas finally said.

A few moments later, I pulled into the driveway in front of my house. As September edged closer to October, the old oak trees of the neighborhood were beginning to shed their leaves, carpeting the road on either side in deep golden drifts.

We got out of my car, crossed through the lawn, and climbed the front steps to the Guard's house. We'd hoped to find Hale at home, but in the foyer we saw that the living room was packed. Lucas and I looked at one another, curious, and walked inside.

A stranger sat in the center of the group. She looked to be in her early fifties, with comfortable curves and soft wispy hair edged in gray at the temples. She was riffling through some papers, chewing absently on her lower lip. When she found whatever it was she was looking for, she pushed her glasses up on her nose and straightened.

"Yes, here it is. Note the date on that page, Mr. Thane." She handed a paper over to Thane, who took it eagerly.

"1628." Thane's breath caught and he pored over the page. "But the original?"

"It was locked in a vault at the Library," the woman answered. "I obtained these copies close to 30 years ago, before they'd done any digital archiving. Thank heaven."

"How much of the library was destroyed?" Hale asked, grimly.

"Oh, it was destroyed in its entirety," she said, surprised at the question. "Leveled, Mr. Hale. Did you expect anything less?"

Dad sat back, unsettled. The woman looked up, peering at us through her spectacles.

"And these young people are...?" she asked.

"My daughter, Braedyn," Dad said quickly. "And this is Lucas Mitchell."

"Pleased to make your acquaintances," she said. "I'm Angela Linwood."

"She's an archivist for the Guard," Dad explained. "Leadership thought we could use a hand." I glanced at Dad, sensing his unease. His eyes warned me to watch what I said. Which could only mean Angela didn't know I was a Lilitu.

"Why?" Lucas asked, glancing at Thane. "You're in over your head?"

"Linwood is the acknowledged expert on Lilitu outliers," Thane said in strained voice.

Hale cleared his throat. "She's been reassigned to our unit."

"Oh?" I asked, trying to keep my voice level. "For how long?"

"Permanently, I expect," Angela said. She adjusted her glasses and gave me a warm smile. "You look to be about the same age as my son. Come here, dear. Let me introduce you."

Angela gestured past us. Lucas and I turned, noticing for the first time that a blond boy was sitting at the edge of the Guard's bay window. He sat, arms crossed, a patchwork of darkening bruises covering one side of his face. I stifled a gasp. It was Seth.

"They go to my school, mom," Seth said. He walked forward, blushing hotly.

"Ah, you've met?" Angela's eyes sharpened, an unvoiced question hanging in the air. She turned to study Lucas critically.

Seth's blush deepened. "It wasn't him. Actually," Seth glanced at me out of the corner of his eye, "they kind of broke it up."

Angela's expression warmed instantly. "Well, then, you have my thanks." She gestured at a pair of empty chairs against a wall. "Pull up a seat. We've got serious business to discuss."

After we were settled in our seats, Hale leaned forward. "You were saying something about precedent?" he prompted Angela.

"Yes, precisely." Angela nodded toward the paper in Thane's hands. "The most recent recorded encounter with a female Thrall was almost 400 years ago. And it happened right here, in Puerto Escondido." She rustled through a few more sheets of tightly scrawled notes. "Roughly the same time as the Guard's only recorded encounter with—where is that page? Ah, here." She looked at Thane triumphantly. "1628."

"You're not saying you think—" Gretchen looked to Thane for confirmation.

Thane took the new sheet of notes from Angela and scanned it for a long moment. "Interesting," he murmured. "Of course, you're assuming a great many things. But it would explain some of the peculiarities surrounding this case."

Lucas and I shared a bewildered look.

Dad noticed our confusion. "I think you'd better go back to the beginning, Linwood."

Angela looked up. "Pardon?" Dad nodded his head in our direction, and she pursed her lips. "Yes, of course. I was intrigued when Terrance told me your group had encountered a woman in Thrall," she explained. "It's been a sort of side project of my work for the Guard, researching curiosities in our history."

"Curiosities?" Lucas said. "That *curiosity* almost killed Braedyn and me."

"I didn't realize," she glanced at Hale. "You mean to tell me these children faced an attacking Thrall on their own and survived?"

"Would you believe it wasn't the first time?" Hale answered. Out of the corner of my eye I noticed Seth turn to give us an appraising glance. "We take their training seriously," Hale said.

"Apparently." Angela adjusted her glasses. "Perhaps Seth could join you for some lessons?"

"Mom," Seth looked pained. "I don't think that's such a good idea."

"I think a few pointers in the self-defense department might do you a world of good."

"A few pointers won't help me," he murmured. He looked so miserable, I felt my heart go out to him.

"I'm confused," I said, pulling Angela's focus back to the subject at hand. "Why is it such a big deal that the Thrall was a woman?"

"Excellent question. I assume you know how a Thrall is created?" Angela asked.

"I do," I said, blushing. It was one of the first things I'd learned about Lilitu, back before I knew I was one of them. Lucas had explained it to me; the first time a Lilitu spends the night with a man, she weakens him severely, but it is possible for him to recover over time. The second time, he becomes a Thrall; a walking shell of a man bound to obey the Lilitu without the will to fight or question her orders. There is no recovery possible, once you've become a Thrall. The third time a Lilitu sleeps with a man, he dies.

"Then you know that a Lilitu's power begins with desire," Angela explained, as though she were telling me how to make a peanut butter sandwich. "And as far as we can tell, the Thrall who attacked you had been a happily married, heterosexual woman."

Angela watched my expression as I mulled this over. When the realization hit me, it was suddenly so obvious. "So, the Lilitu that attacked her, it was male?"

"Very good, Miss Murphy," Angela said. "Rare as he may be, a male Lilitu is known colloquially by another name; incubus."

"Wait," Lucas breathed. "You mean an incubus is here? In Puerto Escondido?"

"That is my theory, yes."

"How do we fight it?" Gretchen asked. "Is he like a regular Lilitu? Will I be able to spot him?"

Angela spread her hands helplessly. "I wish I could answer your questions, but I'm afraid we simply don't know. We need to try to reconstruct as much of the history of your mission as possible. It seems tied to this incubus somehow. I hope, if I can piece together what happened, I can fill in some of the gaps in our knowledge. Seth," Angela turned to her son, beckoning him closer, "did you get a chance to take another set of rubbings in the mission?"

Seth opened his backpack and pulled out a stack of ruffled pages. Some of them were still edged in dirt. He laid them out on the coffee table gingerly.

"What do you see?" Angela asked the group.

Hale frowned. "The stations of the cross. Hand carved. Typical of Catholic missions."

"Yes, but that's only part of the story," Angela said. "Look here." She pointed to a collection of figures in the skinny border of one of the carvings. The group leaned closer.

"I'll be damned," Thane murmured. "What is this?"

"Well, keep in mind that the first set of rubbings Seth collected for me were rougher, so it was hard to make out but," she bent over the rubbings, concentrating. "My goodness. Well done, Seth. There's quite a bit more detail here. Yes, I think—" She fell silent, absorbed in her thoughts.

"Linwood?" Hale prompted.

She looked up, as if suddenly remembering we were there. "I believe there's a second story being told in the borders of these carvings. A story about the missionaries and their fight against the Lilitu." As she narrated her version of the story, she pointed from one rubbing to the next. "You see here. These are the monks who built the mission at Puerto Escondido. Notice the shields they carry? They clearly believed they were here to protect something."

The carving showed the unmistakable silhouette of the original mission sanctuary. Beneath the carving of the sanctuary, I saw a rough circle and my blood ran cold. I was sure it was the seal. I leaned closer for a better look as Angela continued her story.

"In the next carving, there is trouble. You can see here two distinct Lilitu." Two figures stood side by side, facing a row of monks with shields and swords at the ready. Angular, bat-like wings protruded from both of their backs, and needle-like teeth ringed their mouths. "And—yes! I thought I noticed something on the previous rubbing but here there's really no doubt, is there?" Angela turned the drawing around so her audience could better see the figures. She held a hand out to Thane. "Do you mind?" He returned the notes she'd given him to look over. Angela scanned the page in silence for a moment. "Yes, here it is. This is an account of a story told to a traveling friar by one of the monks of this mission. One of only five survivors of the events, if we are to believe him. According to this monk, the mission was attacked by two demons. Siblings."

Angela stabbed her finger back at the rubbing. As I stared, it became clear. One of the Lilitu in the carving had the curves of a beautiful woman, while the other had the triangular chest of a fit young man.

"A sister and a brother," Angela said. "The monk's story seems consistent with the rest of these carvings. There was a great fight against the Lilitu. The monks overpowered and possibly killed the sister, but the brother escaped into the night."

"What are you suggesting? That it's the same incubus who attacked that woman in town?" Dad asked.

"I'm not suggesting anything," Angela said. "I'm merely sharing the preliminary fruits of my research into the mission. Whatever happened to that incubus was lost to history, I'm afraid. The friar who recorded this monk's tale moved on from the mission and the five surviving monks were never heard from again. The later stations of the cross that these monks carved, the ones that presumably continued their story, they were defaced long ago."

"So despite all your research, we know very little," Thane said.

"There is one additionally curious thing," Angela said, pulling another rubbing from the bottom of the pile. "You see here, on the carving of the last station of the cross? This is a common druidic symbol for winter solstice, and here we have a full moon."

"Which means?" Hale asked.

"Well, I don't know what it means, but it appears to be some kind of pagan lunar calendar. That in itself is curious, considering it was carved onto a Catholic religious image, presumably by a Catholic monk." Angela studied the paper thoughtfully.

"You have a theory," Thane said. It wasn't a question.

"Yes," Angela gave Thane a small smile. "But until I've gathered more information, I'd rather not share it. I'd hate to be wrong about this."

"All right." Hale stood, pacing to the living room's great mantle. He ran a thumb along the scar dividing his eyebrow—a souvenir from a fight he'd had with a Lilitu in his youth. I'd come to recognize this gesture as a sign that Hale was wrestling with unpleasant thoughts. "If there is an incubus in town, we need to be on our guard. Keep your eyes open. Until we know more we proceed with extreme caution. I don't want anyone stumbling blindly into more than they can handle."

"Excellent advice for us all," Angela said, glancing pointedly at Seth.

"We can't be too careful."

"Speaking of which, we have rooms for you and Seth here," Hale said.

"Oh, dear," Angela winced. "That is very kind, but I've never done well in communal living situations. I've already rented a small house in town. I think we'll both be a bit more comfortable there."

Hale looked like he wanted to argue. Dad caught my eye.

"Why don't you and Lucas take Seth over to our house," Dad said. "Order a pizza. I have a feeling we're going to be here talking strategy for a while."

Seth glanced at Angela hopefully. She looked resigned, but she nodded permission. "At least order something with vegetables on it, if you don't mind."

Seth noticed me watching him and looked away quickly. My eyes lingered over the marks on his cheek. He'd have a tender black eye in the morning.

But it could have been much worse, a voice inside me said.

I stepped onto the Guard's front porch, drawing my sweater tighter around me. Lucas closed the door, and Seth let out a long breath.

"And here I thought I was the only kid whose life's been ruined by the Guard."

"How do you mean?" Lucas asked.

"Oh, come on," Seth's smile was tinged with bitterness. "They see Lilitu around every corner. I can't go to a movie because a Lilitu might be prowling the theater. No, I get to spend my afternoons taking rubbings of old carvings in deserted churches because they might hold the key to a centuries-old mystery about who-gives-a-crap. Why should I care if some horny loser ends up in bed with a demon? Right?"

Seth didn't read the warning in Lucas's eyes. "You know the truth," he said. "How can you not take a stand?"

"You're kidding, right?" Seth's smile faded when Lucas didn't respond. "Okay." Seth shrugged his shoulders and leaned closer to me conspiratorially. "Guess no one told him not to drink the Kool-Aid, huh?" Lucas turned abruptly and walked toward my house. I could see the tension in his shoulders. Seth watched him go, surprised. "He's serious about this stuff?"

"His brother was killed by a Lilitu," I said, but I couldn't pull my eyes off of Lucas. "Lucas was there when it happened. So was Gretchen." Across the yard, Lucas disappeared into my house. I heard the door close softly, and my heart wrenched for him. Eric's death was a wound that never healed for Lucas.

"Seriously?" Some of the color seemed to drain out of Seth's face.

"The Lilitu who killed him got away," I explained. "As far as we know, she's still out there. Hunting. So yeah, he's serious about this stuff."

"I didn't know." Seth glanced at my house, his expression sober.

"Now you do." I left Seth standing on the Guard's porch, alone with his thoughts.

When I walked into our comfortable foyer, I heard Lucas in the living room. He was planted on the couch with the TV on. He wasn't paying it much attention, though. I sat gingerly beside him. Silently, he draped his arm over my shoulders and pulled me in tighter.

Seth appeared in the entryway to the living room a few minutes later. "Mind if I join you? Or is this going to turn into another make-out session?"

Lucas only glanced at him.

Seth leaned against the wall, crossing his arms. "Let me ask you something. I've been reconsidering my approach to making new friends. The 'putting-my-foot-in-my-mouth' plan isn't working out as well as I'd hoped it would."

"I don't know," Lucas said. "It's better than the 'I'm-an-arrogant-asshat' act you pulled in the mission."

"You think?" Seth said, moving to sit on the leather chair next to the couch. "I was afraid it might be too subtle. Could give people the wrong idea, like I'm some kind of sensitive, decent human being."

"I don't think you have to worry about that," Lucas said, finally breaking into a smile.

"Oh, good," Seth leaned back in the chair. "As long as it's clear I'm a total jerk-face."

"It's clear," Lucas replied. "Who wants pizza?"

"I'll get the phone." I hopped up and went to grab the handset from the kitchen. From the living room, I could hear Seth say something and Lucas laugh in return. The sound gave me a warm feeling inside, easing a tension I'd felt since Seth had looked at me with that aching vulnerability after the fight at school.

It was a roundabout way to do it, but Seth had finally made some friends in Puerto Escondido.

It's strange how, when you've got a major problem absorbing all your attention, the things that really matter to you can fall through the cracks without your notice.

The last chilly days of September sped by, ushering in a crisp October. The Guard kept Lucas and me busy after school with practice, while Cassie and Royal were making themselves comfortable fixtures in the theater building. Outside of class and lunch, we didn't see much of each other. When Cassie made a comment about missing me, I reassured her that things would settle down eventually. The truth was, I was so caught up worrying about the coming war that my non-Guard friends got shoved way down on my list of priorities. And so much of my time was spent with Lucas and Seth that it didn't occur to me I barely saw Cassie and Royal anymore.

Seth started coming over to the Guard's house every time Angela found some new piece of research or wanted to consult with Thane about something. Then he started coming over even if she was nose-deep in some book at their house. Before too long, Seth was catching a ride home with Lucas and me every day after school. He watched us train some afternoons, but each time Hale offered to show him a few things he politely declined and fled back up the stairs to wait for us in the Guard's living room.

Lucas was warming to Seth day by day. It felt strangely comforting to have another friend our age to talk to about the Lilitu. With Seth, Lucas and I could be—almost—completely honest. Hale had warned Lucas and me to keep my secret. Angela and Seth might be part of the Guard, but there was no telling how they'd react if they learned I was Lilitu. And so the days passed as my life fell into this new routine.

I was so focused on my own thoughts that I completely missed the signs that morning.

Amber and her friends were gathered outside the North Hall when I arrived at school with Lucas. I noticed Ally turn to look at me. I hesitated. The other girls with her pulled her back, hands clamped over their mouths to muffle their laughter. Suddenly self-conscious, I nudged Lucas.

"Is something wrong with my hair or something?"

He looked at me blandly. "You look ready for a photo shoot. Isn't that one of the benefits of your genetic heritage?" But when I didn't smile, he tilted his head to the side, trying to catch my eye. "Why do you ask?"

"No reason." When I glanced back at the girls, they were already hurrying into the building, out of sight. Only Amber paused at the door. The look in her face sent a chill down my spine. Her face could have been carved from granite. Her eyes flickered to look across the quad. A moment later they returned to my face and her lips pulled back in a smile that was more of a sneer.

I turned, trying to follow her gaze. I could just make out a group of guys beyond the dining hall, gathered at the edge of the faculty parking lot at the other end of campus.

"What is that?" I murmured, my heart suddenly leaping into my throat. Lucas saw the group a second later. Before he could answer, I was running across campus.

As I got closer, I could hear the jeers of the crowd. They were looking at something on the ground.

I reached the edge of the crowd and shouldered a few guys out of the way.

"Dude, take it easy," one of them said, rubbing his arm.

I elbowed my way through to the heart of the group. Two guys from the soccer team were holding Royal down on the ground while Rick ran a buzzing razor over his head, sheering off the last of his hair.

"*Stop,*" I screamed.

Rick stood, grinning. "My work here is done." The two guys holding Royal down released him and stood, giving Rick high-fives. Someone in the crowd gave a loud *Wooo!*

"Braedyn?" Lucas arrived, winded. The crowd was already starting to disperse.

"What is wrong with you?!" I spun on Rick.

"Chill out," Rick said. "It's just hair. It'll grow back."

"Why?" I was so angry I could barely speak. "Why would you do this?"

Rick smiled a secretive smile and shrugged. "Let's just say I owe someone a favor."

I lunged for Rick, ready to tear that smile off his face.

"Don't," Royal said hoarsely from the ground behind me. He had pulled himself up to his knees, but his hands were shaking. A few stubbly patches of hair crisscrossed his bald head, but my eyes latched onto the red, raw places where the razor had sheared skin. A few spots of blood stood out starkly against his pale white scalp.

"Later," Rick said, walking away with a spring in his step. The last of his friends joined him, turning their backs on us with a last snicker.

I dropped to the ground beside Royal. His shirt was a rumpled mess of dirt and grass stains. I saw a small rip at the shoulder, evidence of the futile struggle against his tormentors. He was staring down. The wind stirred drifts of light brown hair along the pavement. Royal lifted a shaking hand to touch his head. What he found there seemed to break something inside him.

"I don't think—" he looked at me, his brown eyes wide. He cleared his voice, trying for a measure of calm. "Tell Cassie I had to go home. I'll see her tomorrow."

"Royal," I tried to catch hold of his hand, but Royal pulled away from me with more strength than I expected. I stood to follow him into the parking lot. Lucas grabbed me by the shoulder, holding me back.

"What are you doing?" I hissed at Lucas. "Let me go."

"I think—I think you should leave him alone for now," he said. His eyes, tight with concern, followed Royal across the faculty parking lot toward the soccer field. "I don't think he wants anyone to see him like this."

"But I'm not anyone," I said. "I'm his friend." As I heard the words leave my lips, I froze inside.

I'm his friend.

Amber. Amber had done this. A strange calm came over me, as though my mind had pulled some kind of emergency switch, disconnecting my emotions from my body. Like some part of me knew I couldn't be trusted to act with this helpless rage boiling inside of me.

But when I spotted her, hovering in the doorway to the girl's locker room, I moved into action. Amber saw me coming and ducked inside the building.

"Braedyn?" Lucas chased after me, but drew up short when I darted into the girl's locker room. "Braedyn!"

I ignored Lucas, determined to settle this score now. I skidded into the empty locker room. Amber was sitting calmly on a bench, waiting for me.

"Leave my friends alone," I growled, advancing on her.

"It sucks, doesn't it?" Amber purred. "Not being able to help your friends when someone messes with them. Like Parker."

I stopped. "Parker."

"I know you did something to him," Amber said, standing. "You messed with his head. No. With his *mind*." She walked toward me, curtains of ice blond hair framing her face.

"He hurt Cassie," I said. "My friends have done nothing to you."

"So it was revenge."

"It was a mistake." Even as I said it, I felt a twinge inside.

"But you admit it."

Something was terribly wrong. I was the one with the supernatural powers, why was Amber the one controlling the situation? *Just like middle school,* I thought. I winced, remembering the years I'd been powerless before Amber's taunts. I could protect myself now. It'd be easy. So why wasn't I acting?

Because it would be the end of my life at Coronado Prep, I told myself.

"How did you do it?" Amber walked right up to me, so close I took a step backwards involuntarily. "Did you say something to him? Did you kiss him?" I tried to turn and walk away but Amber shoved me back into a bank of lockers. "I want some answers, demon."

"Leave me alone," I said. My voice sounded weak, and I tried to muster some confidence. "Leave us all alone."

"Or what? You can't do anything to me. I'm a girl."

"You have no idea what I can do," I mumbled.

"Oh? You want to fight me?" She flipped her hair back from her shoulders, as though giving me a cleaner target. "Go ahead. You'll be expelled before the lunch bell rings."

"I don't have to hit you to hurt you," I said, dropping my voice.

"Sticks and stones," Amber shrugged. "You think I care what you say to me?"

"That's not what I mean."

"Enlighten me." Amber's eyes gleamed hungrily. When I didn't say anything, her grin deepened. She brushed some imaginary lint off my shoulder. "That's what I thought. You're not as powerful as you'd like me to believe, are you?"

I stepped forward. Startled, Amber fell back a few paces. "You want to know what I did to Parker?" I asked, my voice low and threatening. "I found him in a dream and planted a seed in his sleeping mind."

"A seed?" Amber tried to scoff at this, but her voice wavered.

"Into that seed, I channeled my anger, my hatred for Parker. It was easy; all I had to do was think about Cassie, and what he'd done to her. The seed grew heavier and heavier, until I couldn't hold it any longer. And I left it to grow in Parker's mind like some kind of slow-acting time bomb. It worked on him, until those thoughts I poured into the seed became his thoughts." I took another step forward and this time Amber stumbled back away from me.

"He tried to kill himself—" Amber stared at me. For the first time she seemed aware, really aware of what she was looking at.

"Now you know why," I answered, feeling sick. What I'd done to Parker—I hadn't known what the consequences would be. Yes, I wanted him to suffer for breaking Cassie's heart. I never wanted him to try to take his own life. By a lucky twist of fate, he'd survived the suicide attempt. But the incident had left a stain, literally. I'd returned to my dream garden after planting the seed to find the rose petals had darkened, red reaching farther toward the heart of each rose, a clear symbol of my transgression. "You don't want me for an enemy," I said. "Trust me."

Amber shrank back against the locker bay. "I told you," she breathed. "I told you she was a demon."

An icy wash of fear poured down my back. I turned and saw Ally emerging from an empty locker behind me.

Amber had set me up.

I spun on Amber, who was already regaining her composure. "I think," she said, forcing her shoulders back. "If you could hurt me in a dream, you would have done it already."

I blanched. Amber was right—but not for the reasons she thought. I wouldn't risk my own humanity to punish some self-absorbed prom queen, no matter how satisfying it might feel at the time. Amber, watching my face closely for any reaction, smiled as I confirmed her suspicion.

"That's what I thought," she said.

"Leave my friends out of this," I warned.

"Well, that's up to you, isn't it?" She asked. "You want me to leave them alone, you know what you have to do."

Amber and Ally walked smugly out of the locker room, turning their backs on me confidently. Unless I wanted to sacrifice my future I was no threat to them, and now they knew it.

I skipped lunch. I didn't have it in me to share the dining hall with Amber.

Instead, I retreated back to the edge of the faculty parking lot, sitting under an aspen tree and playing the scene from this morning over and over in my mind.

I was a wreck when Lucas found me. He'd smuggled a plate of food out of the dining hall for me, but I wasn't hungry. After I told him so, he nodded.

"I figured it was worth a shot," he said, joining me at the base of the Aspen tree.

"What's the word on Rick and the others?" We'd been waiting for an announcement from the headmaster.

"This isn't going to make you feel any better," Lucas said.

"Why? What happened?"

"They're claiming it was just a prank that got out of control."

"What?! They held him down and shaved his head completely bald!"

"I know. But apparently Fiedler believes them. They got a three-day suspension."

"That's it?" I pulled back to read Lucas's face, stunned. It was barely a slap on the wrist.

"That's it." He didn't look any happier about it than I was. The bell rang, announcing the end of lunch. We had five minutes to get to fifth period. Lucas stood, offering me his hand. I let him help me stand, and dusted leaves and dirt off the back of my plaid skirt.

"Cassie. Now Royal," I said. I looked at Lucas, my worry evident in my gaze.

Lucas pulled me close. "I'd like to see her try to mess with me."

"I wouldn't."

"I don't know. I think I'd look kind of badass with a shaved head."

I smiled, but my heart wasn't in it.

"Speak of the devil," I heard Lucas mumble.

I looked up and saw Amber walking across the quad towards us. Behind her, Ally walked hand-in-hand with Parker. I looked around, desperate to avoid her, but we were standing at the edge of campus—there was nowhere to hide. Amber's eyes caught on me.

An irrational swell of panic kicked up inside me - all I wanted was to disappear. And just like that, my Lilitu instinct kicked in. Leathery wings—invisible to most mortal eyes—materialized around me, cloaking me from view.

Lucas uttered a startled curse under his breath. "Braedyn? What are you doing?" he whispered.

But my eyes were locked on Amber. She froze, staring at me, stricken. Ally and Parker came to a stop beside her, sharing a strange look. I saw Ally ask Amber something. Amber barely reacted.

"Amber can see me," I hissed. "She's a *spotter*." My skin crawled. I felt naked, laid bare under her gaze.

Lucas turned and saw Amber's face. "Oh, man. You go. I'll deal with Amber."

I didn't need to be told twice. I ran, feeling Amber's eyes on me all the way into the South Hall. The hall was empty; most kids were already in fifth period, waiting for the bell to start class.

I pulled the door closed behind me and slumped against the wall, uncloaking.

I'd thought the hall was empty, but I'd been wrong. Someone gave a strangled cry. I looked up. Seth was there, staring at me, horrified.

"Seth." I held out my hands, trying to soothe him with the gesture.

Seth jerked back. His eyes raked over my face, but whatever he saw there did nothing to calm him. He turned away from me and ran down the hall. So much for keeping my secret. There was no going back. Seth knew I was Lilitu.

6

Seth was nowhere to be seen after school that day.

"I should have run after him, tried to do some damage control," I said, full of self-recrimination.

Lucas, leaning against the hood of my car, shook his head. "Wouldn't have made it any easier. He just needs time."

"How much time?" I worried aloud.

By the time the parking lot had emptied of everyone not staying for an afternoon practice of some variety, I was pacing in front of my car.

"I don't think he's coming," Lucas said. "We should get home."

"He didn't let me explain." All I could see was that look of horror on his face, replaying itself in my mind over and over. "He must think—" I covered my face with my hands. "I don't know what he must think."

"Come on, Braedyn. He's smart. He knows Gretchen's a spotter."

I looked up sharply. Lucas reached out a hand to me, his gaze steady.

"He'll work it out," Lucas murmured. "And when he does, he'll realize you're on our side."

I took Lucas's offered hand and let him draw me close. "Okay." But that left another problem. "Amber," I whispered. "What do we tell the Guard?"

Lucas shook his head, miserable. Spotters were rare—and they were critical to the Guard's mission. You could always train more Guardsmen to fight, but being a spotter wasn't something you could learn. The Guard had lost Dina last year, the spotter for Marx's unit. They'd come to help us battle Ais and Dina had died—killed by Ais in the first moments of our fight. Since Dina's death, no new spotter had been found for Marx's team, which left them dangerously exposed.

"I think for now," Lucas said after a long moment. "We keep it to

75

ourselves."

It was what I wanted to hear him say, but I still felt a twinge of guilt. The Guard needed people like Amber—regardless of what I thought of having her embraced by my friends and family.

Lucas stood and opened the driver's side door for me. With a heavy heart, I drove us both home.

That night, after practice and dinner with the Guard, Dad and I returned home.

"Feel like watching some TV with your old man?" Dad asked.

"I think I'm going to turn in early tonight," I said.

Dad's eyebrows jumped a little in surprise. "You're feeling okay?"

"Yeah. Just tired." That was true, but it was only one part of the truth.

As I lay down in bed, I willed myself into a dream. I was aware of my head hitting the pillow, but the sensation was far away; I was already standing in the odd rose garden that waited for me every night.

I knelt and put my hand on the ground at my feet, sensing for the world beyond this tiny dream. I'd learned that perceiving this place as real—a real garden, with clouds and dirt and roses—made it real to my sleeping mind and trapped me here. But once I could sense the dream for what it was, I'd slip out of my secluded bubble and into the larger dream space shared by all living things.

A pool of darkness opened at my feet, and the swirling stars of other sleepers' dreams came into view. I sat there for a long time, until I sensed the dream I was waiting for spring alight in the darkness.

"Karayan," I said, calling her dream out of the crowd. It rose up to the surface of my pool. I reached down and touched it, willing myself inside.

Karayan turned as I entered her dream, her perfect mouth dropping open in silent surprise.

"I need to talk to you," I said. Karayan's dreamscape was dotted with bluebells, which stirred in a sudden breeze; Karayan's unease manifesting itself.

"How did you—" With visible effort, Karayan struggled to regain her composure. "It's generally considered rude to force your way into another Lilitu's dream," she said crisply.

"You do it all the time," I retorted.

"That's different," Karayan said, waving this away. "I'm like your mentor."

"My—" I stared at her, momentarily stunned into silence.

"Uh, yes?" Karayan's eyes narrowed. "Or are you forgetting coming to me, asking for help with your little extra-curricular revenge project?"

The irritated response died on my lips. Karayan was right; I'd gone to her for help to punish Parker. Karayan was the one who'd showed me how to plant the seed in his sleeping mind—but only because I asked her to.

"Fine," I said, swallowing my pride. "Mentor me." I willed two chairs into being and sat in one of them. The leather felt soft under my fingers, warm and comforting. Karayan eyed the chairs with a strange look in her face, but sat. She ran a hand over the surface of her chair, reluctantly appreciative. "I need to know how someone becomes a spotter," I said.

Karayan turned her beautiful eyes back to my face. "Why? Don't tell me you want more of *them* out there?"

"No," I said impatiently, "there's a girl at school. She *saw* me."

Karayan leaned back, considering this for a moment. "Amber," she said at last. "Of course."

"Why 'of course'?"

"Because of Derek."

"But they weren't even dating when—" I faltered. "When he died."

Karayan gave me a pitying look. "Braedyn. Do we need to talk about the birds and the bees again?"

I blushed hotly. "What does sex have to do with any of this?"

"Everything," she said simply.

I waited, but when she didn't offer anything further, I was forced to speak. "I don't understand."

Karayan tilted her head to study me with a condescending smile. "I know you don't, sweetie."

"Just tell me what you're talking about," I snapped.

Karayan's smile widened, but she settled in her chair to explain. "When two people have sex, they forge a bond whether they want to or not. It's not just a physical act. It's a union of spirit. And when one of those spirits is damaged, sometimes the other is impacted as well." Karayan's eyes grew thoughtful. "Spotters are usually deeply in love."

"When you say Amber was impacted..." I prompted.

"Altered. Unblinded to the larger world, somehow. That change allowed her to see through a Lilitu's defenses after—" but here Karayan stopped.

"After you turned Derek into a Thrall," I finished.

The bluebells on the hill around us shivered. I glanced at them, then back at Karayan, surprised. She'd never indicated any remorse for attacking Derek. But that was definitely an emotional reaction.

Karayan stood abruptly. "You should go."

"I have more questions," I protested.

Karayan glared at me and I felt a strange pressure, like the larger dream world was trying to suck me out of Karayan's dream. My eyes snapped back to Karayan's face.

"Stop," I said.

The pressure ceased. Karayan staggered back almost as if buffeted by a gale-force wind. Her face registered shock.

I was dimly aware of my alarm clock, blaring back in the real world. Time to wake up. I stood, and Karayan took another step away from me, eyeing me like I was some kind of venomous snake.

"If you don't want to talk in dreams, meet me in the Plaza today after school," I said. "Four o'clock."

I opened my eyes. Sunlight crowded the edges of my drapes, eager to flood the room with dawn. I felt a moment's irrational resentment, then sighed. Ready or not, the day was beginning. Pushing back the covers, I rose out of bed.

I tried to catch sight of Seth before first period, hanging out by his locker. He didn't show. First bell rang and I gave up, resigning myself to seeing him in physics. Provided he had even come to school today. *What if he told his mom and she kept him home from school to keep him away from me?* I wondered. *What if I never get the chance to explain?*

I walked into first period. Amber was back in her usual spot in the second row of class, talking with Missy. She pointedly ignored me as I entered, which was fine by me.

Cassie was scribbling notes into the margins around another costume drawing.

"Nice," I said, admiring the design of another tunic, this one encrusted with some kind of rubies.

"Sorry," Cassie said without looking up. "Can't talk right now. My fabric estimates are due today."

"Right." I opened my history book, pretending to look over last night's chapter, feeling awkward and lonely. Not a great start to a very long day.

The morning classes seemed to last forever. I found myself checking the clock every two or three minutes, urging time to leap forward. But when the time came for physics class, I found myself dragging my feet, suddenly unsure about whether or not I wanted to see Seth after all. I got to class just before the bell rang announcing the start of class.

Seth was sitting in a desk near the back of the classroom, head bent over his book. Just in front of him, Ally and Amber spotted me and shared a whispered conversation I'm pretty sure featured me as the main subject.

I was trying to summon the courage to go talk to Seth when Cassie and Royal entered. I felt my heart surge when I saw Royal, and forgot about Seth for the moment. Royal wore a light grey knit skullcap. He gave me a thin smile, tugging on the back of the hat self-consciously.

"Not my favorite choice, but the alternatives were my brother's baseball cap or my mom's beret."

"I told you," Cassie said. "It looks fine." She turned to me for back up. "Tell him, Braedyn."

"Actually," I said, eyeing him critically. "It looks kind of edgy and cool."

"Right?" Cassie turned back to Royal. "You see? Edgy."

"Please. Braedyn's got the fashion sense of a timid nun," Royal said. "No offense," he added to me as an after thought.

"Why would I be offended by that?" I asked mildly. Cassie shot me a grin.

"Okay, folks, class actually started a few minutes ago," Mr. Harris called. He was a compact man, with a penchant for outlandish bow ties. I liked his class; he had a zest for his subject that was contagious. Cassie, Royal, and I took our seats as Mr. Harris wrote "LAB DAY" in big letters across the chalkboard. "I see we have a few absent students, so I'm going to take this opportunity to mix things up a bit."

The class groaned. I glanced around and remembered that Rick and his two soccer buddies were on their mini-suspension. "New lab partners will be as follows." Mr. Harris started reading off names, but when he called Royal and Rick there was an audible reaction from the class. Royal's face drained of color as Mr. Harris grabbed his eraser, suddenly realizing his mistake.

"Nope, sorry." He glanced up at Royal, his face lined with consternation. "Why don't you and Cassie partner up? I'll put Rick with someone else."

"Thanks," Royal said faintly.

"Braedyn, you're with Seth. Amber, you're with Ally." Mr. Harris looked up. "And I think that's it."

I glanced at Seth, who was staring at me, expressionless.

"Let's move this party to the lab," Mr. Harris said. We filed out of the classroom and headed across the hall to the physics lab for what Mr. Harris called our "plumb-bob experiment." It involved hanging a weight from a string to make a pendulum, taping a razor to the edge of the desk to cut the string as the weight swung by, and predicting where the weight would land on the floor—all based on the height of the weight at the start of its swing.

Seth and I worked together, setting up our pendulum almost wordlessly. I started the calculations to predict where the weight would land. Seth glanced around the room, then lowered his voice.

"You're Lilitu, aren't you?"

I looked up at him sharply, unprepared for this question in the middle of physics lab. Seth read my face and nodded. He looked tense, but not scared.

"I'm fighting for the Guard," I said.

"Yeah, I figured that much out," Seth replied. "But you and Lucas? In the mission it looked like—I mean, are you guys allowed to…"

I blushed. "That was a moment of weakness. We know we have to be careful."

Seth nodded and fell silent for a moment. I was about to turn back to my calculations, thinking that's all we were going to say for now, when he turned back to me, eyes alive with curiosity. "So how did this happen? I mean, how did *you* end up with *them?*"

"My dad," I answered. We kept our heads bent over our experiment and I filled Seth in. I told him about Dad, the great

Murphy, a living legend to the Guard. I told him how Dad had been good friends with my biological father, Paul Kells, and how Paul had given his life so I could be born and raised by Murphy to fight for the Guard. When I was done, Seth studied his hands for a moment in silence.

"That makes sense, I guess," he said.

"What about you?" I asked. "How did you end up with the Guard?"

"My father was killed when I was a baby, too," he said. "Mom had been an ancient history professor, but losing my father messed her up pretty bad. The police didn't have any leads, but Mom... something about the crime scene, the marks on his back, the changes in his personality, it all sounded weirdly familiar to her. She dug into some old Mesopotamian research, stuff she hadn't looked at since her grad school days. And there it all was. Beautiful demons who steal men's souls, kill with an embrace," Seth eyed me uncomfortably and shrugged. "She got obsessed with the Lilitu. Quit her job. Became a Guard archivist."

"She seems pretty intense," I offered.

"Yeah. She's totally into this mission project. She keeps finding little bits of information she calls 'clues to the big picture,' but she won't tell me what they are." He shrugged. "She tries to keep me insulated from a lot of this stuff."

"So she's found something?" I asked, suddenly focused on Seth.

"Well, yeah. That theory she mentioned to the Guard? That's all she's been working on for the last month. She thinks she's onto something huge."

"When is she going to tell us what she found?"

"I don't know. When she wants to." Seth smiled a lopsided smile.

"Could you ask her?"

"You think I haven't? What gets really annoying is when I'll hear her say something like; 'how do they keep it locked,' and I ask 'keep what locked?' and she tells me to go outside and play. Like I'm 10 years old again."

All of a sudden the room seemed to lurch. My heart beat painfully in my chest and I put a hand out to steady myself on the desk. "She said that?" I asked, my voice hoarse with urgency. "She said 'locked?'"

"Well, yeah," Seth said, giving me a curious look. "Why? Does that mean anything to you?"

I bit my lip, trying to control the sudden hope that flared inside. Locked. Could she mean the seal? Was there a way to keep it closed? Instead of answering his question, I asked, "Can I see your mom's research?"

Seth shifted his weight, suddenly uncomfortable. "She wouldn't really—"

"She doesn't have to know," I breathed in a rush.

Seth gaped at me. "I—she's got her papers all organized in piles. She'll know if we mess with them."

"Please," I said. "This could be really important."

Seth didn't say anything for a long moment. He was avoiding my eyes. "She doesn't like strangers in our house." I felt a wave of disappointment crash over me, but it vanished in the next moment. "So we'll have to sneak over at lunch. She's on a research trip to the library in Santa Fe. She won't be back until this afternoon." Seth caught my eye, gaining courage with every word. "If we're going to do this, we should do it today."

After fourth period, I spotted Lucas on the way into lunch. I grabbed his hand and pulled him out of line. His shoulders tensed, suddenly alert.

"What is it?"

"We need to take a little field trip," I said.

Lucas followed me to the parking lot, glancing at me with surprise when he saw Seth waiting by my car.

"I'll explain on the way," I said.

10 minutes later, Lucas was caught up. I didn't have to mention the seal—Lucas gave me a look that told me he knew exactly what I was thinking. We pulled up outside the little cement-block house Seth and his mom had rented for their stay in Puerto Escondido. It had a salmon-colored stucco face, with sun-faded roof tiles. Seth led the way to the front door, through a small, gated courtyard.

Seth turned to us, suddenly hesitant. "Let me look around first," he said. "Just to make sure she's not here."

I nodded, and Lucas and I crouched down out of view of the front windows.

Seth disappeared into the house, and reappeared a few minutes later. "Coast is clear."

We slipped into the house and Seth pulled the door closed behind us.

The inside of the house was dated but comfortable. Deep brown tiles stretched from the foyer into the living room.

"The office is this way," Seth whispered, clearly nervous. Lucas gave me a smile as we followed Seth down the hall. He opened a door and stepped back.

A desk sat in the center of the room, surrounded by islands of paper stacked all over the floor. The bookshelf pushed up against the back wall sagged under the weight of a mountain of books.

"Whoa," Lucas said, taking it all in.

"Just watch out for the piles," Seth said, hovering nervously in the doorway. "I have no idea how she organizes this stuff."

"So," I was at a loss for where to look. "Where should we start?"

Seth seemed to understand the question I wasn't asking. "She records her theories in her diary," he said, walking quickly into the room. He stepped nimbly around stacks of papers to the back of the desk. "It should be over here somewhere," he said.

Lucas and I walked into the room, moving cautiously to avoid the paper land mines surrounding us. Books and papers weren't the only things in this room I saw. Mingled among the research were artifacts, some extremely old judging by their patinas.

"That's Mesopotamian," Lucas said, pointing to a small statue of two figures wrapped in a pair of bat-like wings.

"You know your art history," Seth said, rustling papers on the desk. "Mom picked up a bunch of Mesopotamian artifacts over the years. Some of this stuff is from the Guard Library, on loan. Come to think of it," he blinked, looking up at the room around him. "Now that the Library is gone, this might be the biggest collection of Lilitu artifacts in existence."

Lucas and I exchanged an uneasy glance.

Seth saw the look and smiled sadly. "You guys are lucky," he murmured. "Having each other. I've never really had a friend I could trust like this before. Mom's kept us moving around. Even if we were in one place long enough for me to make friends, she didn't want me hanging out with anyone my own age."

"Sounds familiar," Lucas said. Seth met his gaze and they shared a look of understanding.

Seth moved another stack of papers and revealed a worn, leather-bound journal. "This is it," he said.

I moved closer, eager to discover Angela's theories. Seth handed the journal to me and I opened it on the desk. I started scanning Angela's notes. A few minutes later, I pulled the desk chair back so I could sit down. We'd found the mother lode.

I read and read and read, flipping through Angela's journal. She had stumbled onto several disjointed pieces of information that—taken together—seemed to lay out the monks' grand plan. As I read, I'd pause to share the most telling bits of research to the guys.

"She thinks the monks believed they had to perform a ritual to, this is a direct quote from her research, 'thwart the coming of the mother of demons.'" I looked at Lucas.

"Lilith," he said grimly. "What kind of ritual?"

I scanned farther down on the page, then flipped to the next page, which contained an itemized list of the contents of the monks' pantry. The journal was blank after that. I flipped back a few pages, trying to see if I'd missed anything. "It's not here," I finally realized.

Seth, perched on the desk to my left, glanced at his watch for the hundredth time. "Lunch ended a while ago," he said. "I think we should be getting back."

"Just a little longer," I pleaded.

"My mom is going to be home anytime," Seth said. "She'll freak out if she finds us here. Trust me, it's not worth the drama." When I still didn't budge, Seth pulled on my shoulder. "Okay—I'll bring you back the next time she leaves town. I promise. Can we go now?"

With effort, I set the journal down, watching as Seth buried it under the stack of papers where he'd found it.

We hurried out of the house, trying not to leave any sign of our visit. On the way to my car, it finally hit me. What all of this really meant to me, personally.

I froze in my tracks. Seth and Lucas, hurrying toward my car, stopped when they realized I was no longer with them. They turned back.

"Braedyn?" Lucas asked.

"Lucas," I whispered. My hands started to tremble. Lucas crossed the distance between us in half a second.

"What's wrong?"

"If this ritual is real," I said. "That means there's a way to keep the final battle from ever starting." Lucas searched my face, uncomprehending. "My duty to the Guard will be fulfilled."

Understanding entered Lucas's eyes, but he needed to hear me say it before he could believe.

"I can become human," I said.

"What?" Seth, just a few feet behind us, stared at me blankly. "How is that possible?"

But I couldn't answer him. My eyes were locked on Lucas. He pulled me in tight, crushing me to him with the force of his emotion.

Lucas released me, beaming. "Do you really think—"

"We have to find out," I said. "If it's real—if it's really real..." I twined my arms around his neck, afraid to speak the words and break this magical spell. Lucas lifted me off my feet, spinning me in a wide circle. I shrieked with laughter, not caring for the moment that we still knew nothing about this ritual, if it really existed, or if it could be reproduced.

For now, we had hope. That was enough.

7

We'd missed most of fifth period so we waited for the bell before sneaking back onto campus for sixth period. Sixth and seventh period were an agonizing wait, and when final bell rang I felt my shoulders sag with relief. All I wanted was to get home and talk to Dad about this ritual.

It wasn't until I opened my locker that I remembered I'd practically commanded Karayan to meet me in the plaza today. "Crap," I muttered.

"What's wrong?" Cassie asked at my shoulder.

I jumped, startled to find her there. "Just remembered there's something I have to do today. Speaking of which, aren't you working in the costume shop?"

"Yeah, actually I need to get over there." Cassie pulled a folded piece of paper out of her pocket and handed it to me.

"What's this?"

"You tell me. Someone slipped it into my locker by mistake. It's addressed to you."

I looked down at the note, which had my name written on it in a strong, confident hand. I opened the note. It read: *Fair warning. I can't take my eyes off of you. Your secret admirer.*

"Ooooo," Cassie teased, reading the note over my shoulder. "A secret admirer." Something about the note gave me chills. I looked up and saw Amber passing in the hall. Her eyes found my face, haughty and cold as ever. "What do you think Lucas would—"

"I'll catch you later, Cass." I left her standing at my locker, rushing off to catch Amber at the drinking fountain. "Hey," I said, grabbing Amber's arm.

Amber pulled angrily out of my grasp. "Touch me again," she growled.

I shoved the note under her nose, interrupting her. "What's this supposed to mean?" Amber glanced at the note, gave me a disgusted look, and turned to walk away. I stepped around to block her. "Answer the question."

"Why do you think I'd have any idea what that means?" Amber asked. Judging from the look on her face, she'd never seen the note before.

Uncertainty washed through me. "You didn't write this?"

Amber scoffed. "Please. I might be watching you, but there is no universe in which I'd say I *admire* you." Amber pushed past me. This time I let her go.

Down the hall, Cassie was waving at someone. It was Mr. Hart. As he waited for Cassie to join him, Mr. Hart noticed me watching him and gave me a brief, inscrutable smile. Then Cassie was standing beside him and they were walking out of the building toward the performing arts center.

I looked back down at the note and turned it over.

There, drawn by a very capable hand, was a single, graceful rose. My mouth suddenly went dry. The rose was nearly perfect, full of dark red petals with just a touch of white at their base. I knew this rose. There was only one place it grew. My dream garden.

Lucas came with me to the plaza that afternoon. He didn't trust Karayan, and he wasn't shy about letting me know it.

"She wrote that note to scare you," he said. "To show you she can get close to you." Lucas glanced at me, grim. "Or close to your friends. She left it in Cassie's locker."

I bit my lip, unconvinced. "Why, though? Why threaten Cassie?"

"Ask her."

We arrived to find Karayan already sitting at a little table outside an artisan coffee shop. She saw me coming and stood. Her lips thinned when she saw Lucas with me.

"Oh look. You brought your puppy." She gave Lucas a condescending smile. "And no leash. He must be very well behaved."

Lucas glared murder at Karayan. "Watch it," he growled. "I'm a *Guardsman*."

"My mistake." Karayan smiled, but her eyes glinted with something cold and unfriendly.

"Chill out," I snapped. "Both of you."

Karayan waved to the empty chairs at her table. The gesture was impatient rather than inviting. When we sat, Karayan leaned closer, lowering her voice. "Talk fast. I'd rather not be seen with you two."

I slapped the note down on the table in front of Karayan. She glanced at it, then looked at me, bored.

"So you've got a secret admirer," she said. "Am I supposed to throw you a parade?"

"We know you wrote it," Lucas said.

"Me?" Karayan smiled, amused. I flipped the note over. Karayan's eyes found the rose. She stopped smiling.

"So you didn't draw this?" I asked.

Karayan shook her head, picking up the drawing. "Who else has been in your garden?"

"No one," I said.

Karayan pushed the note back across the table. "Well, clearly *someone's* seen your roses. And apparently she wishes to remain anonymous."

"How do you know it's a she?" Lucas asked.

"Because only a Lilitu could force her way into another Lilitu's—" but Karayan suddenly stopped, struck by a thought.

A fist of lead closed around my heart. "The incubus?" I asked.

Karayan gave me a sharp look.

"You know?" Lucas asked. "You know there's an incubus in town? Where is he? What does he want?"

Karayan frowned at him, clearly irked by his presence. "Sorry. I don't know anything about your party crasher."

"Who is he?" I asked.

"That's the kind of thing that's usually included in the blanket 'I don't know anything' statement," Karayan said, as though explaining something to a toddler.

I took a slow breath, pushing my irritation down. "I need your help to identify him."

Karayan crossed her arms and leaned back in her chair. "Well, I'm not actually looking to join the Guard right now. But thanks for the invite."

"Forget this," Lucas said in disgust. "We don't need her."

"That's debatable," Karayan muttered, examining her sculpted nails.

"You think we'd take you in?" Lucas snapped. "After everything you've done? Knowing what you are?"

"And what do you think I am, little Guard dog?"

"A selfish, soulless killer," Lucas shot back. "There's no place for you in the Guard."

"Something we can agree on," Karayan said, her tone dangerously quiet. "I've never been very good at turning off my brain."

Lucas glared at Karayan, opening his mouth to fire back.

"Lucas, please." I laid a hand on his arm. It took a moment before he could pull his eyes off of Karayan. When he'd calmed down enough to listen, I spoke. "Let me talk to her for a minute. Privately."

"Fine. I'm tired of looking at her face." Lucas stood and walked away from our table, shoving his hands into his pockets. I watched as he walked into a bookstore a few doors down.

Someone was standing in the bookstore's window, watching us. I couldn't make out too many details, other than his short-cropped hair, which seemed to gleam platinum under the display lights. But there was something about him... A strange tingle shot down the back of my neck.

"Alone at last," Karayan murmured.

"You don't have to bait him like that," I said, pulling my eyes away from the stranger.

"Oh, I know I don't *have* to." She smiled, taking a sip of her coffee. "But it's so much fun."

"Karayan." I glanced back at the bookstore window, but the stranger was gone.

"Ugh. You're spending too much time with the Guard. It's very bad for your sense of humor."

"I'll work on it," I said. "In the meantime, I really do need your help."

Karayan smiled at some private joke. "That's rich."

"I'm serious."

"Perpetually."

"Do you not care at all about this world?"

Karayan looked down at her coffee, playing with the rim of the cup. "I don't know why you're asking for my help."

"Whatever happened to being my mentor?"

Karayan laughed humorously.

"That's funny?"

"What's funny is you not knowing how powerful you are." Karayan looked up, and for a change, her gaze was serious.

"Don't play games with me," I said.

Karayan rolled her eyes. "Whatever you think I can do, you should be able to do it yourself."

"I'm asking for your help," I said through gritted teeth. "Are you going to give it to me or not?" Karayan looked at me, unimpressed. "Before you answer," I added. "You should know that I can be pretty stubborn. Also? I know where to find you in your dreams."

That wiped the bored expression clear off Karayan's face. After a moment, she forced a smile. "Well. What are mentors for?"

Lucas and I walked into the Guard's living room half an hour later. Hale looked up from the newspaper he was scanning. He frowned.

"You're not dressed? Matthew and Gretchen are already downstairs warming up."

"We need to talk to the Guard," Lucas said. "We've got news."

Hale didn't need to hear anything else. "Get your sister and Matthew. I'll get Thane. Braedyn?" Hale glanced at me but I was already dialing my cell for Dad.

By the time Lucas returned with Matthew and Gretchen, I had Dad on the line and Hale was leading Thane out of the back office.

Two minutes later, when Dad walked through the front door, we were all sitting around the dining table. He joined us, taking the chair next to me.

"What's the news?" Dad asked.

"There's a ritual," I said. "That can lock the seal. It could keep the Lilitu out forever. The monks at the mission knew about it." I had expected a big reaction. Instead, the room fell into silence. Dad and Hale glanced at Thane.

"I've never heard about any ritual capable of locking a seal," Thane said after a long moment.

"Braedyn where did you get this information?" Hale asked.

Lucas and I shared a quick look. "We went to Seth's house," I explained. "He showed us his mom's journal."

"You went through Angela's work?" Dad asked. I could see this disturbed him. "Without her knowledge?"

"Why would she keep this from us?" I asked, voicing the thought that had been nagging me all afternoon. "If it really could shut out the Lilitu forever, why would she even hesitate to tell us about this?"

"Angela is an archivist of the first order," Thane said stiffly. "If she's not ready to share her research, there's likely a good reason."

"Like what?" I snapped.

"Maybe she doesn't have all the necessary information yet," Thane replied.

"But if she told us—if she told you," I glared at Thane. "You could help her. Aren't two archivists working on this problem better than one?"

"I have projects of my own," Thane said.

"As important as this one?" Lucas asked. Thane glanced at him but remained silent.

"They have a point," Dad said.

"Murphy," Hale said. It sounded like a warning. He turned to me. "Braedyn, I understand that this is potentially very significant. But we have to trust our experts to do their work. Angela is—as Thane says—one of the best. She's got a gift for research. She'll come to us when she's ready."

"But," Lucas started.

"Drop it," Gretchen said quietly. "You guys shouldn't have left school."

"Dad?" I pleaded. Dad glanced at Hale. Conflict warred in his eyes.

"Linwood is following protocol," Hale said. "She's doing exactly as she was trained to do."

Dad nodded stiffly. "Hale's right."

"So we're just supposed to trust her blindly?" I asked. "What do we really know about her?"

"Braedyn," Dad said quietly. "We can't give into paranoia. Not when we're so close to the next battle. Let Linwood handle the research. We need to focus on the fight."

"Speaking of which," Matthew interjected. "We got a call from

Marx's people. The first group should be arriving in a month or so. They're going to make some stops along the way, try to ferret out a few other units if they can."

"We need to start preparing for them," Gretchen said. "I think we can fit four cots to a room upstairs if we move out the furniture. It's going to be tight, but we can't sleep everyone downstairs. And we're going to need supplies to handle the crowd."

Hale pulled a notebook out of his back pocket. "I'll make a run to the army surplus."

"Wait." Lucas's voice rang like a bullet, silencing the room. "You're not listening to us."

Gretchen turned to Lucas. "We've had our answer," she murmured. "Give Linwood some time."

"There's more at stake," Lucas looked at me.

"If we can lock the seal," I started. Hale glanced at me. He wasn't used to having his orders questioned. "If we can lock the seal, we won't have to fight. And if we don't have to fight," I caught Dad's eye. "I can become human."

My words ran through Dad like some kind of electrical current. Hale saw it, too.

"It doesn't change anything," Hale said.

"We should, at the very least, ask her," Dad replied.

"You want to avoid inciting paranoia," Thane muttered. "You might not want to tell the archivist we're depending on for answers that we've been snooping through her private journals." His eyes cut to me.

"We need to make learning about this ritual a priority," Dad said. It wasn't a question.

"Thane can research it independently," Hale said after some thought. Thane didn't look happy about this, but he nodded in acceptance. Hale turned to me. "All right?"

"All right." It was the best I was going to get for now.

Dad gave my shoulder a warm squeeze. "Just hang on. We're going to figure this out," he promised.

That promise didn't make life any easier. School became an exercise in patience. Whatever progress Thane might be making on his own, he wasn't talking about it. And Angela still hadn't come forward with any of her theories. But Lucas and I had agreed to give them time. And so we were stuck, waiting. Going through the motions of our everyday lives. School. Training. Dinners spent planning with the Guard. And all the while we were trying to ignore the possibility that all this was unnecessary because maybe, just maybe, there was a way to lock the door between this world and the Lilitu world forever.

One week became two. Two weeks became three. And then it was Halloween. Lucas and Seth came over to watch TV with me. The pumpkins Dad had bought for us sat on our porch, un-carved. Next to them I'd set out a bowl of self-serve candy for any trick-or-treaters brave enough to walk up to our dark front door. It just didn't feel like Halloween without Cassie and Royal. We'd spent Halloween together every year since elementary school, but this year they had other plans. They'd been invited to a big party that some of their theater friends were throwing. Cassie had asked us to join them, but neither Lucas nor I felt up to it, and Seth wasn't exactly well liked around campus. After half-heartedly flipping through some Halloween specials, I told the guys I wanted to turn in early. Lucas, understanding, said he thought it was time to be getting home, too.

Dad offered to make popcorn if Seth wanted to stay and finish the show, but Seth made his excuses and left to drive himself home in the car he'd borrowed from his mom for the night.

Moments later, after hastily brushing my teeth and jumping into bed, I slipped out of this reality and into my dream. I sat in the rose garden, hugging my knees to my chest, next to a pool of flickering dreams. It felt like a small eternity had passed before Lucas fell asleep, but as soon as he did I could sense him. The glimmering light of his unconscious mind rose up and out of the pool at my feet. I closed my hand around it and felt the comfort of Lucas's presence drawing me into his dream.

I found him squinting against a bitter wind, anxious and unfocused. When he saw me his troubled brow eased. He came to me and I buried myself against his chest, holding on to him tightly, drawing comfort from the embrace. I felt Lucas's hand brushing the side of my cheek and looked up. His kiss was warm, urgent. I responded, threading my fingers through his hair—trying not to compare the sensation to what it felt like in the real world. In the dream, everything felt somehow muted, watery. Which wasn't to say it wasn't nice. It just wasn't... real. And yet, it was all we had. We spent the night trying to take our minds off the agony of waiting.

November settled over Puerto Escondido, teasing the last of the leaves off the aspen and oak trees, and we still had no answers about the ritual.

That week in physics class, while Mr. Harris stood at the board going over the math for another experiment, Seth was watching me. I had been trying to take notes, but my pencil kept straying to the margins, filling the page with anxious doodles.

"Something's bothering you," he said. "I think—I think I get it."

I glanced at him. "What?"

"You know, because that ritual is all about shutting the door on the Lilitu world forever. I get why that would freak you out."

"It doesn't," I looked at Seth, surprised. "Why would you think that?"

"Well, if I were you, I mean," Seth shifted in his seat, uncomfortable. "Aren't you curious? About what's on the other side?" Seth studied my eyes. "If my mom figures it out," Seth shrugged, "you'll never get the chance to find out."

"This ritual, it's a good thing," I said, studying Seth sharply. "Do you know something more about it?"

"No. It's just," Seth glanced quickly to the front of class. Mr. Harris had his back to the class, carefully writing out a list of formulas on the board. "Why do you want to be human? I mean," he lowered his eyes sheepishly. "I think your powers are cool."

I looked at Seth. Unfamiliar feelings tickled the back of my mind.

"What?" he asked, seeing my expression.

"Not even Lucas thinks my powers are cool," I admitted.

"Why not? They're a fundamental part of who you are," Seth said. He looked honestly surprised. "I mean, you can turn yourself *invisible*. How much cooler does it get?"

I couldn't help smiling. No one—with the possible exception of Karayan—had ever talked about my powers like this before. Seth looked at me with awe, but not like the boys who were caught in the snare of a Lilitu's beauty. This was different. Seth looked at me, *really looked* at me, and saw all of me as beautiful. The feeling was strange, but nice.

Seth was still watching me, curious. "He seriously can't see that?"

Stubbornly, I defended Lucas. "Lilitu hurt his family."

"Yeah, but that wasn't you. I mean, from what Gretchen says, you saved Lucas's life." I had no answer for him. Seth shook his head. "I thought Lucas was cooler than that."

Try as I might to push Seth's words out of my mind, they stayed with me all day. I found myself watching Lucas at lunch, trying to spot any signs of revulsion or fear. Once, he caught me staring and gave me a faintly bemused smile. I glanced at Seth, who was talking animatedly with Cassie across the table. Lucas followed my gaze, then turned back to me.

"It's nothing," I said in answer to his unasked question. Before he could call me out, I turned my attention to Cassie.

"I've got a few more things to do, but it's ready for a fitting today," she was telling Seth.

"Which costume is this?" I asked, forcing enthusiasm into my voice.

"It's one of Guinevere's dresses, the one she's wearing when she meets Lancelot. You want to see?" Cassie looked suddenly hopeful. "Will you come over today after school? I'd love to show it to you; you haven't seen any of the stuff I've been working on lately."

I felt a twinge of guilt for being so absent from Cassie's life. "I'd love to," I said, and this time my enthusiasm wasn't faked. I could feel Lucas watching me, but I spent the rest of lunch engaging Cassie in stories about what it was like to be a costume designer.

After school, I walked into the performing arts building. There were posters along the walls from former musicals and concerts. From some rooms I could hear violins or horns running scales. At the end of a long hallway, I found the heart of the theater program—the green room.

Cassie and Royal were sitting on an old worn couch, talking and laughing with some kids I didn't know. Cassie jumped up when she saw me.

"Braedyn," she said, "you're here! Come on." Cassie led me back down the hall to a set of double doors. "This is the costume closet," she said, opening one of the doors.

Closet was a bit of an understatement. It was massive—at least the size of a classroom. Shelves and racks lined the walls from the floor to the high ceiling 20 feet above us. The floor in the back half of the room was crowded with rolling racks of clothes, but the front of the room featured a huge worktable piled with bolts of fabric, buckets of tape measures, pencils, scissors, and stick pins. It looked like Cassie's personal heaven.

A dress form stood next to the table, and I recognized Cassie's work instantly. A shimmering, pale grey velvet gown hugged the dress form snuggly to the waist, then the creamy velvet spilled down in gleaming folds of fabric that just barely kissed the ground.

"It's beautiful," I breathed. It was true. The gown was perfect, delicate, pure. "I want to get married in that dress."

Cassie giggled, pleased. "It's not totally finished," she said. "I can't put the trim on until I've hemmed everything up for—oh! Here she is!"

I turned as Missy bounded into the costume closet. "Where is it?" she asked eagerly. I don't think she even saw me standing there.

Cassie gestured at the dress, beaming. Missy squealed when she saw the gown. She threw her arms around Cassie. "You are a genius, Cassie!" Finally, Missy noticed me. "Oh, Braedyn."

"You're in the play?" I asked.

"She's the star," Cassie said.

"Well," Missy lowered her eyes, pleased. "It's really Arthur and Lancelot's show. I'm just the eye candy."

Cassie hit Missy lightly on the arm. "That is so not true," she said, turning to me. "She's got an amazing voice."

Missy tipped her head down, letting the red curls cascade around her features to hide the pretty blush spreading across her cheeks. "Thanks, but we all know who the most talented lady of this production is." Missy threw an arm around Cassie's shoulders and grinned at me. "Right, Braedyn?"

A tight knot of jealousy worked its way into my stomach. I tried to push it aside. Cassie was one of my best friends in the world, but I didn't own her. Of course she had other friends.

"Absolutely," I said, trying to keep my voice light.

Royal arrived at that moment, carrying a huge box. "Delivery for Miss Ang," he said.

"Put it on the table," Cassie said. She pounced on the box with a pair of scissors. When she had it opened, she pulled out a deep blue material. It had a luxurious sheen, but was shot through with the rougher strands distinctive of raw silk. "Very nice," she said with satisfaction.

"Is this the material for the outer dress?" Missy breathed. At Cassie's nod, Missy practically swooned. "I wish we could dress like this every day."

"Yeah, to heck with Women's Lib," I said. "Who needs pants?" Cassie and Missy looked at me. I cleared my throat, feeling awkward.

Royal perched on the worktable, eyeing me. "Look who decided to visit." He still wore the skullcap everywhere, but he wasn't tugging on it self-consciously anymore.

After an awkward moment, Cassie turned to lift the dress off the dress-form. "Try it on?" she asked Missy.

"I thought you'd never ask." Missy took the dress and slipped out of the costume closet to go change.

"So," I said, turning to Royal. "How's it going?"

"It's grueling, but I think I could get used to this assistant gig," Royal said. Cassie snickered. Apparently I was missing out on a joke.

Cassie saw my confusion and explained. "His duties as my assistant basically consist of sitting around and keeping me company." Cassie grinned at Royal. "But yes, he is really good at it."

"You should join us," Royal said. "As you can see, there's plenty of room in the closet for all of us. And no, the irony is not lost on me."

Cassie giggled and I smiled. It was the three of us again, like it used to be. A sudden rush of nostalgia flooded through me. I missed this. I missed Royal and Cassie.

The door opened behind us again. Mr. Hart entered. "Cassie, Missy looks incredible. Sometimes I can't believe you're only 16. You've got the skills of a master craftsman, kid." Cassie's face lit up with pride—and something else.

Mr. Hart noticed her look and spotted me. "Hello, there. Another volunteer for the production?"

"Who, me? No," I said.

"Braedyn's just visiting," Cassie said. Was I imagining the disappointment in her voice?

"Ah," Mr. Hart gave me a pained smile. "I'm sorry, but I'm going to have to ask you to leave. It's a liability thing for the school. If you're not here for the production..." he left the rest unsaid.

"Oh." I glanced at Cassie and Royal. "Right."

"Thanks for understanding." Mr. Hart turned his back on me and went to join Cassie at the table. She smiled up at him warmly, turning away from me.

I walked to the door and hesitated. Most of the girls in the greenroom looked up expectantly, their eager smiles fading into disappointment when they saw it was just me. One or two shot wistful looks at the door to the costume closet behind me, while another pair slumped onto the greenroom couch, disgruntled. Because I wasn't Mr. Hart.

I turned to look back into the costume closet. Unease prickled at the back of my neck. It crowded out the jumble of emotions in my mind. Piece by piece, it all fell into place. Mr. Hart with his easy good looks and charm, winning over the female population of Coronado Prep in one lunch announcement. Cassie, throwing herself into this production to the exclusion of almost everything else, straining to win these precious words of praise from him. He worked at school. How hard would it be for him to slip something into Cassie's locker? Even if someone saw, they'd assume it was a note about costume design or the production.

As if sensing my thoughts, Mr. Hart glanced back at me. "Don't worry, Braedyn. Your friends will still be here tomorrow." His smile was a clear dismissal.

I walked out of the costume closet, down the hallway, and out into the crisp October air. Only when I reached my car did I allow myself to name my fear.

Was it possible? Was Mr. Hart the incubus?

8

An amber glow spilled over the rough dining table from the aging pendant light. I fell silent, looking around the table. The faces of the Guard were solemn as they processed what I'd said. Hale. Thane. Gretchen. Dad. Lucas. Angela. Seth. No one spoke. I'd talked for over an hour, walking them through my realization, laying out the evidence against Mr. Hart. By the time I'd finished, the sun had set, shrouding the house in darkness save for this one light.

Thane glanced at Angela. She felt his gaze and nodded slowly, thinking. After another long moment, she looked back at me.

"Did you sense anything about this man?" she asked. "As a Lilitu, I mean?"

Dad's head whipped around.

Angela smiled a thin smile. "Yes, I know." She glanced at Thane with reproach. "After my initial shock, it became rather obvious that the benefits of working with a tame Lilitu," and here she glanced at me, "no offense, dear."

"Sure," I mumbled.

Seth, sitting across the table for me, blushed. "Sorry. I tell Mom everything."

"The benefits," Angela continued, "balance the potential risks." She eyed me for a moment, then glanced at Hale. Whatever she wasn't saying seemed to grate on Dad's nerves. Hale sensed Dad's mood and cleared his throat.

"You bring up a crucial point," he said. "Braedyn, did you *see* anything about Mr. Hart that backs up your concerns?"

"You mean," I glanced at Gretchen. As a spotter, she was the only other one at this table who could see the smoky wings or faint inky stain that surrounded a Lilitu when she was preying on a human.

101

"Would they exhibit the same markers?" Gretchen asked, voicing my thought for me.

Angela shrugged. "We have no way of knowing. The only account of an incubus we have in our records is the story I've told you about the monks from the mission. They had no spotter with them."

"Braedyn?" Dad asked.

"I didn't see anything," I admitted.

"Not even during lunch, when you claim he was enthralling the student body?" Thane asked. There was an edge of accusation in his voice that rankled me. But the truth was, I hadn't seen anything like the fingers of shadow other Lilitu gave off when they were exerting their power. I shook my head no.

"Well." Angela steepled her hands on the edge of the table. "That leaves us with two possibilities. Either male Lilitu are capable of disguising themselves from female Lilitu when they don't want to be seen..." she shrugged. "Or Mr. Hart is not an incubus."

"All right." Hale nodded, leaning back in his chair. "We'll keep an eye on him." He smiled at me. "Thanks for sharing your concerns with us, Braedyn. It's good to be cautious."

Hale pushed back from the table. The meeting was over.

"But," I glanced around as everyone except for Dad and Lucas stood up. "That's it? We'll keep an eye on him?"

Hale glanced at Dad. "Braedyn," he said, choosing his words carefully. "Until we know more, we can't really act."

"But he's," I turned to Lucas for support. "My friends spend a lot of time with him. If they're in danger...?"

Thane frowned. "Yes. *If.* They're only in danger *if* your suspicions are founded."

"So we're just supposed to wait for him to make a move?" I snapped. "Maybe once he's attacked Cassie you'll believe me and we can do something?"

"Do you have another idea?" Hale asked.

"I... I could try searching for him in the dream," I said. Why not? It was no challenge for me to find a human dream, and when I went looking I'd found Karayan's dream without too much trouble. Maybe if I could slip into Mr. Hart's dream I could find out whether or not he was a threat.

Seth looked at me, intrigued. "Could that work?"

"Interesting," Thane murmured.

"Hang on," Dad said. "We don't know anything about this incubus."

"If we're going to remedy that, we should allow the girl to look for him," Thane said.

"I'm not comfortable with this." Dad's brow creased with anxiety. "What if she tips him off? What if he comes after her in retaliation?"

"I'll be careful."

"We don't know what he's capable of," Dad said.

"We don't know what I'm capable of, either," I answered.

"It's worth a shot," Hale said. When Dad tried to argue, Hale held up a hand. "Braedyn, if you're going to do this, make us a promise. If anything feels wrong, you get out of the dream and report to us immediately. Deal?"

"Deal," I said.

Dad looked like he'd swallowed something sour, but the discussion was over and he knew it.

Dreams are funny things, even for a Lilitu. If I let my mind wander in someone else's dream, I can get swept away in the current of thoughts welling up from the dreamer's unconscious. A few times, with Lucas, I'd released control entirely, letting myself float along in the narrative of his dream. It was exhilarating and terrifying in the same moment. Because regaining control—once it had been relinquished—was a struggle.

I had always felt safest in my own garden. Here, letting my mind wander meant only rest and calm; a chance to escape from the tension of my physical body and simply drift, *being*. This was my sanctuary from the world. This was my fortress.

But as I sat among the roses, I felt cold. Someone had visited this place, without my knowledge or my permission. Worse, I hadn't sensed the trespass. They'd left no trace of their invasion. It was in the middle of these unhappy thoughts that I felt Karayan's presence, hovering at the edge of my dream.

"Finally. I've been waiting for you," I said.

Karayan appeared, looking every bit as beautiful as she did in the physical world. "I said I'd come. I didn't promise to jump at your beck and call."

"Fine."

"Thank you, Karayan," she said, gushing sarcastically. "I don't know *what* I would do without your help. And your hair looked so *fabulous* the other day. I can't do anything with mine." It was meant to be an imitation of me, and I frowned. "Oh, stop," Karayan went on in her own voice, ignoring my grimace. "You're going to make me blush."

"Really?" I asked, giving her a flat stare.

Karayan crossed her arms. "You want my help? I'm here. Let's get this over with. I'd rather not spend the whole night holding your hand."

"Okay." But here I hesitated, at a loss. Where to begin?

"It helps to know what you're trying to do," Karayan prompted. She was not a very patient person. "Do you know what you're trying to do?"

"I need to find the incubus," I said.

"And I already told you: I don't know who that is."

"Mr. Hart," I clarified.

"Oh, little Nancy Drew's gone investigating, has she?" She crossed her arms, waiting. "So?"

I hesitated again. As brave as I'd felt at the Guard's dining table earlier in the night, things were different in the dream. What if he took control and I couldn't fight him? What if he was able to mess with my head like I'd messed with Parker's? Karayan's expression softened. I turned away from her abruptly. The last thing I needed was her pity.

"You know," she said. "If it'll move this thing along, maybe I should just come with you."

I glanced at her, but she wasn't looking at me. A soft wash of gratitude welled inside of me. I cleared my throat. "Sure. Whatever." I knelt and placed my palm on the ground-that-wasn't-ground at my feet. I let my awareness expand beyond the confines of this dream and felt the infinite world of the shared dream lapping at its edges. It was a simple matter to open my mind and let the shared dream inside.

A pool of dark liquid grew under my hand. It looked like water, but felt like glass. For a moment I let the drifting sparks of dreams pass beneath us, undisturbed. I felt rather than saw Karayan watching me, but she didn't speak.

"Mr. Hart," I murmured. Ready or not, it was time to learn whatever I could about the mysterious stranger who'd charmed his way into my school and into my friends' lives.

A brightly gleaming spark of a dream rose from the sea of swirling lights. As it grew closer, I studied it. It looked just like a human dream; there was no bright-blue halo surrounding it as there were surrounding Lilitu dreams. But there was something different about it. I couldn't place what it was, but Karayan noticed it, too.

"Odd," she said. "I can't sense anything from this dream."

She's right, I realized. Whenever I called Lucas's dream out of the dark pool, I could feel *him* drawing near. Or, more accurately, I could feel his essence—the stubborn, loyal, brave core that made him Lucas. With Parker, I'd caught a flash of the cold self-confidence with which he navigates the world. But with this dream? Nothing. No charisma, no open friendliness, none of the dramatic flair that he exhibited at school—none of *Mr. Hart* emanated from his dream. I looked up. Karayan was frowning in thought. Her eyes found mine.

"It looks like a human dream," I said.

"I've never met a human who could shield his dreams this completely."

"What do you think it means?"

Karayan tilted her head to one side with a tight smile. "I love that you think of me as the holder-of-all-answers, but I have to burst your bubble."

"You don't know either." I sighed. "Here goes nothing." Karayan didn't look nervous. I tried to push my own misgivings to the back of my mind. "Together?"

"You're the fearless leader," she said.

Together we lifted our hands and cupped them around the dream. Nothing happened. I mean *nothing*. The only reaction Karayan gave was a small, startled breath. We withdrew our hands at the same moment.

"Is this...?" I asked.

"No," Karayan said. "This is *not* normal." She looked at me, all traces of her characteristic attitude gone. "Even with a really powerful Lilitu who's shielding her dream, you feel something."

"You've never seen this before? A dream that's totally closed?"

"Not only have I never *seen* this before, I've never heard of this *happening* before."

"So what now?"

Karayan pulled her eyes away from the sparkling dream. "It's your show. You tell me. I'm just your backup."

"Okay. Let me think," I said.

Karayan sat back, brushing her hair off one shoulder. Her eyes caught on something behind me. She grew suddenly still. "Braedyn?"

Something in her voice alerted me. I turned around. A slender roll of paper was tied to the stem of a beautiful rose with a red ribbon. I stared at it, uncomprehending.

Karayan's eyes cut to mine. "Was that there before?"

"No." My mouth went dry. Karayan and I were on our feet in an instant, instinctively pressing our backs together, scanning the field of roses for any sign of the intruder. A wind ruffled the roses as my fear found a way to manifest itself across my dream.

"Control yourself," Karayan murmured, not pulling her eyes away from the field.

I forced my fear to the back of my mind. The wind died down. We stood there, back to back, for several long minutes. Nothing else stirred. Whoever had broken into my dream and tied that scroll to my rose—they were long gone.

"How did they get past us? How did they enter my dream without me sensing them at all?" I asked. Karayan shook her head, unable to answer me. I took a step toward the scroll. Karayan caught my hand, stopping me.

"I don't know if you should do that," she said.

"I'm not going to leave it there," I snapped. "This is my *mind*."

Karayan's jaw tightened, but she let me go. I walked to the scroll. It was a thing of beauty. The red ribbon shimmered with the luster of a pearl, and the scroll itself was a thick, cream-colored parchment. I barely had to tug on the ribbon before it sprang loose. Freed, the scroll unspooled. I recognized the bold handwriting instantly. It was the same as the handwriting on the note from Cassie's locker.

It was a simple message: *Apparently, my friendly warning was too subtle. Stay out of my way, little sister, or I'll be forced to sideline you. Permanently.*

I turned back to Karayan. She was watching my face; something like concern had etched faint lines into her brow. Wordlessly, I handed the scroll over. Karayan took it. As her eyes scanned the message, her frown deepened.

"Okay. You played the brave little soldier, good job. Now it's time to back off."

"Back off? I thought this was my show." I snatched the note out of her hands.

"I'm here to help, remember? This is me helping." Karayan pointed at the scroll in my hands. "It doesn't take a genius to see that that's a threat."

"A threat is different from an attack," I said.

"Come on," she lifted her hands, looking around. "The guy can slip into your dreams undetected. You want to tell me he can't slip into your house?"

"If you really want to help me," I said. "Show me how to shield my dreams so he can't come barging in here whenever he feels like it." Karayan looked mutinous. "Please," I said. Karayan gritted her teeth. But instead of arguing, she waved her hand over the pool of dreams. It dried up, leaving the ground unmarked.

"Shielding your dreams isn't something you can do once and then forget about like locking a door," she said. "That's not how this stuff works."

Locking a door? I glanced at her sharply, but she didn't seem to notice.

"You've got to keep it going every time you fall asleep. Close your eyes." When I hesitated, she waved at me impatiently. "Close your eyes. This is easier to do if you can just feel it."

Trusting Karayan wasn't something that came naturally, but I swallowed my suspicion and did as she asked.

"You can sense the edge of your dream, right?"

"Yes," I said. In my mind's eye I stood in the center of a snow globe, its curving wall of glass separating this dream from the infinite dream it travelled through, like a bubble of air in water.

"Okay. You have to hold that edge in your mind. Search it for weak spots. Will it to grow stronger."

As she spoke, I let my mind probe the outer edges of this dream. I found that—unlike the glass wall of a snow globe—this wall shifted under my touch. Some places were thicker, some thinner. And then I came to a small hole in the wall, centered around a silvery cord.

Curious, I toyed with the idea of closing the hole. It started to constrict instantly.

"Stop!" Karayan said. "Unless you're done with this lesson."

My eyes sprang open. "You said to look for weak spots."

Karayan looked exasperated. "You want me in here, you've got to leave one door open."

"Okay, sorry."

Karayan gave me an appraising look. "But that was pretty good," she said. "Don't worry. You'll build up strength over time, and one day you'll be able to push unwanted visitors out of your dream."

I suddenly remembered the time I'd visited Karayan's dream. "You tried to do that to me," I said.

"Well," her smile looked a little strained. "I wasn't trying all that hard." She brushed her hands, as though finished with a dirty job. "That should be enough to get you started. Maybe if you keep your head down, the incubus will leave you alone."

I laughed ruefully. "Yeah, *that's* not going to happen."

"Braedyn," Karayan put a hand on my shoulder. "We have no idea how powerful this incubus is."

"I know."

"Good. Don't be stupid. If he doesn't come after you, don't go after him. That's all I'm saying."

I pushed Karayan's hand off my shoulder. "If he tries to hurt Cassie, I'm going after him."

"That. That right there is stupid." Karayan punctuated the words by poking her finger into my chest.

"Cassie doesn't know the danger she's in," I said. "I do." I turned away but Karayan caught my shoulder and spun me back to face her.

"If you're not careful, your friend is going to get you killed."

"There's no way I'd leave her unprotected," I said, getting angry. "There's no way I'd leave any of my friends unprotected. That's the difference between you and me."

"No," Karayan snapped back. "The difference between you and me is that I'm not wiling to throw my life away trying to win approval from a bunch of old men who'd just as soon see me dead."

"You know, Karayan? Maybe the reason you don't have any family is because you don't understand what *makes* family family."

My words struck Karayan deeply, as I meant them to. She jerked back as if stung. "Believe it or not, I really am trying to help you. The writing is on the wall. If that incubus is as strong as he seems, there's a good chance he'll open the seal like he plans."

Her words drove like spikes into my chest. I tried to keep my expression neutral. "You should go now."

"And once the seal is open and the Lilitu are freed, the Guard is going to be wiped out—you along with them if you're still standing by their—"

With the smallest twist of effort, I closed the hole I'd found in my dream. Karayan winked out of my garden mid-rant. Fury boiled in my mind, but under that, an icy sea of terror opened up. My mind cast out, running along the walls of my dream. Everywhere I passed, I felt the walls of the dream harden, thicken into something like granite, seamless and solid, until no weakness remained.

Standing in the garden, I shivered. I may have cast Karayan out effortlessly, but her words were much harder to banish.

"Get up, Dad." I stood next to Dad's bed, dressed for school. The room was dark and still, filled with the peace of early morning. It grated on my nerves, contrasting sharply with the chaos of my thoughts. "Dad. Time to get up."

Dad groaned. He opened his eyes and glanced at the clock. "Braedyn?"

"We need to see the Guard."

"You found something?" Dad asked, sitting up.

"Hale's up. I saw him coming back from his run." I had waited in my room at the window since five, watching for Hale's return.

"Okay. I'm up."

"I'll be downstairs." I walked to the door, already caught up in another tangle of anxious thoughts.

"Oh, Braedyn," Dad called from behind me. I turned as he swung his legs over the side of his bed, rubbing the sleep out of his eyes. He gave me a tired smile. "Happy Birthday."

I stopped with my hand on the door, running through the days in my head. But of course he was right. November ninth. I was 17 years old today.

It took longer to get everyone assembled than I expected. It was 6:30 by the time everyone had joined us in the Guard's living room. Lucas and Gretchen were the last two down the stairs. When they sat down, Lucas's jaw creaked with a massive yawn and Matthew ruffled Gretchen's short hair affectionately.

"Okay, what's up?" Hale asked.

"It's Mr. Hart," I said grimly. I told them what had happened last night. I even told them the part Karayan had played. When Thane heard her name his expression darkened with fury, but no one interrupted me. More than one of them looked unsettled when I explained how I'd touched Mr. Hart's dream and felt nothing. That Karayan was surprised, too, made them more uncomfortable. "It's him," I finished. "Mr. Hart has to be the incubus."

"Braedyn, honey." Dad took my hand and looked into my face. His expression was deadly serious. "Is it possible, is it at all possible that this dream you had doesn't mean what you think it means?"

"You think I'm making this up?" I asked, crushed.

"No. You believe what you're saying, no question. But I need to know if there's any possibility that Mr. Hart is human."

"I'm telling you what I saw," I said.

"I'm more concerned with what you haven't seen," Dad said gently. "You say you sensed nothing from his dream. Okay, correct me if I'm wrong, but that means if you couldn't sense he was human, you also couldn't sense that he was Lilitu, right?"

I opened my mouth to argue, but I couldn't.

"And neither you nor Gretchen saw anything supernatural about him."

"Gretchen?" I asked. "When did Gretchen see Mr. Hart?"

"I went to his house last night," she said.

"And?" I asked.

"Sorry, Braedyn," Gretchen said. "I was looking hard for anything at all, but," she shrugged unhappily.

I glanced around the table. "That doesn't mean he's not an incubus. Angela told us, we don't know enough about them to know if spotters can even see them."

"Maybe," Gretchen admitted. "But he lives with his wife and two little kids. If he's an incubus, he's gone to some pretty extreme measures to fit in."

"I'm telling you, something's not right with that guy," I insisted.

"Braedyn can you tell me with 100 percent certainty that Mr. Hart is an incubus?" Dad asked, but then held up a finger before I could answer. "Please. Think hard, honey. Because you're asking us to execute a man."

The breath I'd taken to answer with left my lungs. Everyone watched me, waiting. My confidence wavered. What if they were right? What if I was misinterpreting the signs? "Maybe," I licked my lips. "Maybe we should wait a bit longer."

"Okay." Dad glanced across the table and I saw Hale and Matthew relax. I suddenly realized that they had been preparing themselves to kill someone on my word. "Okay. We'll wait."

The doorbell rang, shattering the quiet morning with a peal of bells.

Matthew stood and answered the door in the foyer.

I heard an explosion of voices, and Matthew's laughter. "Holy shit, man, look at you!"

"What about you, dude?" the guy Matthew was talking to answered. "I hear you let some woman put a leash on you. What's up with that?"

I glanced at Gretchen, whose eyebrows hiked up, amused.

"You might want to watch what you say," Matthew said as he and the newcomers walked into the living room. Four men in their early twenties dropped their overstuffed duffels onto the floor. They weren't wearing uniforms, but something about them screamed *soldier* nonetheless. Matthew had his arm around the neck of a handsome black man, steering him roughly into the living room. "That's her over there. Gretchen," he said, "Meet Sam. Sam, Gretchen. I cannot wait to watch her take you apart on the mat."

"We'll see, we'll see," Sam said, grinning. "What do you say, Gretchen? Up for a bout sometime?"

"Looking forward to it," Gretchen said. Her smile was mild, but her eyes crinkled with anticipation.

Sam's eyes travelled around the room, snagging on me. "So come on, man," he said, hitting Matthew in the stomach. "Introduce the crew."

"Right," Matthew said. He pointed out the newcomers as he listed off their names. "Privates Chris, Paul, and Jason. You already know Sam." Matthew turned into the living room, naming the rest of us for the newcomers. "Gretchen, Lucas, Thane, Hale, Braedyn," he ended by sweeping a hand toward Dad. "And this is Murphy." The newcomers reacted, eyeing my dad with more than a little amazement.

"For real?" the blond guy—Chris? Or was it Jason?—asked.

"In the flesh," Matthew said.

"It's an honor, sir," the blond guy said, offering Dad his hand.

"Please," Dad said, shaking it. "We don't stand on formality here. Come in, put your feet up."

The newcomers crowded around Dad and he was stuck fielding questions. I couldn't help but grin. It was still strange to think of Dad as the living legend so much of the Guard saw him as.

"Braedyn?" Hale pulled me away from the crowd. "This probably goes without saying, but you should keep your secret under wraps for now."

I glanced at the soldiers, my smile fading. "What about their spotters?" I asked.

"Marx and his team are recruiting the spotters for their mission. They're just sending the fighters on to Puerto Escondido right now, so we have a little time to get them familiar with you before we drop that bomb."

"Okay." I let out a deep sigh. I wasn't looking forward to another round of "what do you mean she's a Lilitu?"

"Keep an eye on Mr. Hart," Hale added. I glanced at him, surprised. "If he is what you think, we'll take care of it."

I nodded just as Dad managed to extract himself from his band of groupies.

"Why don't you go home, honey," he asked. He was smiling, but I could see his tension. It didn't take a genius to work it out. He didn't want me around the Guard soldiers any more than was strictly necessary.

"Sure, okay."

"I wanted to make you breakfast for your birthday," Dad said. He glanced back at the new Guardsmen. "But I think I need to help sort out the arrangements."

"No, I get it."

"I love you, honey," Dad said, planting a kiss on my head. "I'll make it up to you later. I promise." But before I could tell him it was okay—who needed a birthday breakfast anyhow?—he was walking back into the living room.

My seventeenth birthday went from disappointing to downright depressing.

At school, no one even mentioned it. Cassie and Royal had been so eager to help me plan my sixteenth birthday. But they'd completely forgotten my seventeenth, being so caught up with the theater production.

Lucas was focused on Mr. Hart, waiting for the drama teacher to make any mistake that could reveal his true nature. I was late to lunch, and when I got there only Seth was sitting at our table.

"Where is everyone?" I asked.

"Dunno," he shrugged, shoving another bite of food into his mouth.

I sat down and reached for the nearest bowl of food. Tater-tots stared up at me, covered in a slick sheen of oil. "Actually, I'm not all that hungry," I said, pushing the bowl away.

"Does that mean...?" Seth eyed the tater-tots.

"Knock yourself out," I answered. I pushed back from the table and stood.

"You're not going to eat anything?" Seth asked.

"No." I gave him a smile in apology. "Not feeling too great today."

"Is there anything I can do?" He asked awkwardly, suddenly looking like a frog on a hotplate.

"No, it's okay. I'm going to head over to the library. I've got a quiz to study for." It was true, but when I left the dining hall I didn't feel like studying.

Instead, I walked over to the performing arts building, thinking I might run into Lucas patrolling the halls for some sign of Mr. Hart.

I walked into the building, but it was empty. Which made sense; most of the students were at lunch.

Searching the halls for Lucas, I turned up empty handed. I stopped in the green room, frustrated. That's when I heard the muffled conversation. It was coming from the costume closet. I cracked the door open and peeked inside.

Cassie and Mr. Hart were sitting on the worktable, side by side. He had an arm around her back, and she was looking up into his face. The moment was clearly private, intimate.

Instead of obeying my instincts and retreating, I pushed the door open with a cheerful, "Oh, hi, Cassie. There you are. We missed you at lunch."

Cassie and Mr. Hart sprang apart, caught. Mr. Hart slid off the worktable and gave Cassie a careful smile. "Well. I don't want to keep you from your lunch." He walked past me quickly.

"I lost track of time," Cassie said, laughing nervously. "Sorry. You didn't have to come looking for me." She gathered up her things and headed to the door. "What are they serving today?"

I closed the door before she could escape. She looked at me, startled.

"Cassie," I said. "What was that?"

"What?"

"With Mr. Hart?"

"What? We were just talking." Cassie's cheeks reddened and she wouldn't meet my eyes.

"That's not what it looked like," I said.

"What did it look like?" Cassie asked. I was surprised by the hostility in her voice.

"I just don't want to see you get hurt. Like before."

Cassie looked at me, genuinely confused. "Before?" I realized instantly I'd made a mistake. Her eyes narrowed. "You mean, like Parker?"

"Cassie," I said, reaching for her arm. She jerked away from me, pissed.

"You too?" she said. Tears of anger sprang into her eyes.

"I didn't mean—"

"I needed someone to talk to," she said. "That doesn't mean I'm going to—" she shook her head, disgusted.

"If you want to talk, why can't you talk to Royal and me?" I asked.

"You?" Cassie laughed in disbelief. "You haven't exactly been around lately and Royal... he still treats me like something that's going to shatter if he's not careful."

"Okay," I said, scrambling for the right thing to say. "But I just think Mr. Hart's—"

"What?"

"Not... appropriate," I mumbled under the heat of her glare.

"Listen," Cassie snapped. "You want to be my friend? Stop trying to be my babysitter."

Cassie pushed roughly past me and yanked the door open. I blocked her path, desperate to get through to her.

"Wait," I said. Cassie wouldn't meet my gaze. "I feel like I don't even know what's going on in your life right now."

"Whose fault is that?" Cassie didn't give me a chance to respond. She pushed my arm out of the way and marched out of the costume closet. I stared at the racks of old clothes lining the room. Cassie was right. I'd disappeared from her life, leaving a convenient hole available for Mr. Hart to slip right into. I couldn't have made it easier for him if I'd tried.

My fault. This was all my fault.

9

A storm was gathering across the mountain. Swollen, purple clouds crouched over the earth, casting darkness onto the land below. The anticipation of rain became a building tension that seemed to ache for release. I leaned my head against the school library's picture window, unable to look away. This wasn't a view you could get in most of Puerto Escondido. But here, standing at this window, I could see through the break in the mountains that encircled our town out to the land beyond. It felt soothing, looking down over the desert stretching away for hundreds of miles. A reminder of the larger world beyond my little town.

I saw Cassie's reflection in the window and turned.

"So," she said. She was standing there awkwardly, shuffling her weight from one foot to the other.

I stood. "Cassie, I'm so sorry."

"You don't have to apologize," Cassie said. "I—I know how it must have looked." I could only shake my head, miserable. Cassie looked down at the floor. "But the truth is, I miss you."

"I miss you, too," I said.

"How about we take the afternoon and go down to Old Town."

I brightened. "Yeah? You can do that? What about the show?"

Cassie shrugged. "Whatever. I doubt they'll miss me for one day."

I wasn't going to argue with her. "I'll drive."

Cassie and I made our way to Old Town, and parked on a quiet residential street across from the main plaza. Stepping out of the car, I could smell a wood fire burning in someone's chimney to ward off the November chill. The scent was filled with the promise of winter. When I was a little girl, that had meant snow, hot chocolate, Christmas trees and stockings. Now, the turning of the seasons heralded something different.

Winter solstice. The longest night of the year. A night when Lilitu were at their most powerful. Lucas and I had barely survived the last one. I shivered, trying to push the unwanted memories out of my head.

Cassie looked up from her phone, concerned. I saw her send a text, but then she slipped the phone into her pocket. "Are you warm enough?"

"Yeah." I gave Cassie a quick smile. "So, where do you want to go?"

"I was thinking we could grab a Mexican hot chocolate from Sabrina's."

"Yes!" I said, suddenly eager. "It's been too long."

We headed into the plaza, steering our feet toward the ancient little restaurant on the edge of the square. The front steps led down into a thick adobe building. We had to bend our heads to keep from hitting them on the low door. Inside, the ancient windows were so tiny the space felt almost like a cave. But the roaring fireplace, coupled with candles sprinkled across every tabletop, filled the space with a rosy light. I couldn't think of any building in town as cozy as Sabrina's. It was an historical landmark; the old adobe building was over a century old. But with creaky wooden floorboards and exposed logs supporting the roof, it felt like a home.

"I see a table," Cassie said. I followed her back to a sheltered alcove.

Lucas and Seth sat on one side of the booth while Royal sat on the other. Between them, 17 flickering candles adorned a beautiful cake artfully accented with red rose petals. Red velvet.

"Surprise," Cassie said.

"Guys?" But my voice felt thick, and I couldn't say much more.

"Happy birthday, Braedyn," Lucas said. His eyes twinkled with warmth. So they hadn't forgotten after all.

"What are you waiting for?" Cassie nudged me with her elbow. "Sit!"

I scooted into the bench beside Lucas while Cassie slid in next to Royal.

"I know it's abysmally low-key, compared to last year," Royal said. "But all my ideas got vetoed."

"I love it," I said. "This is exactly the way I wanted to spend my birthday."

"You might want to hurry and blow this sucker out," Seth said, eyeing the wax dripping into little pools at the base of each candle.

"Don't forget to make a wish," Cassie said.

I felt Lucas squeeze my hand under the table. There was one thing I wished for every day. I closed my eyes. *Let me become human soon.* I blew out the candles.

"Excellent," Royal said, clapping his hands. "Now, let's eat. I've been staring at this thing for half an hour."

"Right?" Seth echoed. "It's like an exercise in pain." Royal smiled, giving Seth an appraising look. I felt a warm hope kindle in my chest. Seth hadn't had much time to get to know Royal or Cassie. Yes, he'd been eating lunch with us, but he'd kept his thoughts mostly to himself, only really opening up to Lucas and me when we were alone. It was encouraging to see him engage with my other friends.

Lucas handed me a knife. "You want to do the honors?"

I cut five generous slices of cake and we dug in. While we were eating, a waitress appeared with five mugs of steaming hot chocolate. Sabrina's specialty. The hot chocolate was laced through with cinnamon and a dash of red chili powder. The combination was a delicious one-two punch, leaving a subtle fire on the tongue after each sweet sip.

Cassie pulled a gift bag from under the table. "Happy birthday."

I felt a twist of regret for the things I'd said to her earlier in the day. "Cassie, you didn't have to do this."

Cassie gave me an eager smile. "Open it."

I pulled the decorative tissue paper aside. Gingerly, I lifted a simple black dress out of the bag. "Cassie?" My eyes swept over the dress. Another elegant Cassie Ang creation. The lines were sleek. A shimmering spray of tiny iridescent beads sparkled indigo around the hem. "How in the world did you find the time to do this?"

"She practically lives in that costume shop," Royal said.

"I had a little side project," Cassie explained.

I held it up to my body, but I already knew it would fit perfectly. "It's gorgeous," I breathed.

"I hate it when you go first," Royal said with a sigh for Cassie's benefit. He handed over a box. Judging by the heft, it was a pair of shoes. "Here. They don't compare to Cassie's magnum opus, but they do compliment it nicely."

I opened the box, revealing a pair of elegant heels. They were dyed a deep indigo that picked up on the sheen of the beads Cassie had hand-sewn around the hem of the dress. "I love them," I squealed, my voice jumping up an octave of its own accord.

"I hope we don't have to discuss what you'll be wearing to junior prom," Royal said.

"I'll cross that off my list." I took another moment to admire the beautiful clothes. It was with great effort that I pushed aside the thought that junior prom was a long way off, and so much could happen between now and then. If the final battle had begun, no one would be attending junior prom. Not in Puerto Escondido.

It was a wonderful afternoon. We stayed in that booth for almost two hours, talking and laughing, ordering food to share until we were pleasantly stuffed. As five o'clock rolled around, I got a call from Dad.

"How's it going?" he asked.

"You knew?"

"Of course I knew." I could hear him smiling over the line. "Were you surprised?"

I looked at my friends, laughing over something Royal had just said. My heart was full. This was what it meant to be content. "Yes," I answered.

"I just wanted to let you know, Hale's giving you and Lucas the day off from practice."

"Oops," I said. I'd forgotten all about practice.

Dad chuckled. "Happy birthday, sweetheart. Enjoy it."

I tried to hang on to that sense of well-being, but as we gathered our money to pay the bill, I could feel it slipping away. How long would it be before we were all together like this again, safe and happy?

Royal offered to give Cassie a lift to her place, and they said their goodbyes in the cramped entryway of Sabrina's.

"Thank you," I murmured into Cassie's ear as I hugged her goodbye. "It was perfect."

"I'm glad," she pulled back. "Once this play is over, things will get back to normal. You'll see."

I smiled, not trusting myself to speak. After they'd left, Seth pulled something out of his backpack.

"I've got a present for you, too," he said. He handed over a manila envelope stuffed with papers. "Sorry it's not wrapped."

I pulled the papers out of the envelope and flipped through page after page of photocopied notes. Angela's notes.

"What did you do?" Lucas asked Seth, frowning.

"I figured," Seth looked at me, confused. "I thought you guys wanted to know whatever Mom found out about the ritual."

Lucas glanced at me, uncomfortable. I knew he was torn. He respected the hierarchy of the Guard, and disobeying Hale wasn't easy for him. But if this ritual could help me become human sooner, he'd want to know.

"Has she figured it out?" I asked.

"I don't know. I didn't have time to read everything. But look." Seth took the papers out of my hands and flipped to a photocopied image of a small vase. "She calls this the vessel. I think it's a part of the ritual."

"The vessel?" Lucas asked.

"Yeah. Does that mean anything to you?"

"Let me see it." Lucas took the sheet out of Seth's hand and reacted.

"Do you recognize that?" I asked.

"No." Lucas studied the image with a thoughtful frown.

"Are you sure?" I asked. I could tell something was troubling him.

"I'm pretty sure I would remember a funky metal vase," Lucas said. "But there is something familiar about it. Weird." He shrugged and handed the sheet back to me. "Don't let Hale catch you with that."

"Right." I put the research into my school bag, meaning to hide it in my room when I got home.

But once I started to read it later that night, I couldn't put it down. Angela was convinced the vessel was the key to locking the seal for good. She'd painstakingly reconstructed the history of the vessel through her research. There was an image in the carvings from the mission that she believed to be the vessel, which placed it at the mission for the fight with the incubus and his sister. Later, it had shown up in Boston, around the time of the revolution. Still later, it had resurfaced in California. Present—if her research was to be believed—in San Francisco during the earthquake of 1906. From that time on, it had been in the Guard's safekeeping, though she wasn't sure exactly where.

I became obsessed with her notes. I took them to school with me. I pored over them in my spare time. I stared at the grainy image of the vessel, trying to make out the details of its surface. Some part of me became convinced that this small metal vase would be my salvation.

I hid my obsession from the rest of the Guard. Not even Lucas knew how much of my time I spent thinking about the vessel. There were moments where I could push it out of my mind for a little while, but like a homing pigeon, it always found a way back into my thoughts.

Training seemed to keep the thoughts at bay better than anything else in my daily routine. Matthew and Gretchen had stepped up our practices. Lucas and I spent three hours after school every day in the basement, training. Hale would check in on us, but he'd left our training in the hands of Matthew and Gretchen while he helped get the new Guardsmen settled.

One afternoon, a few weeks after my birthday, we were training in the basement as usual when the door opened at the top of the stairs. I expected to see Hale or Dad, but it was the newcomers: Chris, Paul, Jason, and Sam. Matthew and Gretchen halted our training session.

"Mind if we practice down here with you guys?" Sam asked. They didn't wait for an answer, simply walking deeper into the basement and spreading out. Their practice was fast and brutal. Lucas and I stared, transfixed.

Gretchen was the first to pull her eyes off the soldiers. "Back to work, kids. We're not done yet."

Matthew waved for my attention. He didn't rely on the forms, like Hale and Dad did. Matthew believed you trained in the basics, but fights were about reacting in the moment, as effectively as you could.

"You ready?" he asked. When I nodded, he came for me, shooting a fist toward my face. I knocked the punch aside, launching a fist for his stomach in counterattack. We struck at each other, each trying to land a blow, each fighting furiously to keep from getting hit. I sensed rather than saw an opportunity; Matthew had overcompensated in blocking one of my punches—he was off balance. Acting purely on instinct, I moved. My fist connected with his cheek, rocking his head back with a meaty thunk. He took the punch and danced back, blinking tears of pain out of his eyes. "Good one."

From across the basement, I heard Jason and Chris laughing. They had paused in their sparring to watch us.

"Damn," Chris said. "She tagged you pretty good."

"She's had good teachers," Matthew said with a forced smile. He turned back to me, putting his hands up. "You ready?" he asked again. There was an edge to his voice. He didn't like getting bested in front of his comrades.

"Yep." I didn't take my eyes off of him. He threw himself into the attack, not holding back. It was all I could do to defend, but I managed to keep him from landing a single punch. He pressed the attack. It was the first time I'd been pushed so hard since we'd started training again. I felt my breath coming faster, my lungs working to keep up as my body demanded more oxygen.

I heard a low whistle and was dimly aware that the newcomers were all watching us spar. Matthew feinted and, distracted, I fell for it. As he dodged out of my way, I realized I'd stumbled into a trap. I dropped to the mat and swept out my leg, knocking Matthew clear off his feet before he'd had a chance to strike. Matthew hit the ground with a loud *ooof!*

But it was Lucas who cried out in pain. I looked up. Lucas was reeling back, clutching his nose. Gretchen dropped her fighting stance immediately.

"Oh, Lucas. Let me see." She moved toward him but Lucas drew back. "Let me see," she insisted, when he wouldn't let her get close.

"Just—just give me a second," Lucas said. He took his hand away. Blood streamed freely from his nose.

"Crap," Gretchen said. "Tilt your head back." She reached for Lucas's nose, but he jerked away.

"You ladies are a force to be reckoned with," the Guardsman named Paul said.

"Hey, kid. Come here," Sam called. "I know a trick for bloody noses."

Lucas glanced at Gretchen, then walked over to Sam. Sam probed at Lucas's nose gingerly. I heard Lucas suck in a sharp breath, but he didn't protest.

"Doesn't look broken," Sam said. "Let's go get you some ice." Sam led Lucas out of the basement. Chris and Jason turned back to their practice.

Gretchen sank into a chair, running her hands through her hair. She looked twisted with guilt. Paul, partnerless now that Sam had left the room, walked over to us.

"That was stupid," Gretchen said.

"He wasn't paying attention to his fight," Paul replied. "You did him a favor."

"How do you figure?"

"If he'd been fighting a Lilitu, he'd be dead."

Gretchen nodded slowly, her eyes flicking to my face. Paul glanced at me with a spreading smile.

"Though I totally get the distraction. If she was my girl, I'd be keeping an eye on her, too. I'd better go help Sam. He's got the bedside manner of a warthog." Paul tipped an imaginary hat at me and headed up the stairs after Sam and Lucas.

Hale appeared at the top of the stairs a minute later. "Gretchen?"

"Yeah," she asked, as if expecting this.

"You want to tell me what happened?" Hale walked into the basement, pulling Gretchen aside for the debrief.

Matthew glanced back at me. "We've still got an hour left. Want to try another round?" I didn't, actually. I wanted to go check on Lucas. Matthew seemed to read the conflict in my face. "How about this," he said. "You land three punches, you're free to go to Lucas."

I tried, I really did. But Matthew wasn't holding back. After an exhausting five minute bout, we broke, breathing heavily. A thin sheen of sweat covered Matthew's brow, and I felt dampness spreading down the back of my shirt. I grabbed a bottle of water from my school bag and downed it.

Hale finished with Gretchen about the same time. "Go check on him," Hale said. Gretchen, relieved, nodded. She hurried up the stairs and was gone. Hale glanced at us. "How's it going?"

I shrugged.

"She's doing pretty well one on one," Matt said.

"Let's step it up," Hale said. "Time for another session of two on one."

I groaned inwardly, but once Hale got something into his mind you'd better just deal with it. "Fine."

"Don't worry," Hale said with a smile. "Practice makes perfect."

Matthew and Hale took up positions on either side of me.

To say that my heart wasn't in it would be putting it mildly. But when two skilled fighters come after you, you learn to move. I might heal quicker than the normal girl, but that didn't make the punches hurt any less. The problem was, as soon as I turned my attention to fight off one of them, the other would attack from my blind spots. I'd spin around to defend, only to open up my back to the first.

Thirty minutes of this had left me sore, irritated, and exhausted. Hale finally took pity on me and called an end to the session.

"Better."

"It's nice of you to say," I said, scowling. "But I think we all know that's a load of crap."

"It's not complete crap," Matthew said with a smile. "Just 90 percent crap."

I grabbed another bottle of water out of my school bag, accidentally pulling it off the table in the process. My bag hit the ground and Angela's photocopied notes shot out. I dropped to scoop them up, my heart thudding in my throat.

Hale bent to help. I looked up quickly. That was a mistake. Hale might have handed everything back to me without even looking at it. But when he saw my face, he glanced at the pages in his hands. And his expression hardened.

He stood, glancing down at the image of the vessel.

"Wait. I can explain," I said.

"Get Thane," Hale said to Matthew. His voice was quiet. His eyes didn't leave my face. Matthew snapped to attention and sped up the stairs.

"Hale," I started.

"Don't."

His calm scared me more than if he'd lost it. "I didn't mean to disobey," I whispered. Hale simply looked at me. Chris and Jason were still training behind us. Hale clearly didn't want to alert them to this conversation.

Thane entered a few moments later. "Yes?"

"I need your expertise."

Thane walked down into the basement, glancing at Chris and Jason. They were focused on each other, sparring. They didn't pay any attention to him. Thane joined us, looking at me curiously. Hale handed him the notes. Thane glanced at them, flipped through a few pages, then found the image of the vessel. He stopped and looked back up at Hale, unsettled.

"I take it this is Angela's research?" Thane asked. He and Hale shared a significant look. I got the distinct impression that they knew something they weren't saying.

"Do you know what—?" I started to ask.

Hale cut me off. "Thane?"

"I need to consult with Ian," Thane murmured.

"Go. I'll handle things here." Hale turned back to me, his eyes snapping. He waited until Thane had closed the door at the top of the basement stairs. "I asked you to leave Angela's work alone."

"I know." I felt excruciatingly small under Hale's glare.

"You gave me your word."

"I know. I'm sorry." When he didn't answer me, I drew in a ragged breath. "I didn't ask for it, Seth just—"

"I don't think you understand." Hale took me by the arm and steered me toward the rack of daggers against the back wall, farther from Jason and Chris. "Braedyn, we're going to have to tell the rest of the Guard about you. You know that, right? And I'm afraid it's going to have to be sooner rather than later. There are Guardsmen who will see you as the enemy. In their eyes, you will be guilty until proven innocent. Don't give them any reason to doubt you." He held my gaze, his eyes piercing. "You can't afford to make the same mistakes as other kids your age. If you make a promise, you have to keep it."

His words stung. I nodded.

"Okay." Hale bent and picked up my bag, handing it to me. "Go wash up. Dinner's almost ready."

Thane left the next morning, taking Angela's photocopied research with him. Dad wouldn't tell me where he was going, only that he had to speak with another Guard archivist.

Lucas showed up on my doorstep early. For someone who'd never been too excited about school, Lucas couldn't wait to get to campus. Hale had chewed Lucas out after I'd left to get cleaned up the night before. Whether or not it was fair, Hale made it clear to Lucas that knowing about the research and saying nothing was as bad as taking it in the first place.

"He's not calling it punishment," he said when we got into my car for the drive to school. "But I've got a whole list of new chores. Weapons maintenance every weekend. Oh, and KP every night after dinner. Which, by the way, you'll be joining me for. Hale says it's time we contribute more to the operation of the Guard. But I know the truth. It's punishment." Lucas looked at me, curious. "What was in that research? It must have been nuclear strength secrets or something."

I sighed. "That's the worst part about this whole thing. If there was some big secret in there, I didn't find it."

"No, the worst part about this whole thing is being stuck in the basement with Hale every Saturday morning when I should be sleeping in."

"At least we have our dreams," I said.

Lucas looked at me, his eyes warm. "Yeah. That's something they can't take from us, no matter how badly we screw up."

In physics, Seth tried to slip me another envelope. "Mom made a breakthrough on the ritual," he whispered.

I pushed his hand back, not touching the envelope he offered.

"What's wrong?" His face was a mask of surprise. "I thought you wanted to know this stuff."

"Things have... changed," I said. "With the new Guardsmen around." I sighed. "Plus, Hale saw the picture of the vessel and freaked out."

"You showed it to him?"

"Not on purpose," I said. "It fell out of my bag."

"Crap. I'm sorry." Seth looked glum. He slipped the envelope back into his bag.

"Actually," I started, remembering the look Thane and Hale had exchanged, "I think he might know something about the vessel."

"Really? Why did he freak out at you?"

"He's worried about what might happen if the Guardsmen figure out what I am before he's ready to tell them."

"You haven't told them you're a Lilitu?" Seth looked outraged, but he kept his voice low.

"No," I said.

"But—why do you have to hide from them? You're on their side."

I shrugged, but some part of me felt a grim satisfaction. At least someone else saw the injustice of my situation. "You know that and I know that, but unfortunately most of these guys think of it as their sacred duty to kill my kind. So until they get to know me a little better, we're keeping it on the DL."

"Well, for what it's worth, I think that's stupid." Seth threw an arm over my shoulder companionably. It was nice. Comfortable.

"Thanks." I leaned into him, resting my head on his shoulder for a moment.

My eyes landed on Royal and Cassie. They were staring at us, speculation running wild across their faces. I straightened, quickly, turning my attention back to my notes. But the damage had been done. Cassie caught me alone after class.

"What's going on with you and Seth?"

"What? No. Nothing," I said.

"I told you," Royal said to Cassie, curling his arm through mine on my other side.

"Okay." But she didn't look convinced. "And the part where you snuggled up to him?"

"Snuggled up?" I felt my cheeks growing hot. "It was just a friendly hug, okay?"

"What was just a friendly hug? Who's hugging who?" Lucas asked, joining us in the hall.

"Seth hugged Braedyn," Royal said, sounding bored. "It's not Watergate."

Lucas's eyes lingered on my face for a moment before he turned to Cassie and Royal. "Oh."

"It was totally innocent," I said, feeling the blush spread. "He was trying to cheer me up."

"It's cool," Lucas said, giving me a strange look. "You can hug your friends. It's not a big deal."

"Right. Thank you." But some part of me felt... guilty.

"Look what you did," said Royal, crossing his arms and giving Cassie a small frown. "Like we need more drama at this school."

"My mistake," Cassie said. She and Royal hurried ahead, leaving Lucas and me behind. Lucas took my hand in his.

"It was nothing," I said again.

"Okay."

"You trust me, right?" I asked, suddenly self-conscious. Lucas gave me a pained look, then glanced around. Spotting whatever it was he was looking for, Lucas took my hand and pulled me into an empty classroom. He closed the door, buying us a moment alone.

"Braedyn. I have total faith in you." Lucas brushed my hair back from my cheek. I leaned into the touch unconsciously. Lucas's breath caught. The sound shot like a bolt of energy through my stomach. I felt something stir in response. The Lilitu storm rose within me, stronger than I'd ever felt it. Strong enough to drive me closer to Lucas, blocking everything else out. Lucas read the desire in my face and tipped his head down, lips parting.

"Stop," I hissed. The warning was meant for Lucas, but it was also a command to the Lilitu power, coiled inside me, ready to spring.

Lucas's eyes seemed to clear. He took a quick step back, like you might if you'd just realized you were standing at the edge of a 100-foot drop. "This is getting more difficult," he said. His voice was husky.

"Maybe we should dial it down a bit," I said, clenching my hands to stop them from shaking.

"Dial it down?"

"You know. Limit... physical contact."

"If you think it will help." He sounded shaken. I nodded. We stood there for a moment, recovering. "Time for lunch?"

I nodded again, and Lucas opened the door for me.

"On the bright side," I said, before walking through it. "You've got nothing to worry about. When I touched Seth, I didn't feel a thing."

Lucas's face split into a lopsided grin. "Well," he murmured, "that's a relief."

Lucas and I refrained from touching for the rest of the day, but it was harder than I would have imagined. I'd grown accustomed to holding his hand, leaning against him in the hall, brushing my foot against his in class. The absence of these little touches ended up serving as a constant reminder of what we couldn't share.

After school, Seth's mom was waiting to pick him up. So I drove Lucas and myself home alone. You would have thought there was an invisible gorilla sitting between us, pressing us to the outer edges of our seats.

When we got home, I pulled into my driveway and killed the engine. But neither of us moved to get out of the car. I gripped the wheel tightly. "Lucas?"

"It's not forever," Lucas said. The look he gave me sent a shiver through my core. "I'll see you at practice?"

I nodded. We exited the car and parted, each to our own house.

I didn't see her until I was turning my key in the front door lock. It was the woman in Thrall—the woman who'd attacked us at the mission. She stepped out from behind a wide wooden column. She'd been waiting for me.

"Apologies for the mess," she said. "But as we both know, you don't respond to subtle."

"What?" I asked. But the woman's eyes were blank, empty. Those words had not been her own. They were a message. A message from the incubus who had enthralled her.

The Thrall pulled a knife from behind her back.

Adrenaline slammed into my system and I braced myself for an attack. "Lucas!" I screamed.

The knife gleamed in the afternoon sunlight. With a grunt of effort, the Thrall drove the knife down, burying the hilt in her own belly. Blood blossomed around the blade, glistening with a red so bright it didn't seem real. With a sick, wet sound, the Thrall pulled the knife free.

"The next messenger I send will be someone you care about," she said. Her face registered no emotion as she stabbed herself again.

Another scream ripped from my throat. I stumbled back against the wall of my house, watching as the Thrall pulled the blade out of her middle again. She stumbled to one knee, then drove the knife in again.

Lucas, who'd been at his door when I'd called his name, pounded across my front yard. I reached for him, forgetting the promise we'd made to one another. His arms folded around me, and he pulled me off the porch, away from the Thrall.

She followed me with those empty eyes, the knife still clutched in her bloody hand.

What if that was Cassie? I could taste the bile rising in the back of my throat. "No!"

Lucas pulled me tighter against him. "It's okay. It's going to be okay."

"It's not okay," I whispered. And it wouldn't be, not until the incubus was dead.

10

Fire licked up the sides of three split logs, undulating in waves of amber and blue. Dad laid another log on the pile, sending a shower of sparks into the chimney's flue. I watched, hypnotized by the movement. Some part of me felt the heat, but it didn't warm me.

The Thrall had vanished.

When Lucas had pulled me away, she was kneeling in front of this house, spilling her life onto the porch in great splashes of liquid red. But when the Guard had raced out to confront her, she was gone. Only the thickening pool of blood remained to bear witness to our story. And only a Thrall could have summoned the strength to flee after losing so much. The incubus wasn't done with her yet. He wasn't done with me.

Dad glanced at the clock. It was past midnight, but I was too freaked out to sleep. The Guard had been on high alert all night, canvassing the area, looking for any trail that might lead us to the Thrall. They'd found nothing. Not one single drop of blood to indicate which way she'd gone. Dad had let the others search, refusing to leave my side.

We couldn't have kept Lucas from the hunt if we'd tried. That Thrall had gotten too close to me. If she'd wanted to attack me, I would have been alone, unprepared. I would have been killed. Lucas was driven half-wild with that thought. He'd felt compelled to do something. And so he was still out there, with the last patrol of the night, looking for her. I knew it was hopeless. We wouldn't find her until the incubus wanted us to find her.

"Can I get you something?" Dad asked. "Something to eat?"

"I'm not hungry."

Dad sat beside me on the couch. "Okay." We sat in silence for a few, long minutes. "Braedyn, maybe it'd help if you talked about it."

I felt another wave of terror rising inside. "It was a message," I whispered.

"I know." Dad sighed in resignation. "It was only a matter of time before he figured out we were here, looking for him."

"No." I pulled my eyes away from the fire. "It was a message for me."

"What—what makes you think that?" Dad shifted on the couch, turning to get a clearer view of my face. I could see him holding his panic at bay. This is why I hadn't told him before.

"Never mind." I turned back to the flames, reaching for the numbness of a few minutes ago.

"Braedyn." Dad put a hand under my chin, gently forcing me to look at him. "Honey. Tell me."

"Before she—" I swallowed, battling another rush of nausea. I could see it clearly in my mind's eye, the knife buried in her stomach, her fist clenched around the hilt, pulling it out only to stab it in again... Dad nodded; I didn't have to say it. "She said—she said the next messenger would be someone I cared about."

"Braedyn?" Dad took a steadying breath. His eyes didn't waver. "Is it possible—the night you went looking for him in the dream—do you think he sensed you?"

A shrill giggle bubbled out of me, tinged with hysteria. Dad's eyes creased with worry. "I didn't want you to worry," I said, fighting off another panicked giggle.

"Worry about what?" His voice was hard, scared.

"He's been in my dreams."

"This isn't the first message he's sent you?"

I shook my head no.

Dad bit his lip, and I could see him fighting the urge to yell. "Tell me everything."

"There was a note. He left it in Cassie's locker, but it was addressed to me. He said he was watching me."

"When was this?"

My voice came out in a whisper. "About a month ago."

"*What?!*" Rage and fear leapt into his eyes. I shrank back instinctively. Dad's nostrils flared, but he clamped his mouth shut. I could see a muscle along his jaw jumping with tension. After a long moment he spoke. "He left you a note. Was that all?"

"No," I whispered.

Dad looked at me, too overpowered by emotion to speak. There was something murderous in his gaze, and though I knew it was directed at the incubus, and not me, it struck an icy fear into my bones.

"He left a message in my dream," I said. Dad watched me, gripping his hands tightly together, waiting for an explanation. "He's trying to warn me to back off."

"Back off from what, Braedyn?" Dad's voice was suddenly quiet.

I licked my lips. "I think—I think we're close. I think he knows it. And he's scared. We're onto something with this ritual."

Dad stood abruptly. I fell silent. He paced to the fireplace and stared down into the fire. When he turned back to me his face was tight with anger. "Hale told you to leave it alone. This is *why* Hale told you to—" he suddenly turned and brought his fist down on the mantle. "Damn it, Braedyn! Why is it so hard for you to trust that we know what we're doing?"

"Because no one trusts *me*," I wailed.

"And you think this is going to earn their trust?!"

I stared at him, stricken.

"Do you really believe that we'd ignore something as important as a ritual capable of locking the Lilitu out of this world?" His eyes bore into mine, demanding a response.

"No," I said.

"And do you think I'd hesitate one *micro*second if I thought there was a way to—" Dad stopped, his voice choking with emotion. "Ever since you told me Sansenoy had the power to make you human, *every single day*, I've carried that thought in my heart."

Hot tears spilled down my cheeks. I nodded, scrubbing them away. "I'm sorry." It wasn't enough, but it was the only thing I could say.

Dad crossed to me, sitting down and enfolding me in a big bear hug. "Tell me," he whispered hoarsely into my hair. "You have to tell me when stuff like this happens." I clung to Dad, letting my tears soak into his shoulder. He tightened his arms around my back. "Okay. It's going to be okay."

Pounding came from the front door. My heart leapt into my throat. "Do you think they found her?"

Dad stood. "Wait here." He crossed out of the living room and into the foyer. I heard the door open, and Dad's surprised voice. "Seth?"

"Please, you have to help me." Seth's voice was pitched unnaturally high. His voice cracked, and with a stab of fear I realized he was crying. I was on my feet in an instant. Dad pulled Seth inside and closed the door. Seth stood blindly in the foyer, his slight frame shaking with grief.

"Seth, what happened?" Dad asked.

"My mom—" Seth choked down another sob. "She's missing."

"How long has she been gone?"

"She didn't come home last night," Seth said. "Sometimes she goes on these research jags and forgets to call, so I thought maybe—" Seth shook his head, his eyes wide with terror. "Only the police came to my house just now. They found her car on the interstate, 50 miles from anything. The door was open. They couldn't find any sign of Mom anywhere."

"Oh, God." I backed into the wall, dizzy with panic.

Dad glanced at me. "Stay with him. I'll get the others." I nodded, and the next second Dad was gone, pulling the door closed behind him.

Seth didn't move from his spot in the foyer. He was shaking like a leaf, eyes wide and staring. "Do you think—do you think the incubus went after her? Braedyn?" He looked suddenly younger than his 16 years. "She's all the family I have in the world."

I wanted to reach out to him, to offer him some comfort. But I couldn't move. I know I should have been thinking about Angela, but at that moment, all I could think about was what I would do if I ever lost my Dad.

I went through the motions of seating Seth at our table, making tea, trying to make him comfortable. But neither of us were really present. We were walking through separate worlds constructed by our darkest fears, fears that overshadowed the tangible comforts of my home.

We sat at the table until steam stopped curling from the surface of the tea I'd poured. Dad had returned with Hale a few moments after he'd left us standing in the foyer. Once they'd gotten all the details they could from Seth, they'd left to organize the Guard to go out and find her.

Which left us here, waiting.

"She found something yesterday," Seth said suddenly. "I don't know what it was. She just said she had to go check on something and she ran out of the house. I waited and waited for her, but she never came home. I almost called you," he gave me a faint smile. "I thought maybe she'd figured the whole thing out." His smile faded. "But when the police came tonight—" A ragged sob shook Seth.

"Seth," I said, feeling helpless. "Don't. We don't know anything. Not yet."

"Yes we do." Seth looked up, his eyes wild. "We know my mom's digging into something that the Lilitu don't want us to find." Seth stood, too wired to sit still any longer. "We know there's at least one demon out there, maybe more. If they discovered what she's doing—" Seth slumped against the wall, doubling over in pain. "God—what if he's got her? What if he's hurting her?"

I stood, anxious to calm Seth down. "It's no use making yourself crazy like this. We don't know anything yet."

"What if she's dying somewhere?" Seth pushed off of the wall, stumbling toward the foyer. "We can't just sit here," he gasped. I grabbed Seth's hand. He tried to pull away, panic driving him into a frenzy. "Let go. Please, Braedyn, let me go!"

"*Calm down*," I said. The chiming tones of *the call* seemed to set the air around us aglow. "*Calm down, Seth.*"

It worked almost instantly. All resistance seeped out of Seth. He seemed to forget what he was doing for a moment. Then he blinked and drew in a long, slow breath. "You're right," he said. "You're right."

"I'll be here. I'm not going to leave you alone." I drew Seth into a hug, meaning to comfort him.

Seth's arms tightened around my back, and he buried his face in my hair. I could feel his breath against my neck. I pulled back quickly. Seth released me, but his eyes lingered on my face. The look he gave me was almost guilty. Awareness hit me in the stomach. Cassie had seen more than I'd been willing to acknowledge. Seth had feelings for me.

"Seth," I started.

"I think I'll put my tea in the microwave," he interrupted. "Can I warm yours up, too?"

Seth wouldn't meet my eyes. "Sure," I said. Now was not the time to have this conversation. Seth pulled our cups off the table and retreated into the kitchen. I folded my arms around myself, thinking back over our time together. If I'd given him any reason to hope I might return his feelings, it was unintentional.

I heard the door open in the foyer.

"Braedyn?" Dad called.

"In here," I said.

Dad and Lucas entered. Lucas looked haggard. He must have just returned from the hunt for the Thrall. He rubbed his hands together, blowing over them.

"Where's Seth?" Dad asked.

We heard the microwave beep from the kitchen. A few seconds later, Seth returned with two steaming mugs of tea. He saw Dad and set the cups down, eager for any news.

"Let's get comfortable," Dad said. "I'll fill everyone in, but I think it's going to be a long night." Dad led Seth into the living room. I picked my cup of tea up and handed it to Lucas. Our hands brushed.

"Your fingers are like ice," I murmured. He took the tea gratefully, wrapping his hands around it. "You didn't find her." It wasn't a question. I could see the truth in his face. In confirmation, he shook his head no.

"Hale called off the hunt," he said quietly.

I nodded. "Finding Angela is more important right now."

We headed into the living room to wait with Dad and Seth. Dad filled us in. The Guard had set out in teams to search for Seth's mom anywhere it made sense for her to go. Once again, we were left waiting.

"You're going to stay with us until we find her," Dad told Seth. I glanced at Dad, surprised. He saw my look and inclined his head toward the guest room. "We've got space, and I'd rather have you somewhere safe until we know more."

"What if we can't find her?" Seth asked.

"Now's not the time for those kinds of questions," Dad said, offering Seth a smile full of confidence. "There are still plenty of explanations for her disappearance. With any luck, she'll turn up tomorrow before sunrise."

But the sun came up, and Angela Linwood was still nowhere to be found. After a full night of searching, Hale made the decision to call the Guard in. Half of the team were sent to bed to get what sleep they could while the other half continued the search. They'd take six hour shifts until Angela was found.

Dad left us to join the search a little after dawn.

Lucas and I stayed home from school with Seth that day. There was no way he'd be able to sit through a whole day of classes while his mom was missing, and we didn't want to abandon him. As the sun climbed in the east, our thoughts turned to the possible reasons behind her disappearance.

"What do you think your mom discovered?" Lucas asked.

"It had to be something about the ritual," Seth answered. "It's the only thing she's been able to talk about for weeks."

"Something about the vessel?" I asked.

"I don't think so." Seth's expression turned thoughtful. "I think she would have said."

"Do you know what she was looking at before she left?"

"I don't know," Seth said, miserable. "Some book. She had it at home. But I don't know if she took it with her when she left." He looked up, stricken. "I didn't think to check her office."

"It wasn't your responsibility," Lucas said.

"I didn't want to mess with her stuff," Seth explained, as though we were judging him. "She hates it when people mess with her stuff." His voice wavered, and I was afraid he was on the verge of losing it again. "But—if she doesn't come back?"

I stood. The guys looked at me, startled by the sudden movement.

"I'm tired of waiting," I said. It was true. The fear of the night had been tamped down by exhaustion.

"What choice do we have?" Lucas asked.

"I'm going to find her myself," I said.

"You can't leave," Seth grabbed my hand. Lucas saw the movement and raised an eyebrow, but didn't offer comment.

"Don't worry," I said, lowering myself to the rug. "I don't have to go anywhere."

If there was one thing exhaustion was good for, it was this. I slipped into the dream without any effort at all. My rose garden was exactly as I'd left it, the wall as solid and impenetrable as ever.

I knelt on the ground and placed my hand into dirt that felt pleasantly warm against my skin.

This time I had to will a hole down deeper, through the fortress surrounding my mind, before I could draw a pool of the infinite dream up into the dirt. Star-like dreams dusted across the inky expanse. When I concentrated on them, they began to move.

"Angela Linwood," I called. I'd found Lucas once when he'd been awake. His dream had flickered dimly—his spirit had been more present in the physical world than the dream world—but I'd still been able to find him. As long as we breathe, we are tied to the shared dream. And so when I summoned Angela's dream, I knew something was wrong.

Where her dream should have been, there was only a faint haze.

Confused, I closed my hand around it, willing myself into her mind.

Strong arms caught me from behind. I dropped the books I'd been carrying out of the college library. They fell, falling open like great, multi-winged butterflies. I felt a pang of horror. Some of these books had been printed before my grandparents had been born. But as I struggled to reach for them I felt a ripping sensation at my throat. The next breath came, wet and heavy. And suddenly I was stumbling to the ground. I stared at the dark red spots growing on the pages of my books. It took more than a second to realize it was my blood. More spots had fallen on the creased skin of my hands, and as I studied them I was surprised by how old they looked—

Old hands. Not my hands. Angela's hands. I jerked back out of the haze, stumbling away from the pool of stars at my feet. No. *No.* I wasn't thinking clearly. I needed answers.

"Karayan," I said, willing her to hear me. I sensed her attention turn toward me, then felt her choose to ignore me. "Please." I pulled slightly on the thread of her awareness. The resistance grew. So I pulled harder.

Karayan appeared, gasping. She spun on me, eyes crackling with fury. "So that's how it's going to be? You shove me out when you don't like what I have to say, then yank me back when you need something—no matter whether or not I *want* to come?"

"Karayan." My voice was faint.

"No," she said. "I'm not your little Barbie doll, Braedyn. And I don't want to be involved. One of the Three is coming back, hunting the incubus. You don't want to be anywhere near this thing when it happens, trust me."

Shock still coursed through my body, but her words penetrated into my mind, shedding a ray of hope. "Sansenoy?" I asked. What if he was coming back because we were close? What if he anticipated our success, knew we'd be able to lock the seal, and he was preparing to grant the promise he'd made to me last year?

Karayan shook her head. "It's sick that you find this so comforting," she said. "You do realize they are our sworn enemies, and I mean that *literally*. As in, they swore an actual, literal *oath* to stamp us out."

I turned back to the faint haze that should have been Angela Linwood's dream.

"So that's it? Now I get the silent treatment?" Karayan crossed her arms, still irked. Then she saw the haze, still hovering above the pool of stars. "Oh."

I looked at her, but I already knew what she was going to say. "She's gone, isn't she?"

Karayan nodded. "Dream energy takes a while to dissipate after—" she touched the haze, then winced, pulling her hand back. "A hard death." She glanced at me. "Who was she?"

"A friend." I looked down at my hands, summoning the strength to tell Seth his mother was dead.

I opened my eyes. Lucas and Seth were watching my face, hungry for news.

I sat up, then turned toward them with a heavy heart. They saw the truth in my eyes before I gathered the courage to speak.

"No..." Seth whispered.

"Seth." I ached for him. "I'm so sorry."

Seth fled to the back room.

Lucas stood. "I'll go tell Hale."

"Tell him to have the Guard search the college campus for her body," I said.

Lucas gave me a solemn, searching look. Then he walked to the foyer, opened the front door, and left. He returned a few minutes later. We sat together on the couch, afraid to touch, listening to the harsh, wracking grief that poured from Seth in the back room.

Thirty minutes later, at 10:45 in the morning, Dad called with news. I'd been right. They'd found her body. Angela Linwood had been murdered.

They didn't return until close to nine o'clock that night. The police had questions. The coroner needed to make an identification. There were forms upon forms that needed to be filled out. Rather than put Seth through the pain of seeing his mother's body, Dad and Gretchen had identified it.

When they walked through the front door that night, I could see the toll the day had taken on them both. Wordlessly, Gretchen held her arms out to Lucas. He walked to her and they held each other fiercely. I turned away, giving them their privacy.

Dad pulled me into a hug and I gripped him tight.

"I would die if anything happened to you," I said.

"No, you wouldn't," he said sharply. I pulled back to look into his face, startled by the vehemence behind his words. Dad brushed a loose strand of my hair back behind one ear. "I love you. I know how strong you are. If anything ever happened to me, I know you'd do the right thing."

"Dad?"

"Angela died fighting for a worthwhile cause," he said softly. "That's more than most people can say. The best way to honor her—to honor any of our fallen—is to carry on the fight."

I let him draw me back into another hug, but the room seemed to spin around me. He didn't have to say it for me to know.

Dad believed this war would kill him.

11

The day dawned bright and clear. Sunlight betrayed the grief that filled our house, reminding us that the world outside marched on cheerfully, untouched by our suffering.

I found Seth sitting on the living room couch, wrapped in the blanket from the guest bed. Dark bags circled his eyes, which were swollen from crying. The exhaustion of the night had finally caught him in its clutches. Seth sat still, numb.

He didn't look up when I entered. Something sizzled in the kitchen, and a moment later I caught the faint whiff of butter and eggs. Instead of joining Dad while he made breakfast, I sat on the couch next to Seth.

There was nothing to say. Nothing that would make this easier for him. But I could sit here and offer whatever comfort my company might bring him.

"I can't believe she's gone," Seth said. He didn't move, didn't look at me. But the words unleashed another flood of grief. Seth tipped his head forward, fighting to contain the raw emotion coursing through his body. Tentatively, I reached out and clasped his hand.

Seth threaded his fingers around mine in response. His hand was warm and strong. His shoulders shook. I couldn't just sit there, watching. I leaned forward and wrapped my arms around him. I held him helplessly, knowing nothing I could do would change the fact that his mom wasn't coming back. He straightened, turning to face me. The look he gave me was so piercing, so intimate, that I froze. Being this close to him, feeling his warmth, seeing his vulnerability—something stirred within me. The Lilitu storm.

Seth's eyes tracked me, waiting. I found myself staring at him, noticing really for the first time the powerful lines of his jaw, the perfect symmetry of his face. The storm within me gathered strength, and I found myself wondering what it would feel like to kiss him.

"Braedyn," Seth started. He brushed the fingers of his free hand along my arm. I jerked back, breathless.

"I'm sorry," I whispered. Guilt tore through me. Seth was in unimaginable pain—but I couldn't be what he needed. Not the way he needed. "I—I should call Lucas."

"Lucas." Bitterness edged into Seth's voice. "Lucas tried to kill you when he found out what you were."

I stared, stung. "How did you—?"

"But when I found out—" Seth struggled to keep his voice steady. His blue eyes held mine, full of conviction. "I knew you were still you."

"I—I know, Seth." I studied my hands.

"He doesn't appreciate you. Not the way I could. Not the way I do."

"Things with Lucas—they're complicated." I met Seth's eyes, trying to make him understand. "But what we have—"

Seth stood, turning away. But I saw the expression of pain that crossed his face. "Okay. I get it."

"I'm sorry. If things were different—"

"I've got bigger problems right now," Seth snapped. But then he glanced at me, vulnerable and scared. "Sorry. I didn't mean to—" He swallowed. "That came out wrong."

"It's okay." I stood, folding my arms around myself. "No offense taken."

"I just can't get it out of my mind that Mom was killed for something she found out." He turned to me, pleading for understanding. "I have to know what it was."

"It won't change anything," I said softly.

"If she died discovering something important?" Seth's eyes shone with tears.

"She wouldn't want you to put yourself in danger."

"You didn't know my mom." Seth's hands balled into fists. "If she found something important, she wouldn't want it to be lost just because she died."

"You can't know what—" I started. But he glanced at me with such pain I stopped.

"Please," he whispered. "Please help me."

I opened my mouth to argue, but instead I sighed. "How?"

Seth's eyes lit with hope. "All her research should be at home. Maybe, if we could just sit down with it for a few hours."

"Breakfast is ready, kids." Dad entered from the foyer. He looked surprised when he saw me. "You're dressed for school? I thought you'd want to stay home." His eyes drifted toward Seth, sitting on the couch next to me.

"Oh." I glanced at Seth, feeling like an idiot. "I'm so sorry. Of course. If you want me to stay home with you—"

"No," Seth said. "You go. I'd rather be alone right now."

Dad didn't look happy about this. "You're sure about that?"

"I'm sure." Seth rubbed at his eyes, as though he were on the verge of tears again. Dad looked away, giving Seth his privacy.

"Okay. But if you need anything, you call one of us, deal?"

"Yeah, okay."

When Dad vanished back into the kitchen I turned to Seth.

"It has to be today," Seth whispered. "Please. Sneak out after first period and come get me." When I didn't respond right away, he grabbed my arm. "Braedyn, I'm begging you. Help me."

"Okay."

"Thank you." Seth let out a long breath, then stood and headed into the kitchen. I followed him, and we sat at the kitchen island. Dad had laid out two plates of eggs, toast, and bacon. My stomach growled as soon as I saw the food, but Seth only stared at his plate.

Dad noticed, and put a hand on Seth's shoulder. "You'll always have a place with the Guard," he said. "Don't forget that."

Seth nodded.

Dad pulled me aside. "Be there for Seth today?"

I nodded. If Dad sensed my unease, he must have chalked it up to the events of the previous night. If he'd known what we planned, he'd never have let us out of his sight.

Lucas was waiting by my car when I emerged into the bright morning. He straightened when he saw me, shifting his weight uncomfortably.

"Hey," he offered.

"Hey."

"I didn't know if you guys were going to school today or not."

"Seth wants to be alone, and as for me," I said, glancing at the house behind us, "I need a change of scenery."

"Yeah. Right." Lucas's eyes fell to the dark stain on my front porch. I knew he was reliving the last 24 hours in his mind. "I think we both do."

I unlocked the car. Lucas opened the front passenger door, but didn't get in right away.

"How's he doing?" Lucas asked me.

"About how you probably expect. His mother's dead. He's sad. And angry."

Lucas nodded. "I wish I didn't know how that felt—but I get it." I wanted to reach out and touch him, but I stopped myself. I could see his thoughts turning inward, back to the night of Eric's death.

"He wants to know why she died."

"Yeah."

"He wants," I glanced back at my house before continuing, "he wants to go back to his house. To see what he can find in Angela's research."

Lucas shook his head. "He's upset. He's not thinking clearly."

"But—" I took a deep breath. "What if there is something there?"

"Hale would never let him go back there," Lucas said. "It'd be so stupid. If the incubus did kill Angela for her research, Seth would just be painting a target on his back."

I closed my mouth, suddenly unsure if telling Lucas what we'd planned was a good idea.

"Let's get to school. A dose of normal life will do us all some good."

I forced a smile. Lucas gave me one last look before sliding into my car and closing his door. As I walked around to the driver's side, I knew Seth and I would be making this run solo.

Hiding my plans from Lucas was too easy. He walked me to class, and we hovered at the door until a minute before first bell. He stood so close to me I could feel the warmth emanating from his skin.

"Last night, when I heard you scream," Lucas said quietly. "You have no idea. It was like my world stopped spinning." He brushed the backs of his fingers across my cheek.

I lowered my lashes, savoring the touch. "Lucas." My breath came out in a husky whisper.

"It's you," he whispered. "What I want. What I'm fighting for. Whenever I lose the faith, all it takes to inspire me again is you."

I drank in the sight of him. Lucas's eyes gleamed faintly green in the light of the hall. In them, I could see the depth of his trust. This. If I could only explain this to Seth, he'd understand. Lucas knew my secrets, knew the danger I posed, and he loved me anyway. He saw in me the person I chose to be, and he knew what that choice cost me. That's what Seth didn't get. Lucas did embrace all of me—the good and the bad. Where Seth saw something cool, Lucas understood the consequences of the power I wielded.

Lucas withdrew his hand, and it felt like he'd taken a piece of me with him. "Until lunch," he said.

"Lucas." I grabbed his hand, keeping him from leaving. I almost confessed the whole plot to him right there. But some part of me was just as desperate for the truth as Seth. Lucas looked into my eyes.

"We're going to get through this," he said, misinterpreting the pain he saw. He leaned closer, until his lips almost brushed against my ear. "And everything's going to be worth the wait."

I melted into him, risking another caress. I felt him breathe in sharply. His eyes locked with mine, and I forced myself away from him, battling the desire to simply give in, to lose myself in his kiss. Instead, I pressed my palms flat against the wall at my back. After a moment, my heartbeat slowed and I got my breathing under control. I saw Lucas struggling to do the same. "Promise me." I whispered. I needed to believe.

"I promise, Braedyn."

I forced a wry smile. "Then you'd better go."

Lucas gave me a smile that promised everything. He turned and vanished down the hall.

The bell rang, snapping my thoughts back to the mission at hand. I pushed myself off the wall and slipped out of the building.

I had to move quickly. If I got caught sneaking off campus, Fiedler would call my dad and this whole covert op would be over before it began. I made it to my car and pulled out of the parking lot without spotting another soul on campus.

Seth was waiting on the porch when I pulled up to my house. His face eased when he saw me and I realized he'd started to worry that I wasn't coming back for him.

"Get in," I said, glancing at the Guard's house.

"They're not in there," Seth said. "They got called away about 10 minutes ago."

"Finally we catch a break," I said, pulling back onto the road.

The drive to Seth's house was quiet. Seth drummed his fingers impatiently on the window, lost in his thoughts. Fine with me. I had my own thoughts to wade through.

I pulled up to Seth's house. "No," he said. "Keep driving. We shouldn't park here, in case—the" He glanced at me, leaving the fear unvoiced.

"Right."

I pulled around the corner of the next block and parked under a bare tree, dark as a charcoal sketch against the bright November sky.

"We can go in the back way," Seth said.

I followed him down the street. He slipped between two houses, and I saw a small drainage ditch traveling the length of the block, creating a small alleyway between the rows of houses. Seth sprinted down the ditch and I had to race to catch up. We stopped beside a cinderblock wall halfway down the block.

"My house," he said, breathing hard. Someone had tossed an old milk-crate over the wall a few houses down. Seth picked it up and turned it over, creating a step for us to make climbing over the wall easier. He went first, and I heard his feet crunch into the gravel of his backyard. I followed. The yard was grim and dusty. A few scraggly weeds pocketed the ground, leading us to a covered cement slab—the back porch.

Seth dug in his pocket for his house keys and let us in.

The house was quiet, dark. The curtains were still closed, blocking out much of the daylight beyond.

"In here," Seth said, leading me quickly to his mom's study. "Be careful of the piles—" he stopped, stricken. Angela would never know if we messed with her piles. He looked at me, and the pain of losing his mother rose up again in his eyes.

"Let's just do this," I said.

Seth nodded and turned back to the office. "I don't know if she took her journal with her," he said.

"She didn't," I said. Seth looked at me sharply.

"How do you—?"

"I just know," I said. "Trust me." I hadn't told Seth the details of Angela's death. It had seemed too cruel. But I'd lived those last few moments in her head, and as she'd died, that journal had crossed her mind. I remembered—through Angela—where she'd kept it. I walked to a file cabinet against the back wall and opened the second drawer down. I was looking for a folder labeled *Insurance*. The journal was there, right where she'd left it.

I heard Seth breathe out in amazement. I handed the journal to him. He sank onto the floor, thumbing it open. After a moment, I heard him sniff wetly. I turned away, giving him time alone with his mother's last thoughts.

I spent the next hour walking through the office, looking for anything else that might be important. An ancient copy of *The Old Farmer's Almanac* sat on her desk. I glanced at it, and my eyes snagged on the date printed on the cover. 1793.

Beneath it, half-covered, was a hand-made drawing of the vessel. I pushed the almanac aside. Not a drawing, I realized. A diagram. Each symbol on the vessel had been separated out and annotated. I scanned Angela's handwriting. According to her notes, the carvings on the vessel were some kind of timeline.

"Winter solstice," Seth muttered.

I turned, feeling that fist of ice closing tighter on my heart. "What did you say?"

Seth stood, excitement giving him a burst of new energy. "The ritual. It has to be performed this winter solstice. If we don't do it this year, we won't have another opportunity for 20 years."

"I don't understand. Twenty years?"

"It has to be performed on winter solstice under a full moon," he explained. He brought the journal over to me, laid it open on the desk. He stabbed his finger at a passage in the journal. "They're really rare. Mom says there have only been nine full moons on winter solstice since *The Old Farmer's Almanac* began tracking heavenly events back in—"

"1793," I finished. Seth looked at me, surprised. I pointed to the almanac on her desk.

"Yeah. That's right. So if we don't figure out this ritual in the next month, we won't get another chance to lock the seal for 20 years."

I turned away from Seth so he couldn't see my reaction. Twenty years. If things kept going the way they had been, 20 years from now there might not be any Guard left to fight the Lilitu. And yet, that wasn't what twisted my insides into a painful knot.

Twenty years from now Lucas and I would be almost 40. I couldn't ask Lucas to wait that long. I couldn't wait that long. My life was happening now. And to sit on the sidelines for 20 years? As it was, I was barely able to kiss Lucas without damaging him. What would happen when I grew up? I'd never be able to marry. Never honeymoon with the love of my life. Never have children. My life would pass me by as I watched. No. By the next time a full moon landed on winter solstice, it would be too late for me.

Seth flipped another page in the journal. "Listen to this. She says the vessel holds the secret of the ritual. It's like—like a recipe or something—"

A faint crash came from the front of the house, followed by the tinkling sound of glass falling to the floor.

Seth looked at me, his face going white.

Without thinking, I grabbed Seth and pulled him out of the office. I meant to head for the back door, but a shadow crossed the threshold from the kitchen. Desperate, I pulled Seth into a half-open hall closet. Seth still clutched the journal in his hands. But the almanac—and the diagram of the vessel—were still face up on Angela's desk.

As I stared at the diagram, a figure crossed into the office. I jerked back, battling the urge to scream. The stranger walked to the desk, and fingered the pages spread across its surface. He moved to get a better look, and I saw his face.

Instantly I recognized him as the man in the bookstore window - the man I'd seen when I met Karayan for coffee. He was in his mid-thirties, compact with well-defined arms, handsome. His short-cropped hair was brown, but those same platinum highlights gleamed when he passed through a finger of sunlight poking through the thick office drapes. And there was still something about him—something not of this world. My heart thudded in my chest. I couldn't take my eyes off of him.

I felt Seth reaching for my hand, and gripped his tightly in return.

The handsome stranger picked up the diagram of the vessel. His lips thinned in disgust. "Idiot children," he muttered. He dropped it back onto the desk. He rifled through the other papers there before turning to the bookshelves. He searched Angela's office thoroughly for over an hour. Seth and I were trapped, unable to flee. The closet where we were hiding was directly opposite the office. If we moved to open the door, he would see. So we stayed put, spying on the stranger through a crack in the door. Waiting.

The handsome stranger finally sighed. He pulled a flask out of his pocket. He unscrewed the top, then upended the flask over Angela's desk. I smelled the acrid scent of kerosene. The stranger lit a match and dropped it onto the desk. Fire exploded across the surface of the desk, streaming down the sides to pool on the floor. The stranger walked out of the office as calmly as if he'd just turned on a light.

Seth and I shrank back, afraid to breathe. The stranger turned, stopping in the office doorway, watching as the fire lapped up Angela's life's work. He stood there until the heat of the flames was like a furnace. Then he turned and was gone.

Seth and I sat, terrified, but the heat from the blaze was too much to bear. I pushed open the closet door, cringing back as a wave of searing air blasted us. The coast was clear. I grabbed Seth's hand and pulled him down the hall, out the back door, into the deserted backyard. We ran until we reached the back wall, then crouched there, sucking in great gulps of cool, sweet air.

I turned to look at Seth. Smoke curled from his clothes, and his face was smudged with sweaty soot from the fire.

"You look like hell," he croaked, giving me a lopsided smile.

"Seth?" Worry pierced my adrenaline-fueled panic. Seth looked almost manic.

"I was right," he said. He turned back to the burning house, eyes shining with a fierce satisfaction. "She figured it out. And now I've got what I need to bury that bastard." Seth looked at me. "We're going to make him pay."

I knew that look. It was the look on Lucas's face whenever he talked about the Lilitu who'd killed his brother. I'd seen that look in Gretchen's eyes, Hale's eyes, Thane's eyes. I'd seen it in Dad's eyes, when he'd told me about the night of my biological father's death.

But this time, the enemy was an incubus.

"Let's get out of here," I said. "This is something the Guard needs to hear."

When I pulled up outside my home, Dad rushed out to meet us.

I could tell by the look on his face that I was in deep trouble.

"Inside," he said.

"Just wait," I said. "You have to listen to—"

"*Inside.*" He glanced at Seth, who withered under his look. "You too."

Instead of obeying, I ran to the Guard's front door.

"Braedyn," Dad growled behind me.

I pushed open the door. No one was in the living room. I heard Dad's step on the stair and raced for the basement.

Hale was sifting through a massive crate of ancient weapons, so corroded by the years that they looked almost black. Lucas sat at the armory's table, polishing one of the ancient weapons to a brilliant shine. When he saw me, he dropped the dagger and stood.

"What the hell, Braedyn," he said. Hurt and anger warred across his face. He must have realized we'd left him behind when we didn't show up to lunch. So he'd come home to report us.

Hale turned, his eyes narrowing when he saw me.

"We have to do the ritual on winter solstice," I said. "If we don't, we won't have another chance for 20 years." My eyes slid back to Lucas. He blinked, processing this news. When the enormity of the consequences hit him, he took a step toward me.

"Your father's looking for you," Hale said, advancing on me.

"That's what Angela figured out," I said, losing my calm. "That's why she died!"

"It's true," Seth said from the top of the stairs. Dad gripped him by the upper arm and guided him down the stairs. "Listen to her. Please."

"All we have to do," I gushed when Hale and Dad turned to me, "is find the vessel. It's got all the answers we need."

"We have to find the vessel *first*," Seth said as he and Dad reached the bottom of the stairs.

"First?" Hale glanced at Seth, but Dad turned to me.

"What does he mean?"

"We saw someone at Seth's house." I glanced at Lucas. He was watching me, his expression haggard. "I think it was the incubus."

Dad closed his eyes, letting go of Seth to grab the stair railing for support.

"The Guard has the vessel," I said. "We just have to figure out where it's being kept."

Lucas's eyes lit up. "Of course. It looked familiar because there's a similar design on-"

"*Lucas,*" Dad snapped. "Go call Gretchen. Ask her to tell the others they can stop looking for Braedyn and Seth now." Lucas jumped to obey. Dad turned on me. His eyes were full of fury. "This is not what I meant when I asked you to be there for Seth today," he said quietly.

"But now we know who the incubus is," I said. "We've seen him. And now we know we have to figure out this ritual within the next two weeks. Seth and I can reconstruct Angela's research, we have her—"

"No." Dad's tone silenced me. "This is a matter for the Guard."

"But we're so close," Seth said.

"*It isn't up for discussion,*" Dad roared. I stumbled away from the rage in his voice. I'd never seen Dad this angry before. Seth fell silent, but he glared at Dad, mutinous.

Hale glanced at Seth's face, then turned to include me. "You're part of the Guard," he said. "Decisions like this are made at the top."

"Fine," Seth said through gritted teeth. "So who do we have to ask for permission to save the world?"

"Terrence Clay," Dad answered. Two simple words, but beneath them I could sense a virtual ocean of roiling emotion about this man.

"He's been the head of the Guard for the last two decades," Hale explained. "Something this important, we have to run it by him before we make any decisions."

"Why?" Seth asked. "You're here now, doesn't that make you more qualified to...?"

"Trust me," Dad cut in. "Clay would not like us acting on this without consulting him."

"So how do we reach him?" Seth asked.

"Thane," I murmured. "Thane's already on the way, isn't he?"

Dad gave me an appraising look and nodded. "We think Clay's somewhere in Canada."

"But this is stupid," Seth said, starting to lose it. "We can't wait for permission for some stranger in another country! We're running out of time!"

"He's right," I said. "We've only got two weeks until winter solstice."

"If Angela was killed over this, and you go poking around in it—" Dad stopped himself, but I understood.

"Tell Thane to hurry," I said. "Please."

Dad took a deep breath and let it out in a sigh. He kissed me on the forehead. "I will. I will." He drew me close into a tight hug, then released me. "Go back to school."

"What are you going to do?" I asked.

"Gather the Guardsmen," he said. "It's time to find this incubus."

I led Seth up the stairs. We could hear Lucas talking to Gretchen on the phone in the kitchen. Seth grabbed my arm, stopping me in the privacy of the hall.

He lowered his voice, but the emotion was clear in his eyes. "So, that's it? It's over?"

"It's not over," I said. Let Thane go to Terrence for permission. If he gave it, great. But I wasn't going to wait for some old man I'd never met to decide the course of my future. Even if it meant hiding from Dad. Even if it meant lying to Lucas. "We're going to do this ritual. But we're going to have to do it on our own."

12

The new moon, curved in the sky like a silver thread, had set hours ago. Stars glittered with fierce determination, but their light was too distant to offer much comfort. So different from the vast darkness of the dream reality. There, the glimmering lights of dreams responded in swirling gusts of motion to my every thought.

I sat at my window, waiting for Dad to fall asleep. I could hear him moving through his room, pacing anxiously. It was all I could do not to follow suit. All afternoon I had been plagued by the knowledge that if we couldn't stop this war from starting in the next two weeks, I might not get the chance to become human for the next two decades. I'd watch Lucas grow and age, while the Lilitu within held me back. And if I slipped? If waiting became too great a test of our patience? If I hurt Lucas?

I shuddered, and leaned my head against the window frame. Lucas's light had gone out over an hour ago. I felt a pang of longing to join him in his dream, where I knew I couldn't accidentally hurt him. But I had other plans tonight.

Finally, Dad's pacing ceased. I heard the springs on his bed groan, followed by the faint click of his light switch. I forced myself to wait another half-hour, then eased my bedroom door open. At the door to Dad's room, I could hear the steady, deep breathing of sleep. My shoulders unknotted, releasing a tiny fraction of the tension from the day. At least now I could *do* something.

I hurried down the stairs, slipping down the back hall to the guest room. I could see light spilling out from the crack under the door. I knocked, and heard a soft thud as Seth jumped out of bed. Moments later, the door opened.

"We're good?" he asked.

"He's asleep. What did you find out?"

"You better come in."

Seth opened the door a little wider. I entered the room, and Seth closed the door behind me. His bed was still made, strewn with notes he'd taken while reading his mother's journal. On one page he'd made a rudimentary sketch of the vessel. I picked it up. It was nowhere as detailed as the drawing that had burned up on Angela's desk, but it was a start.

Seth stood behind me to get a look at the drawing over my shoulder. "It's an instruction manual," he said. "The vessel, I mean."

"An instruction manual for what?"

He shuffled through the notes on his bed and came up with a handful of crinkled pages. "For the ritual. Apparently it's kind of complicated."

"No surprise there," I said, an edge of bitterness pushing through my voice.

Seth glanced at me and smiled. "We'll get it. I mean, the monks only had the vessel. We've got the Internet." He handed me the page. "Here. This is the list of ingredients we'll need."

I scanned the notes. "*Ericameria nauseosus, Juniperus scopulorum, Pinus edulis, Rosa canina* hips—" I looked up. "The ingredient list is in Latin?"

"Don't panic. According to Google, it's mostly a bunch of plants." Seth leaned over to point at the page in my hand, translating. "Basically—chamisa, juniper, Piñon, dog rose hips, et cetera."

"So, we just have to go out into the desert and pick some wildflowers?"

"Not exactly," Seth said. "Some of them have to be tinctures, like the juniper and the rose hips. The problem is, we've only got two weeks."

"Hm. Yes," I said. "And that might mean something to me if I knew what a tincture was."

Seth ducked his head. "Right, sorry. A tincture. It's just basically alcohol infused with a berry or something. So, like, take some juniper berries, soak 'em in vodka for a month or two, then strain them out and *voila,* tincture."

"Vodka, huh?"

"Well, the clearer the alcohol, the better. Medicinal alcohol would be best, but vodka works in a pinch."

I shook my head. "Those monks must have really liked their

moonshine."

Seth chuckled.

I returned to scanning the page. "Herbs and tinctures."

"Yes, mostly," Seth said. I heard something in his voice and looked up. He avoided my gaze. "It shouldn't be too hard to get our hands on most of that stuff."

"So what's the problem?"

Seth hesitated, then cleared his throat. "Here." He pointed back at the list. "The last ingredient."

I read it off the page. "*Sanguinis lamia.*" I looked up, suddenly chilled. "*Sanguinis?* Doesn't that mean—"

"Yeah," Seth said. "Blood."

"So, what is *lamia?*"

Seth squirmed in his socks. He couldn't meet my eyes. "It's the Latin word for Lilitu."

"Oh." I turned and sat on the edge of Seth's bed.

"But we don't need much," he said. "Just a few drops should work."

"You think the monks stopped with just a few drops?" My voice sounded faint in my ears.

"I think if more was needed, they would have detailed it in the ingredients list." Seth sat beside me on the bed. "Seriously, Braedyn. They took crazy insane notes about every single ingredient. Which juniper berries could go in the tincture, how to harvest the perfect rose hips—but when it came to *sanguinis lamia...*" he shrugged. "That's all they wrote; no annotation, no explanation." He studied my face, concerned. "Braedyn? I wouldn't ask you to do this if I thought—"

"No," I interrupted him. "It's okay. I'll do it." And as I said the words, I knew that I had to do it. If I wanted to be free of this curse, if I wanted a normal life, this was the way.

"Are you sure?" Seth asked.

"Why? Are you hiding another Lilitu in here somewhere?" I asked.

Seth smiled. "No. 'Fraid not."

"Then it's settled."

Seth let out a long sigh. "The only problem left is—"

"The vessel." I finished the thought for him. Seth nodded, his eyes solemn. "Well, we'll have to cross that bridge when we come to it," I said. "In the meantime, you've got our shopping list. There's a lot we can do to prepare."

"Yes," Seth agreed. "But we don't have a lot of time left."

I could see the worry in his eyes. We had two weeks to find this mysterious vessel, or all the tinctures in the world wouldn't help us lock the Lilitu out.

"Why didn't you tell me what you were doing?" Lucas asked, leaning against the locker bay. It was the first time we'd been alone together since Seth and I had ditched school to search his mom's house.

"You're right. I should have," I said, closing my locker. I was exhausted. I'd left Seth's room at around four in the morning, leaving me just over two hours to nap before I had to get up for the day. I could tell Lucas was upset, but I really didn't have it in me to do this right now. I started to turn away. Lucas caught my arm.

"No, come on." Lucas's eyes searched my face. "You ditched school with Seth, fine. Whatever. But you went to his house, even though you knew how dangerous it was—I mean, seriously, the incubus broke in *while you were there*." I felt his hand tighten on my arm.

"I know." I felt miserable, but what was done was done.

"You could have died." Lucas's voice was tight with emotion. "You should have died. How you guys managed to escape with your lives—"

"I know, Lucas. I know. It was a huge mistake. How many times do you want me to say I'm sorry?" I snapped. Lucas released me, stung. He turned his head, pretending to watch the students hurrying past us before first bell. I'd hurt him. I took a deep breath and let it out, trying to regain my calm. "I—that came out wrong."

"No, I was pushing." Lucas looked down at his fingernails. "It's just that we used to tell each other everything. So, what is it? You don't trust me anymore?"

"No, Lucas." I reached out and caught his hand, risking the touch. "Of course I trust you."

"So why didn't you tell me?"

"Because I knew you'd stop us," I said. "And I need this ritual to work."

"Wait, what are you saying?" Lucas asked, his face stricken. "You're not trying to do the ritual on your own?"

I felt a thrill of fear shoot down my spine. If Lucas told my dad that Seth and I hadn't given up, I'd be lucky if I didn't end up under house arrest. At the very least, it would be nearly impossible for us to gather everything we needed in time. I forced a smile, steeling myself to lie. But as I started to speak, Lucas released my hand and took a step back.

"Wait," he said. "You know what? Maybe we shouldn't have this conversation right now. I don't want you to say something you might regret later."

Lucas turned and left me standing by my locker alone. I closed the locker with a quiet click, reeling.

This is for the best, a small voice in my head said. *The less he knows, the easier it will be on him. Once the ritual is complete, the door will be locked, you'll be human, and there won't be anything left to be upset about.*

So why didn't that thought comfort me?

I kept meaning to talk with Lucas. I felt like I needed to apologize again, or offer him some comfort—or do my best to throw him off our scent. But it was harder and harder to find time to talk with him alone during the day, and by the time I crawled to bed each night in the pre-dawn, I was too tired to try to have the conversation in a dream. Seth and I had our hands full preparing for the ritual; I didn't seem to have any energy left for anything else.

By the time Thursday arrived, I'd reached a state of exhaustion that I wouldn't have believed possible. My irritation had gradually grown into paranoia, which exploded that day in physics class.

I was working with Seth on some experiment, the details of which hadn't been able to penetrate my sleep-deprived mind. He seemed to have it under control, so I let my thoughts wander. Amber and Ally had their heads together in the back of lab. As I watched them, I saw Ally's eyes flick past me, toward the lab table where Royal and Cassie sat working on their experiment. It put my hackles up. Ally caught me staring. A faint smirk twisted her pretty lips, but that was the only indication she gave of having seen me. She and Amber turned back to their lab work. I kept my gaze fixed on their table, waiting for the next indication of what they were planning.

Someone snapped their fingers in front of my face. I turned, furious.

Royal was standing at our desk, giving me an odd look. "Earth to Braedyn, anyone at the helm?"

"What?" I blinked, and noticed that Seth was at the front of the room, talking with Mr. Harris.

"I was saying, I think I might actually have a date to my brother's wedding in January." Royal's eyes danced with anticipation. But something kept scratching at the back of my mind. I glanced back at Amber and Ally, who were bent over their Bunsen burner, concentrating on the experiment. "Okay, I was expecting a bigger reaction to news of my first actual boy date, but clearly no dice. Just let me know when you're accepting applications for friends again." Royal turned and walked away.

"Wait, Royal," I said. But he ignored me, returning to the lab table he shared with Cassie. Whatever he said to her caused her to glance at me, frowning. I groaned to myself. I'd have to do some serious work to earn back their trust. After winter solstice.

A shrill giggle banished thoughts of Royal from my head. I spun around, and this time I caught Amber smirking at me. As our eyes met, she covered her mouth with her hand, as if saying, "oops, you caught me."

Seth returned to our table, looking at our experiment plan. "So, apparently we were adding the wrong—"

"I'll be right back," I said, interrupting him. I walked over to Amber and Ally's lab table.

Amber looked up at me, and genuine surprise flashed across her face before she covered it with an irritated scowl. "What?"

"What are you plotting?" I hissed.

Amber very deliberately picked up her beaker and smiled at me. "I don't know what you're—"

"Don't lie to me," I snapped. "Hurt another one of my friends and you'll move into first place on my 'To Deal With' list."

Amber flicked her wrist, sending her beaker crashing to the floor. At the same time, she flinched back from me. "Braedyn?!" Her shriek cut through the lab chatter.

Mr. Harris looked up, instantly on alert. "Ladies? Is there a problem?"

"What is your damage, Braedyn?" Ally asked, getting into the act. "That was our experiment!"

Mr. Harris walked over to us, his concern deepening. "Braedyn? You want to tell me what you think you're doing?"

"What?" I felt like the room was closing in on me. "That—no, I came over to talk to her—"

"To threaten me, you mean?" Amber asked, eyes smoldering. I didn't have to fake the hatred in my glare.

"Clean it up, Braedyn," Mr. Harris said. "And then you can take your write-up over to the headmaster's office personally. I do not tolerate fighting in my classroom."

The entire class was silent, watching me with bated breath. I wanted to scream. I wanted to wipe that smirk off Amber's face permanently. But instead, I clamped my teeth shut and nodded.

"All right, Amber, I'll get you another beaker," he said.

"Thank you, Mr. Harris." Amber even managed to make her voice quiver a little. When Mr. Harris turned to head back to the front of class, Amber's eyes cut back to me.

"Leave my friends alone," I hissed. "Or you'll wind up with more than a broken beaker."

She tossed her icy blond hair and followed Mr. Harris toward the front of class.

My eyes shifted and I saw Seth staring at me. Concern pulled his forehead into furrows. He gestured silently, offering to help me pick up the glass. I shook my head, resigned. I was about to start picking up the shattered beaker when Amber passed Seth at our lab table. She stumbled, knocking into him. He'd been focused on me and was totally unprepared for the hit.

Seth stumbled back into the lab table, hard. There was a soft *whoosh*, then someone screamed. Amber's face registered horror. Seth had stumbled back into the lit Bunsen burner; the whole back of his shirt was on fire. He arched his back, eyes rolling.

"Get it off, get it off!" Seth screamed, struggling to free himself from the flaming prison of his shirt.

Mr. Harris moved faster than I'd have thought possible. He ripped open a cabinet and grabbed a thick grey fire blanket. In two strides he had it unfurled. He tackled Seth, catching him in the blanket and controlling their fall to the ground. Within seconds, the smell of singed wool filled the lab. Seth finally struggled out of Mr. Harris's grasp, but the blanket had done its work. Blackened strips of ruined cotton covered Seth's back, sending an acrid smoke into the air.

A strange silence fell over the class as Mr. Harris and Seth recovered, rolling to their knees and breathing hard.

Mr. Harris reached out to Seth. "Can you stand, son?" Seth nodded, tears of pain squeezing out of the corners of his eyes. Mr. Harris helped him up. "Everyone turn off your Bunsen burners," he said. "I'll meet you back in our classroom." When no one moved, he glared around the room. "*Now.*"

Students moved toward the door quickly.

Ally passed me on her way out, eyes dangerous slits. "It's like your friends are cursed or something."

I clasped my hands around my arms. Cassie. Royal. Now Seth. Amber was making good on her threat, clearly undeterred by my feeble attempts to get her to back off and leave my friends alone. She'd hurt every single one of them—except for Lucas. With a shiver, I watched the last student leave the lab. Lucas. What did she have in store for him? And more importantly, how could I stop her before she got the chance to hurt him?

If I'd thought Mr. Harris would forget about sending me to the headmaster's office, I was disabused of that notion as soon as he returned to class. After briefly reassuring us that Seth was okay—an ambulance had been called as a precaution but his skin didn't appear to have even blistered—Mr. Harris wrote up a quick note to the headmaster and dismissed me from his classroom for the day.

I walked the note up to the administration building, stewing. I arrived and handed the note to Fiedler's administrative assistant, a woman I'd seen a few times before but had never spoken to. She glanced at me disapprovingly over her glasses and told me to have a seat, Headmaster Fiedler would be with me shortly. "Shortly" turned out to be half an hour, giving me plenty of time to sit with my thoughts. When he finally opened the door to his office and beckoned me inside, my anger had faded, leaving me feeling sick inside.

"So, Braedyn, you want to tell me what's going on?" Headmaster

Fiedler had my record up on his computer, and whatever he saw there had him worried.

"Amber broke her own beaker," I started.

"I'm not talking about the incident in class, although that is going to warrant some discussion." He steepled his hands, studying me. "Up until last semester you were an exemplary student here. Your teachers couldn't say enough good things about you."

He watched me, waiting for some kind of answer. I shrugged, uncomfortable. "I guess it's been kind of a hard year." I heard myself utter the words, then had to bite my lip, suppressing a manic urge to laugh. A *hard year?* Welcome to my entry for "understatement of the decade." In the last 12 months, I'd learned my father wasn't my father and I wasn't human, I'd watched a powerful Lilitu drag Lucas off to kill him, and I'd fought my way through her guards to save him—nearly dying myself in the process. I looked down at my hands, struggling to maintain my composure.

"I understand," Fiedler said.

"No disrespect intended, sir," I murmured, "but I don't think you do."

"You watched a burglar murder your friend Derek in your home," Fiedler said. I looked up, stricken. Derek. He hadn't even crossed my mind. "I can't say I've ever been through what you've been through, Braedyn, but I know that it's affected you profoundly."

A stinging pressure spread through my nose and into my eyes. I bit my lip, holding back the flood.

"And then, just a few months later, you were in a serious car accident with another good friend. Lucas, wasn't it?"

I dropped my eyes, avoiding the necessity of lying. That "car accident" was our cover story for the extensive injuries Lucas and I had sustained in our battle against Ais.

"I'm afraid that we've failed you," Fiedler continued.

"How do you figure that?" I asked.

"You've been through significant trauma—both you and Lucas. We should have mandated counseling sessions for you both."

I felt my head snap up. Fiedler was watching me closely. I swallowed, afraid to speak. It was hard enough fitting everything in as it was, if I had mandatory counseling sessions on top of everything else...

"I think I'm just really tired," I said, trying to sound reasonable and sincere. It helped that it was true. "I haven't been sleeping well. So, I've kind of got a short fuse right now. But I'm going to do better. I promise."

Fiedler frowned. "You know it's not a punishment, right? Speaking with a counselor could really help you sort through everything you've experienced."

Unlikely, I thought.

Fiedler must have sensed my resistance. Instead of pushing, he sighed. "How about this? Promise me you'll consider it. Anytime you'd like, we can set you up with the school counselor. And I mean anytime. During class, during lunch, after school—whatever you need, if you need it."

I forced myself to smile. "Okay. I'll consider it."

Fiedler nodded, then leaned forward, crossing his arms on the desk. It was an oddly informal gesture. "So about this business with Amber."

"Right." I slumped in my seat, steeling myself for the fallout.

"I think we can give you a pass."

"Really?" I looked up, genuinely surprised.

"Just this once. But promise me you're going to take better care of yourself. Get some sleep. And consider visiting the school counselor if you need someone to talk to."

"Yes," I said. "I promise."

"Then I think we're done here. If you hurry you should still be able to enjoy your lunch."

"Thank you," I said, standing. Fiedler nodded, then waved me out. I left his office and my stomach growled. Lunch sounded just about right.

"Braedyn." Seth was waiting for me in the hallway.

"What are you doing here?" I asked. "I thought you were on the way to the hospital."

"Naw," Seth said. "The paramedics checked me out and said I was fine."

"But—" I started, unwilling to believe that was that. I mean, he'd been on *fire* less than an hour ago.

"Look, this is the perfect excuse," Seth said, lowering his voice. "Everyone knows what happened to me. Just call Lucas and tell him you're skipping lunch to come visit me at the hospital."

"Why?" I asked. After this morning, the thought of lying to Lucas turned my stomach.

"Because we've got some fresh *ericameria nauseosus* to collect, and it'll be a lot harder to find it at three o'clock in the morning. Who knows," Seth gave me a conspiratorial smile, "we might even have time to get some sleep tonight."

That settled it.

"I'm in."

We drove out of Puerto Escondido, heading northwest. Seth had been following several "wildflower sightings" blogs, looking for news on a flowering Chamisa (which was also called "Rabbitbrush" by the wildflower enthusiasts). Apparently, they usually flower in September, but someone had spotted a late-flowering bush out here just two days ago.

"It's much better if the ingredients are fresh," Seth said, rereading the notes he'd taken from his mother's journal.

"Yeah, but the ritual's still over a week away," I pointed out. "They're not exactly going to be fresh at that point."

"We're drying them," Seth said, distracted. "It just helps to control the final outcome if we've got fresh flowers to start with. Something about us killing the blooms ourselves, rather than simply finding dried flowers on the bush."

I glanced at him out of the corner of my eye, but he wasn't paying attention. "You sound pretty excited."

Seth looked up from his notes. "Yeah, aren't you? This means you get to become human, be with Lucas. I know that's what you want." Seth gave me a watery smile.

I turned back to the road, thinking for a moment in silence. "It's amazing."

"What's that?" Seth asked.

"When I met you, you didn't even believe Lilitu were real."

"Huh." Seth chewed on his lip for a minute in silence. "A lot has changed since then."

"Yeah." I risked another glance at him, worried.

"Mile marker 63," Seth said, straightening. "Pull off on this access road."

I followed his directions, and in about 10 minutes we were parking off the side of a dirt road.

"It's supposed to be over here," Seth said, shielding his eyes from the sun to look out over the flora of the high desert foothills.

"There," I said, pointing. A bush, maybe seven feet tall, sat nestled at the base of a bolder, crowned with bright yellow flowers.

"That's the one," Seth said.

We picked our way through the scrub brush, prairie grass, and cacti until we came to the bush.

"We want only the most perfect flowers," Seth breathed. He snapped off a small yellow blossom. It looked like a trumpet, opening up into five delicate petals at the end. "Like this one."

"How many do we need?"

"Enough to grind the dried flowers down into a cup or more of powder."

"So... how many?"

"A lot," Seth said. He handed me an empty canvas grocery bag. "We should probably fill a couple of these."

I took the bag with a sick, twisting feeling. "We're not going to make it back for afternoon classes, are we?"

"I'm in the hospital, remember?" Seth shot me a roguish grin. "And my good friend, Braedyn, is keeping me company. You should probably call Lucas. We don't want him freaking your dad out again."

"Right," I said. But I hesitated before reaching for my phone. This was very different from just not telling Lucas what was up. This was deliberately misleading him. And I wasn't sure if it was something I wanted to do. But Seth was right, if he called my dad or Hale, things would get very complicated, very fast. I fished my phone out of my pocket and dialed Lucas's number.

Seth saw the movement and walked a little ways off, giving me some privacy.

Lucas picked up on the third ring. "You're not at lunch," he said. It wasn't an accusation, just a statement.

"No."

"Is it Seth?" he asked.

"Yeah, it is," I answered, glancing back at the skinny boy happily snapping yellow blossoms off the plant behind me. "I'm with him right now."

"Oh, man," Lucas said. "I heard about what happened. Is he going to be okay?"

"I think so."

"How about you? I heard about that other thing, too. You really went after Amber?"

"What? No!" For a moment, anger chased away my guilt. "She totally framed me. Who told you I attacked her?"

"Royal and Cassie," Lucas said, sounding confused. "They said they saw the whole thing."

"Why would I attack Amber?" I asked. "I'd just be making her life easier if I got kicked out of school."

"Right." But Lucas didn't sound convinced. "So, are you going to stay at the hospital for the rest of the day?"

"Um," I took a deep breath, every part of me fighting the lie. "I think I'm going to stay with Seth as long as he needs me."

"You're a good friend," Lucas said, with real warmth in his voice. "I'll ask Royal for a ride home. Maybe he'll actually let me drive this time."

"Thanks," I said, desperate to end this call, "I should probably get back to Seth."

"Okay. Tell him hi from me? We're all thinking about him."

"Yeah."

I hung up, taking a moment to settle my racing heart. *You didn't technically lie to him,* I told myself. And then another thought surfaced. *Great. Now I'm lying to myself.*

Seth and I finished our harvest a little before school got out. I drove us home, then Seth and I smuggled the bags of Chamisa blossoms into his room. He'd already set up a drying station in his closet, but it'd take several more hours to hang all the blossoms up so they'd dry evenly.

"You should probably go to practice," Seth said. "Keep up the routine."

"You don't need help with this stuff?" I asked.

"I've got it." Seth shrugged. "I'm actually looking forward to the solitude."

I studied his face for a long moment, then nodded. "Okay. You know where to find me if you need anything."

It felt good to throw myself into practice after the afternoon's deception. The physical workout felt like a penance. I fought hard, focused only on the next attack, the next defense.

At the end of our normal training session, Lucas sat down and Gretchen and Matthew ringed me for another round of two-on-one. While I wasn't great at anticipating both attacks simultaneously, there was one moment when I was blocking Gretchen's frontal attack that I almost *sensed* Matthew behind me. Instinctively I dropped, dodging the blow before it landed. In the next breath, I swept out my leg, catching Matthew behind the knees and knocking his legs out from under him.

"Nice work, Braedyn," Hale called from the stairs. He was grinning. "I can't think of a better way to end a session."

"I think we're starting to see some progress," Gretchen said, offering a hand to help Matthew up off the floor mat.

"Thanks." I flashed them a brief smile, then picked up my water, draining it. My muscles felt hot, but loose, relaxed. Except for the tender spots—reminders of what happens when I don't move fast enough to block a punch—I felt remarkably good.

Until Lucas cornered me.

"Is everything all right?" He kept his voice low and neutral, to avoid drawing the attention of Hale and Gretchen, talking a few yards away.

"Yeah, why?" I tried to make my voice nonchalant.

Lucas gave me a strange look. "You don't normally train like your life depended on beating the crap out of my sister-in-law."

"What?" I glanced over at Gretchen and saw her rubbing at her shoulder, wincing. "I didn't mean to hurt her."

"Yeah, that's kind of what I mean," Lucas said. "It was like your mind was a thousand miles away, and all that was left was this robot-girl hammering out punches." Lucas dropped his voice even lower. "Is it Seth?"

"No," I said, not thinking.

"But something's bugging you." Lucas scrutinized me shrewdly.

"Lucas." I faced him full on. "Do you trust me?"

Lucas glanced at Hale for the briefest moment before answering. "Of course I do."

"Then *trust* me."

He gave me a smile, and shrugged his shoulders. "Sorry. My radar must be off or something."

I blotted my face with a towel, hiding the guilt I was afraid I couldn't conceal if Lucas was staring into my eyes. When I pulled the towel away, Lucas was drinking his water.

"I should probably get back to my place," I said. "Fiedler's on my case about my grades and I've got a quiz in English tomorrow."

"Right. See you at dinner?"

"See you." I left the basement, hurrying up the stairs. When I got home, Seth was sitting on the foot of our staircase, waiting for me.

"I found the last two ingredients on our shopping list," he said.

"Careful," I murmured. We couldn't afford to get careless, and just blurt things out.

"No one's home," Seth said, shrugging my caution off. "Come on. We can make it there and back before dinner."

"No," I said, more firmly than I'd intended. Seth looked at me, startled.

"Is something wrong?" He seemed to shrink into himself. He made me think of an abused puppy, expecting another kick.

"Sorry," I relented. "Sorry. What did you find?"

"The tinctures," Seth said. "I found an herbalist who's totally anal about her preparations. She's got several varieties of tincture of rose hips, including the dog rose, and she's got the juniper one we need, too."

"Can we go tomorrow instead?" I asked. "It's just, we're supposed to be here, so if Dad gets home and we're gone—"

"Sure. I totally get it." Seth folded up his ingredients list and shoved it into his pocket.

"Did you finish hanging the blossoms to dry?"

"I did, indeed," Seth said. "So what do you want to do now?"

"Believe it or not," I smiled weakly. "Study."

We were both bent over our textbooks when Dad came home that night. He didn't say anything, but I could tell he was pleased. I shoved down the wave of rising guilt. He thought we were playing by the rules; he didn't know the truth. He didn't know we'd spent the day collecting ingredients for the ritual instead of going to class. But with less than two weeks to go before winter solstice, I had to prioritize—and that meant the ritual came first.

The next day was Friday. I couldn't afford to skip another lunch, not with Lucas obviously watching me. But I had a study period right before physics, and if we drove fast, Seth and I could make it to the herbalist's and back before I missed any class time at all.

Sneaking off campus was becoming uncomfortably easy. I met Seth by my car and we pulled out of the campus parking lot, no one the wiser.

We drove straight to the little shop tucked into the outskirts of Old Town.

An old-fashioned brass bell hanging over the door tinkled merrily as Seth and I entered the cramped shop. It was a tiny room, and very crowded. The walls were lined with narrow shelves, and two more freestanding shelves took a big bite out of the available floor space. We had to walk single file down the aisles.

"Hello? May I help you?" I turned as a plump woman looked up from a table at the back of the shop. Her face was weathered with lines born of too much sun-exposure, but her eyes were kind. She wore a loose cotton shirt died indigo and her dark brown hair was pulled up in a comfortably messy bun.

"We're here for a couple of tinctures," I said.

"I called in the order yesterday," Seth added. "Seth Linwood?"

"Oh dear," the woman said, looking at us kindly. "I—thought you were a bit older."

Seth and I glanced at each other, confused.

"My tinctures are alcoholic in nature," she explained. "I can't sell them to minors."

"We're not going to drink them," I said.

"I'm sorry, it's just—" she pointed to a sign that read, *We do not sell alcohol to minors*. "I'm afraid I can't make any exceptions. I don't relish the idea of going to prison."

"But—" I started.

"We'll look around," Seth said. "Maybe there's something else that will work."

"Good idea," the herbalist said. "I'm here if you have any questions."

In the corner of the shop, I looked at Seth. "I thought it had to be a tincture."

"It does," he said.

"So what are you planning to—?"

"Not me. You." Seth met my eyes directly. "Of the two of us, which one can turn herself invisible?"

It took me half a second to figure out what he was asking. "You want me to rob her?"

"No," he said. "I don't *want* you to rob her. But she won't sell us the tinctures, and we need them. Put some money in her drawer if you want. Here." He fished in his pocket and pulled out a few twenties. "That should more than cover it."

"I don't..." I glanced at the woman, nervous. She was watching us closely. I felt like a thief already.

"You're the one who wanted to do this quickly," Seth reminded me. "Just go outside. I'll distract her. You can come back in all cloaked up, do your thing, and we can get back to school."

"I don't even know what they look like," I protested.

"She's got them set aside for me. Check the back."

I examined the back of the shop. There was an open curtain separating the shop from the storeroom. I wouldn't even have to move it aside.

"Good," Seth said, seeing my decision. He turned back to the woman. "So what other things do you have with juniper in them?" he asked.

I left the store, propping the door open with a rock. My heart thumped loudly in my ears. A few pedestrians walked past the shop outside. Too many eyes. I slipped around the side of the building. After a moment, checking to make sure no one was around, I took a deep breath, and felt the ripping sensation spreading along my back. It was the oddest feeling. I never seemed to get used to it. When I concentrated, I could almost feel the glossy smooth leather of my wings. But they didn't exist in this reality—and they wouldn't unless I learned how to make them solid and tangible outside of the dream.

Physical or not, my wings were capable of cloaking me from the sight of most mortals. And since Gretchen wasn't around, I felt pretty safe walking into the store.

The woman Seth was talking to didn't even flinch when I slipped back through the open door. I walked right toward her, but there was no glimmer of anything in her eyes to indicate she saw me. I slipped around her, through the curtained opening, and into the back. It was more of a closet than a storeroom, with row of shelves lining the walls floor to ceiling. On one shelf I saw a collection of simple brown sandwich bags, each labeled with hand-written names. I found the one labeled *Seth Linwood* and clutched it to my chest.

I walked back out of the tiny office, and out of the store, returning to my car and crouching down behind the side door before uncloaking. I stood, shaking, and unlocked the driver's side door, slipping the package into the glove compartment and out of sight.

About 10 minutes later, Seth returned.

"Did you get it?" he asked.

"Yes." I pointed to the glove compartment.

Seth opened it, and pulled two small glass bottles out of the brown paper bag. "That is so awesome." He grinned at me, but I couldn't share his enthusiasm. He didn't seem to notice my reticence. He pulled his shopping list out of his pocket and crossed off the tinctures. "So. That leaves the vessel," he said. He looked up at me, some of his excitement fading. "Which we have no leads on."

"Maybe Thane will find that Clay guy soon," I said. "He might know where it is."

Seth nodded, but he didn't look happy. "I've been trying to reconstruct the instructions, but that photo only shows one side of the vessel, which basically means we only really know one half of the instructions. We need the *actual* vessel if we want this ritual to work. *Someone* has to know where it is."

"Wait." I sat up in my seat, something tickling the back of my mind. "Do you remember when we first told Hale and the others about the ritual—how it has to be done on winter solstice?"

"Yeah?" Seth watched me, waiting to see where I was going with this.

"Lucas said something..." As I replayed the memory in my mind, I remembered dad interrupting Lucas right after he'd started to say something looked familiar in the photograph. "I think Lucas might know something about the vessel."

"Do you think he'll help us?" Seth asked.

I didn't answer. I was already thinking of what I'd have to say to get Lucas to see why we needed to do this ritual. He had to help us. He was our only lead.

13

"When are you going to ask him?" Seth murmured.

"I don't know," I whispered back. "Shhh."

We were sitting in English, hunched over our quizzes. I'd actually studied for this. I didn't want to get an F because Mr. Avila thought I was cheating. Seth sighed and looked back at his own paper.

The final bell rang as I was finishing up the last essay, which was supposed to be a personal reaction to the nature of disguise in Shakespeare's *Twelfth Night*. Viola summed up her thoughts pretty neatly when she said, "Disguise, I see thou art a wickedness..." I had plenty of personal reactions to that, but I couldn't exactly write an essay on what it felt like to be a Lilitu trying to pass as a normal girl in high school.

"All right, folks," Mr. Avila said. "Pencils down. You made it through another day. Bring your quizzes up here and then you're free to enjoy your weekend."

I felt a chill move through me. *The weekend, already?* That meant winter solstice was only eight days away. Suddenly it didn't feel like there was enough time. I walked my quiz up to Mr. Avila then fled the classroom, feeling numb.

Seth was waiting for me in the hall. He read my expression and frowned. "Braedyn? What's wrong?"

I spotted Lucas approaching in the hall. "Now," I whispered. "I'm going to ask him now." I moved toward Lucas and Seth fell into step with me. "Actually..." I glanced at Seth and he flinched.

"Right. You probably want to do this alone."

"I think it'll go a little smoother if—yeah." I gave Seth a quick, apologetic smile. Lucas was already on edge when it came to me and Seth sneaking off to do things without him. This might be easier for him to hear if it was coming from me alone. Seth nodded and turned back the way we'd come.

Lucas waved. "How'd it go?" he asked. "The quiz?"

"Pretty good, I think," I said. "I would have aced it if I'd been able to share my personal feelings about what it's like to have to hide your true nature from all but your closest friends and family, but, you know."

"Shucks," Lucas said, smiling.

"So, actually, there's something I need to talk to you about." I hesitated, unsure how to begin. "You know, maybe we should go outside."

Lucas's smile faded. Concern crinkled the edges of his eyes. "Okay, lead the way."

I walked out of the building, and drew Lucas off the path onto the quad. The wind was picking up, and we huddled against gusts of biting air. December was ushering in the beginning of winter. Heavy clouds edged the horizon, fat with the promise of snow.

"Talk fast," Lucas said, trying to keep his voice light. But I could see the worry lingering in the back of his eyes. I pulled a folded piece of paper out of my satchel. Lucas took it gingerly and unfolded it, revealing the annotated drawing of the vessel. He looked up at me, understanding. "Murphy told you to leave this stuff alone."

"I need your help."

"Sorry, Braedyn." He shoved the drawing back.

"Wait. Hear me out." I caught his hand before he could leave. A warm energy flowed through the touch, and I could see Lucas felt it, too. He hesitated, meeting my eyes reluctantly.

"What do you want?" Lucas asked.

"You," I said. "I want to be with you. Without the fear of what might happen if we touch, or kiss, or—" I lowered my eyes, unable to voice the thought. Lucas swallowed.

"I want that too," he said.

"Then help me. Please."

"Braedyn."

"We have eight days, Lucas," I pleaded. "This ritual could end the war. And that would set me free."

"Could," Lucas said. "If it works."

"It will work."

"How do you know that?" Lucas asked. "We don't know anything about this ritual. Thane's halfway across Canada, and all of Angela's research burned up in the fire."

"Not all of it," I said. Lucas stared at me. "We have her journal."

"We?"

"Me and Seth," I said. Lucas's jaw tightened. "We just need the vessel, and then we can end this whole—"

Lucas pulled his hand away. "Braedyn, no."

"Do you know where it is?"

Lucas shook his head, helpless with frustration. "I don't. And if I did, I wouldn't tell you. Hale and Murphy said no. We have to trust them."

"But this is our life, Lucas. They don't know how hard we have to work, just being this close to each other." As I spoke, I felt my words reaching Lucas. I placed my hands on his chest, urging him to hear me. Urging him to understand. "This is the only thing keeping us from being together. Can't you see that?"

"I—" Lucas looked torn.

"Please." I willed my words to move him. Lucas's green eyes seemed to lock onto mine. His pupils started to open—

"What are you doing?!" Amber grabbed my arm and spun me away from Lucas. As we parted, Lucas staggered back. It was like a spell had broken. "What was that— What are you doing to him?!"

I looked at Amber, shaken. I'd been so focused on Lucas, I hadn't heard her approach. And then the reality hit me. I turned to Lucas, fear leaping into my throat. I must have used my Lilitu powers on him, trying to bend his will. Lucas stared at me. His face lost its color as the same realization hit him.

"Are you okay?" Amber asked, turning to Lucas. "Did she hurt you?"

Lucas couldn't pull his eyes away from my face. "Braedyn?"

I gave a strangled cry and fled. I had to get away; I couldn't bear the accusation in Lucas's eyes. Terror gripped my heart. I hadn't intended to exert Lilitu power over him, so how had it happened? Was I losing my mind? Were my powers growing beyond my ability to control? Or was this simply what it meant to be a Lilitu? To manipulate and control people without any effort at all?

I was dimly aware of Lucas shouting after me. He caught up to me behind the theater building. He spun me around to face him.

"What the hell happened back there?" He was breathing hard from the sprint.

"I'm sorry." I said. He deserved an explanation, but I didn't have one to give. "I didn't realize—" Lucas's hands relaxed on my arms. It was all I could do to choke back a sob. "You should stay away. Stay away from me. I—I'm dangerous."

Lucas shook his head, too angry to speak.

I've lost him, I thought. *I've finally lost him*. Part of me had always believed this was too good to be true. That I didn't deserve Lucas's loyalty, or his love. Of course it was over. We were enemies; a Lilitu and a Guardsman—we could never work. And now Lucas knew it, too.

"I'll leave you alone." My voice quavered as I pulled free from his grasp. I turned away from him, ashamed of the tears threatening to stream down my cheeks.

"I know what you are," he said. I felt his hand on my arm and reacted without thinking, spinning around, ready to strike. "Whoa! I wasn't trying to—" Lucas looked sick at my reaction. "Braedyn, I don't want you to leave me alone."

I lowered my hands, stricken. "I don't understand. I almost—" But I couldn't say the words.

"Enthralled me?"

"I didn't mean to," I whispered.

"I believe you."

"You don't understand. I didn't mean to use any Lilitu powers on you. It just—happened."

"So let's make sure it doesn't happen again."

"Lucas—" I started to protest.

"Like I said. I know what you are. It doesn't change how I feel about you."

I shook my head, unwilling to accept this.

"You're forgetting," he said, his voice barely above a whisper. "I've felt you in my mind. When Ais had me, when I thought I was going to die, you were there for me, giving me strength. I *felt* your love. I know you would never hurt me." Lucas gave a bitter laugh. "That's why I don't care that you're spending so much time with Seth, even though it's obvious the guy's head over heels in love with you."

I felt a hot tear slip down one cheek. Lucas gently thumbed it away, leaving his hand to cradle my cheek.

"Until you tell me you don't love me anymore, I will never doubt you." Lucas enfolded me in his arms, and I responded, circling my arms around his back and holding on for all I was worth. We stood there for several long minutes, ignoring the icy December wind. Finally, reluctantly, Lucas pulled back and looked into my face. "But that doesn't mean I'm going to help you get yourself killed."

"Lucas?" I felt a knife of ice twist in my stomach and knew then that someone—Dad? Hale?—had talked to Lucas, convinced him that the best way to protect me was to keep me from the vessel.

"If keeping you safe means we have to wait a little longer, I'll deal. It's worth it."

"Lucas, you're not listening to me. *Twenty years* isn't a little—" But Lucas cut me off, placing a finger across my lips.

"Braedyn." Pain laced his voice. "I'm too vulnerable to you right now. I'm asking you to stop, please."

I stared at him, suddenly speechless. Lucas brushed his hand against my cheek again, then pulled away from me.

"And—don't take this the wrong way, but I think maybe we should cool it on the dreams for a few nights." Lucas turned and left, without waiting for a response.

I stared after him, at a loss. I had to make him see—that vessel was the key. Whatever he knew, he had to share it with us before it was too late. But before I could summon the energy to follow him, a door opened behind me. It was Mr. Hart.

"Braedyn?" he asked. "I thought I heard someone fighting out here."

"No, it's fine," I said, taking a step away from him before I could stop myself.

Mr. Hart's eyes tightened, and he studied me for a long moment. "Everything okay?"

I stared at Mr. Hart, suddenly remembering I'd been unable to touch his dreaming mind. After Seth and I had seen the stranger in his house, I'd simply assumed we'd found our incubus. Now, looking at Mr. Hart, I couldn't fathom why we'd left this stone unturned.

"Braedyn?" he prompted. "Is there something on your mind?"

"I don't know what you mean," I said, fighting to keep my voice level.

"You don't like me very much, do you?" he asked with a small smile. Before I could figure out how to answer this question, Mr. Hart looked around, then lowered his voice. "Listen, Braedyn. I'm not a bad guy. I mean, you can ask Cassie."

"What does this have to do with Cassie?" I asked, my voice faint.

A group of students rounded the corner of the building. Mr. Hart glanced at them, eyes narrowing. He turned back and caught my gaze. "Just that, whatever you think you know, you should consider the possibility that you're wrong. I know you don't want to see her get hurt any more than I do."

I stared at him. Was that a threat?

"If you think about it, we're really after the same thing," he said. He retreated into the theater, closing the door behind him.

I stood there until my hands ached with the cold, torn by indecision. On the one hand, I wanted to find Lucas and convince him that we needed his help to locate the vessel. On the other hand, I needed to make sure Cassie—who spent every afternoon under the power of the charming Mr. Hart—was okay.

The costume closet, nestled in the heart of the building, was a cozy little den of creativity. I poked my head into the room and saw Cassie hard at work at the table. A sturdy sewing machine hummed as she guided material under the needle with expert moves. She was so absorbed in her work, she didn't notice me enter. I waited until the sewing machine stopped.

"Cass?"

Cassie looked up. When she saw me, she held a finger up. "Hang on." She clipped a few loose threads and turned the creation inside out. It was a large tunic in rich black brocade and velvet. Cassie glanced at it, then turned to drape it over a wide dressmaker's form. "I am insanely overwhelmed," she said. "Our Mortimer broke his leg—compound fracture. They think he's going to be in traction for a week or two. So Mr. Hart had to cast a new Mortimer, who's three sizes bigger than the old Mortimer, hence the mad scramble for new costumes at the last second." She finished draping the tunic and stepped back to give it a critical once-over. "Well, that'll be good enough for a fitting, anyway."

"It's gorgeous," I said.

Cassie turned away from the costume. "What brings you to my kingdom?"

"Just, wanted to check in," I said. "See how things are going." *Make sure you're not turning into a little snack pack for an incubus.*

Cassie wrung her hands. "I know things have been kind of weird between us this semester. I hate it."

I felt a swell of emotion at her honesty. "Me too," I said. "I really hate it."

"Hug it out?"

I laughed, and opened my arms. Cassie and I embraced tightly. When she pulled back, she was smiling. "I'm so glad you came. I'm freaking out about this play."

"Why?" I asked. "Everything I've seen of your costumes looks amazing."

"It's—" Cassie shook her head and I saw that she was really nervous. "I just wish I had more time to get everything right before all my work is paraded in front of the whole school." So it wasn't that she was worried about the costumes, she was worried about putting her talents on display for our peers. "I know that's stupid. People are going to be paying attention to the actors, not what they're wearing."

"Cassie," I chided. But telling her that her costumes were likely to be as eye-catching as the best performances on that stage probably wouldn't help matters. So I bit my tongue.

"Maybe—" Cassie gave me a pleading look. "Do you think you could come to dress rehearsal on Friday? It'd be great to just get an outside perspective on the whole thing."

"I'll be there," I said.

"Knock, knock." Mr. Hart walked into the costume closet. Cassie turned, her face filling with a happy glow at the sight of him. I eyed Mr. Hart, trying to conceal my worry from him. But I didn't have to bother—he wasn't looking at me. His attention was focused on Cassie. Try as I might, I couldn't sense anything supernatural about him. And yet, Cassie looked at him with such devotion.

She straightened, unconsciously straightening the hem of her shirt. "Hi, Mr. Hart."

"I've brought you a Mortimer to fit." Mr. Hart made a sweeping gesture back at the door as a stocky kid waved. Cassie barely glanced at him.

"Excellent. I'm all ready." Cassie turned back to me, almost as an afterthought. "I should get back to work."

"Right," I said, stepping out of the way as the new Mortimer entered to admire the tunic.

Mr. Hart glanced at me with a veiled look. "Anything I can help you with?" he asked.

"Nope." I tried to keep my voice light for Cassie's benefit. "I was just leaving."

"Then we'll see you later, Braedyn." Mr. Hart turned his back to me, watching Cassie measure the new Mortimer's arm length with her tape measure.

Oh yeah, I'd be at that dress rehearsal. It'd give me a chance to kill two birds with one stone; support Cassie, and keep an eye on *him*. In the meantime, I had a bigger problem to solve.

I had to figure out how to convince Lucas to tell me what he knew about the vessel.

Training sessions were becoming the perfect outlet for my pent up frustrations. After our fight, Lucas put a little distance between us. He was still angry, and I totally got that. But it made finding time to talk to him alone impossible. Also, I was respecting his request that I not visit his dreams, which killed any chance of a private conversation entirely. But when Saturday dawned, I was faced with the uncomfortable reality that we only had one week until the full moon. I was running out of time to be patient. Lucas had the key, and if we couldn't talk, he couldn't hand it over.

As I fought Gretchen and Matthew that weekend, I turned my thoughts to the enemy, picking apart our assumptions about the incubus—and who he might be. Mr. Hart didn't seem overtly supernatural, but then again, I hadn't been able to glean anything from his dream. What did that mean? And who was the stranger in Seth's house? That guy *had* seemed otherworldly—could he be spying on me? Whoever the incubus was seemed extremely plugged into what was going on in my life. So—where did that leave us? Nowhere.

Sunday's training session was grueling, but I embraced it. The harder I trained, the less time I had to think about the approaching solstice. For a few hours every day, I didn't have the energy to think about anything beyond the next attack, the next defense.

"It's good to see you applying yourself again," Hale said as we broke for some water. "I haven't seen you this focused since—" Hale hesitated only briefly, then gave me an encouraging smile.

"Well, you know, incubus on the loose," I murmured. Lucas shot a look at me from the corner of his eye. I drank half a bottle of water, then set the bottle down on the back table.

"Okay, let's try another round. Lucas, you can sit this one out," Hale said.

"Gladly," Lucas said, pulling the tape off his hands.

Hale gestured to Matthew. "You take the front attack this time, Gretchen, you attack from behind."

We moved to the mat, and Gretchen and Matthew surrounded me. It didn't go well. I could handle Matthew's attack just fine—because I could see him. But Gretchen kept sneaking up on me and pouncing. She wasn't fighting full strength, but she still left a trail of bruises across my back. After half an hour of this, Hale called a timeout.

"Look," he said. "I've seen Lilitu fighting groups of Guardsmen, and it's like they can see where they are even though they've got their backs to them."

"Well, unless you can tell me *how* they do it, it's not really helping," I muttered.

"You've already done it, though," Hale said. "Don't you remember?"

I looked up sharply, and I did remember—there was that one tiny moment last week where I could sense Matthew lunging for me. I glanced at Matthew and saw that he remembered it, too.

"Want to try again?" Matthew asked.

"Yeah," I said.

"Try to keep from getting touched," Hale suggested. "Don't worry about attacking. This is purely a test of your ability to evade."

We spread out across the mat again. This time I tried to let my focus roam. Instead of keeping all my attention on Gretchen, I let part of my mind wander. And then there it was—I could sense Matthew behind me, springing. I sidestepped him easily and he lurched past, grinning.

"Nice," he said.

Before I had time to savor my victory, I was flat on the mat. Gretchen had tackled me from behind while my attention was focused on Matthew. I groaned, grateful for the mat that softened our landing. Gretchen rolled off, sighing.

"Easy," Matthew said, holding his hands out. Gretchen took one and I took the other, and Matthew pulled us to our feet.

Hale glanced at his watch. It must have been past noon, because he clapped his hands. "Okay. We'll try again tomorrow." Hale waved Gretchen and Matthew over for a mini-conference.

As they started to discuss training strategies for the next session, I walked over to Lucas.

"Do you feel like taking a walk around the block?" I asked. This was my last-ditch effort to do things the nice way. "I was thinking about our fight and everything and—I think we should talk about it."

"I've got an AP History test tomorrow," he said. "I've been studying all weekend but I've still got three chapters to review if I want to pass this thing. You know, just in case the world doesn't end." Lucas flashed me a brief smile then walked up the stairs without a second look back.

I watched him go, steeling myself for what I needed to do. How could it be that the greatest obstacle to Lucas's and my future was Lucas?

Slipping into the dream was as easy as diving into a pool. I took a moment to examine my dream garden's roses, afraid my incident with Lucas had chased the last bit of white out of the petals. They looked almost unchanged, and I let out a sigh of relief. So whatever had happened between us, I hadn't hurt him.

I checked the shield around my dream. It was still solid. Alone. I was completely and utterly alone here. No Guard barking orders, no high school drama, no father to disappoint, no Seth with his endless preparations. I savored the feeling for a moment.

But I wasn't here to relax.

I placed my hand on the ground, willed a pinhole crack to open in the shield around my dream. I summoned the dream I was looking for, and it rose up out of the darkness like a glimmering jewel. But this time, instead of barging in, I placed my hand around the dream and waited. In the front of my mind, I held a request for permission to enter.

I felt the dream world around me shift. There was a tugging sensation, and then I was standing next to Karayan in her dream. Sloping hills dotted with bluebells surrounded us. There was a sweet scent to the landscape, even in the dream.

"Well," she said. "Look who's learned some manners."

I bristled, but managed to force my irritation down. "I—yeah. I wanted to apologize for last time, pulling you into my dream and—"

"Please." Karayan waved my apology away, impatient. "You want something. Just get to it already." I took a deep breath, and let it out. This was the moment of truth. Karayan studied me, suddenly looking interested. "Hm. Things are about to get juicy, I can tell."

"I need to know how to get someone to tell me a secret in their dream."

Karayan tilted her head. "Well, that could be easier or harder depending on how strongly this person feels about keeping their secret, you know, *secret*."

"But it's possible?"

"Oh, yeah. Totally possible."

"And," I dropped my eyes, "is there a way to keep the dreamer from remembering?"

Karayan shrugged. "If you're sure that's what you want to do."

"I don't have much of a choice," I said.

"Okay. Who pissed you off? Dish," Karayan said. "Wait, let me guess. That little blond from your school. What's her name? Treesap?"

"It's not Amber." I shifted my weight, trying to keep my anxiety at bay. "Are you going to tell me how to do this or not?"

"Tit for tat, sweetie." Karayan crossed her arms and gave me a flat smile.

"Fine. It's Lucas." If I'd been in the real world, I'd have blushed. But here, I had more control.

Karayan's eyebrows jumped. "Really? The golden boy's keeping secrets, is he? Not stepping out on you?"

"It's not like—" I stopped myself. I didn't have to defend Lucas to her. "It's not actually any of your business."

Karayan's eyes flicked away. Wait. Had I hurt her *feelings?* "Whatever. I get my fix of teenage drama on TV."

"So, can we get to it, then?" I asked.

"So testy." Karayan held up a hand as I started to respond. "Lesson the first. The easy part—and you should keep in mind that none of this is easy—will be getting him to tell you his secret."

"Okay, how do I do that?"

"It'll be way easier if he doesn't become lucid. Which means you need to slip into his dream and let his mind direct the action." Karayan gave me a suggestive smile. "But I'm guessing that's something you're already familiar with."

"But if he's in control, how do I get the secret out of him?"

"You see the problem. My suggestion? Get him thinking about it before you show yourself in his dream."

"How am I supposed to do that?"

"Well, unless you want to tell me what this secret you're hoping to learn is, that's something you'll have to figure out on your own."

I bit my lip, thinking. Fine. I could work it out. *Without* telling Karayan anything about the vessel or the ritual. "What about keeping him from remembering?"

"Again, much easier if he doesn't become lucid. A memory is like a weed." Karayan gestured in the air, and a tiny pink flower appeared in midair, hovering over the ground, complete from petals to roots. "Once it's planted in the mind, it has a chance to spread."

She lowered her hand and the flower floated to the ground. As it made contact with the earth, the roots dug in. A moment later, another flower sprouted, then another, and another. Karayan waved at the flowers in a gesture that said, "you see?" She knelt beside the first flower.

"If you don't want the memory to survive, you have to pull it out by the roots—meaning you can't leave even a little bit of it behind." Karayan grabbed the flower, her fist closing around the base of the stem like a vise. She pulled it out of the earth. But instead of the simple root system the flower had had moments ago, these roots kept coming. Karayan pulled until first one, then two, then all of the other pink flowers came out of the dirt, the last thread of root trailing free a moment later. "Done and done," Karayan said, satisfied.

"So, I'm looking for a flower?" I asked.

Karayan gave me a look of pure exasperation. "Seriously? It's a *metaphor*, Braedyn. It helps to visualize the memory as a physical thing, so you have something to grab onto."

"How will I know I'm grabbing the right memory?"

Karayan folded her arms. "You're Lilitu. Trust me, you'll know."

"Well, what if I—"

"Lesson's over," Karayan said. "Now go. Conquer." She gave me a grim smile. "And, you're welcome."

With that, I felt a slight pushing sensation. I let Karayan shove me out of her dream. It wasn't worth resisting her right now. Outside of Karayan's dream, I let myself float in the formless expanse of the infinite dream for a moment. It was peaceful watching the tide of dreams swirl in the vastness. They moved like a distant city of fireflies, all going about their own individual lives. I wondered, if I became human, would I still be able to visit this place? Or would I be relegated to my own individual dream for the rest of my life? The thought unsettled me. Pushing it to the back of my mind, I returned to my garden.

I didn't feel any more prepared than I had a few minutes ago, but time was a luxury I couldn't afford to waste. I urged a pool of the infinite dream to gather at my feet, then called Lucas's dream to me. It rose out of the glassy pool, and I could sense Lucas—his essential stubborn, passionate *loyalty*. Before I closed my hand around his dream, I took a moment to ask Lucas for forgiveness for what I was about to do.

I touched the surface of his dream. In it, Lucas was wandering through a crazy house. Its walls and windows connected at odd angles, shifting when his attention moved away from them. Staircases and hallways led everywhere, and each door seemed to open up a vast wing of the house previously unexplored. It felt strange, watching him in his private dream without his knowledge. Voyeuristic. Invasive. But I had a job to do.

First things first. How to make him think of the vessel? As I pictured it in my mind, one wall of the house took on the squiggly lines and symbols we'd seen covering the vase in the photograph. Lucas, walking by the wall, stopped to study it. As he did, the symbols on the wall clarified, changing slightly from what I remembered. Lucas's unconscious mind had taken the hint.

I had to trust that this would work. If it didn't, I'd have wasted one of the very few nights we had left before the full moon. I closed my hand around the dream, and slipped into Lucas's unconscious mind. Instead of steering his sleeping thoughts to lucidity, I let his dream place me, like a prop, where it willed.

I found myself standing beside Lucas, holding his hand, studying the strange wall. Lucas glanced at me, as though I had been there the whole time.

"It's weird," he said. "I know this somehow."

I wanted to speak, to ask him how he knew it, but his dream was in control, and so instead I said, "Let's go back, Lucas. I'm frightened."

"This—I think this is important," Lucas said. He touched the wall, and it fell away, revealing a set of stairs leading down.

My interest piqued, I wanted to peer into the blackness below. But dream-me hesitated, needing Lucas to lead her forward.

"It's okay," he said. "I'm here with you."

Dream-me squeezed his hand harder and followed him down into the darkness. When we reached the bottom of the stairs, Lucas flipped a switch. We were standing in the Guard's armory.

Dream-me looked confused. "What are we doing here?" she asked, finally echoing my actual thoughts.

"Wait here," he said. And I was forced to hover by the stairs anxiously while Lucas walked to the back of the armory. He did something to one of the support posts, and I realized it wasn't actually supporting anything. It swung up, revealing a small hole under the floor. "I need your help," Lucas called.

Dream-me walked tentatively over to join him, even though I would have run if I were in control. There, in the hole, was a small brass box covered with the same curving designs that we'd seen in the photograph of the vessel.

"Should you be showing that to me?" Dream-me asked. I could have screamed. Lucas looked stricken. He released the post and it swung back, covering the hole and hiding the box from sight.

Something changed in Lucas's eyes. "Braedyn?"

The dream world rocked, and I found I was able to move my own body. *Oh no. He's becoming lucid.*

"Lucas," I said. "It's okay. Let's go upstairs."

But Lucas looked around, saw where we were standing... remembered. "No. No," he breathed. "What—what did you do?"

"I'm sorry," I whispered.

"I promised," he said. "I promised not to show you. You can't go after it, Braedyn. Please, tell me you'll forget about this."

I turned away from him, struggling for the calm I'd need to visualize Karayan's memory flower.

Lucas grabbed my arm, turning me to face him. Panic swept across his face. "Murphy... he begged me to keep you safe. I can't believe I—" His eyes seemed to clear. "You invaded my dream—tricked me. You made me *betray* the *Guard*."

The earth rocked under my feet, but Lucas didn't seem to notice.

"Braedyn?" Lucas's grip tightened on my arm. He searched my expression with urgent need.

"I had to," I whispered.

Lucas released me. A roiling fury chased the devastation out of his eyes. "No. No. Promise me you won't go after it."

"Lucas—"

"Promise me! I need to hear you say it." When I couldn't answer, Lucas stepped back away from me, his face contorting with agony. "I can't believe this is happening. How could I have been so stupid?!"

"It's not your fault."

"It is my fault! I'm the one who—" Lucas turned aside, running a hand through his hair. "Okay, no. We'll move it. I'll just tell them and they'll move it, somewhere safe. Somewhere I won't know to look for it."

Even in the dream, I felt hot tears stinging my eyes. Lucas read my expression and stopped pacing.

"What—why are you looking at me like that?" he asked.

"I'm sorry, Lucas. But you won't remember any of this."

"What does that mean? Braedyn?"

Instead of answering, I squeezed my eyes shut and visualized the same flower Karayan had used. The terrible metaphor. I felt something twist in the dream and opened my eyes. The flower bloomed in the cement at my feet, one perfect pink flower. And then it spread, shooting across the basement floor like wildfire, fueled by

Lucas's lucid mind. I grabbed the first flower and pulled.

Lucas doubled over, gripping his head. A terrible scream tore itself out of his throat.

I almost released the flower. But the blooms were already spreading up the stairs. "I'm sorry," I said.

Lucas shook his head, as if his thoughts were suddenly fuzzy. But then his eyes snapped to my face, and I saw realization there. "No. *Don't*. Braedyn, please. *Don't do this to me.*"

I had to work fast. I started pulling. It didn't take as much effort as I'd thought it would. But the roots were deep, and they seemed to spread almost as fast as I could pull them out.

Lucas stumbled to his knees, clutching his head so hard his knuckles went white. "Stop," he panted. "If you love me, please stop. I'm begging you—"

"I can't, Lucas," I said, fighting the urge to give in to him. "I'm doing this for us."

Tangled ropes of roots looped along the cement at my feet, but I was gaining ground against the memory. It had stopped spreading up the stairs. Flowers yanked up out of the cement floor one after another, leaving a scarred mass of dirt and rubble in their wake. It was as though I were pulling the string out of a sweater, creating a bigger and bigger hole.

Lucas had grown quiet. He was watching me with a numb, questioning look.

When I had pulled the last thready root out of the ground, I stopped. Lucas looked up at me, eyes misted over. I'd done it.

Nausea swept through me.

I turned, pushing through the wall of his dream, desperate to escape.

Karayan was waiting in my dream garden.

"So?" She asked. "How did it—?"

"*Why didn't you tell me it would be like that?!*" I screamed. Something inside me broke, and I fell to the ground, wanting to retch, unable to expel anything from this dream body.

Karayan stood over me, silent for a long moment. When I'd stopped heaving, she spoke. "What did you expect?" Her voice was low, strained. "You took something precious from someone who didn't want to give it to you. Of course it was going to be painful."

I looked up, and found Karayan staring down at me, eyes dark and unreadable.

"*Get out.*"

"Braedyn," Karayan said, pity welling in her eyes. She reached a hand out, placed it on my back. "I'm sure whatever reason you—"

I found the tiny pinprick break in my dream's shield and closed it. Karayan winked out.

I was alone again. But the silence did not bring me peace. And then I looked up, and a fresh wave of terror rolled through me.

My roses. The last bit of white was gone from them—replaced by a thin line of black that edged the top of each crimson petal. I lurched to my feet, horrified. Petal after petal... each and every one of them now carried the taint of my betrayal.

14

I lurched awake in my bed, covered with a cold sheen of sweat. Nausea swelled inside me—and this time, my body responded. I stumbled out of my room, barely making it to the bathroom in time. My stomach heaved over and over, as though it could expel this new taint by sheer effort of will.

After half an hour, I leaned back against the wall, wrung out in every way possible. The cold tile felt soothing against my bare legs, even though goose pimples crawled up the skin of my arms. I sat in the dark bathroom, each detail as clear to me as it would have been in broad daylight. A Lilitu's night vision. Deep, hopeless rage boiled inside me. *I was a demon. Why had I ever let myself believe I'd be capable of winning my redemption?* I closed my eyes as another thought stabbed through me. *Why hadn't I taken Sansenoy up on his offer the first time around?* I'd had the chance to become human. It was pure arrogance to turn it down, to believe that I'd be able to hang onto my humanity long enough to make a difference in this war.

I stayed on the bathroom floor until I heard Dad stirring in his room down the hall. It took more effort than I expected to pull myself to my feet. I swooned, catching myself on the sink before I fell. I was weak. Of course. I'd used my Lilitu powers on Lucas, and I'd done nothing to replenish the energy I'd spent. I was depleted. I looked up into my reflection in the bathroom mirror. I didn't need to turn on a light to see the deep circles under my eyes. I pulled open a drawer of the vanity, looking for the compact I'd bought with Cassie last summer. The one that matched my pale skin. I straightened in front of the mirror and began the work of hiding my exhaustion.

Twenty minutes later, dressed for school, I headed downstairs. Dad and Seth were sitting at the kitchen island, eating breakfast. Coffee brewed on the counter, filling the kitchen with a friendly aroma. The warm scent used to comfort me, but it didn't do anything to ease the pain in my chest today.

"How about some toast?" Dad asked. "Gretchen brought over this new jam she discovered. It's—" he picked up the jar and read the label. "Blueberry jalapeno preserves."

Seth grinned. "I know. It sounds disgusting. But it's kind of awesome."

"No, thanks," I said. "Not really hungry."

Dad stood, swiping a newspaper off the kitchen counter. "Suit yourself, kiddo. I've got to check in at the office."

"The office? Really?" I looked up with surprise. Dad used to run a security firm in town, but he'd let most of his contracts go since the day he'd told me I was a Lilitu. I guess I knew he still kept a business office, but I hadn't seen him visit it in months.

"For the Guardsmen," he said by way of explanation. "Town's small enough that someone's bound to notice a flood of new residents who don't seem to have jobs and spend their days wandering the streets. This will give them a uniform and a cover story. Private security, keeping the community safe."

"Right," I said.

Dad leaned over and kissed me on the forehead. "Take it easy today, honey. You look tired." With that, he left, grabbing his keys from the counter on his way out. A few moments later, we heard the front door open and close.

Seth glanced at me, eyes eagerly scanning my face. "So? Did you find out where they're keeping it?"

"Um—" The memory of last night rose in my thoughts so powerfully it blinded me for a moment. I took a shaking breath.

"Braedyn?" Seth watched me, his brows knitting together with concern.

"I have to—I'll be back," I mumbled. I pushed past Seth and raced for the front door, yanking it open. The morning chill was shocking. I stepped onto the porch and slammed the door shut behind me with more force than I'd intended.

I hurried across the yard, slipping through the gate that separated our property from the Guard's. The front door was locked. Surprised, I knocked.

I heard the bolt unlatch. A strange man opened the door. He had close cropped hair and wore jeans and a black T-shirt that stretched across his broad chest. He gave me a curious look, tossing a towel over his shoulder nonchalantly.

"You need something?"

"Is—is Lucas here?" I asked.

"Oh, right—you must be Braedyn." The stranger grinned, then turned to shout over his shoulder. "Hey, kid! Your girlfriend's here." He opened the door wider to let me in. "He's in the kitchen."

I entered the foyer, then stopped. I almost turned and fled. The living room was teeming with guys I'd never seen before. The furniture had been pushed up against the walls, and a series of cots spread out over the floor. But the most jarring change was the atmosphere in the house. Instead of the calm focus I was used to, there was a sort of raucous camaraderie between the men that made *me* feel like the stranger.

"I know. They showed up last night." Lucas joined me in the foyer, frowning at the newcomers.

As we stood there, a pair of guys walked into the foyer. "Have fun at school, kids," one said, reaching a hand out to ruffle Lucas's hair.

"Don't." Lucas recoiled, furious. A few other guys laughed good-naturedly from the living room. Lucas's cheeks reddened.

"Easy, little man," the stranger said. "You should enjoy it. I wish I could go back to the care-free days of high school."

"Damn straight." The other guy clapped a hand on Lucas's shoulder. "Hold onto your innocence as long as you can. There'll be plenty of time for the big fight later." The men walked off into the kitchen.

Lucas fumed, reaching a hand up to smooth down his hair.

"Yikes," I breathed.

"Yeah. Turns out, I like Guardsmen a whole lot better when there are only a few of them around," Lucas muttered. He took a deep breath, then turned his attention to me. "So, what's up? Are we leaving early today?"

"I just—" I unclenched my hands, trying to relax. "How are you feeling?"

Lucas sighed. "Yeah, I'm sorry. I know I've been kind of grouchy. I just needed some time."

"Time. Right." I tried keep my voice level, afraid to show too much concern. "But, how are you feeling today?"

"You mean besides under-appreciated and demeaned?" Lucas's eyes cut back to the living room, full of new Guardsmen lounging and goofing off. "I don't know. Groggy, actually. I don't think I slept very well." He gave me a sheepish smile and lowered his voice. "Maybe this no dream-visit thing's not such a good idea after all." I smiled. Lucas misinterpreted my relief. "Yeah. I've missed our dreams, too."

Hale appeared at the top of the stairs, buttoning up his shirt. He saw me and nodded a greeting. "Morning, Braedyn." He glanced around, then gave me a pointed look. "Maybe you two should be getting off to school?"

"Good idea," I said.

"I'll just get my bag." Lucas raced up the stairs past Hale.

When Hale reached the foyer, one of the men saw him and snapped to attention. Instantly, the others followed suit. Conversation abruptly ended. All eyes focused on Hale. "At ease," he said. The men relaxed, but no one spoke. "We're patrolling in teams of four today," Hale said. "Gretchen will work out the rotation. Get some breakfast, first patrol leaves in 10 minutes."

This was the order they'd been waiting for. Their idle conversation was replaced with purpose, and in moments, most of the men were heading to the kitchen.

Hale saw my curiosity. "We're still looking for the man who broke into Seth's house," he said. "But now, with the added numbers, we've got a much better shot of finding him. Seth gave us a pretty good description, and Jeremy used to work as a sketch artist in North Carolina. Here. Look familiar?" Hale picked up a drawing off the entry table near the door. I hadn't noticed it before, but as I took it from Hale I recognized the face of the man who'd set Angela's life's work on fire.

"That's him." I found myself rooted to the floor.

"We're going to find him," Hale said, taking the image from me gently.

Lucas came down the stairs, slinging a backpack over his shoulder. "Ready?" he asked, not waiting for me to answer before escaping through the front door.

Hale sighed. "It's going to take some getting used to," he said in a low voice. He glanced toward the kitchen, now flooded with around two dozen Guardsmen. "For all of us." His eyes returned to my face.

The first sign of trouble came at lunch. Royal, Cassie, Seth, and I all showed up at roughly the same time, having just gotten out of physics together. So we were digging into a tray of steaming lasagna by the time Lucas arrived.

He dropped into his chair wordlessly. His face looked ashen.

"Dude, what's eating you?" Seth asked. "You look like a zombie."

"I'm pretty sure I bombed my history test," Lucas said. "Which sucks because I studied for it all weekend long."

I felt a clenching fist of fear grip my stomach. I looked down at my lasagna before Lucas could see it in my eyes.

"I should have just gone out to a movie," Lucas said. "Sometimes I don't know why I try. I'm not cut out for academics."

"What is that supposed to mean?" Cassie asked, putting her fork down.

"It means he had a bad day, and he's licking his wounds," Royal answered. "Because he knows you'd kick his butt if he suggested he wasn't smart enough for school. Right, Lucas?"

"Right," Lucas said. "You can stand down, Cass." I could hear the grudging grin in his voice.

I looked up. Royal was staring directly at me. I might have hid my fear from Lucas, but Royal had read me like a book.

After lunch, I stayed behind to clear our table. I knew that look in Royal's eye. If he managed to corner me, he was going to dig and dig until he heard an answer that satisfied him. My best bet was to put a little distance between us and hope he'd forget or lose interest in his suspicions. It didn't work. I walked out of the dining hall and found him waiting for me, lounging on the low brick wall of a school planter.

"So what was that all about?" He held up a finger before I could speak. "And let's skip the part where you play dumb."

"I've got it under control." I pulled my sweater tighter around my shoulders, but the chill spreading down my spine wasn't due to the surprisingly mild December day.

"Ah." Royal looked at me sharply. "So the *something* is a Lilitu thing."

"Royal," I hissed. No one was close enough to hear us, but that didn't soothe my frayed nerves.

"Something you're afraid to tell Lucas." Royal scrutinized me with ruthless focus.

"Can we do this later? I'm going to be late to class." I tried to walk past him. He stepped into my path, blocking me.

"What was the point of the whole 'hey, I'm a teenage demon' share-fest if you're going to shut me out now?" he asked. This time he kept his voice low. I looked into his face and saw genuine concern. "Something's going on," he said. "It's pulling you away from me and Cassie. It's pulling you away from Lucas. Are you sure you want to be driving all your friends out of your life?"

I dropped my eyes. His words stung. "I just—I just need to get through this week," I said. "Then things can go back to normal."

"Just like that?" Royal asked, snapping his fingers. I bit my lip, unsure. Royal sighed. "I thought you and Lucas were two peas in your own little supernatural pod. What could be so bad that you can't tell him?"

Another pair of kids exited the dining hall behind us. We waited in silence for them to pass. When they were out of earshot, I turned back to Royal. "I think I hurt him," I said.

"Hurt?" Royal eyed me, suddenly uncomfortable. "Not—you didn't—?"

"Sleep with him?" I smiled bitterly. "I'm pretty sure if I'd done that you'd be able to tell."

"So what did you do?" Royal looked sickly fascinated.

"It doesn't matter," I said. "I hurt him and I don't know how to make it right. Or if I can make it right." My voice dropped to a whisper. "I don't know what to do."

"Talk to him," Royal said. Instead of answering, I shook my head. "Okay. Think this through. Did you mean to hurt him?" Royal asked.

"No, of course not!" I snapped. Then, when some part of me rebelled against this half-truth, I shook my head. "I didn't realize it would turn out like this. I never wanted to cause him pain."

"So tell him that," Royal said, like it was the most obvious idea in the world.

I stared at Royal. "You don't understand," I said. "Lucas can *never* know what I've done."

Royal shook his head. "I think you're underestimating how much that guy likes you." He turned and walked away.

Why do you think I can't tell him? I asked in my head as I watched Royal walk away. Lucas's love was one of the truly good things in my life. I needed him. It wasn't just that I'd stolen the secret of the vessel from him, or that I'd ripped the memory of my crime out of his mind. I'd made Lucas give up the one thing he'd sworn to Hale and my father he'd protect. I'd made him betray the Guard. And if he ever found out, I'd lose him for good.

Seth eyed me all day, clearly eager to get me alone. I wasn't ready to tell him what I'd learned about the vessel. I'd stolen the secret from Lucas. It didn't feel like it was mine to share. Seth didn't seem to see it that way. I ran into him in the hall between fifth and sixth period, and he pulled me aside before I could enter my trigonometry class. The hall emptied as students entered their classrooms, leaving us mostly alone in the hall.

"So, we didn't get a chance to finish our conversation this morning."

"Our conversation?" I asked, feigning distraction.

"The vessel." Seth prompted. "Did you find out where it is or not?"

"Braedyn? In or out?" Ms. Yates, my trig teacher, called from the doorway.

"Sorry," I said to Seth, concealing the relief I felt. "See you next period?" I followed Ms. Yates into her class without looking back. I couldn't stomach his anticipation. In an effort to avoid him, I made sure I was late to English. I arrived as Mr. Avila started writing notes on the board.

"Braedyn, nice of you to join us. Have a seat." Mr. Avila waited until I'd dropped into a desk in the front row to turn back to the board. I dug in my backpack for the reading assignment, catching a glimpse of Seth's face a few rows back. I shrugged, feigning helplessness. Seth gave me a faint smile. I couldn't tell if he guessed I was trying to avoid him or not. I spent the rest of class staring at the board, but keenly aware of Seth's eyes boring holes into the back of my head.

When the bell rang at the end of seventh period, I took my time packing things up. Seth stopped by my desk, as determined as he'd been that morning.

"I need to talk to Mr. Avila," I said. "Meet you at the car?"

Seth glanced at Mr. Avila and back to me, confused and more than a little frustrated. "Sure."

I took my book to the front of the class. Mr. Avila looked up from his desk. "Sorry about coming in late," I said.

Mr. Avila looked a little surprised. "Thank you for the apology." I felt Seth lingering in the doorway; I couldn't leave just yet. Mr. Avila sat back in his chair. "Is there something else?"

My mind cast around for something to say. "I was thinking about doing an independent study on Shakespeare next year," I said.

Mr. Avila's eyes lit up. "That's a wonderful idea. I actually thought your essay on *Twelfth Night* had some very astute observations. Are you looking for a faculty advisor? I'd love to help you, but you should also talk to Dr. Gloer. She did her PhD on the nature of love and passion in Shakespeare's England, believe it or not. Did you have her for English freshman year?"

As we talked, Seth gave up and left. By the end of my conversation with Mr. Avila, I had half-convinced myself that I really wanted to do this independent study I'd pulled out of thin air just moments earlier. Mr. Avila gave me Dr. Gloer's email address and promised to talk to her about me at the staff meeting later this week.

I made my way to the parking lot. Lucas and Seth were standing by my car, talking. They looked up as I arrived.

"Sorry, didn't mean for that to take so long," I said. My voice came out a bit too cheerfully, but neither Seth nor Lucas called me out. I drove us back to my house. As we were getting out of the car, two Guardsmen raced up the block and into the Guard's house.

"Where's the fire?" Seth asked.

"Seriously." Lucas stared at his house, uneasy. "Maybe we should check it out, make sure everything's okay." We walked into the Guard's house. Two of the newcomers stood guard in the foyer.

"Sorry, kids," one said. "You'd better hang at Murphy's today."

"We've got practice," Lucas said, bristling. He tried to push past the Guardsmen. They stepped closer together, blocking his path.

"Practice is cancelled." Sam entered from the living room, carrying an old leather satchel that looked like it had seen a lot of abuse. As he shifted it in his grip, I heard the sound of metal objects clanging together. It gave me the creeps. Sam glanced down the hallway leading to the basement, then back at Lucas. "You might want to crash at Murphy's tonight, too."

"What's going on?" I asked.

"Gretchen?" Lucas started, trying to push into the house. "Where's Gretchen?!"

"She's fine. But we're all a little busy right now." Sam turned to the two guards with a stern look. "Just get them out of here." Without another word to us, he disappeared down the basement stairs.

"Something's wrong." I strained to see past the guards. "Is someone hurt?"

"Not yet," one of the guards said. The other one smirked.

I felt my blood run cold. "What does that mean?"

The guards exchanged a glance. "Sorry," the taller one said. "Orders are to send you to Murphy's."

"This is my house," Lucas snapped. "You can't send me away."

"Lucas, do as they ask." Dad entered from the living room, looking haggard. His eyes found mine. Something *was* going on—something he didn't want me to see. "You shouldn't be here for this. I'll come home as soon as I can."

Lucas looked consumed by curiosity, but he couldn't say no to my dad. Seth, Lucas, and I left together, walking across the yard into my house in silence.

When we reached my living room, Seth voiced the question I was thinking. "Do you think they caught the incubus?"

"No way," Lucas said. "They'd have said something. Whatever they've got in the basement, they don't want us to know about it." He looked at me askance.

"Lucas," I breathed. With a sickening twist of fear, I pictured Karayan, broken and bleeding on the basement floor, ringed around by Guardsmen. "What if it's Karayan?"

Lucas's lips tightened. He didn't like Karayan, but she'd saved all our lives the night Ais had died. And whatever he might feel for her, he didn't like the thought of her at the mercy of the Guardsmen any more than I did.

"Who's Karayan?" Seth asked.

Lucas and I looked at one another, searching for the right answer. After a moment, I turned to Seth. "A friend." I glanced back at Lucas. He nodded. "I have to know, Lucas."

Lucas blanched. "You can't go over there."

"If I cloaked myself—?"

"No," Lucas said, catching my hand. "Even if they don't have a spotter over there—" He swallowed, looking sick. "You're not going to be able to get her out. You'll just get yourself—" He stopped. But I didn't need to hear the words to know what he was thinking.

"You guys think—you think they're going to kill someone?" Seth asked.

"We don't even know if it's her they've got," Lucas said.

"I'm going to find out." I turned my thoughts to Karayan, composing my mind.

I could feel the barrier between physical reality and dream reality like a shifting curtain. I closed my eyes and pictured pushing against it, meaning to step into the dream to find her. Instead, I felt myself divide into a physical Braedyn and a dream Braedyn, both tied together by my consciousness. It was a uniquely disorienting feeling - I felt like I was halfway between realities. I could sense my body, even as I watched it from outside. And - from this *in-between* perspective - I could also see the vast darkness of the universal dream, swirling with the pinpoints of billions of minds, some awake, some asleep.

I sensed Karayan in my conscious mind, and *felt* her notice me. Suddenly we were together in this in-between space.

Braedyn?

Karayan? Is that you?

You called me, I felt her exasperation through our connection. *I wasn't aware you could drunk dial via telepathy.*

I breathed out in a rush, my body giving voice to my amazement. Seth and Lucas looked at me.

"What? What is it?" Lucas asked.

"I'm talking to her right now," I said.

"Talking?" Lucas gaped at me. I held up a finger. It took all my concentration to maintain the connection.

Are you okay? I asked Karayan.

Yeah... are you okay? There was a slightly mocking tone to her voice, but I didn't care.

"She's okay," I told the guys. Lucas's face eased, and I felt a surge of warmth toward him.

Is there a point to this little tête-à-tête? Karayan's impatience was almost palpable.

The Guardsmen captured someone, I explained. *We were afraid it was you.*

You're checking up on me? I felt Karayan's surprise through our link. And, more than that, I could feel that she was moved by my concern.

Not that it makes us BFFs or anything, I said. And through our link, I could feel Karayan's soft chuckle. *But if they don't have you,* I asked, *who could it be? Are there any other Lilitu here?*

I felt a hesitation, sensed that Karayan knew something and was debating whether or not she wanted to tell me. Finally, I felt her give a resigned sigh. *Not yet.*

That sounds ominous, I replied.

The Lilitu know the final battle is coming sooner rather than later. Like, a lot sooner. And Puerto Escondido is ground zero. In fact, now might be a good time to pack up all your little Guard friends and get the hell out of town.

Nice try, but we've got some unfinished business here.

Don't say I didn't warn you.

How many are coming?

I don't know, Karayan replied. *A lot.*

When you say a lot, what are we talking? Ten? Fifty?

You're not ready for this, Karayan answered grimly. *Almost all of the Lilitu in this world are gearing up for war. That's got to be over 200.*

Two hundred? I felt my breath rush out of my lungs sharply. Lucas and Seth watched me with concern, but I shook my head. I needed to finish this conversation.

Two hundred on this side of the seal, Karayan corrected. *There could be thousands on the other side, lining up for the moment that thing pops open.* For a long moment, my mind was too numb to form a response. I felt Karayan's worry. *Braedyn? You still there?*

We can't fight that many, I told her, feeling faint.

Yeah. I felt her smile humorlessly. *I believe I've already said something to that effect.*

I closed my eyes, steeling myself against the panic that threatened to overwhelm me. *Be careful,* I urged. *The Guard is coming here, too. They'll be stepping up patrols. If you don't want to end up in their basement, you need to stay out of sight.*

What about you? she asked. For once, there was no snarky edge to her voice. *What are you going to do when those spotters get to town? Because, if memory serves, keeping a pet Lilitu is kind of one of the Guard's big no-nos. And you're not going to be able to hide from them, living right next door.*

I trust Hale, I said.

I can't say I share your faith in the Guard. But then she added, grudgingly, *Though, if they're smart, they'll recognize what a powerful ally they have in you.*

Karayan, you could join us, I started.

No.

So you're on their side? I couldn't keep the judgment out of my thoughts, but if Karayan sensed it, she didn't seem to care.

I'm on my side, she said. *Perfectly content with my seat on this fence.*

So what's the plan? Just wait the battle out, see who wins?

I couldn't have put it better myself.

You're going to have to pick a side eventually.

I guess we'll have to agree to disagree about that, she said. *Take care of yourself, Braedyn.*

I released the connection, letting my consciousness flood back into physical reality. Karayan's presence faded from my mind. Lucas and Seth waited on pins and needles. I wished I had better news for them.

Dad came home the next morning to find us slumped on the couch, asleep. We'd tried to wait up for him, finally passing out sometime after two o'clock. I'd fallen into a dreamless sleep. It was rare, but it gave my mind a chance to rest.

Dad didn't look like he'd had any sleep. He gathered us into the dining room. We sat around the table, rubbing our eyes.

"They caught the Thrall," Dad said.

Lucas and I traded a look, suddenly awake.

"What—what did she say?" Seth asked. "Did she tell you who the incubus is?"

"She was a Thrall," Dad said gently. "She didn't say much."

"What about Gretchen? Could she sense any kind of connection between the Thrall and whoever turned her?" Lucas asked.

Dad shook his head, solemn. "It seems like Thane was right. Incubi seem to operate on a different... *frequency* than regular Lilitu."

"But—you were gone all night," I said, stunned. "Didn't you learn anything from her at all?"

"Yes. We learned two things." Dad took a moment to compose himself. "Seth, the first thing we managed to get out of her—this Thrall was the one who killed your mom. There's no doubt in our minds now, the incubus was behind Angela's death."

Seth stared at Dad. It didn't come as a surprise to us, but hearing the confirmation of our suspicions still hurt. He cleared his throat. "Did she say why?"

"Yeah. That's the second thing we learned." Dad folded his hands. It almost looked like he was getting ready to pray. "For the last several years, Angela's been researching rumors of a mythical weapon. That research led her to the story about the incubus who attacked the mission all those centuries ago."

Seth's hands tightened on the edge of the couch with every word Dad spoke. "Yeah, that weird knife. She was obsessed with it for a while. But, I don't understand. What does that have to do with—?"

"We think the incubus is here for that weapon. We think he believes it is the one way to secure victory for the Lilitu. And Angela was the only human alive who knew where it was hidden."

Five days left until the solstice, and we were no closer to finding the incubus than we'd been the day Angela had first told us about him.

That afternoon, after they'd recovered from their grueling night, I told Dad, Hale, and Gretchen about the conversation I'd had with Karayan. They listened to me carefully, sitting around our dining room table. I could see the fear gripping each of them as I related what Karayan had told me. Two hundred Lilitu on this side of the seal, untold numbers on the other side. All waiting for someone to open the seal so they could flood into this world and reclaim what they saw as their birthright. And yet, even after I'd explained everything, the Guard still wouldn't agree that the ritual—our only known chance of keeping that seal closed—was the right move.

"We have to wait for Clay," Dad insisted.

"For how much longer?" I asked, exasperated.

"The solstice isn't for another five days. We can wait a little while longer," Dad said.

"And if we miss our window?" I asked, frustrated.

"Right now, our primary goal has to be keeping that weapon out of the incubus's hands," Hale said. "There will be another window."

I stared at him, stricken. "Yeah, in *20 years*."

Hale looked at his hands, miserable. "The point is, this solstice is not our last chance to attempt the ritual, once we've had time to research it properly."

"But it's *my* last chance," I said. "You want my help to defeat the Lilitu, right? So let me help. Locking the seal could make a real difference in this war." Hale wouldn't meet my eyes. "Dad?" I turned to Dad. He couldn't look at me either. "Dad, please."

Dad stood abruptly. "I can't," he said hoarsely, but he looked at Hale as he said it. Hale nodded, and Dad left the room.

I turned back to Hale. "Why?" It was all I could manage.

"We've been fooled before," Hale said simply. "Whenever something looks too good to be true, it usually is."

"No." Tears burned in my eyes. "Not this time. This time it's real."

"We can't know that," Hale started.

I stood, ready to blurt out everything. That I had the ingredients for the ritual. That I knew where the vessel was. That all I needed was his blessing, and I could bring this whole nightmare to an end. But something stopped me. I could see it in his face. Whoever this Clay was, Hale wouldn't risk going against him, even if not acting meant losing the war.

"Screw it," I muttered. I turned to leave. "I'm going to get something to eat."

"Braedyn," Hale called. "Stop. There's something else we have to discuss."

"What more is there to say?" I snapped, pausing at the entrance to the foyer.

"I'm calling the spotters back."

Icy fear flooded into my veins. "Am I supposed to move into the attic or something?"

"No. We're going to station them at the edge of town with small units of Guardsmen. As far as the Lilitu are concerned, this is now a closed city. No one in, and no one out."

I heard Dad on the stair behind me and turned. He saw my distress and opened his arms wordlessly. I moved forward into his hug, holding onto him, trying to sear this feeling into my memory.

"So this is it. The final battle is beginning." The words felt strange on my tongue. One moment, the final battle was some abstract concept, some epic confrontation for the end of time. Then suddenly it was here, and the Guard wasn't ready to act.

As I hugged Dad, I felt a surge of determination. The Guard might not be ready, but *I was*.

You wouldn't think the end of the world was right around the corner. The Guard had stepped up patrols. We'd see them occasionally in town, walking the streets in pairs, looking for all the world like boys - albeit extremely fit ones - from the nearby college. They kept their daggers concealed beneath their jackets or stashed in their bags, ready should the need for weapons arise. Each day more and more arrived. They came in units of five or seven or 10, filling the Guard's house until the basement alone was lined with cots to sleep 50 soldiers.

When the first spotters arrived, Hale started housing teams in empty homes on the outskirts of town. Lucas started calling them the "outposts" and the name stuck. Dad left to check on the outposts every day. He'd make rounds, gather intelligence, deliver supplies. Each spotter was charged with patrolling the five block area surrounding her outpost. Gretchen was the spotter "assigned" to the five blocks that included my home and school. In that way, Hale insured the entire town was covered—and that none of the new spotters got the chance to lay eyes on me or my secret.

Seth and I were ready. We had everything we needed for the ritual, and I knew exactly where to go to find the vessel. Seth pressed me for its location once, but I shut him down. When the moment was right, I would get it. Until then, better to leave it undisturbed. He didn't look happy, but he dropped the subject after that. We had to perform the ritual on the solstice; Angela's notes were very clear about that. It started at dawn and wasn't complete until the light of the full moon struck the vessel that night.

So there was nothing for it but to wait. Only, the waiting was surreal. Everything else in my life was so achingly, beautifully, pedestrian. Dad insisted we continue going to school, and I can't say I minded. Holding onto that last bit of normalcy made the coming battle feel much more like a dream than a reality.

The one rule that I was forbidden to break was this: I couldn't tell anyone what was coming. Not Royal, not Cassie, no one. The Guard believed that knowing the truth would put civilians in more danger; Lilitu moved through the world silently, their attack was all seduction and manipulation. If we couldn't stop the incubus from getting his weapon, or the seal from opening—the end of the world would start very slowly. Better to let my friends go on, oblivious that the extinction of humanity had begun. The alternative—telling them the truth—would only paint a target on their backs.

And so each day of school became a bittersweet, living memorial to the lives we might soon be setting aside. I tried to push the ritual out of my mind. I wanted to immerse myself in every mundane detail of my life as the days to winter solstice dwindled. Three left. Two left. And then, only one.

Friday, in first period, Cassie gripped my hand tightly as the morning announcements were read. Fiedler reminded everyone to buy their tickets for the winter musical, opening tomorrow night.

"You're still coming to dress rehearsal tonight, right?" Cassie asked. She looked as nervous as Missy did.

I nodded. It seemed like the perfect way to keep my mind off the ritual.

The day went too quickly, slipping away even as I tried to stitch it into my memory. Seth, Lucas, and I shared a quiet dinner after school, killing time until the dress rehearsal began.

When we returned to campus at six, the sun was just dipping below the horizon in the west.

Inside, the theater was a bustle of energy and nerves. Cassie hovered by the glass doors to the lobby's entrance. She lit up when she saw us, and beckoned us inside.

"I've saved us some seats," she said. "Right in the center."

For a dress rehearsal, the theater was more crowded than I'd expected. We walked down the steps of one aisle and took our seats. I felt someone glaring at me. I looked around. Amber and Ally scowled down at me from a few rows behind. Of course they were here; they'd want to support their friend Missy. I turned my back to them, putting them out of my thoughts. I wasn't going to let them ruin tonight.

The lights dimmed, and the music began. I hadn't expected anything too spectacular, so I was completely transported by the musical that unfolded. Cassie's costumes were just one piece of an inspired production. Missy—I couldn't believe how well she sang. Lancelot was played by a sophomore guy I'd never paid much attention to before, but after this performance I was pretty sure he'd be mobbed by girls for the rest of his career at Coronado Prep. Even the new Mortimer was great.

Lucas took hold of my hand halfway through the first song, and we sat together, watching the show, sharing the warm energy of that simplest of touches.

When the lights came up for intermission, I turned to Cassie. No part of me had to force enthusiasm.

"Cassie, it's—it's amazing."

"You think so?" But she was beaming ear to ear. No one in that theater could deny it was a great show. "It's all Mr. Hart," she breathed. "He's the amazing one."

My enthusiasm dampened a little, but I shrugged this off. Out of the corner of my eye, I noticed Amber, sneaking out the back of the theater, dialing her cell. Her eyes snagged on me, and for half a second I saw the glimmer of something that sent an electric current of alarm through my body.

"Excuse me," I said. "I'll be right back."

Seth and Lucas turned to congratulate Cassie. I slipped out of the theater, looking for Amber in the lobby. She was nowhere to be seen. I glanced around, then caught a flash of motion through the glass doors at the entrance to the lobby.

Amber was pacing in front of the theater. I walked out of the building in time to catch the end of her conversation.

"Right. Just be careful. I owe you one." Amber hung up her cell with a self-satisfied smirk and turned back to the theater. When she saw me, she froze.

"What was that?" I asked.

Amber's smile broadened. She shrugged. "A private conversation."

She walked past me back to the theater. But before she opened the door she turned. "Oh, you're going to want to stick around. You won't want to miss the after-show." Amber reached for the handle, but I slapped the palm of my hand against the glass door, preventing her from pulling it open. "Not this again," she said. "I thought it was clear after the last time you tried—unsuccessfully—to threaten me. I don't negotiate with Lilitu."

"I'm not going to let you hurt another one of my friends."

"Yeah, you're kind of running low, aren't you?" She turned back to the door, dismissing me with a flip of her icy blond hair. I grabbed her chin and jerked her face back around until I could look into her eyes. I was about to demand an answer to my question—when I caught a glimmer of Amber's thoughts. It wasn't like the telepathic conversation I'd had with Karayan—because Amber wasn't interested in sharing any of her thoughts with me. She tried to shrink back, but I gripped her tighter. Amber whimpered.

I pressed the index finger of my free hand into the soft skin of her forehead. Images and thoughts spilled out of her mind. Amber tried to jerk free, but I refused to release her. I saw, through her minds eye—

Amber standing at her bathroom sink, looking at her reflection. Ripping the front of her shirt open, scattering buttons across the blue tile floor. Mussing her hair.

Then, *Amber crying in her brother's arms. She'd told him a story—that Lucas had tried to force himself on her. That he'd been stalking her, and wouldn't leave her alone.*

Then, *Amber in the living room of her house, with her big brother and three of his friends. Their faces darkened with anger as she recounted her story again, tearing up in all the right places, until the boys were whipped into a frenzy of rage.*

Then, *the plan taking shape. Amber reluctantly agreeing that something had to be done or who knows what Lucas might try next. And Amber warning them that Lucas was a good fighter, so they'd have to find a way to catch him off guard—and get him alone. Ally would lure Lucas into the trap. Amber would distract Braedyn while it went down. No witnesses. The boys agreed.*

I staggered back, releasing Amber. "You're going to get Lucas killed."

"They're not going to—" she started.

"*Liar*," I roared. "Get out of my way."

Amber shrank away from me, sliding out of my way. I grabbed the handle and wrenched the door open. She glared at me, still stubborn in her conviction. "You could have stopped all of this," she whispered.

If I hadn't been desperate to find Lucas, I don't think I could have kept myself from clawing her sanctimonious face off.

He wasn't in his seat.

Cassie and Seth looked at me strangely when I asked where Lucas was. I realized my voice was edging into hysteria.

"Um, Ally said something to him and he just left," Cassie said.

"Where?" I fought the panic rising in my chest. "Where did they go?"

Seth pointed to the side exit, the one that led to the loading dock. "I think they left that way."

The theater lights started to dim. I pushed my way through the row. When I got to the aisle, I ran straight for the door, throwing it open and charging into the night.

My eyes adjusted to the darkness almost instantly. I saw Lucas standing at the edge of the parking lot.

"Lucas!" I shouted. He turned, surprised.

A car sped around the side of the theater. Headlights caught Lucas, edging him in a blinding glare. Lucas threw up a hand to ward off the light, but the car didn't slow. It barreled straight for him, impacting with a sickening thud. Lucas rolled up and over the hood of the car, flying a good 10 feet into the air before landing on the ground.

"No!" My scream echoed down the loading dock. I raced forward. Before I could reach him, the car skidded to a stop and Amber's brother and his three friends jumped out. One of them had a bat. I pounded forward, choking down a breathless sob of fear.

The boys surrounded Lucas, who rolled to his side, stunned.

"Stay away from Amber," one of them said.

"What?" Lucas reached a hand up to his head. It came away bloody. "Amber?" He looked confused.

One of the boys kicked Lucas savagely in the stomach. He jackknifed with a breathless grunt of pain.

"Stop!" I screamed, reaching the circle of boys. I dropped beside

Lucas, shielding him with my body. "Stop. He didn't do anything."

"Stay out of this," Amber's brother said. "You don't know what you're talking about."

One of the other guys grabbed my arms, hauling me away from Lucas while the guy with the bat stepped up. I spun around, breaking out of his grip—but some instinct kept me from attacking.

"*Amber's a liar*," I said, using *the call* in a desperate attempt to get through to them. The boy standing over Lucas lowered his bat, looking down at Lucas as though seeing him for the first time.

"Dude—?" one of the other boys asked, turning to Amber's brother.

Amber's brother shook his head, fighting *the call*. "No. He tried to hurt her," he said. "She wouldn't make something like that up."

"**Lucas is innocent**," I insisted, willing the power of *the call* to penetrate his mind. It moved slowly, fighting the love he held for his sister. "*Ask your sister.*"

Amber's brother fought it with everything he had. But some part of him must have known she was capable of a lie like this—because after a long moment of struggle, he shook his head. "Yeah. We should ask her," he muttered.

They pulled back, retreating to their car.

I knelt back down to examine Lucas. He clutched his stomach, his breathing ragged.

"Lucas?"

"That sucked," he said. He looked up at me, eyes cloudy with pain. "I have no idea what that was about."

"I do," I said.

Lucas saw my expression. "No—" He shook his head, then winced. "Amber's a wreck, sure, but she's not a psycho."

"It was her, Lucas." The absolute conviction in my voice reached him. He nodded, then reached a hand out toward me. I took it, and helped pull him to a sitting position. A small patch of his hair was matted with blood.

"We need to get you to a hospital," I said.

"I'm fine."

"You got hit by a car."

"Yeah, I vaguely remember something about that." Lucas saw my exasperation and sighed. "Okay. Fine. Whatever you think is best—I just need a minute."

I fought the instinct to run my hands over his body, checking to make sure he was whole. Instead, I sat back, waiting for him to recover. I saw movement out of the corner of my eye. Amber was watching us from the corner of the loading dock. I was on my feet in a heartbeat.

"You," I hissed. Lucas glanced up at me, surprised by the venom in my voice.

"That was *the call*." She stared at me, sickly fascinated. Her mouth quirked up into a smirk. "Finally it all makes sense."

"You couldn't stop pushing," I growled. "Congratulations. You're about to see *exactly* how bad I can hurt you." Amber's smirk vanished. I tilted my head, studying her almost clinically. "You've tried so hard to drive me out of this school. It's going to be poetic justice when Fiedler expels you on Monday."

"In your dreams," she scoffed, but I could tell she was uneasy.

I laughed. The sound was low, guttural. Frightening.

"Fine," she said, struggling for bravado. "So I get kicked out of school. You think that's going to destroy me?"

"Oh right. Miss popular. You must have a pretty awesome social life to fall back on. Let's see what happens when every straight guy at this school decides he hates you." I took a step toward her. She skittered back away from me, watching me with widening eyes.

"You—you can't do that."

"I guess we'll find out soon, won't we?" I took another step toward Amber. She flinched. "I tried to take the high road," I said, my voice full of menace. "But now—you're about to see me get creative."

Amber turned and fled into the night. I heard a sharp breath and turned. Lucas was watching me with a strange expression on his face.

"Lucas?" Concerned, I dropped beside him once more. Lucas startled back, then smiled wryly.

"I keep forgetting how powerful you are," he said. "Remind me not to piss you off. Wouldn't want you using your powers on me."

His words bore a hole straight through my heart.

Lucas groaned and rolled to his knees. "You know," he said. "I think this hospital idea is worth exploring after all. Shall we?"

I helped him to his feet, using the moment to hide my expression before Lucas could see.

Gretchen met us at the hospital; I'd called her on the drive over. When we described the accident to the admitting nurse, she got Lucas in to see a doctor immediately. Gretchen and I took turns pacing the waiting room while the doctors ran Lucas through a variety of tests.

Finally, they called us back to his room.

"Mild concussion," a young doctor said. "We'd like to keep him overnight for observation, but if everything checks out in the morning, he'll be free to go home."

"Thank you," Gretchen said, finally letting herself relax.

"You're a very lucky kid," the doctor said to Lucas. "An accident like that, you could have fractured any number of bones, not the least of which is a vertebrae."

Gretchen closed her eyes, sick with the thought of what might have been.

"You're scaring my sister," Lucas said.

The doctor smiled and closed Lucas's chart, slipping it over the end of his bed. "Well. Time to get some rest." She glanced at us. "Are either of you staying the night?"

"I will," Gretchen said. She turned to me. "Could you go home and update the others?"

I nodded. Gretchen sat next to Lucas on the bed and gave him a gentle hug. I saw his eyes search me out as I left, and I nodded my goodbyes. He gave me a faint smile, but I could tell he was still shaken by the events of the evening. It felt like my place was here, by his side. But something else was pulling me away—something I needed to take care of tonight. I comforted myself with the thought that Gretchen would watch over Lucas—and they'd be away from the house in case anything went wrong.

Dad and Seth were waiting up for me when I got home. They were both relieved to hear that Lucas was okay. I didn't tell Dad about Amber's involvement. That would get too close to the fact that she was a spotter, something that neither Lucas nor I had shared with the Guard yet. As far as Dad and everyone else was concerned, Lucas had been the victim of a hit and run.

After I'd recounted the news from the hospital, Dad decided it was past time for us all to get some sleep. I went up to my room and closed the door. I curled up on my bed, not bothering to change. As I waited for the others to fall asleep, I had plenty of time to run over the events of the past few nights.

I didn't like who I was becoming, what these Lilitu powers were turning me into. I needed to end this war now. If I had to wait too much longer, I feared I would become too tainted—and Sansenoy's offer to make me human would be rescinded. Assuming, of course, that I hadn't already crossed Sansenoy's line.

Sometime after three in the morning, I cloaked myself, walked out of my house, and crossed the yard to the Guard's front door. I gripped the keys I'd taken from Lucas's jeans at the hospital. Silently, I slid them into the front door lock and turned it. With the faintest click, the lock slid free. I cracked the door open. The foyer was empty. I eased into the house as quietly as I could and pulled the door closed behind me.

The living room was dark, but I could see the sleeping forms of Guardsmen stretched out on rows of cots. The sounds of their breathing filled the house like the rustle of grass in a field.

Suddenly, a Guardsman entered the foyer from the dining room. He was holding a cup of steaming coffee. He looked at the door suspiciously. I froze. Of course they'd have left a guard on duty. I was lucky I hadn't opened the door to find a sword spearing me through the heart. I almost lost my courage in that moment. But I couldn't turn back now—the front door was closed, and if I opened it, I'd be giving myself away.

I slipped carefully past the guard and edged down the hallway. The basement door was open. A few nightlights illuminated small sections of the wall, but the rest of the room was shrouded in darkness. I descended into the basement. As I passed a light on the stairs, I realized I cast no shadow. Cloaked as I was, the light of this world passed through me as easily as air. I set my foot on the last step and it gave a loud groan. It took every ounce of self-restraint not to bolt back up the staircase at the sound. My heart thudded painfully beneath my ribs, but I forced myself to breathe out slowly.

None of the 50 or so sleeping soldiers stirred.

I eased myself onto the concrete of the basement floor with relief. It was tedious work to move through the maze of cots toward the back column, taking care to avoid bumping a sleeper and risk waking him. The farther away I got from the staircase, the darker the room around me became, and the safer I felt. I had no trouble navigating the darkness, but the human men around me depended on their sight. They'd be less likely to strike in total darkness, and that thought brought me comfort.

I reached the support column at the back of the room. The closest cot was just 10 feet away. I eyed the wooden column, suddenly aware that I was facing too many unknowns for comfort. How did the column swing? Was it on a hinge? Would it creak with movement? I stood there for several long moments, contemplating my options. But the truth was, I was out of time. This had to happen, and it had to happen tonight.

I leaned my shoulder against the column and gave it a gentle push. Nothing. It didn't budge in the smallest. A rush of panicked adrenaline surged through my body. It took all my effort to calm my heart, take a deep breath, and think.

In the dream, Lucas had come over to this column first, leaving me behind. He'd done something...

I ran my fingers over the back of the column and found a small carving of a rose. It looked like the rose from the mission. I pushed it, and heard a faint click as a latch sprang free inside. I pressed my shoulder against the column again. The bottom edge of the column eased back with a sound almost like a sigh, revealing a hole in the floor.

A small bronze chest was nestled in the hole, covered in symbols like those decorating the vessel. Exactly as it had been in Lucas's dream.

My breath caught in my throat. I lowered myself to the ground, careful not to let the column slip back to cover the compartment. I reached a hand into the hole and pulled on the top of the chest. It was locked.

So I took the whole thing.

15

Moonlight illuminated the world with a ghostly brilliance. The heavy bronze box dug into my skin as I ran. I clutched it to my chest like a child, and didn't stop until I'd locked the front door to my house behind me. It had felt good to move again. I'd waited, crouched in the hall, for nearly two hours before the guard on duty stepped away for another break. It had been a simple matter to escape through the unguarded front door. Much easier than the waiting. Each second of those two hours had been a torture; all I wanted was to get back home and figure out how to open the box. Until I saw the vessel with my own eyes, I wouldn't be able to relax.

Seth was pacing the foyer when I returned, clutching a borrowed robe around his skinny frame. When he saw the bronze chest in my arms he looked at me curiously.

"It's locked," I whispered. Dad was asleep upstairs.

Seth frowned, his dark eyes clouding with worry. He beckoned me back to his room. When I set the chest down on his bed, something heavy shifted inside. Seth eased the door shut until the lock clicked. Then he turned to me, face tight with anxiety.

"Now what?" he asked.

"We figure out how to open it."

We examined the chest for over an hour. The surface was inlaid with an array of different stones that worked in and around the symbols with an elegant grace. One part of me appreciated the artistry with which it had been constructed. But most of me was ready to smash it to get at the vessel I could only hope was inside.

"Forget it," Seth said when we'd made no progress. "No keyhole, no hinges that I can see."

"We can't give up." My voice was strained, but I'd come too far to turn back now.

"Does your dad have a crowbar?"

"In the garage," I said, eyeing the ancient chest. As sad as the thought of destroying it made me, I was right there with Seth. If we couldn't do it any other way, we had to find a way to force the chest open.

Seth eyed the chest, then sighed. "Okay. We'll grab the crowbar on the way out. We should get over to the mission. It's going to be dawn soon, and we want to make sure we're ready when it's time to start the ritual."

I nodded as Seth flipped the light switch off.

"Seth," I breathed.

A small patch of the inlaid stones seemed to glow in the darkness of his room. Seth stood next to me, awed. "It must be some kind of phosphorescent mineral or something," he said.

"But it wasn't glowing in the basement."

"You said it was buried in the floor?"

I nodded.

"Phosphorescent stuff needs light to charge it up," Seth said. "The light in my room must have given the stones just enough energy to glow." He looked at me eagerly. "Do you have a bright flashlight somewhere?"

"Yeah, we keep one in the kitchen."

"Get it." Seth looked back at the box, eyes fixed on the faintly gleaming stones.

I returned with the flashlight a minute later. Seth flipped it on and shined the light on the lid of the chest for a minute or so. When we were done, the glow was stronger, and I could see a pattern.

"The rose," I murmured. Seth looked at me, confused. I pointed to the surface of the chest. The tiny, distinctive shape gleamed on one corner of the box; you wouldn't notice it if the stones weren't glowing. "It's the same as the carving that tour guide showed us in the mission," I said.

"What carving?" Seth asked. I looked at him, remembering he hadn't been with us on the field trip to the mission. He hadn't seen the secret door, or the rose carving that unlocked it.

"Doesn't matter," I said. I ran my fingers over the stones making up the rose. The petals radiated out from a central stone. I pushed, and the stone depressed into the surface of the chest. The chest's lid pivoted over an inch or so. I tried to slide it over farther, but it wouldn't move. "Give me the light," I said.

Seth handed the flashlight over without a word. I held it up to the chest, examining every side. There was another tiny rose-mosaic on the back, containing another release—this time a petal. I pushed it and heard a faint click. The lid of the chest lifted under my hand. As I opened it, I saw that we would have had a difficult time prying it open with a crowbar. Two edges of the lid were lined with metal braces that curled up under the reinforced lip of the base. Sliding the lid to the side also slid those hooks away from the lip so they couldn't hold it closed. The second latch had released something in the chest's complicated hinge, allowing the top to lift up.

"You did it," Seth said.

I stared into the chest. Inside, a small vase was covered with an almost chalky green patina, but I could still make out the symbols carved into its surface. The vessel. It was real. It was here. My heart swelled with anticipation. After today, my hopes could be realized. After today, I could become human.

We hid the bronze chest under Seth's bed, behind a few spare blankets. It would take more than a cursory glance to find it there.

"We should get going," Seth urged.

"Wait." I grabbed some pillows and stuffed them under Seth's covers, repositioning them until they could pass for a sleeping Seth. I'd already done the same in my room upstairs, on the off chance Dad decided to check in on me in the middle of the night. Seth gave me an appraising look, but didn't say anything.

We bundled the vessel and the ingredients we'd prepared for the ritual into a duffle bag. It was still dark outside, but the birds were starting to sing. Dawn was approaching.

I stopped on the porch, stricken. "If we take my car, Dad will know we're gone," I said.

"Only if he looks outside before we get back," Seth said. I started to protest, but Seth held up a finger. "If we do this right, we'll be back here by seven—worst case scenario by eight. With any luck, no one will have missed us. We can sneak back into the house and carry on like nothing happened." Seeing my hesitation, Seth frowned in exasperation. "What? You want to call a cab?"

I shook my head. We moved quickly to my car. But as I opened the driver's side, Seth put a hand on my arm.

"The spotters," he said.

"Oh," I breathed. Goose bumps prickled up along my arms. "I can't go. They're watching the roads out of town."

"You have to go," Seth said. "Your blood—" He looked at me, his eyes pleading. "It has to be fresh."

I bit my lip and looked at the car. "You drive. I'll hide in the trunk." Seth looked like he wanted to argue, but I didn't give him a chance. I unlocked the trunk and climbed inside. It was a tight fit, and I had to hug my knees.

"You're sure you'll be okay in there?" Seth asked. He studied the cramped quarters anxiously, but there wasn't time to discuss it.

"Just watch out for potholes," I said, giving him a grim smile.

Seth's lip twitched in response, but he didn't look amused. Resigned, he closed the trunk.

For the record: not my favorite way to travel. I could tell Seth was taking it easy. He handled the turns slowly, but I still had to brace my hands against the side of the trunk to avoid knocking my head at each corner. Unable to see where we were going, the drive seemed much longer than I remembered.

When I heard the crunch of gravel under the wheels I let out a breath of relief. We were almost there. Seth slowed even more for the rough climb up the foothills to the mission, but the unpaved road made for a nauseating ride. When the car finally came to a stop, I was squeezing my eyes shut, battling the urge to vomit.

Seth unlocked the trunk and fresh air flooded into my lungs. "You okay?" he asked.

"Yeah," I answered. He reached a hand out to me and I took it, eager to escape the cramped prison. I drew the cold morning air into my lungs, one bracing breath after another, while Seth pulled the heavy duffle bag out of the car. After a minute or so, my nausea subsided. "Did you see any spotters?" I asked.

"Not a one. Maybe they're farther out."

"Or maybe they're watching the road, just looking for girls," I said.

This thought seemed to make Seth uncomfortable. He glanced

back down the road. "Yeah. Maybe."

The sky to the east was a rosy pink. Dawn wasn't far away. Seth and I each took one handle of the heavy duffle and hurried to the mission's doors. They creaked as we pulled them open.

The sanctuary was dark, even though the broken window had been replaced with new glass. Seth and I moved into the silence of the place and hesitated. There was a power here; I could feel it. We set the duffle down. Seth walked to the front of the sanctuary. When I didn't follow him, he turned back.

"Help me with the pews?"

"Right." I shook my head, trying to dispel the sense of foreboding. I told myself it was the memory of last winter solstice, nothing more. Seth and I dragged several rows of pews toward the back of the sanctuary until the seal was uncovered.

"Ready?" Seth looked at me, eager.

"Ready or not," I said, "let's do this."

Seth returned to the duffel and dragged it closer to the seal. He dug out the vessel, handling it with a grave reverence. I felt a pang of empathy; Seth had as much invested in this ritual as I did. Everything he did now, he did to honor his mother. Seth placed the vessel on the center of the seal. When it connected with the stone, the vessel rang like a bell. The tone was rich, deeper than I would have thought possible from such a small object. Seth glanced back at me. Another rush of goose bumps climbed my arms. Seth walked back to the duffel bag and pulled out a small camping stove.

"Here goes nothing," he said. He pulled the metal pot we'd pilfered from my kitchen out of the bag and set it on top of the small stove. "Could you hand me the distilled water and the flour?" he asked, lighting the stove. I pulled a thermos and the bag of flour we'd measured earlier out of the bag. The heat from the fire made a nice contrast to the cold stone floor, but didn't do much to alleviate my unease. Seth poured the water and flour into the pot. "We need to whisk it until the mixture thickens," Seth said. "Do you mind?"

"No problem," I said. I searched the bag for the whisk I'd stashed there. By the time I turned back to the pot, the flour was already clumping together. I started whisking the mixture, breaking up the clumps as best I could. I was suddenly aware that Seth was the one with the detailed notes about the ritual. I had no idea how it was meant to be performed, beyond the ingredients we'd collected together. "What's next?" I asked.

"Salt." Seth dug in the duffle bag and pulled out a large container of salt. "Salt focuses the power of the ritual. We need to keep it directed at the center of the seal." He peeled the seal off the spout, then upended the container over the vessel. It took three containers to fill the vessel. Seth leveled the salt off at the rim of the vessel, taking great pains not to spill a single grain. He pulled a good-sized wooden bowl and a wooden stirring spoon out of the duffle.

"Where'd you get that?" I asked. I didn't recognize it; it wasn't from our kitchen.

"The mall." He met my gaze and smiled. He pulled a metal tin out of the duffle and carefully eased the top off. We'd spent hours grinding dried chamisa blossoms into a fine yellow powder. Seth poured the powder into the wooden bowl and I sighed. All that effort, for so little final product. Seth pulled another small package out of the duffle bag. "This was a little harder to find."

"Your special order?" I asked. I'd known he ordered something, but I hadn't seen it arrive.

"Yep. Hydrated lime powder." Seth bit his lip, concentrating. He measured out half a cup and mixed it into the yellow powder. "Now the tinctures." He fished the two small tincture vials out of the duffle. Uncorking first one bottle then the next, he added a few drops of each into the powder mixture. He took up the wooden spoon and started folding the mixture together, gently distributing the moisture from the tinctures throughout the bowl. "How's the flour coming?"

My arm was starting to get tired, so it was a little disconcerting to see there were still several clumps of flower moving through the mixture. "Needs more work," I said.

Seth gave me an encouraging smile. We worked together in silence for 15 minutes or so, then I sat back.

"I think it's done," I said. Seth leaned over my shoulder to look into the pot. The flour mixture was the consistency of a smooth, thick gravy.

"Perfect," he said. "Now for the magic." He scooped a spoonful of the powder from his bowl into the flour mixture. A warm yellow spread into the mixture. Seth continued to add powder until the whole pot was full of the vibrant yellow-gold color.

"It's beautiful," I said.

"Not bad for our first attempt at an ancient ritual, huh?" Seth grinned, then bent over and turned off the stove. "Now we wait for it to cool."

I looked at the windows. Judging by the sky outside, the sun had risen. "Seth," I said. He followed my gaze, and read my concern.

"It's okay. We've got a little time before the sun crests the mountain." Seth dumped the unneeded powder into the empty bag we'd used to transport the flour. Then he poured the steaming mixture from the pot into the wooden bowl slowly, letting the icy air cool the liquid as he worked. Five minutes later, the mixture was no longer steaming.

"One final ingredient," Seth said. He met my eyes.

"Right." I forced myself to smile. "Hand it over."

"I'd say be careful, but..." Seth pulled a small knife out of the bag, and removed the cardboard sheath he'd taped around the blade. He'd sharpened it last night, while I'd snuck into the Guard's house for the vessel. He gave it to me, handle first.

I took the knife, suddenly uncomfortable, awkward. "Where should I—?"

"Into the bowl," Seth said.

I was keenly aware of him watching as I summoned my courage. This was nothing compared to what I'd gone through with Ais. So why was I so afraid?

"Screw it," I muttered. I held my left hand over the pot and sliced the knife across my palm. It was sharper than I'd expected. Pain shot through my hand as the skin of my palm opened up like a ravine. For a moment, nothing happened. Then a torrent of blood swelled out of the wound. Instinctively, I balled my fist, jerking my hand up. Seth caught my wrist.

"Careful," he whispered.

"Sorry," I said. "Reflex. I'm good." Seth released my hand. I held my hand over the pot, then unclenched my fist slightly. Another wave of pain radiated from the wound, but this time I didn't move. Blood flowed freely from my hand, staining the golden mixture a ruddy red. I watched it with sick fascination.

"Braedyn, breathe," Seth said, laying a hand against my shoulder.

I startled, pulling my eyes away from the pot. It felt like I was snapping out of a trance. But Seth wasn't looking at me. His eyes were fastened on the bowl resting on the floor between us.

"Just a little longer," he murmured. Then he sucked his breath in sharply. I looked down. The mixture was changing. It had been pure red moments ago, but now it seemed threaded through with metallic swirls. As I watched, the entire mixture took on the sheen of liquid silver, until even the drops of blood spilling from my hand seemed to transform just as they connected with the surface. "There," Seth breathed. "Hard part's over." He handed me a clean white cloth. "You rest. I've got it from here."

Numbly, I wrapped the cloth around my hand. Seth collected the leftover ingredients, empty bottles, and used equipment back into the duffle bag. He moved with focused purpose; no wasted motion, no hesitation.

When he'd finished packing, he picked up the wooden bowl. He walked it with extreme care to the center of the seal. As I watched, he dipped his fingers into the mixture, then laid them against the stone floor. He began to paint a series of symbols onto the seal. Every once in a while he'd stop, look at the vessel, then return to his work. By the time he was done, there was a ring of symbols gleaming darkly on the dusty stone. The bowl was almost entirely empty.

Seth stepped back to admire his work, wiping the silvery stuff off his hand. Then he joined me at the edge of the seal, crouching to look into my face. "How's the hand?"

But I was still staring at the seal. "Is that it?" I asked.

"Yes," Seth said, giving me an odd look. "Why?"

"I just— " I looked at him, worried. "How are we supposed to know if it worked?" Instead of answering, Seth turned to look at the windows. The sky was full blue now. We could see the crest of the mountain, edged in gold, through the sanctuary's windows.

"Wait for it." Seth's eyes locked to the crest with a burning anticipation. For a few breathless moments, we watched the mountaintop. And then the sun rose that essential hair's breadth farther. Light speared into the sanctuary. "Now... watch." Seth pointed down.

I let my eyes follow his gesture. The silvery glyphs Seth had painted onto the seal seemed to undulate, as if a mirage were distorting them to my eyes. And then—they receded, like water sucked deep into the cracked face of a desert after a storm. Thirty seconds after the sun had touched the seal, none of the marks Seth had painted onto the stone remained.

Without warning, a powerful tugging sensation pulled me toward the seal. I let out a ragged gasp. Seth didn't seem to hear me. *It worked.* The thought seemed to release something inside me. My head felt light, almost giddy.

"Does that answer your question?" Seth asked. Fierce satisfaction burned in his eyes. "Thank you, Braedyn. I couldn't have done this without you."

I stood, feeling shaky. Seth cupped a hand under my elbow, steadying me. I gave him a weak smile. "We make a good team."

Seth grinned back at me. "I think we can even make it back before seven."

"Then let's not waste time celebrating." I moved toward the seal.

"Wait. What are you doing?" Seth asked, catching my hand.

"We have to get the vessel back before the Guard notices it's missing," I said.

"No," Seth said, alarmed. "We can't move it. The ritual isn't finished until moonlight falls on the seal, remember? We don't know what moving the vessel might do, and we can't risk disrupting the ritual."

I looked back at the small bronze vase. If anyone noticed it was missing... Then an idea bloomed in my head. "The chest," I said. "We can return that."

"Yes. Good." Seth picked up the duffle bag and tossed it over his shoulder. "Let's get moving." I followed Seth toward the mission's doors, glancing back at the vessel one last time.

Moonrise couldn't come soon enough.

Once we were back inside the town limits, Seth pulled over and let me out of the trunk. I drove the rest of the way home. Neither Seth nor I felt much like talking. We both knew we weren't home safe until we'd made it back undetected. I killed the engine half a block away from my house and coasted down the gentle slope of our road. I pulled to a stop at the curb where I'd parked my car yesterday. Seth and I traded an anxious glance, then got out of the car. We left the duffle in the back of the car—we'd deal with that later; trying to take it in now would make sneaking inside that much harder. We were starting up the path to the front door when I saw Dad through the dining room window. He was in the kitchen, probably making coffee.

"Get back," I hissed, pulling Seth behind a massive oak tree.

"Any ideas?" he asked.

"We can't go in the front door."

"I figured that much." Seth gave me a pained look.

"I've got an idea," I said. "Come closer."

Seth looked at me, questions springing into his eyes. Impatient, I pulled him close. His breath caught. I felt a stab of irritation, but I'd deal with his crush later. First things first; we had to get inside before Dad realized we were gone. I concentrated on my Lilitu wings, drawing on their power. The familiar ripping sensation spread down my back. Wings both intangible and somehow present unfurled behind me. I arched my back and felt the wings respond, stretching to their very tips. I'd never extended them fully before; the feeling took my breath away. I felt—strong wasn't the right word. *Invulnerable.* Seth was watching me, intrigued.

This wasn't the moment to lose focus. I willed the wings to curve around me, like the folds of a living cloak. Seth choked out a startled breath; from his perspective, I'd just vanished into thin air.

"Hold still," I murmured. I willed the cloak to expand slightly, including Seth under its protection. He breathed out in amazement when he saw me standing before him again. "There. We're hidden." I couldn't keep the satisfaction out of my voice.

Seth looked uncertain. "You think we can walk through the front door without your dad noticing?" he asked.

"No," I said. "But we're not going in the front door. Follow me."

We walked together to the back of my house. I kept Seth cloaked from both Dad and anyone at the Guard's house who might be watching. We reached the backyard without incident. Seth crouched beneath the window to the guest room while I reached up and tried to open the window.

"I think it's locked," Seth said. He looked worried.

I crouched beside him, thinking. "Okay. I'm going to climb into my room. I'll open your window from inside. Just give me a few minutes to throw Dad off the scent."

"Okay." He backed partway into a hedge. It might be scratchy, but it kept him neatly screened from view.

I retreated back to the trellis leading up to my bedroom window. I picked my way gingerly through the thorns of the climbing rose up to the second floor. My window was closed but not latched. I slid it open with my palm, then eased myself inside, taking care not to fall to the floor. I pulled the pillows out from under my covers, throwing the sheets back as if I'd just gotten out of bed. I dug through my closet for a fresh shirt, pulled it on, then headed downstairs.

Dad looked up as I entered the kitchen. "Morning," he said.

"Morning." I picked up an orange out of our fruit bowl and stared out the kitchen window, trying to keep my voice neutral. Outside, I could see a group of Guardsmen hustle into a car parked on the street. "What's up with the Guard?" I asked, glad for the conversation topic.

"Still searching for your mystery man," Dad said. I glanced back at him. He was buttering a slice of toast.

"So they're all on patrol?" I asked. Dad finished buttering the toast. He put it on a plate and slid the plate toward me across the kitchen island. I picked up a piece of toast. "Thanks." I took a big bite of toast. It was warm and crisp and delicious. Dad was watching me closely. I forced myself to swallow. "Something wrong?"

"I know you know it's winter solstice," Dad said. The toast suddenly lost some of its flavor. "You can talk to me," Dad said. "I know how frustrated you've been. How hard it must be for you to trust us." He walked around the island and took my shoulders in his hands. "I just wanted to let you know, I'm proud of you, honey."

I set my half-eaten toast back on the plate, feeling ill. "I should see if Seth's up."

Dad studied me with a searching look, but let me go. "Sure. I'll throw some more bread in the toaster."

I walked into the hallway, forcing myself not to run. Shame and guilt clawed their way through my middle. I paused at Seth's door and knocked. "Seth? You up?" It was an act for Dad's benefit, but I needed to make it sound real. "Sure, I think there's a spare towel in your closet. I'll show you." I walked into the room.

Seth was watching me from the other side of the window. I crossed the room quickly and unlocked it. Seth reached a hand up. I took it and helped him climb into the room. The whole production took less than a minute.

"You're getting ready for a shower," I whispered.

Seth understood immediately. He pulled his shirt off, revealing a chest chiseled with tight, compact muscles. I stared for a moment, stunned. I wouldn't have expected that kind of definition from such a skinny guy. Seth caught me staring and smiled. Blushing, I turned my back on him. I heard him finish taking off his clothes, then pull on the robe he'd been wearing over his pajamas last night.

"It's safe," he said. I heard amusement edging his voice and scowled.

"Your towel," I said, pulling a towel out of the top of the guest room closet and shoving it at his chest. Seth's grin deepened.

I returned to the kitchen. "Seth's going to grab a quick shower," I said. Dad nodded, and joined me at the kitchen island with another plate of buttered toast.

Seth joined us a few minutes later, after the fastest shower in the world. We all ate breakfast together, keeping the conversation light, until Dad had to leave for his daily rounds to the outposts.

The coast was finally clear.

"You sure you want to do this now?" Seth asked.

"If anyone gets suspicious, the first thing they're going to do is check for this chest," I replied.

Seth nodded, and we both pushed back from the kitchen island. We retrieved the chest from Seth's room. I cloaked us for the walk next door to the Guard's house. I hesitated on the porch, opening the door with the key I'd taken from Lucas once again. The inside of the house was quiet. It didn't seem like anyone was home. I pulled Seth inside. In the shelter of the hallway by the stairs, I uncloaked us. The last thing we needed was for one of the newcomers seeing me uncloaking accidentally, and I'd need Seth's help placing the chest, which meant we'd be too far apart for me to keep us both invisible. It'd be a lot easier to explain what we were doing hiding a chest in the basement than it'd be to explain how I could make myself and Seth invisible.

We walked to the basement. The lights were off. Seth and I descended the basement stairs, our only illumination the light streaming down the staircase. I led him to the column and together we slid it aside. While I held it, Seth replaced the chest with my direction. We let the column swing back down, covering the hole in the floor, and heard the soft click as the latch reengaged.

"Done and done," I said, sagging in relief against the column.

Seth turned, suddenly close. His eyes searched my face. The strangest tingle crept over my skin. Seth leaned forward and kissed me. The touch of our lips was like an electric shock, shooting through my whole body, down to my toes. I froze, paralyzed by the swarming emotions that flooded through me. Seth cradled my cheek, his hand warm and firm on my skin. The kiss grew more heated, and I felt myself beginning to respond. I lifted my hands, placed them on his chest—and gently pushed him back, breaking the kiss.

"Seth..." My heart was still pounding, I swayed, dizzy.

Seth stepped back, mortified. "I'm sorry. I thought—"

I lowered my eyes. Why did I want to pull him closer? "I think you'd better meet me back at my house."

"Right." He rung his hands, miserable, then retreated up the dark staircase. I watched him go, sinking against the post again.

Something moved in the darkness beyond the staircase. My eyes adjusted—and it felt like the world plummeted away beneath my feet.

Lucas walked forward slowly. He flipped on the light switch, and his hand lingered on the wall, as though he needed the support to remain standing.

"Wait," I breathed, crossing the distance between us. "What you saw—Seth kissed me. I'm not into him, I promise."

"I know," he said. But he didn't look at me.

"Then, what's wrong?"

"How did you know where to look for the vessel?" His question struck me like a physical blow. I stepped back involuntarily. Lucas turned his head toward me, his eyes heavy and full of pain. "Yeah. I had a feeling, when I couldn't remember any of the stuff I'd studied for my history test."

"Lucas—" I breathed. But it wasn't a denial. Lucas looked sick.

"You made me tell you. After I made it clear how I felt about this." He turned back to the wall, unable to look at me.

I drew in a ragged breath, struggling for calm. "I didn't want to hurt you." My voice sounded thready, weak.

"You took what you needed," he said simply, "then you made me forget."

I put a hand on his shoulder. He pulled away from me abruptly.

"You made me forget." He turned his eyes toward me. "*I trusted you.*"

The force of his words burned through the last of my excuses. "I did it for us," I said faintly. But I knew, even as I said the words, that I couldn't undo this damage.

Lucas laughed, but the sound was brutal, humorless. "That's rich."

"You have to believe me," I said. My voice was shrill, on the edge of breaking.

"No. I don't." Lucas looked at me. It was as if a cement wall had been built behind his eyes. Whatever he was thinking, whatever he was feeling, he kept it veiled. With a wrenching pain, I felt him slipping away. "I don't think I'll ever believe you again."

"You said you'd never doubt me." My throat was tight with emotion. "Not unless I told you I didn't love you anymore."

Lucas met my eyes with a clear, direct stare. "Don't you get it?" he asked. "You just did."

16

Steam curled from an oversized mug of hot chocolate in my hands. Heat radiated through the ceramic. The rich aroma of cocoa and chili powder hung heavy in the air. I observed it all like it was happening to someone else. Nothing had seemed real to me since Lucas had left me standing alone in the Guard's basement.

After the first wave of shock had worn off, I'd fled to my car. I hadn't intended to come here, but my drive had wandered through the neighborhood. Sophia's seemed as safe a place as any. I needed some time alone to think. When Lucas had made it clear we were through, I'd started to question everything. I'd fought so hard to become human, desperate for the chance at a healthy relationship with him. And now that chance was gone.

I took a sip of the scalding liquid. The pain focused my thoughts. Brought me back to the present moment.

Do I even want to become human? I asked myself. *Why sugarcoat it? Everything I'd done, I'd done for Lucas, hadn't I? To be with Lucas. Who now wanted nothing to do with me ever again. So I was free to decide my future unencumbered.*

But even as I thought this, my stomach twisted painfully. A fresh wash of grief spilled through me. I tipped my head forward, ashamed. The life of a Lilitu? To never have a romantic relationship that didn't end in devastation or death? To never get married, never have Dad walk me down the aisle? To never have a child unless I stole the life of another?

No. Lucas wasn't the reason I wanted to be human.

Exhaustion battered at my mind. I stood, leaving the cup still steaming on the table, next to a crumpled five-dollar bill.

How I made it home, I don't really know. The house was empty. Seth was gone. Dad hadn't returned from his rounds. I climbed the stairs, feeling gravity pulling a little harder on my limbs with every step. I collapsed into bed, tumbling into a dreamless sleep only seconds later.

I struggled to wake up, hearing the sounds of voices below. I glanced out the window. The sun was low in the west. I'd slept most of the day away. I considered pulling a blanket over me, seeking the oblivion of dreamless sleep once more. But my stomach growled angrily. I'd had nothing to eat today but that piece of toast at breakfast and a few cups of hot chocolate. I rose, still groggy, and headed downstairs.

Dad and Hale were talking with two others at the dining room table. As I came down the stairs, Thane's face came into view. So he was finally back. The fourth man at the table was a stranger to me, but the others were listening to him with rapt attention.

"It doesn't surprise me that he tried to manipulate your children," he was saying. "It would have been a great coup for him if they'd managed to perform the ritual."

My steps slowed on the staircase.

"When I think what could have happened," Dad said. He shook his head. The others murmured agreement.

"What?" I asked, reaching the bottom of the staircase. "What could have happened?"

Dad turned. "Braedyn. This is Ian Masters. He's Terrance Clay's archivist." Dad gave me a sharp look, urging caution. I walked into the dining room, crossing my arms so I could hide my bandaged hand nonchalantly.

"What are you guys talking about?" I asked again.

"This ritual you were so intent on," Thane said. "The one you thought would lock the Lilitu out of this world?"

"Yeah?" I asked. A strange prickling wash spread across my back.

Thane inclined his head toward the new archivist. "Ian's just told your father and Hale that this ritual is the way to *open* the seal."

"Open?" I asked.

"Indeed." Thane shot a look at my father. "The incubus tried to play you all for fools."

I reached out for the wall, suddenly needing the support. Dad's eyes locked onto my face. I saw the bolt of understanding strike him.

He clamped a lid on his rising panic and gave me a mild smile. "You look tired, kiddo. Go up to your room. I'll bring you some dinner in a minute."

I stared at him, reeling, unable to move.

Thane glanced at me.

"Go on up," Dad said, some of his anxiety breaking through the calm facade. "I'll come see you in a minute."

I turned back to the stairs.

"*Stop.*" Thane was on his feet in an instant. He crossed the distance between us in three long strides, then grabbed my arm and spun me around. My eyes darted to Dad for help, but Thane tightened his grip on my arm. "What did you do?"

"I—I'm sorry," I wheezed.

"*Stupid girl,*" Thane hissed.

Dad pushed back from the table. "*Thane.* Let her go."

"You realize what she's done?" Thane turned to the others. Hale was staring at me, his face full of disbelief. Ian looked from me to Dad, unsure what to make of this. "She's delivered victory to our enemies! She's opened the seal!"

"Braedyn?" Hale turned to me with a look of horror.

"I—it was supposed to lock the door," I said helplessly.

"Please, no one panic," Ian said, standing. "They couldn't have finished the ritual. They'd need the blood of a Lilitu to set the power—"

Hale, Thane, and Dad turned to me. Thane grabbed my wounded hand and ripped the bandage off. I blanched, biting back a gasp of pain. The gash in my palm was healing quickly, but it hadn't yet closed. Thane's breath came out in a low hiss of fury.

"Call the others," Hale said quietly.

Ian looked around the room with a blank look. "Have I missed something?"

Thane glared at Hale.

"Call the others," Hale repeated to Ian, with more force this time. Ian nodded, confused, and walked quickly for the front door. We heard the door close behind him. Thane released my wrist.

"And what about our errant young Lilitu?" Thane asked Hale quietly. "You are, after all, assuming she made a mistake. How do we know she hasn't changed her allegiance? You continue to cling to the hope she is our secret weapon. How do we know she isn't *theirs?*" Dad stepped toward Thane, too angry to speak. Thane backed away reflexively, then drew himself up to his full height. "You still defend her?"

"I will *always* defend her," Dad said.

Thane gave my dad a level look. "Then this is as much your fault as it is hers."

"What's done is done," Hale snapped. "We need to pull the forces together."

"What should I do?" I asked in a tiny voice. All three men turned to look at me.

"Go to your room," Dad said after a moment's silence had passed.

"Yes." Thane said, his voice dangerously quiet. "I think you've done quite enough for one day."

I walked numbly down the hall to my room.

This can't be happening. The thought kept repeating in my head. *This can't be happening. This can't be happening.*

By the time I reached the door to my room, my sight was blurry with tears. Nothing made sense. Angela had been so clear in her journal. This was our way out of the coming war. It had to be. That was the justification for *everything* I'd done. Stealing from that shopkeeper. Going behind my father's back. Trespassing in Lucas's mind. Taking the vessel from the Guard.

How could I have been so wrong? I'd gambled everything so I could become human. I'd gambled *everything*—and I had lost.

I fell onto my bed, curling into a tight ball. Strangely, I found I was too tired, too worn out to cry. Even that release was denied to me.

I noticed something out of the corner of my eye. Something that didn't belong here. It pulled my spiraling thoughts up short. A fuzzy, grey knit skullcap folded neatly on one of my pillows. Royal's hat. I picked it up, and a small piece of paper slipped out. I opened the note, and the message inside stole my breath away. I knew the handwriting. It was the same as the note he'd slipped in Cassie's locker.

One night down.

The incubus. The incubus had attacked Royal.

I held the note in one trembling hand. A growing fury chased the exhaustion out of my body, burning through my veins until even my bones were saturated with rage. He'd tricked me into betraying everyone I loved in this world. He used me to open the door between worlds. He'd won. He'd won, and yet he continued to take from me.

I turned, planting my feet on the floor and standing. *One night down.* Royal wasn't a Thrall yet. I could find him. I could talk to him. He'd be weak, but he'd still be Royal. And that meant he could still be reasoned with. He would tell me who'd attacked him. Royal would lead me to the incubus.

I grabbed a sweater from my closet, thrusting my arms through the sleeves while I crossed the room. I was halfway to my door before I stopped. I turned, glancing at my dresser. I hadn't taken them out since the night Ais had died. It seemed fitting somehow that I'd first hold them again on the anniversary of her death.

I knelt before my dresser and pulled open the bottom drawer. It was a mass of scarves, belts, gloves, hats—things I didn't need often. Things I hadn't touched since I'd last closed this drawer one year ago. I reached behind a pile of scarves. My hand closed on the leather sheath, lying where I'd left it. I pulled it out.

Her blood still stained the hilt.

Flashes of that night crowded out the room around me. The panic, the helplessness, the pain and fear. I stared at the drops of blood along the hilt, and I noticed a faintly metallic glint to them. Metallic—like the mixture we'd made at the sanctuary. A chill moved through me.

In a sweeping motion, I pulled the weapon free from the sheath. I thumbed the hidden release. What looked like one dagger sprang apart into two twining, serpentine blades. They gleamed oddly in the fading light of day. The blades—like the blades of all Guard weapons—had that peculiar sheen that always reminded me of gasoline spreading across water; a sort of dirty rainbow swirl somehow embedded in the metal.

If I found the incubus, I'd be ready. I slipped the daggers back into their sheath, then tucked them into my school bag. I stood, catching sight of my reflection in the mirror above my dresser. The girl who looked back at me was pale, with beautiful blue eyes and long, dark hair that gleamed richly even in this dim light. But there was something cold and hard in her expression.

I turned away from the mirror, not liking what I saw there. I hurried out of my room and into the hall. The men were still arguing at the dining table downstairs.

I didn't have time to deal with them, their bickering, or their interference. I cloaked myself and descended the stairs. No one heard me. When I reached the front door, I hesitated, risking a glance back into the dining room. Only Dad was visible, but his back was to the door. No one would notice me leaving. I pulled the front door open, and slipped into the night.

Twenty seconds later I was behind the wheel of my car, speeding off toward school.

The campus parking lot was packed. It looked like half the school had turned out for opening night. I pulled into the first parking spot I could find and killed the engine.

I'd thought this through, and if Royal was even partly himself tonight, he'd be here.

I got out of my car and ran across the parking lot for the performing arts center. Campus seemed deserted; everyone must be inside watching the show. My shoes slapped against the pavement with a sharp, staccato sound that echoed across the parking lot. I'd realized on the drive over that I didn't know if "one night down" referred to today or last night. If it had been last night, and the incubus had found Royal again today... *No.* I was going to find Royal first. I wouldn't let myself consider the horrible thought that it might be too late to do anything for him.

The lobby was empty. I could hear the musical intro for the second song through the doors to the theater; the play was well into the first act. I bypassed the theater entrance and headed down the hallway that led backstage.

The main lights were off in the greenroom, replaced by blue backstage working lights to help the actors and the crew find their way. And even though they were much dimmer than the lights in the lobby had been, my eyes needed no time to adjust. I scanned the faces of everyone I passed, looking for Royal. No luck. I turned to see if he was in the costume closet. The door ahead of me opened, and I froze.

Cassie emerged from the costume closet with Mr. Hart, her arm curled through his. As I watched, she gave him a kiss on the cheek, then slipped into the chaos of backstage, ready with the mantle that Guinevere wore in the next scene. I felt my blood run cold. All the denials, all the secrecy—but what I was seeing seemed pretty clear.

Mr. Hart watched her go. His eyes swept over the crowd of students, all busy with their jobs for the show. Then he saw me and froze.

I hurried after Cassie, catching up to her in a few strides.

"Braedyn?" Surprise flashed across her face. "What are you doing backstage? We're in the middle of the—"

"Where's Royal?" I asked, cutting her off.

She read the urgency in my eyes. "What's wrong?"

"Is he here?"

"No," she said slowly. "He missed crew call. I tried to reach him but—" her eyes searched my face. "Something's wrong. What's going on?"

"I don't know yet," I said. "You—you should focus on the show. I'll look for him."

"Tell me what's happening," she said, grabbing my arm before I could escape.

"Shhh!" The stage manager, hunched over an annotated script, shot us a withering look and jabbed his finger at the stage, just beyond the double doors in front of us. He held a finger to his lips and gestured for me to leave. "Scene change in two pages," he whispered to Cassie.

Cassie looked torn, but she grabbed me by the arm and led me away from the stage, oblivious to the stage manager's panic behind us.

"I knew something was wrong," Cassie breathed.

"When's the last time you saw him?" I asked.

"Last night," she answered. "He was working costumes backstage so I could watch the dress rehearsal. He was supposed to come tonight to help me prep, then he was going to watch the show—"

A sudden thought sprang into my head. "He said something about a date—"

"What?"

"A date to his brother's wedding," I said.

"Yeah?"

"Have you ever met Royal's guy?" I asked. Cassie shook her head.

Another student dressed all in black tapped Cassie on the shoulder.

"10 seconds, Cassie," she said. Cassie looked at me, worry distorting her features.

"Go," I said. "I'll find him."

Cassie didn't look happy, but she nodded and left.

I glanced back to the costume closet. Mr. Hart was still standing there, watching me. After a moment, he approached me. "Braedyn," he said. "I'm surprised to see you here."

"Why is that?" I asked, thrown.

"I thought you'd want to be with your friend. I imagine he must be pretty traumatized."

Royal's face flashed across my thoughts. Mr. Hart gave me a look full of pity.

"He seems like a nice kid, I hope he makes it through. Something like that—it could scar a person for the rest of his life."

Fury darkened the corners of my vision. Mr. Hart laid a hand on my shoulder. I recoiled.

"*Don't touch me*," I hissed. "I know what you are."

Mr. Hart's eyes went flat and cold. He glanced around. Suddenly the crew leapt into action for the scene change. No one was paying any attention to us.

"All right, Braedyn," Mr. Hart said. "You want to do this now? Fine." He grabbed me by the arm and pulled me into the costume closet. I jerked out of his grasp and stumbled back into the worktable. Mr. Hart closed the door and flipped the lock. He turned to face me, spreading his hands wide. "There. No one will interrupt us. Why don't you get it all off your chest."

I fought to keep the fear out of my eyes. "Keep your hands off of my friends or— or—" but what could I do to an incubus?

"I'm not loving the threats," he said. "Why can't we talk about this like two reasonable people?"

"Reasonable?" I stared at him, incredulous. "You still think we're on the same side?"

"We are," he said. "You just can't see it yet."

Something inside of me snapped. I lunged for him, fueled by the helpless rage I'd felt since finding Royal's hat on my bed.

I shoved him hard, and Mr. Hart hit the ground, curling his arms around his head. "What the hell?!"

I dropped onto his chest, straddling him. In the same motion, I pulled the dagger out of my bag. "What did you do to Royal?!"

Mr. Hart eyed the dagger, but he kept his voice calm. "Put it down, Braedyn. I don't believe you want to hurt—" but his voice cut off as I grabbed his hair and leveled the dagger at his throat. He squeezed his eyes shut.

"Why?" I asked. "Why him?"

"I don't know what you're talking about," he whispered, looking for all the world like a terrified victim.

"Don't lie to me!" I jerked his hair and his eyes flew open. "You completely shielded your mind. No human could do that. Most Lilitu can't do that."

Mr. Hart met my gaze. "Please. Put the knife down."

"I'm going to ask you one more time," I said. I glared straight into his eyes—and suddenly his pupils began to dilate.

"I don't know what you want to hear," he whispered.

I gripped his hair tighter, but a sick fear was working its way into my stomach. His pupils—what if I'd made a terrible mistake? There was one way to test him—to know for sure.

"*Tell me the truth,*" I said. "*What did you do to my friend?*" The *call* burrowed through the air between us, cracking through this reality with sounds like little chimes.

"She needed someone to talk to," he answered. His words came haltingly, but they came. "About Parker. Someone who wouldn't judge her."

"Not Cassie," I growled. But I'd done my work too well, he couldn't stop. He told me the entire story of their relationship, from the first time he found her crying at the worktable, to the day he joined her for a session with the school counselor. He recounted the day I'd seen him and Cassie talking in the closet. He'd worried then that it had looked like a compromising situation, and he'd decided to find a time to talk to me about it. He'd wanted to allay my fears, knowing that the last thing Cassie needed right then was more suspicion or judgment. He thought he'd gotten through to me that day behind the theater—*the day I'd fought with Lucas,* I realized. Based on the story he told, Cassie had truly come to depend on him this past semester. And why not? Royal wasn't the confidant she needed for this, and I hadn't been there for her. I didn't want to believe him. Part of me kept looking for the glimmer of the incubus behind his words. But as he finished the story, I realized it was true. It was all true.

Mr. Hart was human.

"I've been afraid she's got a crush on me, but I'd never—" he blinked, and a tear slid free from one of his eyes. "I'd never hurt one of my students. *Never.*"

I lowered the dagger back into my bag and released his hair. "I'm sorry," I said. "I—I was wrong."

He blinked and looked up at me, shaking off the power of *the call* with some effort. "Braedyn?"

The lock flipped and the door opened. "Mr. Hart? Are you in—?" Cassie entered and saw us. Her expression went slack. "Oh. I didn't—I didn't know." She turned, fumbling to pull the door closed.

Mr. Hart's eyes found my face. "No. No—Cassie! Wait!" He pushed me off of him and rolled to his knees, standing a few moments later. But when he reached the door, he turned back to me, torn. "This—this could end my career."

"I'll go after her," I said. "I'll explain."

Only, when I left the costume closet, I couldn't find Cassie anywhere.

I scoured the backstage, then moved out into the theater's lobby. At the next scene change, I could hear the chaos backstage—and the growing panic when it became clear that the costume department had gone AWOL.

I crossed the lobby toward the glass doors. When I opened them to exit, a sudden, frigid wind greeted me, blowing in from the east. It bit through my sweater, driving straight into my bones.

"Cassie!" I shouted. No one answered. I ran out into the parking lot, looking for any sign of movement that might give her away. But Cassie had picked her hiding place well, and if she could hear me, she was choosing not to answer. Finally, I was forced to admit it; Cassie was gone. But Royal needed me more right now. Whoever the incubus was, he was still out there. Only—I had no idea where to look for Royal. And if he was with the incubus right now, they could be anywhere in the town.

I slumped against the trunk of one of the school's aspen trees, wracking my brain for any ideas. My eyes rose to the sky. The moon hadn't risen yet.

My breath caught in my throat. *The moon hadn't risen yet.*

We hadn't been able to return the vessel because according to Angela's notes, the ritual wasn't complete until moonrise. What if the seal was still closed?

I pushed off the tree and ran for my car. I might not know where Royal was, but I had a pretty good idea where the incubus might be. He'd gone to great lengths to get us to perform the ritual for him. I was willing to bet that he'd do whatever it took to make sure no one disturbed the vessel until the ritual was complete.

Unlocking the driver's side door, I slid into the car and keyed the ignition. The Firebird roared to life, and another thought pushed into my mind. I *was* betting—I was betting with Royal's life. Because if I was wrong, and the incubus was with Royal right now instead of where I guessed he was, Royal would be lost to us forever.

But if I was right? If I was right, there was still time to stop the seal from opening.

17

A sprinkling of stars dusted the sky overhead, frozen in place against the velvety black backdrop of night. My mind felt fractured. Yes, my hands gripped the wheel, some small part of me navigating the streets in a haze—but my thoughts were miles away at the mission. I relived each moment of the ritual, wincing as the knife sliced through my palm in memory. I gripped the wheel tighter and my hand throbbed in protest. The pain goaded me on, a sharp reminder of our terrible mistake. But what we'd done, we could undo. I had to believe that.

I turned onto my street. My body strained against the seatbelt, compressing the air out of my lungs. I hit the brakes, suddenly aware of how fast I was driving. The Firebird lurched as the wheels locked up, tires squealing against the road. I slid for a few feet, but my speed was back under control. My heart thudded in my ears, louder than the sound of the Firebird's engine as I tapped the gas. Moments later, I turned up the driveway in front of my house and killed the engine, leaving the keys in the ignition. I opened my car door and caught a whiff of burnt rubber, but paid it no mind. I charged up the path to our front door, reaching for the doorknob. Unlocked, it turned under my hand. I shoved the door open and burst inside, expecting to find Dad, Hale, and Thane still arguing at the kitchen table.

Instead, I found Seth and Lucas sitting in silence. Seth hunched over a steaming mug of herbal tea as Lucas glared at him. The spicy aroma filled the foyer. He looked beaten down, defeated. They must have told him what we'd done by performing the ritual. Lucas turned as I entered. The look he gave me was so impersonal it stopped my breath for a moment.

Seth looked up half a heartbeat later. His face lit up and he stood. "Braedyn!" And then the memory of our day crashed in on him and his face twisted in misery. "Oh, God. I'm so sorry. I can't believe we—"

I strode into the dining room. There wasn't any time to waste. "Seth, don't. It's not too late. We can still stop it." Seth gave me an incredulous look. Lucas turned his back on me, pulling a cell phone out of his pocket.

Seth glanced at Lucas, startled. "Lucas? Did you hear what she—"

"They're out looking for her." Lucas cut him off shortly. "I'm just going to tell them where she is."

"Who—who's looking for me?" I asked. The memory of Thane's rage was still fresh in my mind. Could he have set the entire Guard after me?

Instead of dialing, Lucas glared at me. "Don't worry. Even after everything you've done, Hale wouldn't let Thane spill your secret. Congratulations. Some people still have faith in you."

"Fine." I turned away from him, unable to meet the anger in his gaze. "Call them. They're going to want to hear this anyway."

"What's going on?" Seth asked, walking over to me.

"It's not over," I gushed to Seth. "We can still stop the ritual."

Lucas hesitated, phone in his hand, listening.

"Come on." I pulled Seth toward the door. "I'll explain at the Guard's house. We're going to need all the Guardsman we can get to help us."

"You need the Guard?" Seth glanced at Lucas, stricken.

"What?" I asked, sensing their sudden tension.

"Sam spotted the guy in that sketch down in Old Town about an hour ago," Lucas said. "Everyone not looking for you is out looking for *him*."

"But—" I felt the panic pressing up through the base of my skull. There was time before the moon rose, but not a *lot* of time. "We've got to get to the mission."

Seth stepped back, pulling away from me. "You want *me* to go back there?"

"We don't have much time," I said.

"But the seal is open."

"No, it's not," I snapped. "You said it yourself, the ritual isn't complete until moonrise. There's still time to stop it. *But we have to go now!*"

"I—" Seth eyed me, looking small and terrified and fragile. "I can't."

"We have to," I said, staring at him with disbelief. "Seth, this is our fault. We've got the chance to make this right. We have to take it."

"I'm not like you," Seth whispered. Shame burned in his cheeks. "I'm not a fighter."

"Seth," I pleaded with him.

"I'll go," Lucas said. I turned to look at him, but he was bending to pick up the jacket he'd tossed over the back of one of the kitchen chairs.

"Thank you," I said.

Lucas ignored me. "Call Hale," Lucas said to Seth. "Get him to pull the rest of the Guard back. Tell them to meet us at the mission." Seth nodded. Lucas glanced at me, shrugging into his jacket. "Let's go."

I ached to reach for him, but held myself in check. "Right. My car's right out—" Lucas brushed past me wordlessly. I fell silent, stung.

"What's that all about?" Seth murmured quietly into my ear, watching as Lucas paused in the foyer to zip up his jacket.

"He knows what I did," I said simply.

Seth bit his lip, awareness entering his eyes. "Oh."

"You coming?" Lucas stood in the foyer, one hand on the doorknob. I turned to join him, but he didn't wait for me. He opened the door.

Cassie stood on the doorstep, her eyes puffy and red-rimmed. "Where's Braedyn?"

Lucas glanced at me, zero curiosity in his gaze. "Make it fast," he said. He walked past Cassie. She spotted me and entered, fists balled at her sides.

"You know, after I saw you and Mr. Hart together," Cassie stopped, her voice shaking with rage. She took a deep breath. "I didn't think I wanted to see you ever again. But now—"

"It's not what you think," I whispered.

"Don't." Cassie's eyes were bright with fresh tears. "Don't lie to me, Braedyn."

"I know what it looked like," I said, raising a hand, trying to appease her.

Cassie snapped. "The door was *locked*," she screamed. "You were on top of him! When you *knew* that I—" She turned away from me, scrubbing the back of her hand against her eyes furiously.

I could feel Seth's eyes latched onto me, burning with curiosity. My cheeks grew hot. "I know," I said.

"You're supposed to be my best friend," she whispered.

My heart wrenched, but at that moment I heard my car engine roar to life outside. "I'm so sorry—but I can't do this right now."

"No, of course not. Why would you make time for a conversation that could save our friendship?"

"Cassie—"

"Don't bother," she said, turning away. I grabbed her arm—I couldn't let her walk out like this. But before I could say anything, she spun on me, pure venom in her eyes. "You're a hypocrite, Braedyn Murphy," she growled. "You give me all this grief about Mr. Hart, when *nothing ever happened* between us. Then you turn around and—" Cassie brought her hands up to her face again, as if she could scrub the memory out of her head. "You could have any guy you want. Why him?"

Lucas honked the horn outside. I glanced out the door, torn.

"Just tell me *why*," Cassie said. "It's the very least you can do."

"I'll tell you everything," I said. "When I get back."

Cassie shook her head, too overwhelmed to speak. I glanced at Seth, pleading silently for help.

"I can handle this," he said. "I'll stay with her." I nodded, grateful. Seth caught my hand before I could leave. I saw the fear in his eyes. "Take care of yourself," he whispered.

I gave him a faint smile, but I'm pretty sure it didn't reach my eyes.

A gloomy carpet of desert stretched out before us as we sped down the highway away from town. The night was quiet, eager. Waiting for the moon and its illumination to bring life to the darkness.

Lucas drove in silence, hands gripping the wheel tightly. The soft glow from my dashboard lit his features, reflecting pinpoints of light in his deep hazel eyes. I couldn't tear my gaze away from him. The seconds ticked past, and the silence between us grew so thick it threatened to suffocate me. I had to speak.

"I'm glad you're here, Lucas."

"You shouldn't take it personally," Lucas said. "This is my responsibility as a Guardsman."

It felt like he'd slapped me. I stared ahead, my stomach in knots.

"You should call Murphy," Lucas said after a moment. His jaw twitched, a sign I knew all too well. He was holding himself in check, clamping down on his emotions. My eyesight blurred, but I fished my phone out of my pocket. The ringer was off. As I glanced at it, I saw I had five missed calls from Dad. I hit redial, turning to stare out the window.

Dad picked up on the second ring. "Braedyn?! Where are you?!"

"Hale hasn't called you yet?" I asked, surprised.

"Hale?" Dad sounded mystified. "What's going on?"

"The ritual. It's not complete until the moon rises. We still have time to stop it," I said.

"Stop it how? What are you planning?" Dad asked.

"I—I just assumed we could—" I lowered my voice, suddenly embarrassed. "Move the vessel or something."

"You're dealing with ancient Lilitu ritual magic," Dad said. "I don't think it's going to be that simple. Hold on. Let me see if I can get Ian on the line."

I stole a glance at Lucas out of the corner of my eye. He had his eyes fixed on the road. You'd think he was driving alone. I turned away from him again. It hurt too much to be ignored by him.

Dad returned a moment later. "Ian, are you there?"

I heard the older man's voice. "Yes. Braedyn? Your father tells me you believe it might not be too late to stop this ritual."

"We think it's not complete until moonrise," I said.

"Interesting. Can you walk me through the ritual? Tell me everything that you did," Ian said.

"I—" I swallowed, glancing at Lucas. "Right." As we sped toward the mission, I described every step of the ritual to Ian. Lucas listened. His expression darkened with each passing moment, and his knuckles grew whiter against the steering wheel. The only detail I changed was the bit about the Lilitu blood. I told Ian we'd gotten a vial somewhere, but Lucas glanced at my bandaged hand. I described what had happened when the dawn sun had hit the floor of the mission. Lucas glanced at my face then, with a look of startled horror.

Ian was silent for a long moment. "Salt," he said at last. "That was a clever move. Clever and dangerous."

"What—?" I started to ask. Ian cut me off.

"The salt, contained within the vessel, should focus the power of the ritual. It also serves as a protection against supernatural interference."

"What—what kind of supernatural interference?"

"Angelic," Ian said simply.

"Sansenoy," I breathed. I suddenly remembered Karayan's warning that one of the Three was hunting for the incubus. I conjured the image of the angel in my mind. He'd appeared—both times I'd seen him in the flesh—as an old man with a scraggly beard and eyes more ancient and mysterious than the ocean.

"Perhaps," Ian said. I heard the curiosity behind his words.

"Salt?" Dad prompted. "Are you suggesting there might be a way to break the ritual with the salt?"

"Yes," Ian said, coming back to the point. "As I'd started to explain, the salt makes the ritual both more powerful, and more vulnerable. You see, as long as the vessel remains undisturbed, the salt will increase the power of the ritual such that—as you saw with the dawn light—the transformative aspects of the ritual should happen almost instantaneously."

"Meaning?" Dad asked. I could sense that he was trying to hurry Ian along without losing his patience.

"Meaning," Ian said. "If the moonlight falls on the seal, the seal should open immediately. Typically in a ritual of this sort, the transformative aspects of the ritual happen more gradually. So for instance, the symbols you painted on the seal would have taken most of the day to sink into the stone."

"How can she stop the ritual?" Dad snapped.

"Take advantage of the incubus's arrogance," Ian replied, unperturbed. "Simply take up the vessel and scatter the salt over the surface of the seal. That should prevent the door from opening."

"All right," I said. "We should be there in about five minutes."

"*What?!*" Dad's voice shot up several octaves. "You've left town?"

"Hale and the rest of the Guardsmen should be on their way," I explained. "Seth called them after we left."

"Braedyn, I don't want you anywhere near that mission."

"Dad," I countered. "This is my fault. I don't have a choice." I lowered the phone, ready to end the call.

"Braedyn!" Dad shouted into the phone, as though he could sense my finger hovering over the "end call" button. "*Braedyn!*"

Reluctantly, I raised the phone back up. "I'm here."

"Don't do anything foolish. Just wait for me. I'm coming to you right now."

I heard the line go dead. After a moment, I shoved my phone back in my pocket. More silence. Lucas kept his eyes focused on the road ahead.

"I'll never be able to make it right," I said. "What I did to you. I know that. But I want you to know," I swallowed, trying to keep my voice from shaking. "I regretted it the instant it happened." Lucas didn't even blink. "Lucas?" No response. I bit my lip, letting my eyes fall to my hands in my lap. After a few moments of silence, he spoke.

"It didn't *happen*."

I looked up, hope leaping into my heart. But Lucas's face was stony. "I—I don't understand," I said.

"It didn't *happen*," he repeated. "*Accidents* happen. This was deliberate. This was you, going into my mind and taking a secret you knew I didn't want to give. And then you clawed the memory out of my mind. Along with everything I'd studied for that history test, and God only knows what else."

His words bore into my heart, unleashing an unexpected wave of pain. "You—you think I took—?" I stopped, suddenly sick.

"I don't know," he said. "I don't *know* what you took. That's the whole point, isn't it?"

I shook my head helplessly. "I wasn't trying to hurt—"

He suddenly hit the steering wheel, so hard I jumped in my seat. "You screwed with my *mind*, Braedyn. How can you sit there and say you weren't trying to hurt me?"

Of course he was right.

"You know, we probably shouldn't talk about this," Lucas said. "I just want to stay focused on stopping this thing from happening."

"Okay," I said. Silence filled the car once more. I kept my eyes focused on the road ahead. Lucas's words settled in my stomach like a lead weight. The small hope I'd nourished—that he might forgive me someday for this transgression—guttered and went out.

"Someone's following us." His voice cut across my thoughts.

"What?" I glanced at Lucas. He was scanning something in the rearview mirror.

"They've been on our tail since town. I thought they might just be traveling through the pass, but they missed the last turn off. The only thing up here is the summer campsites and the mission. So either they really like sleeping in the snow, or they're heading the same place we are."

I turned to stare out the back window at the car behind us. One of the front headlights was drooping to the left, evidence of a bad repair after a fender bender. I knew that car. It belonged to Mrs. Ang.

"It's Cassie," I whispered, a new fear clutching my stomach.

"Are you sure?"

"I'm sure."

Lucas shook his head, but whatever he was thinking, he kept it to himself.

"How far to the turn off?" I asked.

"We're here." Lucas slowed and gave me a look. "Suggestions?"

"We can't stop," I said. "The moon's going to rise any minute now."

"If Cassie follows us—" He slowed even farther as the turn off leading to the mission came into view. "She's not prepared for what might be waiting for us up there."

He was right. Cassie had no idea that Lilitu existed. She'd be incapable of defending herself from an attack, and if Lucas and I had to fight the incubus inside, we might not have the luxury of offering her protection. She'd be walking into a life-threatening situation, completely oblivious to the danger she was in. I glanced at the crest of the mountain. It was just barely edged with silver. The moon was rising behind it, and as soon as it crested the mountain, the ritual would be complete. We were out of time.

"Don't stop," I whispered. My voice sounded hollow in my ears.

"It really sucks being your friend," Lucas said quietly. He pulled onto the dirt road. In moments, we were driving up the foothills toward the mission. Lucas hit the high beams, illuminating the desert far ahead into the night. As we came around the final turn, the headlights fell on the mission.

"Turn them off," I said.

Lucas did as I asked without comment. Flickering light emanated from the mission.

"Someone's inside." I breathed. Adrenaline shot through my system, leaving a bitter taste on the back of my tongue. Some part of me had held onto the hope that we'd arrive to find the mission deserted. No such luck.

Lucas pulled the car over at the edge of the parking lot, killing the engine. It was unlikely whoever was inside had heard us. The doors were closed, and those old mission walls were thick adobe. But they might have seen our headlights. Which meant they might know we were coming.

"How do you want to do this?" Lucas asked.

"I'm going in. You keep Cassie from following." I leaned over and pulled my school bag from under my seat. I reached a hand inside and withdrew my daggers.

"Not to state the obvious or anything," Lucas said. "But you do realize there's probably an incubus in there. We don't even know if those daggers work on them."

"Careful, Lucas," I said, opening my door. "You're going to give me the impression that you care." I got out of the car and walked toward the mission. I didn't look back.

18

A minuscule fleck of ice left a tiny kiss on my cheek. I looked up. It would be a stretch to say it was snowing. Tiny ice crystals must have blown in from an approaching storm. They were so light that even a wave of my hand could disturb their plummet to the ground. They vanished as soon as they met the desert floor.

I heard Cassie's car approaching. Wheels crunched through gravel as she drove into the parking lot. Headlights swept past my feet, sending my shadow stretching toward the mission. I didn't turn back. Lucas would deal with Cassie. I had a job to do.

My eyes cut back to the mountain. Silver light outlined the ridge against the black sky, but the rising moon hadn't breached the crest. Yet. There wasn't much time left.

I reached the mission's massive doors. I grabbed hold of the ancient brass loop serving as the door's handle with my good hand and pulled. The door didn't budge. Surprised, I took the ring with both of my hands and squared my shoulders to the door. This time I pulled hard, throwing everything into the effort. The door creaked softly, but did not open. It was locked. Only, I knew this door did not have a lock. Not the kind you could open with a key. Someone must have set the massive timber across the doors from inside.

"... between me and Braedyn!" Cassie's voice cut through the night. I spun around, my nerves frayed. Lucas called softly to Cassie, grabbing her arm. She pulled out of his grip and walked away from him. She was making a beeline straight for me. Lucas saw me watching and threw his hands up in a gesture that said, "what do you want me to do?"

I tucked my daggers through the back of my belt, then rushed forward to intercept Cassie before she got any closer to the mission. "What are you doing here?" I whispered. "You're supposed to be waiting at my house with Seth."

Cassie eyed the mission behind me. "So this is the big emergency? You just had to come visit some obscure tourist attraction in the middle of the night?"

"Cassie, you shouldn't be here." I tried to nudge her back toward her car.

Cassie ignored the urgency in my voice and crossed her arms, looking mutinous. "I'm tired of being stuck in your shadow." This was so far out of left field I could only stare at Cassie. "You think I'm blind?" she asked. "I've seen how everyone looks at you. Lucas. Seth. Even Parker was obsessed with you first. But Mr. Hart?" Her eyes tightened with pain.

Lucas joined us, glancing at the crest. "Braedyn, should you really be doing this right now?"

"I know," I hissed, turning to him. "But the door is locked."

Lucas gave me a piercing look, then passed us, running for the door.

"Go home, Cassie." I turned and followed him.

"Hey," Cassie protested.

Lucas and I reached the door. He tried to pull it open.

"I told you," I said grimly.

Cassie grabbed my shoulder, trying to force me to look at her. "He was a decent man until you sunk your claws into him!"

"What is wrong with you, Cassie?" I spun on her, snapping. "You *know* me. Do you really believe I'd do something like that?"

"I really believe," Cassie hissed. I stared at her, at a loss for words.

"Wait a minute." Lucas's eyes narrowed. He grabbed Cassie and turned her to face him. "Cassie, look at me for a sec."

"And you," Cassie spat. "You're always defending her—"

Lucas slapped Cassie across the face, hard. Cassie staggered back, clutching her cheek.

"Lucas!" I spun on him. But he was watching Cassie, unsettled. Something about his expression sent a shiver chasing over my skin.

"She's been enthralled," he said.

"How—?" I started.

"Unless she's into girls, how do you think?" Lucas looked grim. Cassie rubbed at her face. She seemed to be coming back to her senses.

"The incubus?" My mouth went dry. "But we only left her 20

minutes ago." Another realization struck me then, stabbing fingers of ice into my heart. "Lucas, Seth was with her." Lucas read my anxiety and turned back to Cassie.

"Where's Seth?" he asked. Cassie didn't answer. Lucas took her by the shoulders and shook her roughly. Cassie's eyes slid to his face, frightened. "Cassie, where's Seth?" he asked again.

"I don't know," she said. "I'm not sure what—" She looked around, confused. "What's happening?"

I heard it then, a faint sound from behind the wooden doors. I grabbed Lucas's arm. "Listen." We pushed closer to the door, straining to catch the sound again. Cassie hung back, curling hands around her arms. She looked shell-shocked, lost. But I was focused on the door, and the sound I'd thought I'd heard coming from behind the thick panels of oak.

"Braedyn?" It was Seth, his voice hoarse with tension. "Braedyn, is that you?" He must have been whispering through the seam between the doors.

"We're here," I whispered back, kneeling to press my eye to the crack of the door. I could make out Seth, sprawled on the floor, arms bent behind his back.

"You have to get me out of here," Seth moaned.

"Are you hurt?" I asked.

"Uh, I don't think so," Seth said. I saw him struggling on the floor. "But I can't move. I'm tied up."

"What happened?"

"I don't know. One minute I'm talking to Cassie, the next minute—It's him, Braedyn. I don't know how but he found us." Panic threaded through Seth's voice. "Cassie. Braedyn, I think he got to Cassie."

"She's okay," I said. I glanced at Lucas and he nodded.

"She was enthralled," Lucas murmured through the door. "But there's no permanent damage."

Seth made a throaty sound that was half-whimper, half-sob.

Lucas glanced at me, tense. "Seth... how did you guys get here before us?"

"He—" Seth's throat seemed to tighten. Each word was a struggle. "We were in the kitchen. Then we weren't."

"The dream." I looked at Lucas, feeling a chill spread over my shoulders. "He must have stepped through the dream and pulled Seth with him." Lucas nodded, his expression stony. It took more than typical Lilitu power to use the dream space to create a bridge from one physical place to another. It meant the incubus was strong. Very strong.

"Get me out of here," Seth pleaded. "Open the door."

"We can't," I said. "It's barred from the inside."

Seth slumped against the floor, suddenly petrified. "You—you should go," he whispered. "Before the seal opens. Run."

"Don't," I said. "Seth, just—hang tight. We're coming."

I stood and faced Lucas. Lucas nodded once; he wasn't leaving either. "The secret door?" he asked. He didn't need my response. It was the only option.

"Cassie, go back to your car," I said. I didn't stand around to see if she obeyed. We raced around the side of the mission to the place where the secret door should be. Only we couldn't find it. We wasted minute after precious minute looking for it.

Finally, Lucas shook his head. "We're running out of time."

I glanced at the crest. That line of silver edging the mountain ridge was bright, heralding the coming moonrise. I looked back at the mission and bit my lip, thinking. It was a solid building, much more of a fortress than I'd ever considered before. The high garden wall, maybe 10 feet tall, skirted the back of the mission. The walls were sheer cliffs of stucco, with no available hand or foot holds until maybe 15 feet up the sides, where support beams for the balcony level protruded from the sides of the mission. The only real weaknesses were the windows. The stained glass I'd kicked the Thrall out of earlier was on the other side of the garden wall—but anyone inside would see me coming. The other stained glass windows were at the top of the sanctuary.

"You've got to get in there," Lucas said in a strained voice.

I spun on him, out of patience. "I'm open to suggestions."

"Step through the dream world."

It wasn't what I'd expected him to say, and for a moment I could only gape at him.

"You've done it before," Lucas said, reading my face. It was technically true. I'd stepped through the dream world out of desperation, knowing my father's life hung in the balance. Leaving aside the fact that I wasn't sure *how* I'd done it the first time, there was a bigger obstacle facing us than Lucas realized.

"I—I cant," I said.

"Excuse me?" Lucas gave me an incredulous look.

"I can't do it," I repeated. "We have to find another way in."

"There is no other way," Lucas said, raising his voice. "So unless you want the final battle to start tonight, you'd better—"

"I don't have the energy," I said, cutting him off.

Lucas grabbed my shoulders, forcing me to meet his gaze. "What are you talking about?"

Shame burned in my cheeks. "You asked me not to visit your dreams, and I've never gone to anyone else—" I swallowed. "It felt—It felt like cheating."

Lucas released me. He looked suddenly ill. "You're telling me—?"

"Even if I knew how I did it the first time, I couldn't do it now. I'd need a solid week of dreams to build up that kind of power—"

"Take it from me," Lucas said. The muscle of his jaw jumped again. He knew exactly what he was offering. "Kiss me."

"*No.*" A vision flooded my head; a field of black roses, stretching as far as the eye could see. If I kissed him, if I allowed myself to draw the energy I'd need to step through the dream, I'd risk doing Lucas permanent damage—and I'd risk burning through the last shreds of my humanity.

"You see an alternative?"

"Not this—"

"You think I want this?" Lucas met my gaze solemnly. "We have one shot to stop a horde of Lilitu from flooding into this world and it expires as soon as the moon crests that mountain."

I could almost feel the moonlight pressing against the mountain behind us, threatening to flood over the crest at any second.

"That much energy—" I looked deep within his eyes. "I'll hurt you, Lucas."

"Do what you have to do." He was willing to sacrifice whatever was needed to keep the seal from opening. A swell of emotion rose through me.

I faced Lucas, bringing my hands up to cradle his face. He flinched slightly, his bravado slipping. He was afraid, but he kept his feet planted firmly on the ground. I leaned forward and kissed him lightly on the cheek. I pulled back and saw the confusion behind his eyes.

"Tell my dad I'm sorry," I whispered.

I turned and ran toward the garden wall surrounding the mission. I planted a foot against a protruding stone in the wall and kicked off with my other foot. The force of the kick propelled me up the side of the wall and I just managed to loop my hands over the top. Pain shot through the palm of my injured hand, but I pulled with all my strength and scrabbled clumsily up to the top of the wall.

"Braedyn?!" Lucas shouted from the ground below. I didn't look back.

I ran along the top of the wide wall and leapt for one of the protruding beams. I misjudged the distance, landing hard across the beam and jack-knifing around it. Reflexively, I clutched my body around the beam and miraculously kept from falling. I drew in a painful breath, then swung one leg around to straddle the beam. Carefully, I stood, pressing my palms against the stucco wall for balance. From this vantage point, I could just barely touch the edge of the Mission's roof. I took a deep breath and jumped. As soon as my feet left the beam, a paralyzing fear coursed through my body. If I missed, I'd fall nearly three stories onto the packed earth below. I felt my body shift as gravity started to pull me back down.

Convulsively, I threw my arms out, trying to grab hold of the edge of the roof. I slid back, stucco scraping into the skin of my forearms- but my hands latched around the roof's edge. I had to pull myself up with my arms. My muscles burned, and the pain in my palm blazed white hot with the effort—but I was able to pull myself up to the edge of the roof. I rolled over the lip of the mission's roof, landing on the hard stucco surface. I collapsed back, my body pooling like liquid. For a few moments I just lay there, sucking in deep gulps of air. I felt an instant's gratitude for Hale, Gretchen, Matthew, and their ruthless training schedule.

No time to wait for my heart to slow. I stood and edged along the roof toward the stained glass windows set into the walls of the sanctuary's elevated ceiling. The windows glowed from within, and I could make out the figures of saints against the night sky.

One of the figures near the end of a line of windows caught my eye. A woman, holding an arrow over her heart. It was the figure poised over the balcony where Lucas and I had stolen a moment's privacy all those long months ago on the field trip. I made my way to the window, then searched the roof for something I could use to break it. There was nothing.

I stared at the window.

It's only a short fall, I told myself. *Just to the balcony. Maybe eight feet down. No problem.*

I pulled the back of my sweater up, wrapping it around my head and shielding my face with my arms. I took a deep breath. Then I ran straight for the stained glass window, twisting at the last second to impact it with my shoulder.

I crashed through the glass and my first thought was one of triumph—the thick sweater had proved an effective shield for my head and face. But then I began to fall, my arms pin wheeling, and I realized I'd overshot the balcony. The railing whizzed past my head, too fast for me to reach out and make a grab for it. I was plummeting toward the stone floor and death or serious injury below—when the strangest thing happened.

Time slowed.

I had an unwelcomed moment to consider my immediate future. Shards of falling glass twinkled in the air around me, shimmering like diamonds suspended mid-air. We fell together, slowly, slowly. I found I could force my body to move, even though it was trapped in this molasses-slow stream of time. I twisted against the gravity pulling my body down. I managed to get my legs under me before I connected with the ground. Each second was drawn out. My ankles bent, then my knees, then my hips, each joint doing what it could to absorb as much of the shock of my fall as possible. I felt my muscles bunching, my sinews straining against the force of the impact. And then the critical moment passed, and the force of impact lessened. I had survived. I saw Seth, lying bound on the floor by the mission's massive oak entrance. His eyes were locked above me, face registering shock. Ever so slowly, his eyes trailed downwards. Just as I realized time really had slowed-

It kicked back to real-time. I fell forward, sprawling on the floor in surprise.

"Braedyn!" Seth shouted.

I heard a meaty impact and searing pain lanced into my leg, sending a shockwave through my body. A horrible, guttural scream tore itself from my throat. I whipped my head around to see the gleaming length of stained glass protruded from my thigh. I stared at it, paralyzed by the sight.

And then my eyes shifted, and I saw *him*.

The stranger. The man who'd set Angela's office ablaze. He sat on the steps of the altar, just beyond the seal. Watching me.

The seal. I realized-with a roiling wave of panic-the vessel was gone. Without the salt from the vessel, I couldn't stop the ritual. The door might not open instantly, but once moonlight struck the seal, the ritual would be complete. The ancient magic would work on the seal slowly until dawn. And then the seal would no longer prevent Lilitu from entering this world by the thousands.

"No," I whispered. The world seemed to tilt. My head was spinning. Dimly, I knew this was shock. I'd taken a serious injury and my body was trying to cope with the trauma by numbing my senses. But I needed my head clear.

I closed my hand around the base of the large glass shard buried in my thigh. I pulled. The glass came free in a slick rush of blood, and another wave of adrenaline slammed through my system. I felt my nostrils flare, and my vision seemed to sharpen.

I reached for the daggers I'd tucked into the back of my belt. My hand closed on thin air. I must have lost them in the fall. Desperate, I scanned the floor, but I couldn't pick out my daggers amid the scattered shards of glass.

Across the room, the stranger spoke. "I wondered if you would return," he said. His voice, though soft, was full of power. He drew a sword from its scabbard. The soft metallic ringing sent a chill through my bones.

And then, as though he had all the time in the world, the stranger stood.

19

Blood seeped through my fingers, still clamped tightly against my leg. The adrenaline was doing its job; pain receded from the front of my mind and I was able to scan the sanctuary, taking silent inventory of my options. They were few. Votives cast a flickering glow around the seal even as they chased dark shadows into the corners of the sanctuary.

The stranger moved toward me, the tip of his sword just inches from the ground. Something about the way he carried it left no doubt in my mind; he was a master swordsman, and I had only moments to get out of his reach.

I planted my good foot against the stone column to my left and kicked. At the same time, I thrust my arms forward, doing my best to aim my body toward the only shelter I could see. The force of the kick sent me sliding across the slick stone floor toward the pews Seth and I had crowded at the back of the sanctuary earlier that day. My aim was true. I reached the edge of the pews as the stranger's footsteps pounded against the floor behind me. I scrambled under the first heavy pew, every nerve in my body buzzing with the need to get away from him.

The pews were long and solid. Every four feet or so, a pair of sturdy legs propped up the pew, straining to support the weight of the thick wooden bench. I grabbed onto the feet, using them like a horizontal ladder to pull myself forward rung by rung, shimmying farther under the pew for protection.

I reached out for the next leg-when the entire length of the pew lifted off of me. I bit back a scream whipping onto my back. The stranger had hauled the pew up and sent it flying to one side. It hit another pew, the force of their collision knocking both pews over. They impacted against the floor with a resounding crash. The stranger glanced down at me, unfazed by the effort it must have taken to toss the massive pew aside. Panic drove me to move. I rolled under the bank of pews, desperate for whatever shelter they could provide, knowing it was only a temporary reprieve. I felt his hand close around my shoe, but I twisted my foot and kicked back, hard. My shoe came off in his hand. I scrambled deeper under the mass of pews, back toward the front of the sanctuary. My eyes lit on the small rose carving, the release to the secret door. If I was going to survive this, I needed to get out of here. *Now.*

I heard wood scraping harshly against the floor as the stranger picked up another pew and tossed it aside. I clawed my way forward, fingernails digging uselessly for purchase against stone. I reached the edge of the pews, hauled myself free, and stood.

I choked back another scream as white-hot agony shot through my leg. I forced my body to move, darting across the seal toward the mission's secret entrance. I couldn't afford to look back. I poured everything into reaching that far wall, that small carving of the rose.

Each step shot arcs of pain through my leg, but I shoved the pain to the back of my mind. My vision blurred at the edges, my breath coming ragged and forced. But, somehow, I reached the carving. I pushed my good hand flat against the rose, felt the slight give as a latch released within the wall.

And then he caught me.

He grabbed the back of my sweater and whipped me around like a rag doll. I hit the ground, rolling back across the seal and skidding to a stop in front of the bank of pews I'd just escaped from.

Stunned, I couldn't do more than roll onto my back. Red and gold swirls clouded my vision. I could hear him coming, but my senses were disoriented. I reached a hand up to the edge of the pew and struggled to sit.

The stranger grabbed the front of my shirt and hauled me to my feet. My hands clamped around his fist instinctively. I found myself staring into his eyes.

"Where is it?" It was a command more than a question. I stared at him, uncomprehending. His expression hardened, and he pushed me back with the slightest effort. I sprawled onto the pew. Before I could regain my balance, he leveled the sword at my throat, resting the icy blade against my neck. "It will go easier for you, if you cooperate."

"I don't know what you want," I said, my voice hoarse.

"The *vessel*."

My mouth opened, but the protest died on my lips. Behind the stranger, I could see Seth edging along the dark wall of the sanctuary, holding something in his hands. A surge of hope filled my chest.

The stranger, seeing something in my expression, turned.

Before he had time to spot Seth in the shadows, I kicked the sword out of his hands. It skittered across the floor. The stranger turned toward it and I lunged to my feet, meaning to dart the other way. But he was faster than I had anticipated. His hand closed around my throat, hauling me up until we were face to face for the second time.

"I will not be baited," he said. I clawed at his hand, but it was like a vise around my throat. If he put any more pressure into his grip, I wouldn't be able to speak.

"The salt," I screamed at Seth. "Scatter the salt on the seal! You can stop the ritual!"

The stranger froze, giving me a sharp look. Something was wrong.

He turned back towards the seal, giving me a clear view into the heart of the sanctuary. We saw Seth at the same instant, returning the vessel to the center of the seal. The stranger released me, lunging for Seth.

"Spill it," I screamed. "Seth, you have to spill the salt!"

Seth looked up, confusion clouding his eyes. He stepped back as the stranger barreled toward him.

Moonlight speared into the sanctuary, flooding the seal with silvery light. The stranger skidded to a stop just beyond the seal, transfixed.

Smoky black ribbons rose up around the vessel in twining spirals of shadow.

"No," I whispered. "*No.*"

The ritual was complete.

The stranger retreated across the stone floor to take up his sword. I limped toward Seth, fighting the growing pain in my leg. "We have to get out of here," I whispered.

Instead of replying, Seth tensed. "Look," he said. I turned, and my breath caught in my throat.

A slender form stepped through the rift between our worlds, gaining substance in half a heartbeat. She had long, pale blond hair that fell in undulating waves down her back. She was small, shorter than Seth by a good six inches. Her limbs were delicate, perfectly proportioned. She was achingly beautiful. *Of course,* I thought numbly. *She's Lilitu.* She held a weapon loosely in one hand. It was shorter than the stranger's sword, but too long to be considered a knife. The curved blade was tarnished with age, but the edge tapered to a cruel point. Strange glyphs ran the length of the blade. The handle, what I could see of it, was a dark and twisted metal.

The Lilitu looked up. Her dark eyes landed on Seth and she moved. The weapon spun through the air directly toward him. I acted without thought, diving into Seth. We hit the floor as the weapon skittered to the ground behind us. Seth let out a surprised gasp. I rolled off of him, back up onto my feet.

"Stay back," I hissed. I couldn't spare the time to check if he was injured. I spun back around, expecting the Lilitu's attack any moment.

Instead, she was eyeing the stranger.

He stood at the edge of the seal, as if unwilling or unable to step onto the stone. He lifted his sword, ready to strike.

"Go back, Lilitu," he said, his voice ringing with authority. "Tell your sisteren that this land is not for-" The stranger's words choked off with a wet cough.

I fell back against one of the sanctuary's columns, struggling to make sense of what I was seeing.

The blade of the Lilitu's weapon speared out from the front of the stranger's chest. His sword fell from his hands to clatter against the stone floor. A second later, he followed, dropping to his knees. He raised a hand to his chest. It hovered helplessly near the base of the blade. An expression of genuine shock crossed his face. I stared. His blood was strangely light, almost pearlescent. Not human. Not Lilitu.

Seth stepped away from the stranger, his face grimly satisfied. He dragged his hand across his jeans, wiping off a spattering of the pearlescent blood. Almost as an afterthought, he kicked the stranger's sword out of his reach. The stranger watched, numb, as his sword skittered to the far edge of the room.

A piercing scream ripped through the sanctuary.

I tore my eyes away from the stranger, searching for the source of the sound. Lucas and Cassie stood in the open doorway of the sanctuary's hidden entrance. Lucas found the opening after I unlatched it. Lucas caught Cassie and held her tightly. She turned into him, burying her face against his shoulder. Her scream choked off, and the sudden silence was broken only by the ragged breath of the dying stranger.

My thoughts felt sluggish, thick. I looked back at Seth.

He walked past the stranger, ignoring him as though he held no more threat than a statue. Seth's confidence seemed to grow with each step. The Lilitu opened her arms. A smile curved across her sensual lips.

"Brother," she said. Her voice was richly amused. "You look well."

"I am better now," Seth replied. "Illydia. It's been far too long."

They embraced, and Illydia's laughter rang through the sanctuary like peals from a golden bell.

My eyes landed on the large square carving directly across the sanctuary from where I stood. In the border, I saw the pair of Lilitu Angela had identified for us. The brother and sister who'd attacked this mission all those long centuries ago. My eyes shifted back to Seth and Illydia. Brother. Sister.

Seth was the incubus.

20

The world seemed to tilt, and in an instant the floor was rushing toward me. I moved sluggishly, just managing to throw out my hands before impact. I sprawled on the floor and felt something warm and slick beneath me. *Blood,* an inner voice noted dimly. *My blood.* The thought left no residual emotion in its wake.

I saw two forms slipping along the wall of the sanctuary. Lucas and Cassie. Somewhere inside me, a shock of alarm blared. My body tried to motivate me to move, to get up, to escape. But the impulse was buried deep, muted by the thick blanket of shock settling over my thoughts.

Lucas dropped beside me, murmuring something into my ear. His hands moved to my thigh, gently easing the blood-soaked fabric of my ripped jeans aside to reveal a deep gash. I heard him curse quietly, then he was wrestling his sweatshirt off, tearing at the fabric with his teeth. Cassie hovered behind us, eyes wide and terrified. I couldn't feel anything.

I turned to Seth and Illydia. They pulled back from their embrace, greeting one another with genuine affection. I saw their lips move, heard the lilting sounds of their speech, but none of their words registered. We were of no consequence to them; they didn't even glance at us as Lucas worked feverishly to tend my wound.

He fashioned a makeshift tourniquet from the ruins of his sweatshirt, then tied it around my leg. That got my attention. Pain slammed my consciousness back into place, driving the haze from my mind. I couldn't hold back a growl of pain.

Lucas's face twisted with empathy. "Can you stand?" he whispered. I shook my head no. I'd burned through all that adrenaline. It had left me wrung out and weak and slow.

"Take Cassie and go," I said.

"I'm not leaving you."

"The seal," I started. I didn't need to finish the thought.

Lucas winced. "We'll worry about it later," he said. "Put your arm around my neck."

I tried. I clung to his neck. Lucas stood, hauling me to my feet. We took one step, then another. And then my arm lost what little strength it had and I started to slide back to the floor. Lucas caught me around the middle, guided me down safely. He looked into my eyes, helplessly.

"Lucas." I gripped his hand tightly, trying to force him to understand. "If you wait for me, none of us will make it out of here."

"I'll carry you."

"Someone has to get out," I insisted. "Someone has to warn the Guard."

Lucas clenched his jaw, glanced at Cassie. But any hope he might have had that she could deliver the news evaporated when he saw her. She had collapsed against the base of a column, her arms wrapped tightly around her knees. Lucas turned back to me.

"They need you more than they need me," he said.

"What does that—?"

Lucas caught my face in his hands and kissed me. This was nothing like our last real kiss, the night Gretchen had found us together, the night she had outed me as Lilitu to the unsuspecting Lucas. That kiss had been passionate, tender, full of hope.

This kiss—Lucas gave his whole self to it, like he didn't expect to see another sunrise. He crushed me to him with a growing urgency. The passion of this kiss smoldered, burned through my resistance—almost brutal in its intensity. Everything we'd fought to contain and control, everything we'd struggled to suppress, flooded free in an instant. My body responded, starved for his touch—

And equally starved for the life energy he was offering.

I felt the draw of power as the Lilitu storm rose within me. My arms fastened around Lucas's neck. He gripped me harder, and I heard a soft moan escape him. It was everything I wanted.

I shoved Lucas back, *hard*. He sprawled onto the floor, gasping. I pushed myself away from him, stronger, but not whole. Not by a long shot.

Lucas gave me a searching look.

"Not like this," I said, shaking. I felt sickened by the thought of what I could do to Lucas. It'd be so easy to draw out his energy, drain him of vitality. I forced myself to look away from him, fighting the wild desire to pull him closer again.

"Fascinating." The Lilitu's voice sounded behind me, full of amused curiosity. "I see you did not exaggerate."

I turned. Illydia and Seth were watching us, smiling with the same arc to their lips. The family resemblance was striking. Seth might have been taller, but their facial structure, their dark eyes, their skin tone—they could have been twins.

"She'll come around," Seth said.

The Lilitu shrugged, uninterested. She turned from me and walked toward the stranger. He slumped on the ground, still kneeling, his breath coming in short, ragged pants. She crouched before him, tilting her head to peer directly into his face.

"Senoy?" she asked.

The stranger's eyes flicked up to her face, full of pain and failure. I sucked in a sharp breath. It couldn't be.

"I thought I recognized that pugilistic arrogance." Illydia gave a delighted laugh. "Well done, Sethayl." She turned to Seth and her smile sharpened, a hungry glee sparkling in her eyes.

"Two down, one to go," Seth said, inclining his head in acknowledgement of her praise.

"No," I whispered. A vise seemed to grow in my chest, gripping my heart tighter and tighter until it felt like I would die. This was all wrong. Karayan had warned me. She'd told me one of the Three was coming, but it should have been Sansenoy. Sansenoy, whom I recognized. Sansenoy, who knew me as an ally. Not this stranger.

Illydia stood, turning her back on the dying angel, dismissing him completely from her thoughts.

Senoy looked up, meeting my stare levelly. The skin of his face was slick with sweat, and his lips had grown pale, but his eyes were as determined as ever. He gave me a look full of meaning and then—very deliberately—flicked his gaze back toward Seth and Illydia.

Illydia was between us and the mission's secret door. Which left one possible escape route for my friends.

I turned to Lucas. "You'll have to get the crossbeam off the front doors. It's the only way you and Cassie will be able to escape." Lucas's eyes tightened, but before he could argue, I reached down and caught his hand in mine. "Help Cassie, please. I can handle this."

Lucas met my eyes. After a long moment, he nodded.

Haltingly, I stood. My leg held. Whatever energy I'd pulled from Lucas had worked on the wound, accelerating the healing process from inside. There was still pain, the wound was not gone, but I could put weight on the leg without swooning. Progress.

Without looking back, I walked toward Seth and his sister. Seth's eyebrows hiked up with faint interest. Illydia turned, eyeing me critically.

"Any time you want to reconsider my advances..." Seth let his eyes travel over my body. I felt suddenly exposed. I stopped moving, rooted to the floor. His eyes returned to my face. "We could do everything you've been missing from your *relationship*," and here he raised his fingers, quirking them in air-quotes with a sardonic smile before continuing, "with Lucas. Believe it or not, I really am fond of you."

I felt a blush spreading across my cheeks, but I was conscious of Lucas and Cassie behind me, trying to escape. The one thing I could give them now was time. I glared at Seth. "It was all an act."

"I know," Seth sighed wistfully. "Too bad they don't give Oscars for passing as human. Although, I did get the vessel, so in the greater scheme of things, I still win."

"So, that's why you wormed your way into the Guard?"

"Uh, yeah." Seth gave me a pointed look. "You thought I was hanging around for the food?"

"Then... the Thrall? Getting Angela Linwood killed? That was you, too?"

"Dig a little deeper, Braedyn." Seth crossed his arms, smirking. "I've been playing this game on multiple fronts. The Thrall, Linwood, those were the obvious moves."

My mind churned sluggishly. "Mr. Hart?"

Seth inclined his head with a slight smile. "You suspected him early on. I just gave you a little shove here and there. The key was keeping you out of his dream. Admit it, once you tried to get into his dream you freaked out a little bit, didn't you?"

"You shielded his mind?" I didn't have to feign my curiosity.

"Useful trick, that," Seth said. "I also shielded Amber's mind, but you never went after her, not even after all those threats about what you *could* do to her."

"Amber?" Something shifted in my mind. I cast my thoughts back, suddenly numb. "What does she have to do with—?"

"Oh, come on," Seth chuckled. "You didn't really think she was *that* evil did you? I mean, the girl's got her moments, sure. But trying to get Lucas killed? I thought I might be tipping my hand there, but you bought it." He shook his head.

My palm throbbed in protest and I glanced down, unaware until that moment that I'd balled my hands into fists. I raised my eyes back to Seth, seething with white-hot rage.

"You're angry with me." Seth gave me a look of pity. "It's a bit misdirected, though. You really only have yourself to blame."

"How do you figure?" I managed, my voice thick with outrage.

"Well, manipulation is one of my strong suits, but you did make it easy for me." Seth spread his hands wide. "The key is to identify what it is someone finds desirable. You," he pointed his finger at me with a knowing smile. "You like the wounded boys." He glanced pointedly at Lucas for emphasis. "So I faked up a sad history, topped it off with the *tragic* death of a fake mom, and *voila*. Putty in my hands."

I shook my head as a thousand new questions flooded my thoughts. Before I could put one of them into words, Seth said something that stopped me cold.

"Royal—now he was a bit more fun." Seth rubbed his hands together with pride. "Royal likes his boys witty." I stared at Seth, horrified, but he went on. "Convincing him to hold his tongue? Not as easy as you'd think. He was so eager to tell his besties all about our magical tryst."

"Royal is your friend," I said, reeling.

"No," Seth said, as though explaining something to a child. "Royal is human. That makes him my enemy."

"But he's not," I protested. "He's not in the Guard, he's no threat to you. Why? Why hurt him?"

Seth sighed. "It was supposed to keep you occupied until moonrise. I'll admit, it was a desperate move." He shrugged. "But I hadn't counted on you figuring out the ritual would open the seal—or that it could be stopped. Too smart for your own good, by the way." Seth wagged his finger at me in mock admonishment. "Once you knew the truth, I needed to give you something else to think about. Though, I have to say I'm surprised. I thought you'd try a teensy bit harder to find him." Seth gave me a sour smile. "Guess I overestimated how much he means to you."

I hurled myself at Seth.

He moved with stunning speed, dodging my attack and clubbing his forearm down against my leg. Pain exploded across my thigh. I staggered to the floor, unable to draw breath for a moment. Across the sanctuary, I saw Lucas and Cassie struggling with the beam laid across the mission's main doors. Even under their combined effort, it wasn't budging.

"Do yourself a favor," Seth said. "Stay down."

An overwhelming despair cut through me, hollowing out my middle and leaving me cold. *I need help,* I thought. The Guard wasn't going to make it in time. *Karayan,* I willed the message to reach her. *Karayan, please, help me.*

"Hello." Seth snapped his fingers in front of my face. "Are you still with us?"

"Huh?" I breathed. The connection I'd tried to forge with Karayan snapped.

"Eloquent little thing," Illydia sniffed.

"Patience," Seth said, giving his sister a patient smile. He turned back to me. "As I was saying, I have a proposition for you."

"Let me guess. You want me to join forces with you?" I asked, conscious of every moment I could buy for Cassie and Lucas.

"I'd settle for you agreeing to sit this battle out," Seth answered.

"And if I do—you'll just let me go?"

"Seems very generous," Illydia said. "Perhaps you should require a show of good faith first, brother."

Seth looked at me shrewdly. "Not a bad idea." He glanced at Illydia. "Any suggestions?"

Without taking her eyes off of me, she raised one graceful hand to point straight at Lucas. "Kill that one. Then you are free to go."

I stared at Seth incredulous. "Seth?"

A slow smile spread across his face. "Hm. I kind of like this idea." Seth turned his eyes toward Lucas and Cassie, still struggling uselessly against the massive mission doors. "Look, they're dead one way or the other."

Cold terror spilled down my spine. I scrambled away from Seth, meaning to sprint to Lucas and Cassie. Maybe if we could get the doors open they could run.

I made it two steps before Seth caught me in a headlock. He leaned slightly forward, compressing my throat against his forearm, cutting off my breath. I clawed at his skin.

"Take a moment to consider your options," he said. "I don't mind waiting."

He eased back, and sweet air flooded into my lungs. I took a deep breath, then shifted my weight, meaning to leverage him off his feet. Seth sensed my intentions. I felt his body tense as he drove his fist into my lower back.

I cried out as fiery pain lanced through my core.

Lucas turned at the sound, eyes clouding with rage. He started toward us, but Cassie grabbed his hand, stopping him. Lucas shrugged her off.

"Kidney," Seth said grimly. "Hurts, doesn't it?"

I choked back a sob, my mind grasping for a way out. Lucas was barreling toward us. If I didn't act soon, he'd be Seth's next target and no one would be left to get Cassie to safety.

Seth still had me in a tight grip. I let my body go limp, my knees buckling. As I started to fall, Seth released me. He must have bought the feint, because he wasn't prepared when I kicked my good leg up with all my might.

My foot caught him squarely in the chest and I heard a satisfying snap as one of his ribs cracked. Seth hissed, stumbling back as a wave of pain crashed into him. I rolled to my feet, ready to press my advantage.

"Get Cassie out of here!" I shouted to Lucas. He skidded to a stop, eyes narrowing. I needed him to take care of her. "Please," I said, pouring all my desperation into the word. Lucas clenched his jaw, but he nodded. A rush of relief flooded through me when he turned away.

I'd forgotten Illydia.

She snaked her fingers into my hair and wrenched me back. I fell, sprawling onto the floor. She dropped on top of me, hands latching around my throat. Unlike Seth, Illydia had no interest in conversation—no interest in me. She squeezed. In seconds black spots were crushing out my field of vision. I scrabbled uselessly against her grip; I couldn't pry her fingers from around my throat.

I reached up, a last ditch effort. One of my hands caught a fistful of her long blond hair. I jerked her closer, felt her grip loosen in surprise. I clapped my free hand against her forehead.

Images and thoughts rushed into my mind. *Illydia and Seth, passing for wealthy land owners, traveling across the New World chasing rumors of a recently discovered seal. They'd carted their prize across two continents looking for a door to the other plane, keeping the vessel carefully hidden for close to 100 years, biding their time. Then, victory so close they could taste it, they began the ritual. But the monks guarding the seal laid a trap for them—and Illydia fell into their clutches. With the seal half-opened, they'd cast Illydia out of the world of men and into darkness, then worked to reverse the ritual before the seal was rendered impotent.*

I shivered as the images of that other plane filled my mind. *No sun fell in their world. It was a place of envy, hatred, pain. Illydia had raged against the darkness for centuries. Her banishment seemed permanent—until she and Seth had found one another again through the dream, and he'd come to her with a plan.*

Illydia's hands released me and I scrabbled away from her.

I risked a look back at the main sanctuary door. Lucas was using a large candlestick holder as a lever, trying to pry the wooden crossbeam out of its seat. Cassie was huddled against the wall, staring at me with numb horror. I felt a wave of concern for her.

Illydia was studying me, her face registering shock. Seth, recovering, noticed this with a dry chuckle.

"I told you," Seth wheezed. "She's stronger than she looks."

I rubbed a hand against my throat. It hurt to swallow. With some effort, I stood, facing them down.

"I'd like to give you one more chance," Seth said, straightening. His eyes gleamed with hard triumph and I knew—flush with the energy he'd taken from Royal—he'd already managed to heal the broken rib. "You're powerful, Braedyn. More powerful than I think you realize. That makes you a great ally. It also makes you a dangerous enemy. So you can see the unfortunate position that puts me in."

"Because you're fond of me?" I asked, my eyes narrow slits.

"Yeah. Exactly."

At that moment, Lucas managed to pry the crossbeam free. It hit the floor with a resounding thud that echoed throughout the sanctuary. Seth glanced at Lucas, who tossed the candlestick aside and reached a hand out to Cassie. Cassie was slow to react, and Lucas had to pull her to her feet. Seth sighed, almost sounding bored.

"Tick tock, Braedyn," he said.

"You know me," I whispered.

I saw some of the amusement dim in Seth's eyes. "I do." He looked almost wistful. "I was just hoping I might be able to appeal to your sense of self-preservation. Come on, Braedyn. You can't fight the whole Lilitu race single-handedly."

"She won't have to."

I turned, my heart surging with new hope. Karayan strode in through the mission's secret door behind Illydia. She glanced at me, taking quick stock of my visible injuries. Her mouth tightened.

"Got your call," she said. "It took me a minute to figure out where you were. Future reference? You might want to include an address with your S.O.S.."

"Right," I said. A slow smile spread across my face.

Seth looked from me to Karayan, considering. "This must be your 'we-don't-know-what-she-is-so-we'll-call-her-a-friend' friend," he said. "Karayan, is it?"

"And you must be the incubus." Karayan looked thoroughly unimpressed. "I thought you'd be taller."

Seth's smile didn't reach his eyes. "Braedyn and I are talking right now. Look, I don't mean to be rude, but I can tell you're low-born."

Karayan's cheeks flushed, but she met Seth's eyes defiantly. "So?"

"So," Seth gestured to Illydia. "Our mother was Lilith-born. Unless you're ready to hang up those sexy stilettos for good, you'll turn around and walk out of here right now."

Karayan's eyes cut to me, uncertain. Then her gaze dropped to the ground.

Satisfied, Seth turned back to me. "Where were we? Oh, right. You were just about to give me your decision."

A sudden ringing echoed through the sanctuary—the unmistakable sound of metal sliding against stone. Karayan had kicked something across the floor, directly toward me. I stopped it with a foot. It was Senoy's sword. I bent to pick it up, sliding my hand up the handle toward the guard. The sword was perfectly balanced. I swung it around, regaining the feel for the weapon from my few sessions with Hale.

Seth took an involuntary step back, suddenly cautious. I might not be the master with this weapon that Senoy was, but it didn't really matter. An angel's blade could do serious damage to a Lilitu. Including, it appeared, incubi.

I looked up, meeting Karayan's fierce grin.

"Sorry," I said to Seth. "I'm sticking with the home team."

"Well," Seth said. "You can't blame a guy for trying."

The next instant, Illydia turned and attacked Karayan. I heard Karayan's short grunt of pain, but I didn't see what happened with her—Seth used the distraction to rush toward me.

I locked my eyes on him, clenching the sword tighter in my hands. Seth feinted to my left and I swung clumsily out with the sword. I saw his smile return; he knew now that I wasn't gifted with this weapon. I adjusted my grip. *I just have to nick him,* I told myself. *Even a scratch will slow him down.*

But Seth didn't give me a chance. It became quickly clear why he never joined us for sparring sessions in the basement. He was a brilliant fighter, his instincts spot on. He might have managed to hide his skill from me when he'd let those boys at school beat him up—*One more trap he'd laid for me,* I now realized—but he'd never have been able to hide his skill from Hale or Matthew or Gretchen in a sparring match.

Seth danced around me, striking my lower back again. I stumbled, clinging to the sword like a crutch. Dimly, I realized it was holding me back. Insane as it seemed, I had to get rid of the sword. I needed my hands free to be able to defend myself, or Seth would slowly take me apart.

I fell back, circling Seth until I was between him and the mission's main entrance. Behind me, Lucas and Cassie were still struggling to move the beam locking the mission's massive doors shut.

"Lucas," I shouted. He turned, hearing me. I threw the sword toward him with all my might, then spun back to Seth.

I heard the sword clatter behind me, then—half a heart beat later—I heard it scrape against the floor as someone picked it up. Satisfied that Lucas had some way to defend himself and Cassie, I brought my hands up in loose fists. Seth's smile deepened.

"I've actually been looking forward to this," he said. "After all that training, I'd love to see how you hold up in a real fight." He darted forward, jabbing for my face with brutal speed. I jerked back, struggling to keep my footing. Seth fought fast. He didn't pull his punches. I struggled to keep my defenses up, blocking blow after blow. "You're not half bad," he said, smiling with exertion.

Press the attack, I told myself grimly. If I kept him on defense, I'd have a better chance of controlling the fight. I lunged forward, feinting. When Seth moved, I drove my other fist into the side of his face. He took the punch like a boxer, shaking it off with a hard grin.

"You're ready to play rough? That's cool," he said. Any illusions I had about controlling the fight dispelled rapidly. Seth drove me back, foot by foot, until I knocked into one of the sanctuary's columns. He buried two fists into my stomach, one after the other. I gasped, my body trying to double over, but Seth grabbed the front of my shirt and slammed my back against the column. He pinned me there and stared levelly into my eyes. "A for effort."

An overwhelming swell of terror pulsed through me. It was all I could do to keep my feet. Behind Seth, Illydia approached, inspecting her nails nonchalantly. My eyes darted to the back wall where Karayan slumped, breathing raggedly.

"That was fast," Seth said.

"I was expecting more of a challenge." Illydia shrugged.

"You break all your toys." Seth shook his head, amused.

"Speaking of..." Illydia's eyes shifted to my face.

"Right." Seth glanced back at me, shrugging. "Nothing personal, but I can't leave a powerful Lilitu just lying around. Last chance. Wanna help change the world?"

I slammed my knee up into his groin. It connected solidly. Seth's eyes bulged and he dropped to one knee, releasing me instantly. I pushed off the column, diving for Illydia. She spread her arms, ready for me. We collided, and Illydia staggered back a few steps. She recovered quickly, latching her arms around me.

"Mine," I heard Seth hiss behind me.

Illydia sighed, irritated. She twisted, dropping to one knee without letting go of me. The force of her movement ripped me off my feet. She released me and I hit the ground, rolling to my side and sliding a few feet away on the cold stone floor. Before me I could see Seth straightening. Murder glinted in his eyes. I stood, ears still ringing from my fall.

Illydia and Seth moved in. They ringed me around, and a dull fear roiled through my stomach. I turned my head, trying to keep both Seth and Illydia in view. It wasn't possible. Seth swung and I focused on him, blocking the blow and skittering back. Illydia swiped a claw across my back. My sweater took the brunt of the attack, but I felt a cool draft along my back as her claw sliced a hole through the knit. They took turns striking at me. All I could do was react, shying away from one directly into the path of the other. If I glanced at Illydia, Seth pressed his attack. If I focused on defending myself from Seth, Illydia raked a claw against my back. It was less than a minute before Illydia's claws finally ripped through the fabric of my shirt, slicing deep grooves into my skin. I let out a hiss of pain, spinning to face her.

"Stop." I panted. "Stop toying with me."

"Are you sure that's what you want?" Illydia asked. "I don't think you'll like the alternative."

I heard Seth chuckling at my back. I spun around to face him, and Illydia caught my arms and wrenched them back. I jerked against her, but she held me fast.

"So, here we are," Seth said. "I was hoping this would end differently, but I'm not totally surprised."

Karayan? I closed my eyes, willing her to hear me.

Yeah, yeah. She sounded tired, and I could feel the pain of her injuries through the link. But she stirred on the floor. She looked up, and her eyes found me. *That doesn't look good.*

My daggers, I thought at Karayan, picturing my fall through the window from the roof above.

Awesome. Crawling through broken glass, she responded. But I felt her push slowly to her hands and knees.

"Sorry there's no time for a long goodbye, but I'd rather *not* be here when the Guard arrives." Seth rested a hand on my cheek. "It's been real."

"Seth," I whispered, my voice catching in my throat.

His eyes didn't leave my face. "I'll make it quick."

"Get your hands off of her," Lucas said. He stood at the edge of the seal, Senoy's sword in hand.

"Easy, lover boy." Seth looked at him, irritated. "I'll be around to deal with you in just a sec."

"You'll have to deal with her first," Lucas said, nodding at something behind us with his head. Seth and I turned at the same time.

Karayan approached, a Guard dagger clutched in each of her hands. "So I'm wondering," she said, keeping her voice light. "If we can't see your powers, can you see ours?"

Karayan's curving wings snapped down around her slender figure, trailing a smoky haze through the air as they passed.

Seth jerked away from me, suddenly tense. "Illydia?"

"A ploy," Illydia said, tightening her grip on me. "She's got no fight left."

"Care to make a bet on that?" Karayan moved forward with sure steps. Illydia released me, turning to face Karayan. "No?" Karayan asked, her tone mocking. Illydia glanced at Seth, uncertain.

With her back to me, I grabbed Illydia's arm, locking her elbow straight and throwing my weight forward against her. Illydia let out a shrill growl and cloaked herself instinctively, stumbling forward.

It made no difference to us—both Karayan and I could see through the hazy protection of her wings without any effort. Karayan moved, slicing one of the daggers across Illydia's wing. Instantly Illydia's cloak vanished. She stood, reeling and wounded, in the heart of the mission.

Seth ran toward Illydia. He grabbed her hand and pulled her away from us. "We'll pick this up later," he said, heading back toward the seal.

Karayan, I thought to her.

Way ahead of you, she replied. *Keep them separated.*

I sprinted for Seth. He saw me coming half a second too late. I jumped him and we fell crashing to the floor as Illydia stumbled away from us. The impact knocked the breath out of both of us.

Here, I heard Karayan in my mind. I looked up as Karayan tossed the dagger to me. I focused on the flash of metal. The arc of the dagger seemed to slow, tumbling end over end in an almost lazy spiral. It was a simple matter to push my hand forward and clasp the dagger's hilt. Time snapped back into full speed. Seth's eyes fastened on the blade. He scrambled away from me-right in front of the cloaked Karayan.

"Sethayl!" Illydia screamed.

Seth dropped flat to the floor, but the dagger sliced a line across his back. He howled in agony. Illydia barreled for Karayan, dropping her human aspect. Her face changed, coal-black eyes glared murder, gleaming black claws protruded from hands as pale as a corpse.

Illydia smashed into Karayan, clawing at her face. Great gashes tore open along Karayan's cheek. She screamed, trying to bring the dagger up to defend herself. But Karayan had never been trained to fight with weapons—and since this opponent could see her, she was outmatched. Karayan's cloak fell away as the concentration she needed to maintain it snapped.

Seth scrambled back from the fighting Lilitu. He eyed the secret door, still standing open, then glanced back at his sister. I could see the conflict in his eyes. He wanted to help Illydia—but he was getting ready to bolt.

I took a step toward Seth. His eyes snapped to my face, his features tensing.

Then I heard Karayan's ragged gasp of pain. I had a fraction of a second to decide. I abandoned Seth and leapt to help Karayan.

Illydia swiped for Karayan again, her wicked claws still gleaming with Karayan's blood. Karayan dodged back, but she was slowing and her eyes were lidded heavily with pain.

"Behind you!" Seth shouted.

Illydia turned on me, claws poised to strike-but I *had* trained with these weapons. She pounced. I knocked her hand aside and buried the dagger in her heart. I felt the impact all the way to my shoulder. I jerked back and the dagger came free. A small pool of dark blood stained the front of Illydia's shirt. Her face went slack. A moment later, she pitched forward onto the sanctuary floor.

"No." Seth's face was ashen, staring at the body of his sister. His eyes rose until they found me. They burned with pure, roiling hatred.

I tightened my grip on the dagger reflexively.

Outside, we heard a car squeal to a stop.

"Short-sighted, Braedyn." Seth's voice was calm, but something in it made my skin crawl.

Behind us, someone pounded on the mission's front door. "Braedyn? Are you in there?" It was Dad.

"Go around the side," I shouted. "There's another entrance."

Seth stepped back away from me, eyeing his escape route. "Don't forget who won this round," he said. "The seal is open." He turned and stepped onto the seal. Twining ribbons of shadow swirled up and around him, pulling him out of this world. Another car squealed to a stop outside, followed quickly by a third. Doors opened and slammed outside, voices filling the night.

Karayan handed my dagger back with a shaking hand. "I think that's my cue."

"You're hurt," I said.

"You think?" Her voice dripped with sarcasm, but she smiled.

"Karayan." I laid a hand on her arm. "Stay with us. We can take care of you."

"Sorry, Braedyn," Karayan said. And she did look sorry. "But I've been down this road. It didn't work out so good."

"Braedyn?" Dad raced through the mission's secret door. His eyes scanned the room until they fastened on me. I sensed Karayan cloaking herself, withdrawing into the shadows.

"Dad." I wanted nothing more than to run to him.

But as I started across the floor, someone else spoke.

"Daughter of Lilith." The powerful voice froze my steps. I turned. Senoy was looking directly at me. "Braedyn." His voice thick with pain. "Come closer."

21

Senoy's eyes followed me across the room. I approached hesitantly, stopping several feet away from where he knelt on the cold stone floor.

"Are you really—?" But I knew the answer. "You're one of the Three."

I heard Dad breathe in sharply at the secret door.

"You have nothing to fear from me, Lilitu," Senoy said. "I would speak with you." A spasm of pain contorted his handsome features. Almost without thinking, I knelt beside him.

"Braedyn?" Dad took a step toward me, his voice tight with fear.

"Get help," I said. "He's hurt."

Dad hesitated, then turned and ran back out through the secret door.

"He has genuine love for you," Senoy said. Then his face wrenched with another wave of pain.

"Maybe you should save your strength," I said. "The Guard is here, they've got med kits in every car."

"There is no need." He glanced down, as though mildly irritated by the blade protruding from his chest. "The wound is fatal."

"Don't say that," I breathed. I let my fingers slide forward, catching his hand. His skin was cool and smooth. It felt almost like marble. "You can't die."

He looked down at our hands, then back at me, bemused. "You are mistaken."

"I'm so—I'm so sorry," I whispered. I felt his hand squeeze my fingers lightly. It was a comforting gesture. I stared. He was dying, yet Senoy was comforting *me*.

"It is the sacrifice required of me." His gaze bore through me. "You are, I think, a friend to the Sons of Adam?"

I nodded.

"Then you must be strong, Daughter of Lilith." His gaze softened. I detected a deep sadness in the look he gave me. "In this fight, many more sacrifices will be required." His eyes seemed to cloud. His strength faded. I caught his shoulder before he hit the floor. As gently as I could, I lowered him to the ground, cradling his head in my lap.

Senoy closed his eyes as another spasm of pain wracked his body. I laid my hand against his cheek, brushing the hair back from his face. He let out a long breath, his features easing. And then the hand cradling his wound fell away, and he grew still.

"Senoy?" I whispered. There was no flicker behind his eyes. I bit my lip and looked up. Karayan was nowhere to be seen. Lucas was crouched over Cassie, trying to comfort her. Dad hadn't returned.

I was the only one who'd noticed the angel die.

The floor of the sanctuary bucked beneath us. I lurched as the stone floor heaved. It split into a web of fractures, radiating out from Senoy's body across the sanctuary, bypassing only the seal. The force of the fractures kicked up chunks of stone and dust. I couldn't summon the energy to lift my hands and shield my face.

The mission's front doors slammed open behind us. I heard Cassie scream outside. I couldn't look up from Senoy's face.

"What's happening?" Cassie was wailing. "What was that?!" I heard Lucas's steady voice as he tried to calm her, but I couldn't make out the words. "No!" Cassie's voice was shrill, unappeased. "Tell me what's going on!" I don't know what Lucas told her. I couldn't focus on his voice.

Senoy's features were smooth now. Death had chased the pain from them, but it felt wrong.

"We need you," I whispered.

"Lilitu," Gretchen shrieked behind me.

I tore my eyes away from Senoy's still face. Karayan, cloaked, must have been trying to slip past the Guard out the mission's front doors. She spun at Gretchen's scream, her cloak vanishing. Dad and Hale had their daggers out in half a second.

"No!" Lucas launched himself between Karayan and the Guard, hands held high. "She's on our side," he shouted. I watched this all as if trapped in some kind of trance.

Karayan retreated back into the sanctuary, re-cloaked, darting for the secret door and her escape.

"She's getting away," Gretchen hissed.

"She saved our lives," Lucas insisted. "It was Seth. Seth was the incubus." That got their attention. As Lucas recounted the whole story, I noticed Karayan stumbling away from the secret door. Someone had just stepped through it.

Thane. He did not see Karayan through her cloak. But he saw me. His eyes shifted to the dead angel, still cradled in my lap, then to the vessel planted squarely in the center of the seal.

"You stole the vessel," he said quietly. He stepped into the sanctuary and I noticed something hanging from his hands. Another sword. Semangelof's sword. I stared at it, sickly mesmerized. "You opened the seal."

My eyes flicked from the sword to Thane's face. His features could have been carved from granite. A cold fire burned in his eyes—righteous indignation. Thane walked toward me, adjusting his grip on the sword.

"Thane!" Dad's desperate cry stabbed through the haze of my thoughts. When I saw his face, a wrenching regret twisted my insides. He'd had such faith in me, and I'd failed the Guard. Dad shoved through the others and pounded forward, but he was too far away. He wouldn't make it in time.

Thane hefted the sword above me. His muscles tensed as he started the downward swing. Dad threw a hand out toward me, but he was at least 10 yards away.

"Stop!" Karayan caught Thane's arm, uncloaking herself as she did so. Thane recoiled, but Karayan didn't release him. "She's not your enemy. And neither am I."

Dad hauled me off the ground, spinning me away from Thane. He enfolded me in his arms, choking back a painful sob of relief. I could see Thane and Karayan over his shoulder.

"You plague me," Thane whispered to Karayan. "Each time I think I've dug you out of my heart, I find your claws buried still deeper." His voice grew tighter. "You are the single greatest failing of my life."

Karayan winced, but she didn't let him go. She reached up and eased the sword out of Thane's grip.

With a growl of rage, Dad moved. He pushed me behind him and drew his daggers. "Thane." The murder in his voice made the hair on my scalp prickle.

Karayan spun to face my dad, shielding Thane from his wrath. She held the sword point down, offering it up to him. I felt Dad tense, preparing to strike whether or not Karayan was standing in his way.

"Don't," I said, grabbing his arm. "Dad, please." After a tense moment, Dad relaxed.

Thane glared at Karayan. "You think this makes you an ally?" he sneered.

"I think you need all the help you can get," she snapped back. Then she looked at me, as though uncertain she was making the right decision. "Assuming you still want my help."

I smiled, a tiny hope rekindling in my heart. "I do."

Gretchen and Hale moved forward to join us. Lucas followed them a few moments later. Only Cassie held back. She watched us all with a numb expression on her face, still huddled by the mission's front doors.

Dad eyed Karayan. "You're thinking about coming back to the Guard?"

"Not my idea," Karayan said. She jerked her chin at me. "Blame her."

The Guardsmen turned to me. I glanced at Hale. "We need her," I said.

Hale gave me a searching look, then turned and offered his hand to Karayan. "Here's hoping I don't live to regret this."

"Yeah. You and me both." She took his offered hand and they shook. Everyone else stared in silence. "Well, don't everybody cheer all at once," Karayan said.

A tiny smile tugged at the corners of Dad's mouth. He held out a hand. Unsure, Karayan took it. "Welcome back," he said, giving her hand a firm shake.

Lucas clapped a hand on Karayan's shoulder. "I owe you one," he said.

"Two, actually, but I've never known Guardsmen to be terribly good at math." Karayan's smile was tentative. For the first time I'd ever seen, Karayan looked a little uncomfortable in her own skin. She didn't seem to know what to do with her hands. Finally, she shoved them in the back pockets of her jeans. She glanced at Thane, and everyone seemed to hold their breath.

Before Thane could speak, the air cracked with a sound like thunder.

Sansenoy appeared before us—not the scruffy old man I'd first met, but revealed in his true form. He towered over us, a gleaming pillar of light.

The others—who'd never seen an angel in his own aspect—scattered back, falling to the floor in the face of his radiance. As my eyes adjusted, I could make out his figure, the chiseled cut of his jaw, the perfect symmetry of his form. I'd seen him revealed like this once before. It still took my breath away.

He turned away from us, kneeling by the side of his fallen comrade.

"Senoy." His voice reverberated with sorrow. It broke something within me, and in moments I could feel hot tears slipping down the sides of my face. "Rest, my friend."

Sansenoy laid a hand to the other angel's forehead. Suddenly Senoy's form began to transform into tiny pinpoints of golden light. The motes swirled up and away from us, dissipating high above our heads. The air filled with a *presence*. I recognized it as Senoy's, even though I'd only spoken those few words to him. It moved through me, filling me with hope. Faith. Courage. And then it moved on, and I felt... bereft. I let out a long sigh. Mine was not the only one.

As the last of the lights faded, the strange Lilitu weapon fell to the ground with a dull clang.

Sansenoy stood. The light of his angel aspect faded. Moments later, when he again turned to face us, I recognized the scruffy old man I'd first met on the street last year. His expression was solemn.

"The seal is open," he said simply. "The ground for the final battle has been chosen."

"Are you planning on joining us for this fight?" Thane said, stepping forward. "Or are you going to leave us to our own defenses yet again?"

"You do not face this fight alone." Sansenoy glanced at me.

"Her?" Thane's voice jumped an octave higher. "She is the reason your friend was killed. She is the reason the seal is open!"

"That's insane," Dad said, anger flushing into his cheeks.

"Is it?" Thane asked. "Do you really think we would be standing here if she had heeded even one of our warnings?"

"We're here because you insisted we keep her in the dark until you'd confirmed your suspicions," Dad growled.

Sansenoy ignored the men. He looked at me, waiting. Waiting for my explanation.

"I trusted Seth," I said, my words coming haltingly. Everyone else fell silent. "Even when it meant hurting my friends. I gave him my blood for the ritual. And I fought Senoy because I thought—" but here my words cut off. "Thane isn't wrong," I finished in a whisper. Dad's forehead furrowed with tension. Thane relaxed, a smug smile of vindication settling on his face.

Sansenoy looked at me for a long moment, then nodded, as though answering a question for himself. He turned to the others. "Gird yourselves, Sons of Adam," he said finally. "You will need all your strength for the coming fight."

"You—you're going to let her live?" Thane's voice sputtered. "After what she's done?" Sansenoy gave Thane a level look meant to end the conversation. Thane shrank back. But when Sansenoy turned to leave, he couldn't help himself. "Why?" he asked.

Sansenoy paused, then turned back. He gave me a smile that flooded me with peace. "Because I have faith in what she may yet do," he said.

EPILOGUE

Christmas Eve brought with it a piercing cold that seemed to hover over Puerto Escondido like a shroud. No wind stirred the leafless branches of the oak trees lining our street. The sky was black and cloudless, and I could see the stars glitter from one horizon to the next. I stepped onto the front porch of the Guard's house, needing a respite from the commotion inside. I closed the door, muting the sounds of conversation within. The silence was a balm to my nerves.

Marx's team had returned to Puerto Escondido earlier in the day. There had been many warm reunions as Matthew reconnected with the members of his old unit. They'd spent the day catching each other up to speed. Marx told us they'd managed to locate just 93 Guardsmen on the continent. The last of the units they'd made contact with were on their way.

Hale had told Marx and his team about the seal. Since the night of the solstice, 50 Guardsmen had taken up residence in the mission. They watched the seal 24-seven, heavily armed and ready to turn back anything that made the attempt to cross into our world. But, since Seth's retreat, not one single Lilitu had entered from their plane.

They were waiting for something. We just didn't know what.

Feeling another surge of anxiety, I turned my eyes to the neighborhood. *Luminarias* lined the front walks of most of the houses on our street, simple paper lanterns made from candles and paper lunch sacks. They glowed merrily despite the cold, scenting the air with the comforting smell of melting wax. I took a deep breath, the freezing air stinging my nose and the back of my throat.

My mind turned back to Royal. He'd been a constant fixture in my thoughts these last few days. *One night down.* The words haunted me. And Seth was still out there. He knew what Royal's friendship meant to me. Which made Royal a target, an easy way for Seth to take his revenge. Once again, I put my friends at risk, simply by caring about them. Cassie—she'd fled from us that night, unable or unwilling to accept what she'd seen. Maybe that was for the best. Maybe if she stayed away from me for good, she'd be safe. The thought stabbed through my heart, leaving an aching emptiness in its wake.

The door opened behind me. It was Lucas.

"Hey," I said. Lucas had been distant since the mission. At first, I'd held out hope that everything we'd experienced together that night would—I don't know. Earn Lucas's forgiveness for what I'd done to him. But once we'd retreated to the relative safety of our homes, Lucas had shut me out again.

He stepped onto the porch and closed the door behind him. He stood there in silence, staring out at the dark night.

"I'm angry," Lucas said finally.

I nodded, dropping my eyes to the porch's rough wooden planks. What could I say?

"What you did to me..." He stopped.

"It was unforgivable," I said, tired. I felt another sting behind my eyes, but this time it wasn't from the cold. "I get it. I'd hate me, too."

"I'm *really* angry," Lucas said again. "But the fact that I can be this mad at you," he glanced at me, "it tells me you left my free will alone."

I met his eyes, and we just looked at one another for a long moment. Then Lucas sighed.

"The truth is, I've been running through everything in my head, and if it had been me in your place, I'm not sure I would have done anything differently," he said. "You fought to do what you thought was right. I mean, you should have listened to your dad and Hale. But Seth screwed with your head." Lucas shrugged. "I guess what I'm trying to say is—I can't say I don't understand why you did it." Lucas let his eyes drop to look at his hands. "Plus—I miss you."

My breath caught in my throat, but Lucas stopped there. "What does that mean?" I asked.

"I don't know."

"Does that mean you might be able to forgive me someday?" I asked. My voice cracked, raw with emotion.

Lucas looked up into my eyes. In answer, he held his arms open. I reached for him, and his arms circled around me, pulling me close. I lay my head on his shoulder.

"I'm sorry," I said. "I just wanted—I wanted to become human." Tears traced a warm path down my cheek. "And now I don't know if it will ever happen."

I felt Lucas's arms tighten around me. "I've been thinking about something for a long time," he murmured into my ear. "Even if you never become human, we can still have one night together."

I jerked back, shocked.

Lucas met my eyes with a steady gaze. "Just once," he repeated. "So we have to make it perfect."

"I don't want to hurt you." I shook my head, overcome.

"Like I said," he whispered. "I've been thinking about this for a long time. I can recover from one night."

"Lucas." I breathed. "Should we even be—? The final battle is coming."

"I don't want to die with this regret," he breathed. "Can you honestly tell me you don't want this, too?"

"I—" But I couldn't deny it. I swallowed. "We have a duty to the Guard," I said. "What we want is secondary."

"Maybe. It doesn't make me want it any less. You?"

I opened my mouth to answer, but I didn't need to. Lucas could see the desire in my eyes.

"One night." Lucas pulled me close again. "When we're both ready."

I clung to Lucas, conflicting desires roiling within me. All I knew for certain was I was the reason the final battle was beginning, and I would do whatever was required of me in the coming fight.

It was the only way I'd have any hope of making up for my mistakes.

The following is an excerpt from

SACRIFICE

Daughters of Lilith:
Book 3

Jennifer Quintenz

1

Color bled out of the sky, casting everything in the indigo glow of twilight. It was a tranquil moment, perfectly balanced between day and night—a moment full of promise. Lucas shifted toward me, and the world around us seemed to drop away, fading into the shadows at the edge of my perception.

His fingers brushed the hair back from my face. I bit my lip. Lucas pulled back to study my face.

"What's wrong?" His eyes shone, shifting from gold to green as he held me.

My heart beat a wild staccato rhythm against my ribcage. "Are you sure about this?"

In answer, his lips brushed against my ear, sending another shiver across the surface of my skin. His fingers traced the line of my jaw, catching my chin lightly, tilting my face up. Even knowing this was what we had planned, what we both wanted, I hesitated. Lucas stopped, waiting for me to decide.

Then I moved, and our lips brushed.

Sensation roiled through me like molten gold, shooting white-hot licks of fire into my veins… only it didn't hurt. The flame it kindled was intoxicating in its warmth. I let it burn. An involuntary reflex, my fingers tightened around him.

Lucas let out a soft moan. He shifted his weight, pulling me down onto the soft grass beside him. I encircled his neck with my arms, pulling him closer. He shifted again, and I moved with him. The warmth of him—the weight of him—it felt right. Natural. Like this moment was meant to be.

We broke the kiss, breathless. I smiled up into his eyes, feeling weirdly bashful. Lucas gave me an equally shy smile.

Wordlessly, I tugged at the fabric of his t-shirt. Lucas shifted, helping me pull his shirt off. My eyes dropped to his chest. I felt a slow blush burning in my cheeks. Look, I knew Lucas was fit. We trained hard enough with Hale and the others that we were both lean and strong. But knowing it, and seeing it in the flesh...? Two very different things.

Lucas smiled. Amusement played around the corners of his mouth. "Do you need a minute?"

I punched Lucas in the shoulder. He laughed out loud. I sprang, rolling him over, straddling him, pinning his wrists to the ground. My hair hung down around us in a silky curtain. Lucas's eyes twinkled. He didn't resist.

I smiled down into his face. "I think you overestimate your effect on the ladies, mister."

Lucas gave me an infuriating grin in response. "All evidence to the contrary."

I released his wrists and started to withdraw. Lucas caught me around the waist and kept me from escaping. He sat up, meeting my eyes. In his gaze, I saw a smoky intensity that stole my breath. His smile faded.

His gaze dropped to the buttons of my shirt. Gingerly, he lifted his hands and undid the first button. When he had worked it free, he glanced up with a question in his eyes. I reached for the second button, pulling it free. We worked together, until my blouse hung open.

A muscle jumped along Lucas's jaw. Slowly, and ever so gently, Lucas lifted a hand to slide the blouse off my shoulders. I felt the cool evening air wash across my skin. Lucas traced his finger along one satin bra strap.

He pulled me close, pressing me to his chest. I melted into his embrace, relishing the feel of his skin against mine. Lucas lay back down on the grass. I curled myself against his side, running my fingers lightly down the firmness of his stomach. My hand hesitated at the button of his jeans.

Lucas watched me, waiting. "We don't have to do anything you're not comfortable—"

I covered his mouth in another kiss, drowning out his words. Another swell of fire rose inside of me. Lucas responded, curling one hand in the soft tangle of my hair. Without breaking our kiss, I slid my hand back down his stomach, seeking the top of his jeans. My fingers strained to work his top button free—

"Wake up." Gretchen's voice cut through the haze of my desire.

I pulled back, suddenly cold. The world around us flared into bright daylight.

"What's wrong?" Lucas looked at me, startled. He rose to his elbows, squinting against the sudden brightness.

"Braedyn. Wake up!"

Lucas studied me, concerned. He couldn't hear her voice.

"Gretchen needs me." I felt a sudden urge to smooth my hair and straighten my clothes, which—of course—was completely unnecessary.

Lucas sat up, alarmed. "Be careful, Braedyn."

I leaned forward and gave him one more kiss. "We'll have to pick this up la—"

I lurched awake with a ragged gasp of surprise. Fingers of icy liquid clawed through my hair and down the neck of my shirt. It wouldn't have been a great feeling anywhere, but it was especially unpleasant in the frigid night air of the stone mission. "Gretchen?!"

"The Seal." Gretchen eyed me grimly, holding an empty-and-dripping soda cup in one hand. She turned. I forced my anger aside and followed her gaze.

We were sitting against one of the large stone columns ringing the sanctuary of the old mission of Puerto Escondido. Beyond us, blending almost seamlessly into the stone floor, was the gateway between this world and the realm of the Lilitu. For thousands of years, the Seal had kept the beautiful demons out of our world. Now, it stood open.

It had been three weeks since the Seal had been breached. The Guard stationed soldiers and spotters here around the clock to watch for escaping Lilitu. But in those three weeks, we hadn't seen so much as a shadow cross the Seal's perimeter.

Until now.

I stood. Gretchen was at my side in a moment.

"What is that?" I strained, trying to force my eyes to focus on a smear of shadow marring the air above the Seal.

"I was hoping you could tell me." Gretchen kept her voice low. I could sense her shifting her weight, and out of the corner of my eye I caught the gleam of her Guardsmen's daggers.

Following suit, I drew my daggers out of the sheath I'd strapped to my jeans earlier in the evening. They came free in a soft ssshhing. I pressed the daggers' hidden release and the two blades sprang free of one another, revealing two cruel, serpentine edges. One dagger in each hand, I stepped closer to the Seal, hoping to get a clearer view.

It was like trying to make out the image in a blurry photograph. No matter how my eyes tried to adjust, the smear of shadow wouldn't come into sharp focus.

And yet—

"Something's in there." I glanced at Gretchen and saw the grim set of her lips. She saw it, too. Movement at the edges of the mission's dim sanctuary caught my eye. Three Guardsmen had seen us approach the Seal. They straightened, drawing their own daggers. Three. Only three. I glanced at Gretchen, keeping my voice low. "Where are the rest of the soldiers?"

"Rounds."

I nodded, frowning. Every hour, Guardsmen would walk the perimeter, leaving three of their fellows behind to guard the Seal alongside the spotters. They mostly chased away high school kids and college kids looking for a private place to hang out or drink. It only took about five minutes, but it was worth it to keep clueless civilians away.

Gretchen motioned for the Guardsmen to keep their distance from the Seal.

Misgiving shifted in my stomach. "Maybe we should hold back until the others get back from patrolling—"

It leapt through the smear of shadow. Adrenaline shot through my system as my brain struggled to process fragments of the scene before me. Long brown hair streamed back from her face. Silvery claws extended from her fingers, glinting even in this dim light. And her eyes—black and soulless as a shark's—were fixed squarely on me.

I stumbled back a step before planting my feet. Hale's training kicked in; even as panic raged through my head, my muscles moved, performing motions as exact as a clock's.

I felt the Lilitu connect, but before her claws could slice through my skin, time seemed to slow. I'd managed this once before—the night the Seal was opened. Memories flooded through my head—

Crashing through the stained glass. Racing toward the stone floor 30 feet below. And then time slowed, as though I—and everything around me—was caught in molasses. With effort, I had shifted my weight, managed to turn in the air and land with my feet on the ground before everything slipped back into normal time.

Like that night, I felt the air pressing in on me. I focused all my attention on shifting my wrist, redirecting the Lilitu's force away from vital organs and arteries. While our bodies were twisting in achingly slow motion, I marked the placement of the other Guardsmen in the room. Gretchen was turning toward the Lilitu; she'd just started to raise her blades in response to the attack.

The three soldiers hadn't yet moved. Their expressions ranged from shock to fear. Less than a second had elapsed.

As the Lilitu's expression started to shift, I concentrated on bringing my other hand around, dagger poised to slice across her ribs—noticing too late that she'd swept her foot behind my ankle to break my stance.

I lost my focus. Time slammed back into full-speed.

My wrist shot out, blocking the Lilitu's claws from ripping through my skin. But her kick, already in motion, succeeded in sweeping my foot out from under me. A sharp, stabbing pain shot through my left wrist. One of my daggers slid across the floor, but I couldn't spare the time to chase after it. I hit the ground hard, rolling away from the Lilitu, meaning to give Gretchen a clear shot at the demon.

But the Lilitu was focused on me. She ignored Gretchen, instead throwing herself after me. We tangled in a sprawling mass on the floor before I could kick free. I scrambled awkwardly backwards, still clutching one dagger in my good hand, until I collided with the sanctuary wall. My left wrist throbbed—best case scenario it was sprained. There was no way I'd be able to fight with it.

The Lilitu clawed her way toward me, her long brown hair gleaming in the mission's candlelight.

I shifted the dagger in my good hand, but before I had a good grip on it, the Lilitu knocked my wrist aside, sending the blade skittering into the darkness behind a line of pews. She circled one clawed hand around my neck. A wash of terror flooded through me, almost instantly muted by the thought drifting across my mind; she could rip out my throat. She could kill me right now.

I looked into her eyes. The purity of the hatred I saw there stabbed straight into my heart. It felt—personal.

"I'll admit, I expected... more." Her beautiful mouth twisted in disgust.

"Who are you?" I searched her faces—both the perfect human mask and the deeper, demonic visage hidden beneath it. I wracked my brain for any memory—no matter how faint—of having seen her before. Her human face would be considered beautiful by any standard. Long brown hair swirled luxuriously around her shoulders. Her fair skin was marred by no visible imperfection. Her human eyes gleamed a startlingly vibrant blue. The demon beneath? As all corrupt Lilitu, her skin pulled tightly over angular bones, white save for where it melted to black at her lips and down toward her fingertips. But neither face called up even the smallest flicker of recognition. She was a perfect stranger.

Gretchen gestured to me wildly over the Lilitu's shoulder. I shifted my gaze to her face. When our eyes connected, Gretchen held one of my dropped daggers up, then set it on the ground and kicked it over to me. The Lilitu turned as the dagger skated across the floor. I moved, slamming my fist into her throat. She dropped back, gagging. I lunged for the weapon, but just as my hands were about to close on the dagger's hilt, the Lilitu grabbed my ankle and pulled me sharply back. The dagger overshot my reach. Almost lazily, the Lilitu stopped its wild slide and picked it up.

Gretchen and the soldiers raced forward.

"Braedyn!" Gretchen flung her hand out, gesturing for me to move. I didn't need the prompt. I was already clawing my way forward, struggling to get to my feet.

The Lilitu tackled me from behind, slamming me chest-down onto the cold stone floor. She grabbed a fistful of my hair and wrenched my head up, exposing my neck. She placed the dagger tip against my carotid artery.

"Stop!" Gretchen threw a hand up and the soldiers froze in place.

For a moment, the only sound was the heavy breathing of the six of us. I was hyper conscious of the dagger at my throat, afraid of making any movement. Even small scratches from these daggers could do serious damage to a Lilitu; it wasn't something I wanted to experience firsthand.

Gretchen watched the Lilitu on my back with the same caution you'd show a rattlesnake. "Ball's in your court, demon."

"You fight to protect her, spotter?" I could hear the bemusement in the Lilitu's voice.

"I won't lie, it took a little getting used to." Gretchen didn't relax her grip on her dagger. Gretchen's eyes dropped to mine. I willed her to keep talking. Somehow, Gretchen seemed to sense my plea. "And it hasn't been smooth sailing the whole time. But she's earned my trust."

"She is Lilitu."

"That hasn't escaped my notice." Gretchen's even voice belied the tension visible in her slight frame.

"And you do not mind that she shares dreams with your ward?" The Lilitu's voice was light, taunting.

I felt my breath catch. Clearly this Lilitu had been watching me for a while. But why? I eyed the doors. The rest of the Guardsmen should return at any minute.

Gretchen winced slightly but forced a smile. "My ward, wow. That's so... Batman and Robin."

"Dreams wherein they share intimate knowledge of each other's—"

"I don't need the details," Gretchen snapped. I saw her cheeks flush with anger. "Look, that's the deal. They can have their dreams. Just as long as they keep their hands to themselves in the waking world."

"Do you honestly believe you can contain a Lilitu's desire in a simple dream?"

Gretchen's eyes shifted to my face once more. For a fraction of a second, I saw her doubt.

The mission's main doors opened as the patrolling Guardsmen returned. I felt the Lilitu above me shift, giving a low hiss of frustration.

In one motion, I caught hold of the hand wielding the dagger and threw my head back into the Lilitu's face. I heard a satisfying crunch at the contact, followed by an air-rending shriek. The Lilitu recoiled, releasing her grip on my hair and dropping the dagger.

I clutched the dagger tightly and rolled out from under her, kicking out. My feet connected. The Lilitu went skidding back into the sanctuary wall.

I was vaguely aware of the Guardsmen racing to join the fight, but I kept my eyes locked on the Lilitu facing me. Slowly, I stood and edged away from her. If she attacked again, I'd be ready for her.

The Lilitu clamped a hand over her nose. Dark blood seeped through her fingers, spotting a few oily-metallic drops on the ground at her feet. But then she straightened. She lowered her hand, staring me down haughtily, completely ignoring the fact that her nose was streaming blood.

"I had envisioned great power. Instead?" She shrugged. Again, I saw disgust flicker over her face. "I find a simpering fool, eagerly wearing the Guard's collar. You are no Daughter of Lilith. You are weak. Pitiful. You will be destroyed."

Anger swelled in my chest. "You're one to talk. Maybe you haven't noticed, but you're kind of surrounded."

"Them?" The Lilitu, glancing around at the half-dozen Guardsmen ringing her, looked like she might actually laugh. "They are like ants; they are no threat." Two smoky, bat-like wings unfolded in the air behind her.

"She's cloaking," Gretchen shouted.

The smoky wings snapped closed around the Lilitu. She blew me a kiss, then barreled toward the closest Guardsman.

"Chris!" Gretchen raised her daggers. The Guardsmen ringed Chris, trusting their training to protect them against the demon they could no longer see. They moved through the ancient Mesopotamian fighting form at the root of all Guard training. Their blades, slicing through the air in perfect synchronicity, narrowly missed the Lilitu. She dropped to her knees and slid through an opening on the far side of the line of Guardsmen.

"Braedyn?!" Gretchen, trapped on the other side of the fray, gave me a desperate look.

"I'm on it!" I raced forward, chasing the Lilitu back toward the Seal. She'd lost some time, scrambling to her feet. I closed the distance between us before she reached the Seal. As her foot crossed the edge of the Seal, I grabbed her arm, spinning her around.

"I don't care how many of you try to convert me," I hissed. "I've made my choice."

The Lilitu smiled, but the effect was chilling. "You mistake my purpose. There is no place for you among our number, traitor."

"Then—?" I glanced over my shoulder. The Guardsmen were edging closer, still uncomfortable with a cloaked Lilitu in the room. "Why come here? Why attack me?"

"I owe you no explanations." The Lilitu took a step backwards, toward the heart of the Seal. I gripped her arm tighter, but she pulled me onto the Seal with her.

When my foot connected with ancient round stone, I felt a wash of power. It circled through the Seal like a vortex, drawn into the heart of the stone. Standing there, I felt it pulling on me—but it wasn't until my foot actually slid forward that I realized the sensation wasn't simply in my mind. There was something else—something drawing the power inwards. Something deep within the Seal.

Alarmed, I let the Lilitu go, stumbling off the Seal. As soon as I'd stepped off the ancient stone, the draw of the power released me. It was like someone had flipped a switch, turning off a powerful magnet. I stumbled, unbalanced.

The Lilitu's cold smile deepened at my confusion. Then, she slipped back through the shimmering veil over the heart of the Seal, and in the blink of an eye, she was gone.

"Braedyn!" Gretchen rushed forward and steadied me. "What did she do to you?"

"It—it wasn't her. It was the Seal. It tried to pull me in."

Gretchen's eyes slid from my face to the stone at our feet. I felt her hand tighten on my arm.

"Gretchen." I covered her hand with my own, as much for comfort as to draw her attention back to the Seal. "Do you see—?"

Gretchen's breath came out in a hoarse curse. As one, we stumbled several paces back from the Seal.

"We have to tell Ian and Thane." Gretchen's eyes found my face. She looked haunted, sick. "You go. I'll finish the shift."

I turned and ran for the mission's doors. But I couldn't stop myself from steeling another look back. There, in the center of the Seal, the shimmering veil between our world and the Lilitu plane was crisp and clear now. And through the veil of shadow, Gretchen and I had seen dozens of gleaming eyes in the darkness. Watching. Waiting.

The question was, what were they waiting for?

End of excerpt.
If you would like to read more, grab your copy of
Sacrifice (Daughters Of Lilith: Book 3) at Amazon.com

A NOTE FROM THE AUTHOR

Thank you so much for taking the time to read this book. If you were entertained or moved by the story, I'd be grateful if you would please leave a review on the site where you purchased this book.

Even a few sentences would be so appreciated—they let me know when I've connected with readers, and when I've fallen short.

Reviews are also the best way to help other readers discover new authors and make more informed choices when purchasing books in a crowded space.

Thanks again for reading,
Jenn

ABOUT THE AUTHOR

Originally from New Mexico (and still suffering from Hatch green chile withdrawal), Jenn includes Twentieth Television's *Wicked, Wicked Games* and *American Heiress* among her produced television credits.

Outside of TV, she created *The Bond Of Saint Marcel* (a vampire comic book mini-series published by Archaia Studios Press), and co-wrote *The Red Star: Sword Of Lies* graphic novel with creator Christian Gossett.

She's also the author of the award-winning *Daughters of Lilith* paranormal thriller YA novels, and is currently realizing a life-long dream of growing actual real live avocados in her backyard. No guacamole yet—but she lives in hope.

Follow her on Twitter: @jennq
Visit her blog: JenniferQuintenz.com

You can also sign up for her newsletter at JenniferQuintenz.com to be among the first to hear about new books, deals, and appearances.

Printed in Great Britain
by Amazon